# BREAKING THROUGH

THE BREAKING SERIES BOOK 3

JULIANA HAYGERT

# COPYRIGHT



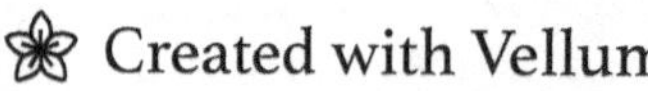 Created with Vellum

English - Portuguese

For a complete list of words used in the series <u>click here</u>!

Note that some words and expression don't have a perfect literal translation. The translation you see here is the one that fits the context of my novels.

Ai – ouch

Ainda bem – thank goodness

Até depois – see you later

Beijinho – a sweet made with condensed sweetened milk

Bem – fine, good, well

Boa noite – good night

Boa sorte – good luck

Boa tarde – good afternoon

Bom – well

Bom dia – good morning

Bomba – item to drink chimarrão with

Bombacha – typical pants used by gaúchos

Branquinho – same as Beijinho

Brigadeiro – a sweet made with condensed sweetened milk and cocoa powder

Café colonial – continental breakfast

Calma – calm down

Carreteiro – typical dish made of leftover steaks from barbecues

Chato – a name for someone who annoys you

Chimarrão – herb-based drink from the south of Brazil

Churrasco – Brazilian barbecue

Churrasqueira – a type of a grill where Brazilian barbecue is made

Claro – of course

Credo – jeez/damn

Cuia – kind of cup to drink chimarrão with

Dança folclórica gaúcha – typical dance from the south of Brazil

De nada – you're welcome

De novo – again

Delícia – delicious

Desculpa – sorry

Deus do céu – Lord above/Oh my God

Droga – crap

E aí – what's up?

É assim – this way

Eita – whoa

Então – so?

Eu não vou me atrasar – I won't be late

Eu te amo – I love you

Eu vou te matar – I'll kill you

Feijoada – dish made with black beans

Feliz Páscoa – Happy Easter

Filha da puta (daughter of a bitch), mimada (spoiled), china (it's like *prenda*, but in a bad way), rapariga sem vergonha (girl without shame), invejosa (jealous) – insulting names for women/girls

Filho duma puta – son of a bitch

Gaúcho(a) – people from the south of Brazil

Graças a Deus – thank God, thank goodness

Grande coisa – whatever

Guria – girl

Idiota – idiot

Irmã – sister

Irmãzinha – little sister

Mãe – mother

Me dá – give it to me

Me deixa em paz – leave me alone

Merda – shit

Meu Deus – my God

Morena – brunette, but in Brazil this term is used in a caring way, like darling or sweetie

Não – no

Negrinho – same as Brigadeiro

Nossa – wow/whoa

O que – what?

O que é isso – what is this?

Obrigado (a) – thanks

Oi – hi/hello

Ótimo – great

Pai – father

Pão de queijo – cheese bread

Parabéns - congratulations

Peão/Peões –cowboys in Brazil

Perfeita(o) – perfect

Pois então – well/you see

Por favor – please

Por que/por quê – why

Porque – because

Porcaria – crap/jeez/damn/shit/bad stuff

Porra – fuck/shit

Prazer – Pleasure, a short way of saying "nice to meet you"

Prenda – just like a gaúcha

Presta atenção – pay attention

Preta – black

Puta merda – fuck/shit/bullshit

Puta que pariu – goddamn it, holy shit, fuck

Que droga – crap/jeez/damn/this sucks

Que foi – what?

Que mentira – what a lie

Que nada – nonsense

Que porcaria é essa – what the hell is this?

Querida – dear

Rio Grande do Sul – southernmost state in Brazil

Sem rodeios – without rodeos, means without dillydallying

Senhorita – miss

Sério – really

Sete de Setembro – Brazil's Independence Day

Sim – yes

Tá bom/bem – okay

Tá tudo bem – it's okay

Também – too/also

Tchau – bye

Tche – common expression used by gaúchos – it can mean many things. A salutation, an exasperated exclamation, or even addressing someone

Te amo – I love you

Te comporta – behave

Tia – aunt

Tio – uncle

Tudo bem/Tudo bom – how are you?

Um minuto – one minute

Vai com – go with

Veado – deer. In Brazil, it's a nickname for homosexuals. Between friends, it's used as a friendly, teasing name.

Vestibular – an extensive and hard test Brazilians take to enter college – each college has its own vestibular test and if the student doesn't pass it, he/she doesn't enter that particular college.

Você – you

 Created with Vellum

# AUTHOR'S NOTE

I hope you enjoy reading *Breaking Through*!


Don't forget to sign up for my Newsletter to find out about new releases, cover reveals, give-aways, and more!

If you want to see exclusive teasers, help me decide on covers, read excerpts, talk about books, etc, join my reader group on Facebook: Juliana's Club!

# THREE YEARS EARLIER

## HILARY

HANNAH SHOVED THE HALTER AND REINS AT ME. "Go. The fourth stall to your right. It's Belle. She's easy and gallops fast. Just ... hop on her, get her going, then put on the harness."

I just stared at her. "What?"

"Just go." She pushed me again and turned to the wall, grabbing another halter and reins for her. She retreated.

"I don't understand."

"They probably run faster than us, but they won't run faster than a horse," my sister explained, walking to another stall. "Now go!"

Still confused, I whirled on my heels and counted four stalls to my right.

A light brown mare stood behind the closed

stall door, her ears alert. She wasn't too tall, nor did she look deadly, but that didn't quiet my fear. And right now, I was swimming in a pool of fear.

I heard Hannah cursing. "Shit." Then, she cried, "Argus!"

Okay, no time to overthink this. It was a question of life or death, and for my life, and Hannah's, I would face this mare.

I opened the door and stepped in. The mare didn't move.

"Hi, Belle," I said, shaking for more than one reason. I wanted to ask her for permission to slide the halter above her head, but we didn't have time for that. Still, my fear of horses stopped me from rushing to her and hopping on her.

The mare snorted, and I decided to take that as a sign that she was okay with me here.

Noises from the stable caught my attention—hurried footsteps, Hannah's muttered curses, a horse whining.

I took a deep breath and did what Hannah would have done. I ran a hand over Belle's neck, hoping she didn't notice how much I was shaking, and pushed the halter on her head. Next, I flipped a bucket around, not caring about all the grain spilling on the ground, and used it as a step stool to mount. Without a saddle. Surprisingly, the mare didn't rear or throw me off.

I tightened my hands around the reins and kicked her sides. "Go, Belle."

We exited the stall and I pulled the reins, forcing Belle to a stop.

Pete, Eric's bodyguard, entered the stable and the other man was closing in. Hannah grabbed a whip from one of the hooks on the wall and raised it in front of her like a sword.

Pete halted and pointed his gun at my sister. "Don't move!"

She froze. I froze.

Hannah's eyes met mine. "Go, Hil." She lowered her head, stepped to the side, and brought the whip down on Pete's arm.

The man cried out as he let go of the gun and cradled his arm. The second bodyguard entered the stable.

I extended my hand to Hannah, but she didn't see it.

"Go, Hil," she said, her eyes on the man pulling his gun from his waist.

"But—"

"NOW!" she yelled, interrupting me.

I jumped, too afraid, too confused, too unsure. However, the mare had thoughts of her own. She turned her head to the back of the stable, pulling against my reins. I loosened my grip and let her take control. The mare took us out through the back gate.

As soon as she stepped out, Belle broke into a faster pace and I hissed, holding on with all I had. Struggling not to fall off, I looked over my shoulder, trying to see Hannah, but Belle turned to the right, taking the back gate from my sight.

My heart sank. I couldn't do this. I couldn't run away while Hannah was dealing with two armed men. Not to mention Eric, who would be on her at any moment.

Oh, God, Eric. I couldn't wrap my head around what had happened.

Eric was my sister's hot boyfriend of over two years. He was the perfect guy. I had a platonic crush on him since I was fourteen. He was the charming man I modeled my future husband after.

And he had just beat me, pulled my hair, licked my face, nuzzled my neck, and slid his hands all over me. I shuddered, thinking about what almost happened. Of what I had escaped.

I started sliding to the side. "Hey," I said. "Slow down." I pulled on the reins, not to make Belle stop, but so I wouldn't fall. The mare slowed down.

I heard tires squealing before I could see an SUV stopping in front of the stable. A guy jumped out of the SUV, holding a baseball bat. Holy shit, another guy wanting to hurt my sister?

A sudden rush of energy surged through me. I had my phone with me! I let go of the reins with one hand and grabbed my phone from the hidden pocket under the belt of my summer dress. It was hard to dial 911 while bouncing over a saddleless horse, but I did it.

"There are three, no, four armed men at my sister's ranch. They are hurting her!"

The dispatcher asked for the address and told me someone was coming our way. She also told me to remain calm. I almost laughed at that—a hysterical laugh did bubble in my throat, but I swallowed it.

I returned both hands to the reins and pulled Belle to a stop.

In the distance, I saw the baseball bat guy fighting Eric. Oh, so he was here to help. Then, Argus was there, right behind Eric. The baseball bat guy jumped back, taking Hannah with him, while Argus reared and descended his legs on Eric.

I gasped, my hand over my mouth.

I kicked Belle's side and pulled the reins,

guiding her back to the stable as the other horse collapsed to the ground too.

Over the baseball bat guy's shoulders, Hannah's eyes met mine. Even across the distance, I saw the relief and the sadness in them.

At that moment, I knew nothing would ever be the same.

# 1

HILARY

THIS PART OF THE EVENING WAS OKAY. FAMILIAR, even.

I sat in the driver seat of my car and looked at the house in front of me. I had known this house since I was a baby, and it had always been associated with good memories—even if it was a ranch beside a smelly stable.

That all changed three years ago.

Right after the incident, I had a panic attack just thinking about coming to my sister's house. Noticing my anguish, and probably wanting to erase her own memories, Hannah had a huge house makeover. Everything about the house was different, except for the foundation. She had re-decorated the bedrooms, the kitchen, and the living room. Even the exterior color of the house wasn't the same anymore. There were no signs of that terrible day.

I took a deep breath.

I hadn't gone to my therapist in five weeks, but I did call this morning when I realized what we were doing tonight and begged her to see me. She was able to squeeze me into her busy afternoon for a twenty-minute session. It seemed too little, but anything was better than nothing.

She told me I could do this, so I kept repeating that mantra in my mind.

*I can do this.*

I cursed under my breath.

*Stop being a wimp, Hilary.*

I just had to face this evening as if it were normal, as if there wouldn't be anything different.

I glanced to the side where the girls' cars were parked. Only Hannah's sports car and Bia's Grand Cherokee were here. I looked around. Leaving my car in this area of the parking lot would mean I would have to stay until it was over. I turned on the engine and parked my car in the farthest spot from the house, closer to the entrance road—it would be easier to leave later.

I made my way to the house and knocked on

the door to announce my arrival before opening the door and letting myself in.

"Hannah? Bia?"

"In the kitchen!" Hannah yelled.

I closed the door and went to meet them in the kitchen. Hannah, Bia, and Gabi—I kept forgetting she was visiting—were around the kitchen island, preparing our food and drinks for the evening. I could hear the popcorn popping into the microwave.

"Hey you," Bia said, coming to embrace me. "How is L.A.?"

I forced a little smile. "It's okay."

Gabi gaped at me. "L.A. is just okay? Ugh, I wish I lived in L.A. too."

Bia chuckled. "Gabi, as far as we know, you wish to live anywhere in the country, as long as it's this country and not Brazil."

"*Sim*. Sad but true," Gabi said, laughing.

The microwave dinged. "First batch of popcorn is ready!" Hannah announced. "Let's put some more in."

We usually had a girls' night out once a month for the last three years. Even when Bia was living in Fort Murray, Hannah and I kept up the tradition, even if that meant I had to come up from Los

Angeles more often. Then Pedro started dating Iris, and she was welcomed into our little group.

Not to mention Gabi. She wasn't around much since she lived in Brazil, but she was part of our group nonetheless.

After Hannah made tons of popcorn and Bia made *chimarrão*, we went into the living room.

It was impossible not to look around this place. Eric had assaulted Hannah and me here. I confess the changes Hannah made in the house made me feel better, but I still avoided the corner in the living room where the couch had once been. Now it was a bookcase full of happy pictures and a few trophies.

Soon, Iris arrived, and we put on a sappy romantic comedy about desperate single people.

Besides Gabi and me, Ri and Gui were the only single ones in our group. We had our bets on when they would finally meet girls who were able to tie them down and add two more to our group. Though with Ri, we knew it would take some time for him to forget what Joana had done and move on, so we didn't really count him.

The bet was more for Gui. Knowing how much he loved the three Ps—polo, parties, and pretty girls—I had bet that it would take him another ten years to start thinking about settling down.

As for me, I wondered if they had bets about me too. If I had to guess, I would say the options were that I would be single much longer than ten years. Maybe forever. Well, even I thought that was possible.

I sighed and tried focusing on the movie.

The main couple was kissing. I sighed again. The last time I kissed a guy had been before that day. Over three years ago. Gosh, that was too long. I still couldn't think about touching a guy, let alone kissing one.

Bia stretched and nudged my knee with her foot. She slipped her phone to me, and I read the message on the screen.

Leo: *We're arriving.*

I reached to the curtain behind me and spied out. I could see the cars' lights approaching. Right before they turned the last curve on the private road inside the ranch, they turned their headlights off.

I picked up the remote control from the side table and raised the volume, hoping it would drown out any noise coming from outside.

Hannah lifted an eyebrow at me. I shrugged. Let her think I was enjoying this sappy movie. Thankfully, she returned her attention to the TV.

I spied out the curtains again. They had

parked their cars closer to the stable. In three seconds, they were out and unloading the equipment.

I shifted my gaze back to the TV and pretended to enjoy the movie, even though all I wanted to do was bite my nails. Or go out there and help. But that wasn't part of the plan. My part of the plan was to make sure Hannah didn't see or hear anything until it was time.

Ten minutes passed.

Bia looked at me with a crease on her forehead. She checked her phone and shook her head. Gabi, seated on the floor, looked fidgety too, but she didn't stop staring at the screen. Good girl.

Twenty minutes.

I spied outside again. Besides all that was going on out there, I couldn't see much with the cloudy sky. The only lights on were a couple inside the stables, probably so it wouldn't catch Hannah's attention. How they were setting everything up in the dark, I didn't know.

Thirty minutes.

Bia typed a message on her phone.

The movie would end soon, and there wouldn't be anything to cover up their noise then.

Bia smiled at her phone before passing it to me so I could read it.

Leo: *We're almost done. When the movie ends, bring her out.*

I smiled and handed the phone to her.

Gosh, this was really happening. I could barely sit still. Taking a deep breath, I closed my eyes and thanked God for moments like this—moments that gave me hope life could be pretty again someday. Hope that the darkness of the past would someday relent and let go of me. Hope that someday I would be open to fall in love again and find my own Leo.

A shudder ran down my spine and that magical feeling was gone, along with all the hope. Damn it. I would never get better.

Bia nudged me with her foot. Pushing back the demons inside my mind, I looked at her. She nodded toward the TV. The couple was kissing again. The makeup and final kiss before the movie ended.

I sat straighter on my corner of the couch.

Ten.

Nine.

Eight...

The movie ended. Hannah and Iris exhaled a happy sigh.

"Ah, that was so good," Hannah said, taking the remote control from the side table.

She stopped the movie and I held my breath, sure she would hear the banging and whatever from outside. There was nothing. Not even crickets.

"Hannah," Bia said, jumping from the couch. "I forgot something in my car I need to show you."

"Oh-kay," Hannah said. "Bring it in."

"I can't." Bia clicked her tongue. "It's too heavy. Just come and see."

Bia turned around and marched to the door. Hannah glanced at me, a what-the-hell-is-she-doing look on her face. I shrugged and followed Bia.

For dramatic effect, Bia paused at the door until Hannah was right behind her. Then, she opened the door and stepped out. I took Hannah's hand and pulled her outside.

The lights came on, illuminating everything in the parking lot between the house and the stable. Hannah gasped, Bia and Gabi laughed, Iris shrieked, and I smiled.

Loud country music started playing from big speakers set on either side of the precarious wooden stage assembled in the middle of the parking lot. The light beams came from four high metal pillars installed on the four corners of the stage.

Holy crap, the guys had really put some effort into this.

Dressed in jeans, boots, plaid shirt and hat, Leo came up on the stage, a wide smile on his face and a microphone in his hand.

"What's going on?" Hannah whispered, her tone suspicious. She looked around, her eyes wide, slowly taking in all the people around the stage. Our parents, Leo's family, Jimmy, close friends. There were around a hundred people in her ranch's parking lot. "Hil, what's going on?"

Before I was able to say anything, Leo raised the microphone to his mouth, and on cue, the music stopped. "This is for you, *morena*."

Then the other guys joined him on stage. Ricardo, Pedro, Guilherme, and even Garrett, all dressed like Leo. A new song started and the guys began dancing.

I tugged Hannah's hand and pulled her through the crowd until we were right in front of the stage.

My sister had an open-mouth smile as if she couldn't believe what she was seeing, as if it was too good to be true, too crazy to be true.

Well, I still couldn't believe my eyes, and I had known about this since the beginning.

The guys swayed and stomped their feet and

moved their hips while Leo lip-synced—it was like looking at the country version of the Backstreet Boys. With the difference that these guys were actually way more handsome than the real Backstreet Boys.

My smile widened. I was always a little relieved when I ended up noticing things like that—if a guy was handsome, or hot, or both. Perhaps it sounded silly, but in my case, it gave me hope that I would be okay. Someday. In the far future.

The lights blinked when the song changed. Then the guys were undressing. Looking like they had just gotten out of a Magic Mike movie, they threw their hats to the people around the stage, and opened their shirts button by button, while still moving their hips to the beat of the song. They all had a white tank underneath, one that hugged their torso—damn, playing polo sure gave a guy some impressive, lean muscles.

The women screamed and catcalled while Gabi uttered an "ew" behind me.

I smiled. Yeah, my therapist would be happy. There was still hope for me.

Leo threw his shirt at Hannah, and she caught it with a huge smile. I loved seeing her like this. Pedro and Garrett threw theirs at their girls, Ri held on to his, and Gui threw his randomly. The daughter of one of my mother's friends from the club caught it, and she screamed like crazy. I shook my head, a little jealous that she got that excited about a smelly shirt.

Two minutes later, the song stopped and a spotlight fell on Leo.

He raised his microphone to his lips once again. "I got a second chance when my family and I moved to the United States three years and some months ago. At first, I thought it was a second chance at polo, but then, after I met you, Hannah—" Beside me, Hannah bit her lower lip, holding her breath. "—I realized it was a second chance at everything. A second chance at life. I didn't even know I was looking for someone to share this new life with until I found you. I found you, and it was like my life was complete." He took a deep breath. "*Morena,* I think I loved you the first time I saw you right outside this ranch." He pointed to the road leading out, and we all followed his gesture with our eyes. "And I'm sure I love you more each day I am by your side."

On cue, Bia, Gabi, and I pushed Hannah forward. Ri and Pedro jumped down from the stage, wound their arms around Hannah's back, and lifted her. Leo was ready—he caught her outstretched hand and pulled her onto the stage.

Then, he did it.

Leo knelt in front of my sister, holding a black velvet box. "Hannah, my love, will you marry me?"

Eyes wide, Hannah's hand flew to her mouth. We all waited with bated breath for her answer; although, she must have forgotten she was supposed to say something. Hannah stared from Leo to the ring and back at Leo, a couple of tears running down her cheeks.

"Say something!" Bia yelled.

That jerked her from her stupor. Hannah lowered her hands, revealing a big smile, and nodded her head. "Yes!" she said in a confident, strong voice.

With a matching smile, Leo stood and embraced Hannah, burying his face in her neck. He spun her around once, twice, before setting her down and putting the ring on her finger.

Hannah stared at the ring on her hand for a few seconds before turning to us and wiggling her fingers. We all cheered and the real party started. Music was once again playing on the speakers. Leo and Hannah came down from the stage, and people lined up to congratulate the couple. Waiters distributed champagne and hors d'oeuvres. After greeting the happy couple, the guests started mingling and dancing.

A sudden panic bubbled inside me.

It was too much, too quick. Bodies close together, suggestive touches, loud giggling, and too many fake smiles. My eyes darted around and all I saw were the men, the guys at the party, grinning at their victims. After a moment, their faces blurred and become the face of only one man. Eric Bennett.

A shudder shook my body and I let out a deep breath.

"What a great surprise," my mother said from behind me. I turned around and found my parents grinning at me. She handed me a champagne glass and clinked hers on mine. "Well done."

I shrugged. "The only thing I had to do was come over this weekend and entertain Hannah while Leo and the guys set up everything."

"The details don't matter," my father said. "We're just glad it was memorable."

"It was, wasn't it?"

My mother tilted her head and narrowed her eyes. "Now it is your turn to find your prince charming."

I rolled my eyes. "That again?"

"Joyce," my father said, his tone almost reprimanding. "If she says she's not ready, she's not ready."

"But it has been three years. Of course she's ready."

Oh my freaking God. "I think I see Bia calling me," I said, turning around. I marched away before my mother could say anything else. Or maybe she did, I just wasn't there to hear it.

I snaked through the crowd, nodding my head to the people who patted me and congratulated me on the engagement of my sister and for helping organize the surprise party. I almost flinched every time someone got too close, let alone touched me, but I swallowed the flinch, the disgust, the panic.

Even though the living room lights were on, I doubted there was someone inside my sister's house right now. Even if there were, it was probably to use the bathroom or grab something in the kitchen. I could sneak up the stairs and hide in the guest room upstairs, or go to Hannah's room and watch TV. I guess she would be occupied at the party for a little while—unless Leo got tired of dancing and wanted to enjoy his fiancée. Well, I had seen them sneak off at parties before. The guest room and my phone would do the trick.

I left my untouched champagne glass on a table and was about to climb the porch steps when Gabi's hand closed around my wrist.

"There you are," she said, pulling me to the side right into the Fernandes group standing by the end of a precarious bar set up along the porch.

Ricardo drank a beer, Pedro had his arm around Iris's waist while they swayed to the beat of the music, and Garrett and Bia laughed at something Gui had said. Reese and Malcolm, players for the Knight House, were here too, talking to Gui, and Gabi danced among them all. We were just missing Leo and Hannah, who were still making the rounds and talking to everyone for a little bit.

I looked around, feeling too self-conscious to dance. I squeezed between the group, hoping to disappear. I raked my mind, trying to think of something to say to distract my mind so I wouldn't panic over being among too many people.

"Tomorrow is Mother's Day," I said. Gabi looked at me. "Won't your mother be mad at you that you're so far away from her?"

Gabi's perfect brows knitted. "Probably. But this isn't the first time I've been away during a special date, and it certainly won't be the last. Are you spending tomorrow with your mother?"

"Not sure if all day, but I'll definitely have lunch with her." I scanned the area, trying to find where my mother and father had gone. There were too many people here. It was impossible to find them from here. I returned my attention to Gabi. "And how's polo?"

She shrugged. "The same. Women's polo in Brazil is a joke. We spend weeks without any training, and there's only one tournament a year."

"That sucks," I said, trying to be sympathetic. Not that I didn't care. I did. It was just hard to focus on someone else's problems when fear and panic flared up my spine every thirty seconds.

"It does." Then, surprising me, Gabi leaned closed to me and whispered, "I see Reese stealing glances at you."

"What?" I squeaked. "No."

"Sure he is. You're blind if you don't see it."

I glanced at Reese. He was talking to Gui and Malcolm. Garrett and Bia also participated in the conversation every now and then. Ten seconds in and the guy glanced at us. At me, actually. Okay, that could have been just him looking around. But another ten seconds, and he looked again and this time he held my stare. Oh-kay, not so subtle, were we? I turned to Gabi.

"Told you," she whispered.

I closed my eyes and inhaled deeply for a brief second. I could do this. The guy was even cute, I guess, so it wouldn't be too hard. It shouldn't be too hard. I could flirt a little.

Once more, I dared a peek at him. This time he was waiting, looking at me. When he saw me looking at him, he smiled. Gui noticed his friend's reaction and followed his line of sight. Gui's usual content expression became closed, and he slapped the guy's chest with the back of his hand. He said something I couldn't hear over the song, but the gesture was enough to make my courage go away, to make disgust and fear come back in full force.

"Excuse me," I said before rushing away.

I darted inside Hannah's house and hid in the guest bedroom. I lay on the bed, took my phone from my pocket, opened a reading app, and continued reading a romance novel about trust and redemption.

# 2

HILARY

TWO HOURS LATER, THE PARTY WAS STILL FULL throttle, even though it was past midnight. It would be better if I left before I fell asleep. Not that Hannah would mind, but I preferred my own bed—especially since the dorm beds back at my school weren't great and I missed my bedroom.

Not wanting to run into anyone—in case they asked me where I had been and what I had been doing—I went down the stairs step by step. Someone was exiting the first-floor bathroom, so I waited behind the stair's wall until the person walked outside. I felt like a thief, or like a sneaking teenager, and to be honest, those two options were way better than the truth.

Quietly, I left through the kitchen's door to the

back and stayed in the shadows of the backyard until I reached the side of the parking lot. Cars were parked side-by-side, lined up in long rows—and many of these cars were blocking others. Gosh, how many people had come tonight? Everyone drove his or her car? Thank goodness I had the foresight of parking near the outer road.

Along the first row of cars, nearest to the party, I saw Gui leaning on the hood of his black Jeep talking to a girl. I smiled. Of course, Gui was talking to a girl. When wasn't he? When he was playing polo. Even then, girls flocked the field, drooling over him, waiting for the game to end.

I shook my head and continued walking to my car with my phone in my hand, the lantern app turned on, illuminating the way.

"Hey, girl," a voice came from my right. A guy's voice.

I froze for about three seconds before panic returned. In slow motion, I turned toward the voice. It was Lucas, a member of the country club and a polo player wannabe. I had never really talked to the guy, just seen him around and greeted him when it was called for.

That fact should have put me at ease. However, his eyes were glazed over, his movements sloppy, his steps wobbly, and the grin on his face sleazy. It put me on high alert. My heartbeat accelerated and my hands shook.

"H-have a good night," I said, my voice sounding weak, but I didn't think he noticed. Without waiting for a response, I walked on, hurrying my steps.

"Hilary, wait," he called again. I didn't stop this time, but I heard the gravel crushing under his shoes. He was following me.

I inhaled sharply and continued walking, fishing my car keys from my purse. I could already see my car at the end of the row. I just needed to keep going—

A hand closed around my elbow and jerked me back. I yelped.

"Hey, what's the problem, girl?" Lucas asked, his grin still on.

"N-nothing." I tried pulling my arm back, but his grasp was firm. "I was just leaving. You should go back to the party though."

"I was leaving too," he said. "Until I saw you. I thought to myself, why is that pretty little thing alone on a night like this? You shouldn't be alone, Hilary. You're too pretty to be alone."

I yanked my arm free and took a step back. "I'm fine alone. If you're looking for company, I'm sure there are plenty of interested girls at the party."

He stepped closer, closing the gap I had created. "None of them is as pretty as you."

"Well." I glanced around, searching for something I could say that would save me. I knew this guy. At least, I thought I knew him. Just like I thought I had known Eric. A shudder ran down my spine and I stepped back again. "It's a shame I have to leave now. It's getting late and I need to be up early tomorrow."

"Tell you what." He took a step forward again. "How about you give me your number? Better yet, agree to go out with me tomorrow night."

"I-I don't think that's a good idea."

"Hey, don't leave yet." He reached out and grabbed my phone from my hands. "Here. I'll enter my number for you."

I extended my hand to him. "Give me back my phone. Please."

"Just a second." He messed with my phone. Damn it. It was probably unlocked because I had activated the lantern a couple of minutes ago. "Entering my number."

"Please." If he didn't give me my phone back in thirty seconds, I would leave without it.

"Sending a text to me," he narrated the steps.

One second later, his phone beeped from his jeans' pocket. "There! Now I have your number and I can call you tomorrow." How he had typed the numbers right with the way his eyes seemed so out of focus, I had no idea.

Finally, he handed me my phone.

I closed my fingers around it as if it were a life jacket. "Okay," I said, retreating. "I'll talk to you to-morrow, then." I would probably delete his number as soon as I got out of here. Or I would simply not answer him tomorrow. However, right now, I was worried about getting away.

"Wait." He caught up with me and grabbed one of my hands. "Until tomorrow, baby." He kissed the top of my hand, his lips too warm and too slobbery. I jerked my hand back, but he didn't let go. Instead, he gave my hand another kiss, one inch higher. Then another, higher. And another higher.

My heart slammed against my rib cage. "Please," I whispered, losing my voice to my fear. "L-let me go."

Without releasing my hand, he wound his other arm around my waist and pulled me flush against him. "Not without a goodbye kiss." He leaned over me, and I turned my face to the side so he wouldn't kiss me on the lips.

My heart beat so fast, it hurt. My breathing came in small gasps, making me dizzy. I pushed against him. Was he too drunk that he didn't realize what he was doing? For some reason, that made everything worse.

I closed my eyes to stop the desperate tears from falling. "Please, let me go," I croaked in a raspy, desperate voice. Even if I were able to scream, nobody would be able to hear me over the music coming from the party.

His lips touched my cheek and I shoved him hard, but he was too strong. Just then, a gentle hand gripped my waist and held me firm while the guy was pried off me.

"She said to let go, dude."

I opened my eyes and gawked. Gui let go of my waist and stood between the guy and me.

"I just wanted one goodbye kiss," the guy replied, his voice more slurred by the second. Like a huge wall in front of me, Gui blocked the guy from my view, so I didn't see it, but I heard him making kissing noises that twisted my stomach.

"Just go back to the party, Lucas."

"Want her all to yourself, huh?" He made a clicking sound with his tongue, though it came out more like a big wet smack. "Not cool, dude. I just got her number, and we're going out on a date tomorrow."

Gui glanced over his shoulder to me, an eyebrow raised, and I shook my head.

"Yeah, sure," Gui said, going with it. "But now you need to go back to the party."

"Why, when we're having so much fun here? Right, baby?" Lucas sidestepped Gui and reached for me.

Fast as lightning, Gui held Lucas's arm back and shoved the guy away. "Go, damn it. Now."

Lucas tripped on his feet and laughed out loud as if someone had told the most hilarious joke he had ever heard. Even so, the guy didn't leave. Shaking his head, Gui put his arm around the guy's shoulder and steered him toward the party. Still trembling from head to toe, I watched as the two of them walked away.

I let out a strangled breath mixed with a painful groan. Because it hurt. My mind, my resolve, my strength—they all hurt. I wanted to run, to scream, but the fear was still present, gripping me and keeping me in place, shaking like bamboo in the wind.

*Calm down, Hilary.*

I could do this. I was strong enough, I knew I

was, and I would win this. I wouldn't have a panic attack right now. No. Not now, not here.

I closed my eyes, counted to twenty slowly while taking deep breaths, and conjured a good image in my mind, just like my therapist had told me. I thought of my family, of how we had become close the past three years, of how we had become more than people with the same last name, of how we could count on each other now. Even though I was away at school most of the time, I still came home every two or three weekends to have a Saturday family brunch or dinner with them—it depended on my parents' busy schedule. In addition, there was my extended family and friends—Leo's family. Bia, Ri, Pedro, Gui, and even Gabi had become synonymous with family. I was glad my sister agreed to marry Leo.

I let a long breath out and opened my eyes.

It was hard to hang on to the good feelings the image gave me once I was back in reality, but the worst was gone. I was still scared, shaken, and feeling as if I might faint with fear, but I wouldn't have a panic attack. Not anymore. I had stopped shaking so hard, and my breathing was almost back to normal.

My therapist had shown me this technique when I had a panic attack right in front of her during one of my first sessions with her. It was simple and quick, and it worked in most cases, but not all of them.

I raced to my car and unlocked the door when I was still a few feet away. I opened the door and was ready to slide inside when Gui called out.

"Hey." I turned around and saw him jogging to me. He stopped a good distance from me, probably aware of how I needed more space than most people did, and he put his hands inside his jeans' pockets. "How are you? Did he hurt you?"

I shook my head. "I'll survive." I tried saying it as if it were a joke, but as soon as it left my mouth, I knew the words were the truth. I had survived before, and I would survive now too. "I ... I don't think he would have really pushed me to ..." I blushed. "But I'm glad you saw it. Thanks."

"I was glad I was nearby too." He glanced at the party. "I think Lucas is way too drunk. I practically carried him back to the party and I had to seat him in a chair. I handed him some water, but I think he's probably passed out on the table right now. He was really out of it." I knew that, I did, but that still didn't excuse his behavior. Gui returned his eyes to me. "I'm sorry."

"Me too," I whispered.

"Is there anything I can do for you?"

"I don't think so. Thanks for asking, though." I jerked my chin toward the party. "You should go back." Then I remembered. "Wait. What about the girl? She's probably pissed right now."

Gui frowned. "What girl?"

"The girl you were talking to by your Jeep."

"Oh, that girl. I don't know." He shrugged. "I had gone to my car to pick up a gift I bought for Leo and that girl followed me there. I have no idea who she is."

"Oh. I thought you were ..." I shook my head. "Never mind." I threw my purse inside the car. "I ... I'm going home now."

Gui gave a step toward me, and then retreated again. "Are you sure you're okay? You want me to drive you home?"

"No, no. Don't worry. I can do it."

"Are you sure? I can call Hannah if you want."

I smiled, though it wasn't a true one. "I'm sure. Thanks."

"All right," he said. "Just ... drive safe."

I nodded and slid inside my car. I turned on the engine, put on the seat belt, and backed the car from the parking spot. Through the rearview mirror, I saw Gui standing there while I drove away until he was consumed by darkness.

As soon as I turned the car onto the highway

from the ranch, a sob made its way up my throat, and as much as I fought against it, I couldn't control it. It ripped through me, bringing on more tears and more shaking. Ten minutes later, I pulled over at a gas station, braced the steering wheel, and cried.

WHEN I WOKE THE NEXT DAY, HANNAH WAS ALREADY at the house. Well, I did get up a little past ten in the morning—very unlike me—and we usually had brunch close to eleven.

In the shower, I tried not to think about the previous night, but it was too hard. The events kept replaying. The way Lucas acted, how drunk he was, and how mad I was about his behavior. How Gui swooped in and saved me. The way I bravely left the party by myself, but broke down once I was out of sight. I had cried for fifteen minutes, but I stayed at the gas station for over an hour because I didn't trust myself to drive until I stopped shaking and lowered my frantic heartbeat.

Closing my eyes, I let the hot water wash away my problems, my doubts, my fears. I would put them behind me. I would because Hannah was here, and this was supposed to be a good, happy day we had together.

By the time I had showered and put on a dress and sandals, my parents and Hannah were seated on the chaises in the sunroom.

"There you are," my mother said, smiling. "If I hadn't heard you walking around your room, I would have gone in and pulled off your comforter."

Smiling, I took the chaise beside Hannah. When I was a bitchy teenager and didn't want to get up early to go to school, my mother did that. Pulled off the comforter. And if it was winter and rather cold, she even opened the windows, so I would have to get up to either grab another blanket or get dressed.

My sister—dressed in her usual jeans, tank top, fitted plaid shirt, and cowboy boots—was radiant.

I turned to her. "How are you?"

She beamed at me. "Wonderful." She showed me the ring.

I had seen it before, but now on her finger, it looked even more amazing. It was shaped like a flower with a huge diamond in the middle, and smaller ones all around the bend. Leo didn't tell Bia, Gabi, and me how much it had cost, but Gui, who had been with him when he had chosen the ring, said it had cost a small fortune. Good thing that was nothing for them.

I took her hand in mine. "Congratulations."

"Thanks. And thanks for helping out with the surprise. I really don't know how you guys pulled off all that without letting a single detail escape."

"Well, I imagined the huge smile you have now, and it was easy to keep quiet, then."

She squeezed my hand back. "Thanks again."

"No problem."

"I have something to ask you, though." Hannah stared at me with a serious face. "Would you please be my maid of honor?"

I smiled from ear to ear. "Of course!" I leaned forward and embraced my sister while my mother let out a loud, delighted gasp in the background. "Thanks for thinking of me."

She pulled back and looked into my eyes. "Thinking of you? You're my sister. My wedding wouldn't be the same if you weren't the maid of honor."

My cheeks heated up. "What about Bia?"

"Even though she's like a sister to me, she isn't you," Hannah assured me. "I'll ask her, Gabi, and Iris to be bridesmaids, though."

"Oh, my heart, I can't wait for us to start planning this wedding," my mother said, a hand over her chest. "It's going to be amazing!"

"Have you two decided on a date yet?" my father asked.

"Not yet, but we're thinking about the end of summer. That way it'll be easier for Leo's family and friends to come from Brazil, and also for Hilary—" She turned to me. "—in case you take summer classes."

"That gives us—" My mother paused and made the calculations in her mind. "—four, five months to plan it all."

"It should be enough," I said.

"If you girls don't plan the next royal wedding, yes," my father muttered, and we all laughed.

Rosa walked into the room. "Brunch is served."

I stood. "Morning, Rosa."

She offered me a warm smile. "Good morning, Miss Hilary." She turned and left.

Rosa had been with my family for many years, but recently she had become someone I thought of. Cared for even. Before, when I was a selfish little bitch, she was just a maid. She didn't get good mornings or please and thank you. After though, Hannah showed me Rosa could be a good friend.

I sighed. It was hard to think about before and after—it all revolved around that day, that forsaken day Hannah and I had lived through. My therapist tried to show me the good that came after that day. She said it wasn't an excuse, that I could still hate it, but according to her, not all the change in me had been for the worse. I had matured, become more open to my family, and I had stopped being bitchy.

However, I had become fearful, easily scared, tense, afraid of everything, quiet, and sometimes a little lonely.

Hannah stood and took my hand, guiding me to the dining room.

My phone rang in my hand. I checked the number on the screen: Gabriela Fernandes. I frown.

"Excuse me a minute," I said, glancing at my mother. Hopefully, whatever Gabi wanted would be quick and my mother wouldn't be pissed about me talking on the phone instead of having brunch with them.

I stepped aside and entered my father's study.

"Hi, Gabi," I answered the call.

"*Oi guria*, how are you?"

"I'm fine. How about you?"

"I'm great!" I could hear the smile in her voice. "The party was great, wasn't it? *Meu Deus*, I wished I lived here with you all."

I chuckled. "Then move here."

She snorted. "Right. My parents would kill me." I didn't answer that, waiting to see if she would reveal what she was calling for. "So," she started, and I imagined her picking her nails. "Gui told me you weren't feeling too good last night and left the party in a hurry."

"Oh," was all I said.

"Yeah. I'm calling to see if you're all right. Are you feeling better now?"

"I am." I didn't know if I should smile or frown. Why was she calling me, really? Had he put her up to it? More importantly, what had Gui told her about last night?

"Are you sure?" She paused, and then asked in a low voice, "Gui seemed pretty worried about you."

This time, I did frown. "I'm sure. It was probably something I ate. I'm much better now. Thanks for asking."

"No worries. Glad you're okay."

An awkward silence filled the line for a few seconds while I searched my brain for what to talk about next—when I should just say goodbye and go to the dining room before my mother had a fit.

Finally, I remembered something. "Hm, you're going back to Brazil next week, aren't you?"

"Not yet. I'm leaving Santa Barbara next week, but I'll spend a week in Hawaii, then Cancun, and then I'll go back to Brazil."

"That sounds fun."

"Nothing like taking a year off to just travel around."

"I bet. I'm going back to school this afternoon, and I won't be back this next weekend, so I guess I won't see you again. Not until you decide to come visit again, that is."

"Hopefully, that will be sooner rather than later."

"Hopefully," I said and I meant it. Gabi was a nice girl, and I would miss her. If she really lived here, I could see her becoming a permanent part of our group and becoming what Hannah and Bia were to me. "Have a great trip."

"Thanks. Drive safe."

We said goodbye. I pressed the red end button on my phone and stared at the screen. What the hell was that about? I went to my contacts page and searched for Gui's number. Since we were friends, I had all of their numbers, but never really called any of the guys, just Bia and Leo. The thought of calling Gui and asking what he had told Gabi pounded in my mind. I pressed his name and the phone started dialing. Before it had made the call, I canceled it. What was I thinking? As if I had the balls to call him and demand anything. If he had told his sister something, it didn't seem like she was about to tell anyone else. I hoped.

I sighed, pocketed my phone, and joined my family in the dining room. "Sorry about that."

"I was about to call you," my mother said.

I pulled out my chair and took my place across from Hannah. "So, what were you all talking about?"

# 3

GUI

"SO?" I ASKED GABI AS SHE STEPPED BACK INSIDE from the balcony and dropped her phone on a side table. "How is she?"

"She says she's okay," my sister said.

She frowned at me, probably wondering why the sudden interest in Hilary. Truth be told, the interest was old, very old, probably born the first time I laid eyes on her—one afternoon at the club, before Leo and Hannah started dating. Back then, she was only sixteen, almost five years younger than I was. Too young. However, my brain took notice of how beautiful she looked, but I did my best to ignore it then.

With the passing of the years, it was harder and harder to ignore how lovely she looked. Just when I thought she couldn't get more beautiful, I saw her again and she took my breath away.

What happened to Hilary and Hannah had been fucked up. Sometimes, I wished I had been there with Leo, so I could have beaten the life out of Eric. That guy didn't deserve to live. At least, Hannah recovered from it, but Hilary hadn't. Well, she did seem better the last couple of months. She started coming to our dinners and get-togethers, though she didn't talk much, and whenever we decided to go to a bar or club, she bailed on us.

After last night though, I was not only interested but also worried about Hilary. She had been shaking like crazy when she left. I almost followed her to make sure she wouldn't get into an accident, but I discarded that idea because it was too much. Yes, I had been interested in her for over three years now, but that was all it would be. Just interest. I would never act on it. She deserved better than me. Besides, I had never seen her with a guy, not even before the incident with Eric. Sometimes I wondered if she was going to become a nun, or if she liked men at all.

Which didn't matter, because I shouldn't care about any of it.

Gabi went to the kitchen, where Bia was checking on our lunch, and Iris talked about dresses from across the kitchen island. I had no idea when or how Bia had learned to cook, but some of her dishes were just too freaking good. Like the lasagna in the oven.

While we waited, I joined Leo, Ri, Pedro, and Garrett in the living room and played video games.

"I saw you talking with Paula last night," Ri said, his eyes on the screen.

"You know her?" I asked, taking the joystick from Pedro. He was fucking terrible at this game. I didn't know why he still tried playing it.

"Iris knows her from college. Apparently, she's friends with Megan."

Megan was one of Hannah's oldest friends from the polo club. Though they weren't best friends anymore, they kept in touch.

"She crashed the party, then?" Leo asked.

"I guess Megan brought her," Ri said. "Anyway, did you hook up with her?"

"Nope," I said.

Ri paused the game. "Say that again?"

Garrett chuckled. "A hot girl was all over you, and you didn't go for it? That's a first." A spatula flew in front of my face and landed on Garrett's shoulder. "Ouch!"

"That serves you right," Bia said from the kitchen.

We all laughed. Bia was too fucking jealous. Even when we were talking about girls for me, she paid attention to what Garrett said.

"Yeah, well, I was going to, but—" I cut myself off. What the fuck? I almost spilled the beans about Hilary. One, I wouldn't tell them what happened last night. Hilary probably didn't want anyone to know. Two, if I told them I had blown Paula off to go help Hilary, they would be on to me. They would know I liked her.

"But?" Leo asked.

I frowned. "Just play the fucking game."

Worse than talking about Paula was remembering how Reese flirted with Hilary last night. When I saw him smiling at her, I wanted to punch his teeth right out of his mouth.

"Uh, someone is touchy today," Pedro teased. I threw him a glare. "What the hell?" he muttered.

The guys teased me some more, saying Paula had turned me down in the end, or that I couldn't get it up. Yeah, right. Inside, I was fuming and ready to punch them all, but for Hilary's sake, I held my ground and gritted my teeth.

Ri tsked. "If it had been me."

Thankfully, the conversation shifted to Ri and his love life. It took him a while to bounce back from the damage Joana had inflicted on him, and on our family, but I couldn't say it was for the best. While I was known for having a few affairs, Ri was known for having many. He had even moved out, to his own apartment on another building two blocks from here, so he could have his own bachelor pad.

Nevertheless, I was still fuming during lunch. I needed to blow off some steam, but playing violent video games wasn't doing the trick anymore.

When we were finished, I was the first to jump up from the table. "How about we go to the ranch and race our monster trucks?"

The guys all agreed, and then Bia, Gabi, and Iris announced they would join us for the game. Ten minutes later, we were driving to the ranch.

# 4

HILARY

AFTER HANNAH LEFT TO GO TO THE FERNANDESES' ranch for a monster truck race—the Fernandeses loved their monster trucks—my mother and I drove all the way to Santa Barbara and stopped by the women's center. I came once a month, but my mother was here at least once a week, and most of the time, Hannah was with her.

Helping other women who had gone through much more dramatic events than what Hannah and I had gone through was part of the healing process, my mother always said, and my therapist agreed.

There were days I was glad I came, like the days I saw women stand up and fight for their freedom, to be respected, to be loved. Then there were the days I wanted to curl up in a corner and cry. Those were the days when a new woman—or two —arrived at the center. They came because they didn't know where else to go, but they were so battered, so broken, so hurt, they had to be sent to the hospital first. Sometimes they came back; sometimes they didn't.

Today was one of the good days, thank goodness. I couldn't handle more drama here after what happened at the party last night.

"Is Evie here?" I asked Leila, the receptionist.

"She should be in the garden out back," she answered. "You know the way, right?"

With a smile, I nodded and then waved at my mother as I went to meet Evie.

The garden was a special place. Each woman was invited to plant a new flower when she first came here and to tend it. To see so many flowers in bloom was inspiring. The staff didn't let the non-cared-for flowers alone for long. They took care of them, as if they were a sign of hope, or they weeded them out, leaving space for someone else to plant her flower.

Evie was kneeling beside a pot, tending her flowers.

"Hey, there," I said, sitting on the wooden bench a couple of feet behind her.

"Hilary!" She stood and smiled at me. "How nice to see you! How are you?"

"I'm good, and you?"

She pointed to her flowers. They were tall, bright, and strong. "Do they answer your question?"

"They do." I was glad she was having a good day. In the year I had known Evie, I had only seen her smile twice.

Her name was Evangeline, but she preferred Evie.

Evie had gotten pregnant when she was eighteen. Her father and mother wanted her to have an abortion, but she couldn't. So, after a big fight with her parents, Evie left and went to live with Mike. However, she lost the baby, and for quite some time, she was depressed and alone.

As far as I knew, Mike had been a sweetheart then and helped her through it. She slowly got better, but then Mike started changing. He became jealous, possessive, and aggressive. His harsh words transformed into slaps and punches. Now, at twenty-three, Evie was again depressed and alone, and she was still with Mike.

She knew better. The therapists and staff here at the center talked to her about leaving him for good. I talked to her about it a lot too, but she never did. She couldn't. It was as if Mike held an invisible and unbreakable collar around her neck.

I understood. My sister had been through something similar, and it had taken her a long time to stand up and do something about it. I didn't agree with it, but I understood.

What I wanted though was to see her win. Even if it took years, I would be here to help her be free of her terrible husband, one way or another.

---

WITH ONE EARBUD ON PLAYING A NEW POP SONG AND a large to-go coffee cup, I focused on my drawing pad and my pencil at the small table in the corner of the coffee shop. I did my best to ignore the noise around me and concentrate on the last details of my project. It was better than staying cooped up inside my dorm room, especially when Mariah, my roommate, was there. She was too chatty, too loud, too spread out, and it was hard for me to be comfortable around her. At least, we got along well enough to live together without any major drama.

This was my second semester in fashion design at the College of Art and Design in Los Angeles, and I loved it. The classes, I mean. I couldn't care less about living in L.A., or the other students, parties, frat houses, and whatnot. Thankfully, my professors seemed to like me. One even told me that, if I continued to impress her, I had a chance of getting a spot in their annual exhibition, where students showcased collections they created. Not all students participated, and this year was too late for me, seeing as the exhibition was next weekend. Even so, it was rare for second semester students to be invited to the showcase. So, I worked hard on my projects due at the end of the semester in a couple weeks, aiming to woo my professors. If I roped them in now, there was no doubt I would be in the showcase next year.

"Oh, I like this dress. It's pretty," Mariah said, taking the seat across the table. She set down her books and coffee and squinted at my pad. "Hm, if you put a slit here." She pointed to the left side of the long skirt. "It would be even prettier."

I rolled my eyes. Of course, she would suggest a slit. Next would be to increase the cleavage, and maybe some holes over the stomach. Wait, no, cut the midriff and make it a top and low-waist skirt. There, just her style.

"I thought you had class," I said, not bothering to look up.

"The professor gave us one last assignment before the finals and let us go to work on it. Can't believe it's only a few more days until finals." She opened one of her books, spreading her things over the small table as if my A3-sized pad wasn't taking a whole lot of space already. "Better start."

For a few moments, it was okay. Mariah started reading and I kept on working on my drawings. At some point, she got up, ordered a coffee and a pastry, and then returned to her studies.

A few minutes later, I noticed she had stopped reading and was looking at the coffee shop customers.

"You really don't see it, do you?" she finally said.

I looked up from my drawing pad. "See what?"

She groaned, as if mad at me. "The guys! All of them look at you. All of them."

"No, they don't." I started drawing again, but my focus was gone.

"I swear, they do. I'm telling you, if you went to some parties with me, you would have every man flocking around you."

"I'm not interested," I said, making the mistake of looking at her again. She squinted at me. "What?"

"Sorry, but I have to ask. Are you gay?"

If I had been drinking my coffee, I would have

sputtered. "No, I'm not. Nothing against gays, I don't judge. But, no, I'm straight."

"Then what? Why won't you go out with at least one of the many gorgeous men around campus?"

I pressed my lips tight. What could I tell her? Not the truth, but I had to give her something so she would stop bugging me.

"I was burned before," I started, hoping it was vague enough, but not too vague to allow for more questions. "It hurt too much, and I don't feel like I'm ready to put myself out there. Not yet."

There. The truth.

She stared at me, probably trying to see something in me, in my eyes, in my body language. Did she think I was lying to her? Who cared if she did? I didn't owe her any explanation.

Finally, Mariah shrugged and returned her attention to the people in the coffee shop.

"Oh, I almost forgot," she said after a couple of minutes in blissful silence. She reached inside her purse. "I stopped by our building before coming here and checked our mailbox." She handed me an envelope. "This one is for you."

Frowning, I took it. It was an off-white envelope made of thick paper with a watermarked F and W on the front—I had seen this logo before—

and my name and dorm address stamped in golden ink on the back, surrounded by elegant swirls. Very elegant, very expensive.

Biting my lip, I opened it.

*Dear Hilary Taylor,*

*Every spring, students from all over the United States send me their portfolios in hopes to secure a summer internship with me. Even though you didn't send me a portfolio, I recently came to know your work and was impressed.*

*If you would be interested in an internship with me during the summer, please come to my studio for an interview next Friday at 11 a.m. Please bring your portfolio.*

*Best regards,*
*Fallon White*

I hugged the letter and let out a squeal.

Mariah stopped whatever she was doing and stared at me as if I had grown a second head.

"Did you just squeal?" she asked, skeptical. I nodded. "You never squeal. Okay, spill. What's in that letter?"

"An invitation for an interview with a famous fashion designer whose studio is in Santa Barbara!"

"Oh, wow. That sounds cool. Congrats!"

"It is!" I looked at the letter again. Wow, this was unexpectedly great.

My mother had taken Hannah and me to have dresses done by Fallon White a couple of times—our christenings, our debutante balls, and our sweet sixteen—and Hannah was talking about having her wedding dress done with her too. If I got an internship there this summer, maybe Fallon White would let me help with it.

There was only one problem. I had my first final exam on Friday morning. Crap.

Praying for my professor to be nice for once, I pulled out my cell phone from my tote and sent him an email, saying I had an emergency and had to head to Santa Barbara on early Friday morning.

I bit my nails until he answered later that day, saying he had another session of the same class on Monday and, if I wanted, I could go to that final exam instead. After checking my schedule and making sure I didn't have another class at that same time, I squealed once more and emailed him, confirming the switch.

It had been so long since I had felt this good, this satisfied. I held on to that feeling with both hands, hoping it wouldn't be able to escape me so soon.

---

IN THE SUNLIGHT, THE WHITE BUILDING SHONE bright, almost blindingly, on the warm Friday morning. It wasn't massive, but suddenly, the three stories had become intimidating. The first story had floor-to-ceiling windows displaying the newest collection, a huge silver F and W logo hung in the middle of the second story, and asymmetrical long, but thin windows decorated the third story.

I gulped, wishing I could swallow my nervousness.

While driving here, I had called my therapist. Not because I was on the verge of having a panic attack—exactly the contrary. For the first time in three years, I felt good. I felt confident, powerful, in control. I could do this. I could live my life. I could let go of my fears. I wanted to tell her that, make her proud of me.

"I'm proud of you," she had said, "and I'll be even more if you tell me you're proud of yourself."

Was I proud of myself? I guess so. I was still curious about how Fallon White found out about me, but did it really matter? Bottom line was she had found me, and now I was here to sweep her off her feet. Who knew? Maybe she would love me so much, she would ask me to come back every summer. Then she would offer me a permanent position within her studio, one that I would gladly accept—for some time, just to learn more and more with the best. Then, when I felt ready, I would open my own studio.

I had never told anyone about this dream, not in three years, though I guess people assumed I would like to have my own studio since I was working in the fashion industry. My only doubt was, to open it in Santa Barbara and be near my family but have to compete with Fallon White, or to open a studio in Los Angeles where I could have more clientele—and also more competition.

I shook those thoughts from my mind, because they were out of place. This was not the time to daydream about so far away in the future. I would worry about that when the time came. Now, I had to focus on the next step of my journey.

My cell phone beeped—I had set a reminder

for 10:55 a.m. After a deep breath, I stepped inside the studio.

A receptionist, dressed in a beautiful white and light gray casual dress, smiled at me from behind a white, curved reception desk.

"Good morning. How can I help you?"

"Hi. I'm Hilary Taylor. I have an interview with Ms. White in a few minutes."

The receptionist—Sonya, the silver tag on her chest read—glanced at the computer screen for three seconds. "Yes, I see you." She gestured to the large white sectional to the side. "Please have a seat. I'll let Fallon know you're here."

I turned and sat on the sectional. From here, the studio looked quiet, as if it was empty, except for the receptionist. To the left, a three-foot wall rose, and white lines like fringes hung from the ceiling, meeting the wall. The lines were dotted with small lights blinking in a slow, alternating pattern. The wall and light curtain separated the dresses being shown in the windows.

"Miss Taylor," the receptionist called me. I jumped from my seat and found her standing in front of the desk. "Fallon is ready for you. Please, follow me."

She stepped to the left of the front desk and opened a white door for me. The door led into a long, white corridor with several doors on each side and one set of double doors at the end. Of course, Sonya took me there.

"This way," she said, opening the doors.

Seated on a tall, white leather chair behind a long glass table, Fallon White was just as I remembered. Tall with generous curves, a sharp nose, white hair cut into an asymmetrical bob, and dark brown eyes behind white-rimmed glasses. Even in her late forties, she looked young and elegant.

"Hilary Taylor," Fallon said, walking around her desk to meet me. "It's nice seeing you again."

"You too, Ms. White."

She huffed. "Please, call me Fallon." She gestured for me to sit on one of the white chairs in front of her table. "How are you, dear?"

"I'm doing well. Very excited to be here."

She took the chair beside mine. "I'm excited too."

Sonya appeared by my side. "Can I get you anything, Miss Taylor? Coffee, water, juice?"

"I'm good, thank you."

Sonya nodded then left the room, closing the doors behind her.

"So," Fallon said. "Let's talk business."

I ARRIVED AT THE BISTRO SIX MINUTES LATE. BIA was already at a table in the middle of the little restaurant, looking at the menu. She probably got here six minutes before the agreed time. I had to walk past the bar and noticed several men having lunch alone—most were drinking beer at noon on a workday, and some were looking at the females in the bistro. Including Bia and me.

A little spark of fear made its way down my body, and I tried to remember that was normal. Guys were like that. They looked at pretty girls. And Bia was stunning. She deserved to be looked at.

Still, I couldn't shake the fear and the disgust that took root in my gut.

I halted beside the table and pulled out my chair. "Hi."

"*Oi guria*," Bia said, lowering the menu. "Are you going to end my misery and tell me what you are doing in Santa Barbara?"

"What do you mean?"

"Usually, you have class Friday mornings and, when you come home to spend the weekend, you don't arrive until late in the afternoon. So, when you invited me to have lunch, I knew something was up. Spill!"

I smiled. "I just had an interview for an internship with the greatest fashion designer in Santa Barbara. Hell, she's one of the best in the country."

"Really? That's great! Good luck. I hope you get it."

"Me too. Although, if I get it, I'll have to cancel my registration for the two classes I was going to take this summer. Which is no big deal. I had just signed up for them so I had something to do. It never occurred to me to apply for an internship after just one year of college."

"I'm sure you'll get it. Your designs are incredible. She would have to be insane to pass you up."

I rolled my eyes. "Okay, okay. Let's change the subject. I need to stop thinking about this interview, or I'll bite my nails off. I probably won't hear about it for another week or so, and I'll drive myself crazy until then."

While we looked over the menu and ordered our lunch, Bia told me about her week. She and Garrett shared an apartment and went to vet school together—though he was one year ahead of her. I couldn't imagine being together all day and all night, but they managed okay. In fact, I thought they always ended up cranky whenever they spent some rare time apart.

Bia and I had just finished our post-lunch coffee when my cell phone rang.

I looked at the screen and didn't recognize the number.

"Hello?"

"Hilary? This is Fallon White. Hello again."

With wide eyes, I stared at Bia and pointed to my phone. "Hi, Fallon. Did I forget something at your studio?"

She chuckled. "No, dear. I'm calling you to let you know you got the job."

I froze. "W-what?"

She chuckled again. "The internship is yours if you still want it."

My heart skipped a beat before going into overdrive. "I do!"

"All right, then. I'll send you some forms via email. Bring them in when you start, the week after your spring semester is over, okay?"

"Sure."

"Great."

"Thanks, Fallon."

"My pleasure, dear. I'll see you soon."

I lowered my phone, but couldn't stop staring at Bia.

"You got the internship," she said. Not a question, but I nodded even so. "That's awesome! *Parabéns!*" Her voice was loud enough to make some heads turn our way. That brought me out of my stupor.

"Oh my gosh, I didn't think this through."

"What do you mean?"

"My house is ninety minutes from here. I can't come and go every day. It would be insane."

"Then stay with Garrett and me!" She sounded excited. She looked excited with those big, sea-green eyes shining bright.

"I don't know," I said, trying to reason what the best option here was. I knew she meant it, and she would really like it, but I also knew me. I would feel like a third wheel on their well-oiled machine. I wouldn't feel comfortable.

Coming and going back from my house was out of the question, though. To spend three hours per day in my car coming and going wasn't for me. There was also Hannah's ranch, which was only twenty-thirty minutes from town, but like with Bia, Hannah had Leo and now that they were engaged … gosh, I didn't even want to think about it.

It would be better to stay in a hotel for the summer months or …

"I could rent a furnished apartment."

Bia's smile fell. "You don't want to stay with me?"

"I really, really appreciate the offer, but I prefer having my own place, even if temporary."

She frowned at me, her mind working, I was sure. "Okay, I understand, I guess." She stood up, a smile on her pretty face. "Let's go apartment hunting!"

"Now?"

She caught my hand and pulled me up. "*Sim,* right now."

# 5

---

HILARY

"I'M SO HAPPY FOR YOU," MY SISTER SAID, embracing me.

"Thanks." I squeezed her. "I think it's great that I'm going to be here this summer. This way I can help out more with the wedding preparations."

"That *is* great." My sister let me go and turned back to the island-slash-bar that divided the kitchen from the dining table, where she was preparing a whiskey with coke for her and Bia.

The guys' large apartment was in a fancy building in the nicest neighborhood in Santa Barbara. It had a big family room, dining area, and open kitchen, an office, and four suites. Bia's apartment was close, only two blocks away, but hers was much smaller, with only two bedrooms in a quieter building. Ri's new apartment was also close and more like a loft. It was nice for parties, but the neighbors always complained about the noise every time we met there. So every time someone planned a get-together, we ended up at the Gui's and Pedro's place.

"You should have seen the apartments we looked at yesterday afternoon," Bia said, seated on one of the high bar stools lining the kitchen's bar counter.

"And this morning," I filled in.

Yesterday, she hadn't relented until we went looking for furnished apartments. I didn't think we would find many, but we ended up finding some gems. All of them only a couple of blocks from either hers or the guys' apartments.

"And this morning," she repeated. "Have you decided on one yet?"

I shook my head. "I don't know. They all have good things and bad things."

"Oh yeah," Bia said. "That one with the white flooring had a funny smell. And the one with the big bedroom had centuries-old furniture that will probably break as soon as you use them."

"Exactly. Besides, I haven't even talked to my parents about this idea. I guess they are assuming I'll either stay at home or crash at Hannah's."

"You know my house is your house," my sister said.

"I know, but I already told you. You guys have your own routine, customs, and whatever. If it were for only one or two weeks, it would be okay, but for three months? No. That's too much and I wouldn't feel comfortable."

"She told me the same thing when I offered for her to stay at my place," Bia said.

"See? Besides," I continued, "you and Leo just got engaged. I can't imagine how steamy things are around that house right now. I don't want to imagine."

Bia scrunched her nose. "Ew!"

My sister barely paid attention to the last words I said. With dopey eyes, she gazed at Leo, probably imagining all the steamy things they were doing around that house. Double ew!

Leo was seated beside Gui in the living room, a joystick in their hands, their eyes glued to the big screen hanging from the wall.

"*Não! Veado, não é assim!*" Ri yelled at them. "You're ruining my high score!"

Gui flipped the middle finger at him. Ri jumped over the ottoman and lunged at Gui. Ready, Gui dropped the joystick and braced himself. Ri and Gui started fighting—playfully. Apparently, it was always like that when they played whatever epic game they were addicted to. The girls didn't even bother separating them anymore. They would exchange a few weak punches, try to kick at each other, swipe someone under his feet, and then they would just yell they were done in Portuguese, and resume playing as if nothing had happened. Sometimes Leo and Pedro got in those fights too.

Garrett never got involved in the fights, though. Bia thought he was afraid of being expelled from the group if he beat one of the guys up. It was nonsense, but he didn't want to hear it.

"Boys," Iris whispered, coming to the kitchen to pick up some appetizers.

Bia got her drink from Hannah. "Tell me about it. I grew up with these jerks."

I shook my head. "I still can't believe they were always like that."

"It got better with age," Bia said. "When they were teenagers, it was so much worse."

"I would have liked to see that," Iris said. She turned to the microwave to heat up a cheese sauce she had brought for a bread and chips dip.

Bia snorted. "I guess there were times when it was fun, but mostly, it was annoying."

The four of us watched as Ri pulled off Gui.

Instead of arguing more, he picked up another joystick and started playing too.

"Okay," I said, taking a Coke Zero from the fridge. "We've got an important subject to talk about."

"What?" Hannah asked.

"Your bachelorette party!"

The girls made aahs and oohs and yeahs, drawing the guys' attention.

"Did I hear something about a bachelorette party?" Garrett asked from the dining table.

"Maybe," Bia said, batting her eyelashes.

"Speaking of which, we have to plan yours too, huh," Gui said, slapping Leo's back.

"We also have to talk about your dresses," Hannah said.

"Did you invite anyone else to be your bridesmaids, or is it just the three of us?" Iris asked.

"Don't forget about Gabi," Bia said.

"Oh yeah." Iris nodded. "She's rarely here so I keep forgetting."

Hannah nudged me with her elbow and raised her voice to be heard. "I guess it'll be just you guys. Or maybe Gui and Ri will fall in love with some girls soon, and we'll include them in our little group."

Ri let out a loud guffaw.

Gui huffed. "Yeah, right."

"Ri and Gui falling in love?" Pedro started. "That'll happen when hell freezes over."

Everyone chuckled.

"Or when Victoria's Secret sells granny panties," Bia said.

More laughs.

"Or when it rains pocketknives," Leo said. The Brazilians laughed, but the Americans stared at him. He shook his head. "It's a Brazilian thing."

We talked a little more about the dresses and the bachelorette party—it was all too early to decide anything—and ate some appetizers.

Finally, the guys turned off the video game and put on some music videos. Much better for what was supposed to be a fun get-together.

Hannah went to sit on the couch with Leo, Bia went to sit at the table with Garrett, and Iris went to the balcony with Pedro. Ri kissed his beer bottle, but Gui stood from his seat on the couch, making disgusted faces at the couples, and came to the kitchen. He took a beer from the fridge and sat on the stool where his cousin was seated before.

"We both always hold candles to these guys," Gui said.

I frowned. "Hold candles?"

"Oh yeah, the expression is different here, isn't it? In Brazil when we say someone is holding a candle, it is the same as saying you're a third wheel here."

"Oh, okay, now it makes sense." I glanced around. Sometimes these parties did feel like make-out sessions. "Yeah. Ri, you, and me are the third wheels here.

"Ri doesn't count. He'll be single forever."

Poor guy. I could understand why, but I liked to believe he would find his match one day. I picked a chip between my fingers but didn't eat it. "You could solve that, couldn't you? Just play eeny-meeny-miny-mo with your phone's contact list and pick some girl," I teased.

"Ha, funny." His forehead wrinkled, and then he stared at me. "How about you? Don't guys line up to ask you out?"

I frowned, trying to decipher what he was implying, but it was always impossible with him. "I don't think so." My voice came out much softer than I intended. Then, for some reason, I became self-conscious and my only wish was to crawl under the table.

Gui kept staring at me, his deep blue eyes keeping me prisoner. "Are you okay? I mean, after that day—"

"I'm fine," I said, interrupting whatever he was going to say next. "I'm ... gonna be fine. Don't worry about me."

"Easier said than done," he muttered so low that I wasn't sure I heard him right.

"How's Gabi?" I asked. "I have barely talked to her since the last time she came to visit."

"She's fine," he said, then shook his head. "I mean, she's okay, but you know she wants to find a way to move here."

I nodded, knowing about the drama. The guys had a visa because of their abilities in sports. Even though Gabi also played polo and was good at it, the women's division in Brazil was too small to be considered extraordinary, and at the moment, there weren't any clubs here that were interested in bringing foreigners to play for them—especially because most of them didn't have any women's team. Therefore, she couldn't apply for the same visa, and she couldn't apply as Gui's dependent. Right now, there was no way for her to come live here legally—other than a student visa. And that wasn't what she wanted.

"Maybe she'll find a way."

"Maybe. Until then, my parents are happy she's mostly in Brazil."

"She has been traveling quite a lot, huh?"

Without actually saying the words out loud, we all knew what Gabi was doing. She was my age and should already be in college. But she didn't want to go to college; she wanted to play polo. So, while polo was still in limbo in Brazil, she decided to take a gap year and travel the world—with several stops in Brazil, since it was the only condition her parents had imposed.

"She has to my parents' dismay." Then, surprising me, Gui changed subjects. "I heard about your internship. Congratulations."

"Thanks."

"I also heard you're looking for a furnished apartment to rent."

"I am."

"So it happens there's one in this building."

"There is? How haven't I seen it at the realtors?"

"Because the owner didn't put it up for rent yet. He's getting a few things done around the apartment, and it should be ready in a week or two."

That was perfect! I still had one more week of finals—probably enough time for the owner to finish the repairs. And if after that he still needed one more week, or even two to finish it, I could stay at Hannah's or Bia's until the apartment was ready. Then I looked around and realized something. "Wait. Your apartment is huge. I won't rent a four-bedroom apartment just for me."

"There are four different floor plans in this building," he said. "His is a nice sized two-bedroom."

"Now I'm interested. Do you think he would show me the apartment, even with the repairs going on?"

He fished his cell phone. "I can see about that right now."

"No, no. You don't need to."

"Just give me a second." He typed away on his phone. Then it dinged a couple of times. "He can leave the keys here tomorrow morning. I can show it to you then."

"You're going to show me the apartment?"

"Why not? I know the guy, I know the apartment, and I'll be around."

I considered that for a moment. Why not? The wheels in my mind spun, and I think a trickle of fear ran through my veins. Letting Gui show me the apartment meant I would be alone with him in a closed space. I took a deep breath.

*Come on, Hilary. This is Gui! Leo's cousin. You can trust him. Can't you?*

I could.

"All right," I said. "What time should I come over?"

"Ten sound good?"

"It does." It actually did. At eleven, I had to meet my mother at the club for lunch with her friends. I shuddered just thinking about that torturous event.

"It's a date." He froze, eyes wide, realizing what he said. "I mean, not a date as in—"

"I know what you meant." My cheeks flamed, probably from embarrassment and anger at the same time.

"Okay, good," he said quickly.

I took a few steps back and leaned on the counter behind me, putting more distance between Gui and me, because the way he had said it, the way he corrected himself so quickly, just made me wonder how terrible it was for him to imagine himself out on a date with me. Was I that disgusting? That bad looking? That repulsive?

The air in the kitchen thickened.

In my head, I was trying to come up with a plan of how to go to another part of the apartment, or leave and go home all together.

I was saved when Bia stood from the couch. "Let's go to that new club that opened a couple of weeks ago?"

"Which one?" Ri asked.

Gui turned on his stool, facing the living room. "The Suite?"

"Yeah, that one," Bia said. "It's only ten minutes from here."

Hannah sighed. "I'm not really in the mood."

"Oh, come on," Bia said. "We should all go for once. It will be fun."

Leo nodded to Hannah and she relented. "Okay, but we aren't staying until three in the morning."

"Pedro? Iris? You in?" Bia asked. They shared a quick glance then nodded. Then she turned to the kitchen. "Gui? Hil?"

"I'm in," Gui said without hesitating half a second.

"I can't go. You know that," I said, relieved I had an excuse. "Under twenty-one over here."

Bia narrowed her eyes at me. "I gave you a fake ID a few months ago. Use that." Damn, I had forgotten about that. To be honest, I didn't even know where it was. "You're coming, right?"

I wasn't going; that I was sure of. Places like that, with so many people, so many men with only one thing in their minds. I started feeling the threads of a panic attack starting, just thinking about going to a nightclub. However, I was tired of always saying no, of always having them beg me to go, only to see the disappointed looks on their faces.

"Okay," I lied.

Bia gasped. "For real?"

Hannah stared at me as if I had grown a second head. "Are you sure?"

"Yes," I lied again.

Gui glanced over his shoulder at me with a sympathetic smile. What? Was he pitying me? The damaged girl was finally facing her fears. I wished …

Garrett pouted. "You didn't ask me if I want to go."

Bia laughed. "I'm going, so of course you're going too."

He rolled his eyes, but had a happy grin on his face.

Iris grabbed her purse from the long sofa table behind the couch. "This is going to be amazing. Everyone ready?"

"We're going now?" Ri asked.

"Yes, right now," Bia said.

We all moved. Bringing glasses and plates to the kitchen, turning off the TV, closing the balcony doors, turning off the lights, and then we were all in front of the two elevators, waiting for them to arrive at the fifteenth floor.

The guys went to the underground floor to grab their cars, while Hannah, Leo, Bia, Garrett, and I went to the front of the building, where we had parked our cars.

"You want to ride with us?" Hannah asked, pointing to Leo's Grand Cherokee.

I shook my head. "I prefer going in my own car, in case I want to leave early."

"Or late," Bia said with a wink.

As if …

I smiled at them. "Meet you all there."

I slipped into my car before they could see the lie and drove away. I turned onto the street leading to the club, so they thought I was going there, but once out of sight, I turned around and headed home.

# 6

GUI

THOUGH WE USUALLY GOT VIP LOUNGES AT MOST clubs, The Suite didn't have any VIP areas available when we arrived. However, after walking around the place for twenty minutes, we found a large table in the back, where you could barely see the dance floor, but was rather close to the bar.

As we settled in our seats, Hannah checked her phone.

"I sent her a couple of texts, but she's not answering," Hannah said, typing on her phone again.

"I'm sure she's just lost in here," Bia said. She grabbed Garrett's hand. "We'll walk around a little and look for her."

Hannah nodded but didn't stop staring at her phone.

"Would you feel better if we went outside and waited for her there?" Leo asked. Hannah nodded again. Leo jerked his chin toward the front doors, and I gave him a thumbs up.

Being taller than most in here, I didn't sit. I leaned my back against the wall beside the table and watched the crowd in search of a blond head. I became tense as the minutes passed. We ordered drinks and French fries. Bia and Garrett came back from their patrol, and Hannah and Leo came back inside.

It was clear Hilary went straight home.

For some reason, that knowledge didn't sit well with me.

I ordered another whiskey and sat alone at the table while the couples went dancing, and Ri went hunting, as he always said. In a matter of minutes, he would have a girl under his arm, and then he would take her to his apartment. Everyone teased me about being free and flirting a lot, but Ri was much worse. They just didn't bother him as much because Ri took offense. Nobody joked about him and his many ladies. It was a fact of life by now.

I groaned.

Why did it fucking bother me to know that Hilary wasn't coming? With her problems, she was better off at home, wasn't she? I didn't really know.

I glanced at the bar, already thinking of my next shot of whiskey, when a trio of girls caught my eye. One looked my way, opened a huge smile, talked to the other two, and they turned to me. The first one scolded them, probably because they weren't supposed to look while I was looking—Bia and Gabi did that all the time when they were younger. So fucking annoying.

The three of them kept talking, and then the other two were pushing the first one away. After a few more harsh words, she straightened and strutted my way. With a boldness I wouldn't have guessed she had, the girl slid into the booth until she was only a foot away from me.

"Hi, there," she said with a smile.

She was cute. Tanned skin, brown hair to her shoulders, with curled ends, and hazel eyes. I hadn't stared at her before she sat down, but she had nice cleavage and a somewhat slender figure.

A good candidate to brighten my suddenly shitty night.

"Hello," I said.

"I'm Rachel." Her smile trembled. "I'm sorry for coming over like this, but my friends and I have a dare game going on, and well, they dared me to come over here."

"I'm Gui." I glanced at her friends. They were

watching us like hawks. "Well, you came. You won the dare."

She scrunched her nose. "Not quite."

I raised an eyebrow. "Hmm, there's more to the dare?" She nodded. "What is it?"

"I ... well," she stuttered, pressing her hands together. "I have to get you to kiss me."

"I see. And what happens if you lose the dare?"

She sighed. "I have to finish their projects in our history class. It's a huge project."

I chuckled, but my laughter died as Rachel looked at me expectantly. Why was I even considering this? It was just a fucking kiss. I bet that if I wanted, I could have this girl take me home where we could do more than kissing. However, something made me hesitate.

*Don't be a fucking* veado, *Gui.*

I settled my whiskey glass on the table and turned to her. I reached over, cupping her face, and leaned into her. She sighed as my mouth fell on hers. She parted her lips and let me in without hesitation. Yup, if I wanted, I could sleep with this girl. I explored her mouth, while my other hand explored her waist. I kissed her intently and deeply, and when I pulled back, for a brief second, I was shocked to be looking into hazel eyes—not green.

"There," I said with a grin. "Now you won the dare." I turned back to my drink and stared out at the dance floor.

The girl humphed then scurried away to her friends.

I felt bad for being such a freaking jerk to her, but I knew I would feel even worse if I had done more with her.

After a while, Ri disappeared completely, and Pedro and Iris came back to the table to order more drinks and fries. And I simply stood, bid them good night, and left. I went straight home to my bed.

---

HILARY

THE NEXT MORNING, I WOKE UP TO A COUPLE DOZEN missed calls and messages, all asking me where I was, if I was lost, if something had happened, until the last couple of messages when it was obvious Hannah and Bia had figured out I had lied to them and went straight home. Still, they wanted me to call or text them as soon as possible. Thank goodness I had my phone programmed to not ring during the night so it wouldn't disturb my sleep.

At 7:30 a.m., I sent a text to Hannah and Bia, though if they really went out last night, I was sure they wouldn't see the messages until much later.

I stood in the middle of my closet, searching for something to wear. Why was it suddenly so difficult to find something to wear? Later I would have lunch with my mother and Hannah and a bunch of other women at the club. I never had a problem choosing a pretty dress to wear then. What was the problem now?

I huffed. The problem was I had a pit stop. Gui planned to show me an apartment in his building. I couldn't wrap my mind around the fact that I was worried about what I would wear to meet him. It was ridiculous. Totally insane.

I shouldn't and I wouldn't care what he thought of my clothing.

In the end, I decided to forget I was going to meet him and chose a simple dress and sandals, as if I was just going to the club instead.

At 8:30 a.m., I left my house and drove all the way to Santa Barbara. At least the club was right there; otherwise, this drive would have been crazy. From Gui's building, I would go to the club, and from the club back to Los Angeles.

I arrived at ten in the morning in the guys' building and found Gui on the sidewalk in front of the main entrance. He was wearing jeans and a dark blue polo that accentuated the vivid color of his eyes. He wasn't wearing a baseball cap, which was unusual, and I noticed his dark brown hair was cut shorter on the back and sides, while on top it was still neatly unkempt. I knew that if it wasn't for my panic attacks, and if we weren't practically family, my heart would have beaten faster each time I saw him.

I parked my car half a block away—it was the only free spot around—and walked back. With a smile, he met me halfway.

"*Bom dia*," he said.

"Morning," I replied, smiling too. "Do you have the keys?"

He jingled them in his hand. "I do."

"I confess, I'm curious about this apartment."

"Then let's end your curiosity." Gui opened the front door of his building for me, guided me through the lobby, and pressed the elevator button, as if I didn't know my way around. A low ding sounded overhead and one of the elevator's doors opened. He gestured for me to go in first, then followed me, and pressed the button to the fifth floor.

He leaned on the mirrored wall at the back of the elevator. "So, you ditched us again last night."

I grimaced. "Yeah. Sorry."

He tsked. "You should say that to your sister and Bia. They were really pissed at you."

"I know," I whispered.

"But ... you were all right, right? I mean, you just didn't go because you didn't want to, right? Nothing happened?"

One corner of my lips curled up. "Yeah, I was all right."

He nodded. "Good."

I forced myself to keep up with the small talk. "Did you guys have a good time?"

"Yeah, I guess."

"You guess?"

He lifted one eyebrow. "I might be going mad, but sometimes I think going out like that is getting a little old."

I gasped to tease him. "What? Gui Fernandes is saying he's tired of partying? No way!"

With a lopsided smile, he shook his head. "Shut up."

Once in the hallway of the fifth floor, Gui turned right and stopped in front of apartment 503 —there were six apartments per floor here, while on his floor, which was the last floor, there were only two.

"Here we go," Gui said, opening the door for me.

We entered a living room, which opened to a small breakfast area and a small kitchen, imitating the guys' apartment, but on a much smaller scale. The floor was hardwood throughout, and the walls were being painted a pale beige tone. There were paint cans, brushes, and low ladders in a corner, and the furniture was pushed together in the middle of the room, covered with blankets. There was no balcony, but I didn't need one. It was easy to see that the kitchen had recently been upgraded, and the appliances and cabinets looked brand new. A hallway opened to the left, leading to a linen closet, a tiny laundry room with a new washing machine and dryer, a bathroom, one bedroom that was a small studio with a desk, chair, and sleeper sofa, and one suite with a queen bed, dresser, armchair, a small walk-in closet, and a nice attached bathroom.

Nothing much, but unlike every other apartment Bia and I looked at, I couldn't see one thing wrong with this one. Could it be this easy?

"What's the trick here?" I muttered.

"What did you say?" Gui asked.

"I'm just wondering ... there must be something wrong with this apartment. Or maybe the building." I turned to him. "What's wrong with the building? Does the elevator break every week? The management doesn't clean the hallways and lobby too often? The neighbors suck?"

Gui chuckled. "The neighbors are awesome," he said, gesturing to himself. I shook my head with a smile. "Seriously, though, I can't think of anything. Maybe the guys and I are more reserved than the other residents, but we don't hear any loud noises or gossip. And they never complained about us and our parties either. As for the building per se, everything is always clean and the elevator has never stopped working once in the three years we live here."

I glanced around the living room, trying to imagine my regular day if I lived here for three months. Me coming in the front door every afternoon, taking my shoes off, throwing my purse on the couch, going into the kitchen, fixing something to eat, maybe taking a warm shower, then lounging on the couch or the bed and watching some TV, or reading a nice book, or maybe drawing a little more. I liked it.

"It can't be this easy."

"You say that as if nothing was ever easy in your life," Gui said, serious.

"It's not that. It's just ... this is all happening too fast, and the pieces are all fitting so perfectly. Unfortunately, nothing in life is perfect."

"Maybe things don't need to be perfect, but just right for you." Gui took a piece of paper from his pocket and handed it to me. "Here. The name and phone number of the owner. Who knows? Maybe the price he's asking for rent is absurd. There goes the perfection."

I laughed, amused over how Gui could always make any situation less dire. "Thanks." I picked up the paper and put it in my purse.

"When he left the keys, he mentioned that the repairs should be done by the middle of next week. Sooner than planned."

"That's ... great."

"Want more time, or did you see everything you needed?"

"I think I'm done here."

Gui locked the door and walked to the elevator a few steps in front of me. His cell phone rang as the elevator doors opened. He picked his phone up to check, walking into the elevator with his eyes on the screen. I reached for the control panel, intent on pressing the lobby button since Gui was busy, but he did it too, and his fingers brushed against mine. A shock ran up my arm, warming my core.

I pulled away lightning fast. "Sorry," I mumbled.

With a lopsided smile, he glanced at me. "It's okay."

It was okay, just it wasn't. Suddenly, I became aware that the two of us were alone, trapped inside the elevator, even if only for a couple of seconds. He could change. He could become angry and violent. He could advance on me, hit me, kiss me by force. He could push me against the wall and—

Hands shaking, I let out a shuddering breath. No, no, no. I wouldn't let my mind go there. Come on, this was Gui. Leo's cousin. Leo, who was perfect and was marrying my perfect sister. Gui couldn't be a bad guy. He just couldn't.

I noticed Gui looking at me from the corner of his eyes, his forehead creased. Gosh, what was he thinking? Option one: What is the problem with this girl? Option two: I want to hurt her.

As soon as the elevator doors opened, I bolted and didn't stop until I was on the sidewalk outside the building.

His hands in his jeans' pockets, Gui caught up with me, though he must have sensed the war in me, the way the panic weaved through my system, because he kept at least five feet between us.

"T-thank you for showing me the apartment," I said, my voice showing a hint of my instability.

"You're welcome."

"Bye." I turned to leave and walked a couple of steps, concentrating on putting one foot in front of the other.

"Hil?"

I glanced over my shoulder. "Y-yeah?"

He stared at me for a moment. "Drive safe."

I nodded and walked away. My feet screamed at me to run, to bolt, and to hide in my car before anyone saw me freaking out. Worst, before Gui saw me freaking out. But like a good girl, I took one step at a time, focusing on slowing my breathing and the hard beating of my heart.

I slipped inside my car and took a deep breath. I would have let it out, my panic, my fear, my cry, if it weren't for Gui still standing in front of his building, watching my car.

Quickly, I closed my eyes and conjured happy images to my mind. Me, the apartment, a warm meal, a good book. And the internship a few blocks away. The perfect setting. The perfect life.

It worked. My heart rate didn't go back to normal, but it didn't hurt anymore each time my heart pumped against my ribs, and the shaking of my hands was almost gone.

Finally, I peeled away from the curb and merged with traffic, leaving Gui and my panic behind.

***

HAVING TO STOP MY CAR BY THE SIDE OF THE ROAD or a gas station was becoming routine. Once again, I had to do that before driving to the club to meet Hannah, my mother, and some of her friends.

Lunch here always had the same rhythm. First, we all—around thirty women ranging from teens to high sixties—met at the balcony overseeing the tennis courts to have appetizers and drinks while engaging in small talk. About an hour later, we were ushered to the main dining room, to three long tables along the far back, where four floor-to-ceiling windows were always open, rain or shine, with a distant view of the main polo field. Here we were served several courses, slowly, then dessert and coffee. If there were a tournament underway, we would then make our way to the polo field. If there weren't, we would walk out together. Some women stuck around to talk to other members or watch tennis matches, but most left.

This time, my mother wanted a seat at the balcony again to chat with another member. Hannah excused herself, saying she had to get back to the ranch before Jimmy made a mess of everything. When I tried coming up with an excuse, my mother cut me such a hard look, I shut my mouth, afraid she would disinherit me. So, I stayed seated beside them around one of the tables, inserting one ah or oh here and there, just so they thought I was paying attention to whatever they were saying.

Eloisa, one of my mother's closest friends, looked past my mother and me and smiled. "Oh, here comes my son."

Reese, the newest and youngest player of the Knight House, stepped onto the balcony. Instantly, the memory of him watching me at the engagement party invaded my mind, along with the memory that I had tried flirting with him and failed miserably. My cheeks flamed.

"Hi, Mother," he said, kissing her on the cheek.

"Hi, dear. You remember Mrs. Taylor and her youngest daughter, Hilary, don't you?"

He turned to my mother and me with a courteous grin. "Of course. Hello, Mrs. Taylor, hello, Hilary, how are you?"

"I'm doing quite all right, Reese," my mother said with a wide smile. "Thank you. How are you?"

"Can't complain," Reese answered. Then his eyes turned to me. "I heard you got a summer internship here in Santa Barbara. I hope that means you will come to the club more often."

I smiled, though internally I was cringing, wondering how the hell he already knew about my internship. Had my mother blabbed to the whole club? To the entire town and region perhaps? I didn't doubt that.

"Yes, that would be lovely," Eloisa said.

"We'll see what my schedule will look like once I start."

"Don't worry," my mother said. "I'll make sure she comes more often."

He flashed his smile at her. "I'll count on that."

I stared as my mother winked at him, and he gave her a thumbs up. What the hell?

Eloisa checked the time on her wristwatch. "Don't you have practice soon, Reese?"

"Yes, ma'am." He bowed to my mother and me. "It was good to see you, ladies."

"You too, Reese," my mother said.

"Excuse me," he said, retreating a few steps with his eyes on mine, before turning around and walking from the balcony in the field's direction.

"Isn't he gorgeous, Hilary?" My mother patted my hand. "He's wonderful, Eloisa. I can see you raised a fine boy."

"Oh, thank you, Joyce." Eloisa shrugged as if it wasn't a big deal. "I can say the same about your girls."

I tuned them out as they exchanged silly pleasantries, and watched as Reese walked away, trying to decide what to think of this encounter. I took a deep breath, shutting down the tingling fear that always assaulted me whenever a guy showed interest in me or was close enough to do harm, and thought for a second. Reese was cute, and as a professional polo player, his physique was in top shape too. He seemed kind, polite, and into me. But was that enough? Enough to help me push back my fears so I could feel more for a guy? For him?

I wasn't sure. I didn't think I would ever be sure. I even had this nagging feeling that if Liam Hemsworth dropped in front of me from the sky, professing his undying love, I still wouldn't be sure.

My mother started talking about Hannah's upcoming wedding, of course, and Eloisa seemed interested in it. Bored and trying to find an excuse to leave, I looked over the club, not really searching for anything. Until my eyes crossed one of the paths going to the main parking lot and found Gui stepping out of his Jeep.

For some reason, the Fernandes boys didn't like to dress up to come to the club, even though it was a rule imposed at every corner—except for them. Gui was wearing jeans, a polo shirt, and cowboy boots, and he carried a white and dark blue bag with the Montenegro logo on it. He walked with an easy gait, and still looked confident, masculine, and handsome.

I inhaled sharply as his eyes found mine, and

one corner of his lips tugged up. My heart sped up, and I stifled a gasp when I realized it wasn't from panic.

Despite my best efforts to remain impassive, I smiled at him. Until a shadow caught my sight, and I looked past him.

Lucas had just arrived too and was walking up the path a few feet behind Gui.

The smile faded from my lips. A knot appeared between Gui's brows, and he looked over his shoulders. He halted upon seeing Lucas and waited until Lucas was right beside him to keep walking. They started chatting and Gui didn't look at me again.

I focused on my mother and Eloisa. They were now discussing honeymoon options. My mother thought Hannah and Leo should do a classic trip through Europe, while Eloisa thought they should do something more exotic, like going to the Maldives or some other stunning beach.

Okay, I was done. After coming up with an acceptable excuse, I bid my mother and Eloisa goodbye and walked to the parking lot, eager to get away from here.

I was nearing my car, keys already in my hand, when someone called me.

"Hilary, wait."

I turned around and saw Lucas jogging toward me. Images of the engagement party flashed in my mind and panic rushed through me. Clutching the keys, I stepped back, bumping into my car.

"H-hi, Lucas."

My expression was probably of a scared woman, because he halted a good distance from me, his hand turned up as if in surrender.

"I just want to say I'm sorry." He shook his head once. "I don't remember anything about that night, but Gui and Malcolm told me what I did. I'm so, so sorry."

My palm was wet around the car keys. "I-it's okay now. Thanks for apologizing."

"I know there's no excuse for it, but I want you to know that I usually don't drink that much. It's just ... my girlfriend, ex-girlfriend, had just broken up with me the day before, and I was ... I wasn't in the right state of mind. That mixed with too much alcohol ..." He ran a hand through his hair. "Not good. I'm really sorry."

I nodded. He was right. It was no excuse, but it made me feel a little better to know that he usually didn't drink that much. Hopefully, he didn't try to kiss every girl who crossed his path at parties and clubs.

"Okay," I muttered, not sure what else to say.

"All right. Yeah. I just wanted to apologize." He started turning around. "I need to go ..." I nodded again and he waved at me. "Bye."

Lucas jogged back to the club. Stunned and still a little shaky, I kept watching him and, in the distance, I saw Gui standing near the main polo field, watching me.

**8**

―――――――

GUI

USUALLY, WE SHOWED UP AT THE CLUB AN HOUR before a game, but today I decided to go even earlier. I arrived at the club almost two hours before the scheduled afternoon game. And I kept telling myself it wasn't because Hilary was probably still here with Hannah and her mother for their bimonthly lunch. Because that would be freaking stupid and girl-like.

*Não.* I had arrived early because I wanted to go for a run around the club before the game. Yes, that. I wanted to work out a little before the game, but I still wanted to have some time between the workout and the game. Right.

I parked my Jeep in its usual spot at the back of the parking lot, under a large tree and its sweet shadow, and walked to the main building. And there she was, seated beside her mother, and some other woman on the balconies overseeing the tennis court.

As if Hilary knew I was looking at her, she turned her head and her eyes met mine. I should have looked away, but she held my stare, and I just couldn't look away.

Then, her eyes shifted, falling on something behind. I glanced back and saw Lucas walking from the parking lot, a few yards behind me. When I looked back at her, Hilary was still staring at the floor, her hands pressed together on her lap. She was probably remembering the engagement night, when this fucked up drunken dude hit on her. I had almost hit him then, and for some reason, I almost turned around and hit him now.

Instead, I paused long enough for him to catch up with me.

"Hey man," I said.

He looked up at me, his brows furrowed. "Hey. What's up?"

I shrugged. "Nothing. Going to the field to get ready for the game. You?"

He launched in a tale of watching the Knight House practice as I shifted most of my focus on Hilary. I saw as she stood and started walking toward her car. Lucas noticed too.

"Wait." He halted. "I have to go talk to her."

I didn't like that. "I think that might not be the best idea."

"I know but, I need to apologize for the other day. I feel too bad, and, shit, she probably hates me right now. With good reason."

All right, I could understand that, so I didn't stop him when he jogged back to the parking lot and called her.

I took one step, willing my body to go to the field or the lockers. Anywhere. But my mind had another idea. I whirled around, on the side of the polo field's main path, and watched Hil and Lucas, just in case.

The conversation was quick and when Lucas turned around and started back this way, Hilary's eyes found mine. I held her brief stare, and something like longing, like want, bloomed in my chest. I wanted ... I wanted to go to her, hold her hands, and tell her she was okay.

Then she broke the stare, slipped into her car, and drove away.

I let out a long breath as I resumed walking. Soon, I was on the side of the building, going through the side entrance, to the locker rooms. My brain tried to come up with excuses as to why I should have gone back to the front and talked to her before she left, but nothing made sense, and finally, I told my brain to shut the hell up. It wasn't happening. It was better if I kept my distance.

I changed into shorts and a sleeveless T-shirt and went running. Hopefully, the exercise would clear my head.

## 9

HILARY

I RAN ACROSS CAMPUS, DOING MY BEST NOT TO BUMP into anyone. My first exam on Monday was at ten in the morning, so I usually slept in a little. However, today I had last Friday's test scheduled at 8:30 a.m., and I had totally forgotten about it!

Because of that, I ran like a crazy woman, my tote firmly under my left arm, my coffee mug in my right hand.

I stepped into the classroom at 8:33 a.m. and the professor was handing the tests to the students. My eyes scanned around, searching for a place to sit, but I froze. The classroom wasn't full, but there were only boys here. Only men. About a dozen or more.

I barely registered as the professor said, "Miss

Taylor, you're late." I opened my mouth to explain to him what happened, but no words came out. He sighed. "Take a seat."

I glanced around. Would I take a seat? If I didn't take this test, I would fail this class. Wasn't I strong enough to push through my fear, my panic, to pass a class? I wasn't so sure.

Shaking so hard I was sure I was going to fall on my face, I finally moved, taking the nearest empty seat I could find to the door. Just in case. Just so I could tell myself nothing was going to happen and that I was safe. This was a healthy environment, a respectful college. Besides, the professor was here, and he would never allow anything to happen to one of his students, would he? Well, he was also a man.

I closed my eyes and tried my therapist's technique. The tap-tap of a pen, the chuckle of someone behind me, the whispers at my side, the footsteps of the professor ... It was useless here.

*I can do this. I will do this.*

I took a deep breath and willed my heart and my breathing to slow down. Not so easy.

*I can do this.*

Just as I grabbed a pen from my tote, the professor handed me the test, then walked back to his table in front of the class. "You may begin," he said.

I turned to my paper and started reading the words. I read the same sentence five times and still couldn't absorb what it said, not when I was surrounded by men. Men who were stealing glances at me every few seconds. Men who smiled at me as if I were their prey.

Okay, okay. I was imagining things. Wasn't I?
*Calm down, Hilary.*

I dared to peek to my sides, and sure enough, most of the guys in the classroom were watching me. Some scribbled a little, then looked at me for a few seconds, then returned their attention to their test, and the cycle went on. But a couple were blatantly staring at me, as if they could see the answers to the test in my face? I wasn't sure.

Stifling a shudder that started in the base of my neck and fought its way down my spine, I did my best to block the men out of my sight and my mind.

*Focus on the test. Focus on the test.*

I stared at the words on my paper and repeated that mantra for about five minutes, until my hands shook a little less and my heart didn't pound so painfully against my rib cage. Still paying attention to my pencil and the paper in front of me, I finally started the test. It was a challenge to ignore the world around me and immerse myself in economics 102, but I managed.

Until thirty minutes later, when the professor's cell phone rang, and he excused himself, saying he needed to get this call. He exited the classroom and closed the door behind him, leaving me alone with over a dozen strangers. A dozen men. Men who probably had sex on their minds.

My hands started shaking again, and I sucked in a ragged breath.

*Focus, Hilary. Focus!*

But I couldn't focus, not anymore.

Then, a guy's hand reached over my desk, and he dropped a folded piece of paper on my test. He quickly went back to his seat on my right, but not without brushing his hand over mine first. Wincing, I jerked back and dropped my pencil on the floor.

Shocked, I stared at the piece of paper as if it could bite me. The fold wasn't too hard and the paper was half-open.

*Go out with me, beautiful*, it read.

I felt sick to my stomach.

Another guy, from my left this time, knelt down and retrieved my pencil.

"Here you go," he whispered, putting my

pencil on my desk. He lingered close, as if I would talk to him.

Something snapped inside me. I jumped from my seat, bumping into my desk and causing my test and my pencil to hit the floor. I didn't care, though. The only thing I cared about was getting away from here.

I swiped my tote from the floor and rushed to the door. With my shaky, sweaty hands, I fumbled with the knob, fear clogging my throat. Why wasn't it opening? Was the door locked? From the other side, the professor opened the door.

"Miss Taylor," he said then paused. He narrowed his eyes at me. "Are you all right?"

I could barely breathe, much less talk.

Instead of answering, or even acknowledge him, I ran. I ran from the building. I ran across campus. I ran to my dorm building and into the safety of my room.

---

ALTHOUGH I STILL SHOOK WHILE RECALLING WHAT had happened, now that I looked back at it, I felt stupid.

"I overreacted," I said to Dr. Walker, my therapist. I was seated in her comfy armchair, positioned strategically in a corner of her office, from where I could gaze through the window and admire the view of the park below.

If I closed my eyes, I could still see myself in that classroom with those guys, and the seemingly locked door, and the missing professor. I knew I had seen and felt the situation in a more dramatic way that it had been, but that didn't stop me from shaking all over again.

After the test, I locked myself in my room for the rest of the day. I even missed another final exam. Mariah came into the room twice, saw me in that state, and left without saying a word. During our first week living together, I had a major panic attack and I had to tell her about them, but I never told her why, what had first caused the attacks. And I never would.

At night, I got an email from Fallon White about my first day at her studio. That finally snapped me out of it. Immediately, I called Dr. Walker and asked for her help—with my current state and with contacting my professors and asking them to reschedule my exams. Thankfully, one of the professors listened to my therapist and let me take the exam another time, without many questions, but the other professor didn't want to hear it. He gave me an incomplete and said he

would email me soon about retaking the exam—
or the entire class next semester.

This morning, I was out of my dorm and had already moved into my apartment in Santa Barbara. However, before I could settle in my new temporary home, I had to do a pit stop at my therapist.

I was trying to focus all my thoughts and energy on the fact that I had an incomplete. Me, the perfect A student, who barely ever missed a class my entire life. I felt pathetic for having an incomplete, and the possibility that the professor would just decide it wasn't worth it and ask me to retake the damn class. However, hovering around those thoughts was the main reason I had come to the therapist: my dear panic attacks.

From a chair a few feet from mine, Dr. Walker pushed her red-rimmed glasses up her nose and stared at me, her dark brown eyes calm. "It's normal for your fear and panic to surge again during situations like this."

"Will I always react like that to these kinds of situations?"

"In extreme situations, probably. Yes. But you will be able to control your reaction. You won't shake as much, or feel like fear is seizing you."

"Hopefully," I muttered.

"Be positive, because positive thinking brings good results. Say definitely."

I scrunched my nose at her, not believing her. "Definitely."

She winked. "I'll pretend you meant that."

I let out a little laugh and sighed. "I don't know what's wrong with me. Why do I think every male, regardless of age, only thinks about sex, about having sex *now*? That they see a pretty girl and immediately lust over her and imagine her naked?"

"Well, the truth is, most males do. But that doesn't mean they are all perverts." She gazed out the window. "Try to remember how you were before the incident when you met a strange person for the first time, or the people you walked by on the street. Even if not consciously, you processed how attractive they were, and you weren't even aware of it." She returned her kind eyes to me. "That's the same with most men. They don't will their minds to go there, to lust over girls and imagine taking them to bed. It just happens, and most of them are so used to it, they don't even notice it anymore. Unless the female in question is absurdly stunning, and they can't take their eyes off her. Then I bet they are conscious of their thoughts."

"It all sounds so technical, as if there was a

manual for male and female, and we had to conform to it, no questions asked."

She chuckled. "Something like that."

This woman knew how to push my buttons, and that was what made her a great therapist for me. I had tried four others before finally feeling like she got me, like she understood me.

"All right, I admit I do remember looking at guys and thinking whether they were attractive. To be honest, I still do sometimes. These moments give me a little hope that I will get over the incident and my fears someday. However, when I was sixteen, I wanted to do something about it if they were attractive, like talk to them, dance with them, get their phone number, whatever. Now, I want nothing. I just acknowledge they are handsome and move on."

"At least the feeling is there. You think men can still be handsome. That's a big step." She pulled a notepad and pen from her table. "I suggest we make a list of all the things that you fear. Even silly, minor things, like spiders, cockroaches, fear of the dark, fear of horror movies, anything. Then we work our way up to the bigger things, like for example, your fear of being alone in a room with a man you don't know. Then last items would be to kiss a boy you're attracted to, and finally trusting a man completely."

I blushed, thinking of how silly it would be to have a list I shared with my therapist about kissing boys. I wasn't sixteen anymore.

"Just make a list?"

She shook her head, a slow smile taking over her sharp face. "Then, you go item by item from smallest to biggest and check them off."

"W-what? No!"

"I understand your hesitation, but listen to me. Even if you don't get to the biggest items, even if you stop in the middle of your list, you'll still have faced many fears and you will feel stronger, more confident. You will know for sure that you can defeat all of your fears, one by one. And then one day, you'll end up checking off the biggest items, even if you didn't intend to, I'm sure."

I narrowed my eyes at her. "It still sounds a little silly."

"And that's why you have to do it. Silly doesn't go well with fear. You don't need to fear this list. It'll be perfect."

I considered that for a moment. Well, she was right. It sounded so silly; I didn't have to fear it at all. And I could always stop in the middle like she said.

"Okay," I said, my tone low, guarded.

"All right." She sat up straighter, her pen poised against the notepad. "What shall the first item be?"

I forced a smile. "That the professor will turn my incomplete into a fail and I'll have to repeat the class?"

Dr. Walker returned my smile, but hers was real and it said, "Don't be silly."

Hard not to.

---

HANNAH AND BIA HELPED ME BRING MY THINGS from my car—and the rented U-Haul trailer—to the apartment. It wasn't much, just my clothes and toiletries and books and other things from my dorm. And Hannah had brought a few of my things from our parents' house too, like some more of my clothes, fitted sheets, and pillow covers, towels, etc.

At one point, I left them working while I went to the grocery store and bought all the necessary stuff: milk, bread, eggs, rice, pasta, red sauce, ice cream, soap, shampoo, and more. I also bought plastic cups, cutlery, and plates. Tomorrow, I would go shopping for real cups, cutlery, and plates, and for pans and all the little gadgets that made life easier. I had no idea what I would do with all these things after I moved back to the dorm, but right now, I didn't care. I just wanted to enjoy my first time living by myself. Really by myself. No parents or roommates.

For dinner, Iris came over and brought some takeout. Now we were just missing Gabi—we even called her to say hi and she yelled at us, telling us she hated us for getting together without her. Then she laughed.

The girls and I ate while they all helped me unpack my things. They didn't know where I wanted my stuff, but the fact that my clothes were out of the boxes and suitcases and neatly folded on my bed made things much easier.

"Excited?" Hannah asked, munching on her pasta with the help of the plastic fork.

"I am," I said.

I felt a mix of excitement and nervousness. I was finally by myself. I was finally doing something by myself. Sure, going to college in L.A. was more than anyone expected of me at this point, but I knew I could control the situation there—somewhat. I just had to avoid everything. Go to classes, go back to the dorm. Period. And spend most of my weekends in Santa Barbara at my parents' house.

Here, though, in this apartment, with this paid internship, I could finally feel like I was working toward my independence, toward my freedom—from my parents, from myself, from my past. Times like this, I really thought I would make it. Someday, I was going to heal and I would lead a normal, healthy life.

I hoped.

**10**

---

HILARY

"HERE IS WHERE THE MAGIC HAPPENS," FALLON said, opening one of the doors in the long corridor.

I gasped in surprise.

Her entire studio had been all white and elegant so far with gray or silver details. Because of that, and the fact that I had seen Fallon and Sonya in white and gray, I had chosen a gray pencil skirt, a white button-down shirt, and dark gray pumps for my first day.

This room though, the real studio of her studio, was an explosion of colors. Large, rectangular tables took over the center of the room, fabrics of all colors and textures spread over them. On one side of the tables stood three mannequins, and on the other side, there was a computer with a big screen. The walls were lined with more fabrics in neat order, like a giant box of crayons, shelves with several jars of buttons, zippers, and other knick-knacks that could be used as details or accessories, and a large, magnetic whiteboard with several written notes and pinned drawings.

Two women and one man worked in four of the seven stations.

"Come meet my team." Fallon beckoned me to follow her. "Guys, say hi to the newest member of our team." The fact that she didn't say the new intern didn't escape me, and I was excited about that. As they walked toward us, Fallon pointed at me. "This is Hilary Taylor. She just finished the second semester of fashion design at an art school in Los Angeles. She'll be here with us this summer."

"Hello," I said, a little intimidated. These people worked with Fallon, which meant they were probably very good at what they did.

"This is Christine." Fallon gestured to a petite woman in her thirties with strawberry blond hair to her shoulders streaked lime green. In my mind, the two colors didn't really go together, but with her pink lips and bright green eyes, she made it work. Christine waved at me. "This is Margot." Fallon introduced me to a black woman, also in her thirties, with long, curly, gorgeous black hair. Her smile was warm and it made her dark brown eyes shine. "And this is Karl." Fallon showed me the only male in the team. As I suspected, he was gay. He was tall and slender, and his brown hair was cut short on the sides, and styled to the right on top. He had about six or seven piercings in his ears, and tattoos running up his arms until they were hidden by his rolled-up sleeves. I wasn't sure if it was the fact that he was gay or his easy grin, but I didn't feel any panic while near him.

They all said hello and asked me how I was doing and how I liked school so far, and other normal questions for when you just meet someone for the first time.

"We don't have a hierarchy here," Fallon said, stirring me to one of the empty stations. "I assign projects as they come and won't breathe down your neck while you're working, although I do expect updates here and there." She gestured to the large wooden table in front of me. "This is your workplace."

I ran my hands on the smooth top, as if I could sense the magic we would make together. "This is great. I mean, not just the table, but everything in here."

She smiled at me. "This is not just my workplace. This is my life. I try to keep a friendly, fun atmosphere here. I won't allow drama or downers. You're warned."

"Understood," I said, nodding.

"Let me show you some of the projects we are working on right now." She beckoned me to follow her.

We walked around the room, and she pointed to models and drawings explaining each one to me. Right now, she was getting ready for three big fashion shows, working on a few dresses for Hollywood actresses for their movie premiere or awards events, seven dresses for women with big names—aka heavy wallet— a couple of others that she called small orders like local weddings and other events. She also had a yearly fashion line. She designed several pieces, produced one of each, and sold them here in her studio. According to her, a big, luxury department store was trying to sign a line with her, but she didn't like the idea of having several of the same dresses out there.

"Your first week's task will be to walk around us like a ghost and take in everything you can," she said as we made our way back to my station. "Ask many questions, and even make suggestions if you have any. We are here to help you learn and grown, and vice versa."

"And the second week?"

Her smile stretched wide. "Then I'll assign you your own project."

My jaw dropped and my heart beat faster, but it wasn't from fear, but out of joy, eagerness. Oh my gosh! This was so exciting!

"That's ... great," I said, hoping I didn't sound too silly.

Smiling, Fallon checked her wristwatch. "Time for an important meeting." She beckoned me to follow her. "Come with me and learn."

I was packing up after an exciting first day when Christine, Margot, and Karl approached my table.

"So," Karl started. "On Thursdays, we usually go to a bar and have a happy hour kind of thing. But today seemed like a good day to have an extra happy hour, you know, being your first day."

I looked to them, meeting their eyes, trying to make sure of what they were saying. "You're inviting me to go to a bar with you guys?"

Karl shrugged, but Margot smiled and answered for him. "Yes. It's actually a restaurant with a nice bar area. It would be nice to get to know you without all the formality of this place."

I glanced around. They thought this place was formal? Gosh, I wished I could take them to a real law or accounting office. Then they would see formal.

"What do you say?" Christine asked, popping her gum. "Are you coming or not?"

Go to a bar with three strangers. A bar, where men went to get drunk and pick up girls. With three strangers.

I opened my mouth to say no but snapped it shut again. Today had been a good day, and I could close it with a golden key—if all went well.

I had just started going out to dinners with the girls about a year ago. I had gone to a bar three times in the last six months, and I had left early—twice on the edge of a panic attack. I had gone to maybe seven or eight private parties in a house that belonged to someone I knew—going to Hannah's house for girls' night in and the guys' place for a get-together didn't count. I hadn't gone to a nightclub—yet.

I could take small steps. I could go with my coworkers to a bar, and if I started feeling uncomfortable, I could leave, couldn't I?

I raised one finger, asking for a moment, and

reached inside my purse. I picked up the small notepad and pen on the side pocket and scribbled something.

If a stranger read it, it wouldn't seem like a big deal. Hell, if my sixteen-year-old self read it, she would laugh in my face and call me insane. But to my nineteen-year-old self, it was a big deal. A huge deal.

I added a new item on my fear list: Go out to a bar with strangers.

And so I went.

---

HANNAH HAD SENT ME A TEXT WHEN I WAS AT THE studio, asking me to come over for dinner later. I thought it was only for me, so I was a little surprised when I saw Bia's and Iris's cars parked in front of my sister's house.

The girls were all in the kitchen, preparing drinks and appetizers.

"What's the special occasion?" I asked, joining them around the island.

"There you are!" Hannah smiled at me and handed me a glass with whiskey and coke. She was wearing a pink apron reading Soon to Be Married. "How was the first and second day?"

"Good." I set down my glass. "Fallon showed me around mostly and told me what she expects of me, and all that."

Bia grasped my glass and poured the contents on her own glass. "Excited?"

"Yes." I smiled, letting them know I was telling the truth. At least I had one good thing to look forward to. Well, two. The internship, and Hannah and Leo's wedding. "Excited about the job, but worried about my incomplete." I rolled my eyes. "My professor emailed me this afternoon."

"So?" Hannah wiped her hands on her apron and turned to me. "When do you have to go back to retake the test?"

I shook my head. "No tests to retake. He talked to another professor of mine from the design department, and they agreed that instead of retaking the test, I have to work on a design project."

I almost had a heart attack reading the email when I left work late this afternoon. Apparently, I had until the end of summer to come up with an original design project, and the design had to have a history or a story. I would have to explain it to them during a presentation that we would schedule later, but would probably be one or two weeks before classes started again in the middle of August.

More things to worry about. More work to do.

"That sucks," Iris grumbled. "The working for college part, of course. Not the design part, right. You're probably excited about designing something, aren't you?"

I narrowed my eyes, realizing they were right. This was a design project. I should focus on what I loved—designing—and not worry that it was for a class and that I would have to present it in front of a committee later on.

"I wasn't excited, but now I think I might be," I confessed. Smiling, I looked at them. "So, what is this? A girls' night during the week? That's new."

Hannah shrugged. "Just wanted to get my bridesmaids and maid of honor together, do some more bonding, and get in the mood for the wedding preparations."

"Oh, Gabi will kill us when she finds out we're together without her again," Bia said.

Poor Gabi. I knew how much she wanted to move to the U.S., but we couldn't stop meeting just because she wasn't here. Otherwise, we would get together what, two or three times a year?

I turned to the fridge and grabbed a can of Coke. "You know mom will kill you if you don't include her in all the preparations."

"I know. I plan on including her of course, but

she doesn't need to be waist-deep in everything. Just her toes will do. You, on the other hand. I want you to be neck-deep in all this."

I smiled, but inside, I was cringing. I was excited about the wedding, but I was so afraid of messing it up. I had never planned a wedding before, and the bachelorette party? Could we just rent a movie and do a drinking game instead of having a stripper over or going out to a club?

"All right. I promise to work on your wedding when I'm not at the studio. Deal?"

Hannah handed me another glass of whiskey and Coke. "Deal."

When she turned around to grab cookies from the oven, I passed my glass to Bia, who was already waiting for it, her hand outstretched. She winked at me and I rolled my eyes.

"What are the boys up to?" I asked, spying in the oven. Oh, I could see Bia's awesome *Pão de Queijo* in there. My mouth watered.

"Guess?" Iris said, her tone a little irritated. "Monster truck racing, as usual." Even though she wasn't an apt rider, she loved horses too, but she didn't get the monster truck thing.

"As usual," I repeated, nodding.

The rest of the evening went by fast. We talked about the wedding, of course, and about the guys, and about polo and horses. We also texted Gabi and, as we suspected, she was sad that she couldn't be here with us.

Not surprisingly, I was the first one to leave.

I climbed down the front porch steps, my eyes looking in the distance for the stable. At night, only a handful of lights were on, expanding the shadows and making it look like something out of a horror movie.

I shuddered. What went down at this house and this stable three years ago could be considered right out of a horror movie. I shuddered again, exhaling. It was okay. It was over. No one would hurt Hannah or me anymore.

As I walked to the parking lot, I stole glances at the stable, focusing on what was inside. I had a terrible fear of horses. I still didn't know how I had the courage to mount Belle and ride away on her that forsaken night. I guess I only did it because it was that or worse. After that one time though, I hadn't gone near Belle. I hadn't even stepped into the stable. Only went to the gates a couple of times with Hannah and the others. But never inside.

Fear of horses was the next item on my list.

I stopped beside my car, still gazing at the stable. I had to face this fear. It was one of the easy ones. Well, no fear was easy to face, but this one was on the less difficult end of my list. If I were nervous about even planning on how to face horses and defeat my fear, how would I advance on my list? I closed my eyes for a second and took in a long breath.

*You can do it, Hilary. One fear at a time.*

I just wished it were that easy.

## 11

I parked my car beside Hannah's, knowing she would be out with a tour group. I couldn't do this if she were here. I don't know, maybe it was because I wasn't sure I could go through with it, and if she was here, she would keep saying, "You can do it," and I wasn't ready for someone else's pressure. I was already having trouble with my own.

I looked around the parking lot. For a Friday afternoon—Fallon had sent us off to enjoy the weekend early—the ranch wasn't as full as I thought it would be. Besides Hannah's car and mine, there were six other cars parked near the stables, probably belonging to the riders who were out in the field with my sister.

After taking a long breath, I slid out of my car

and looked down at my clothes. Jeans, a plaid, fitted shirt, and cowboy boots—the only ones I had, which had been a gift from Hannah when I was fourteen and miraculously still fit. Back then, she still had hopes that I would fall in love with horses like her, and we would ride into the sunset together.

I didn't think I would ever fall in love with horses, but I was here to face my fear, to try and defeat my fear of horses.

Exhaling deeply, I walked into the stables. I wrinkled my nose once the smell hit me and I almost bolted right then. Gosh, how did Hannah spend all day here and didn't gag? It was crazy.

I had been inside this stable only a handful of times, but I still remembered every detail. After the fire that killed our grandmother and destroyed the entire thing, Hannah took over the ranch and had the stable rebuilt exactly as it was before. To her, it was to preserve our grandmother's memory. I would have preferred if Hannah had built it differently. Maybe it would have been easier to step into it right now.

"Miss Taylor?" Jimmy, my sister's right hand at the ranch, stepped out from a side room, startling me.

I gasped, my hand over my pounding heart. "Jimmy, you scared the hell out of me."

"I'm sorry, miss." The old man looked all around but directly into my eyes, seeming uncomfortable around me. "Miss Hannah is out with a tour group. She should be back in about two hours."

"I know."

"Oh." He shifted his weight. "Can I help you, then?"

"Well ..." I looked around. "For now, I just want to walk around the stables, if that's all right."

He narrowed his eyes at me, probably thinking I was crazy. "Of course." He stepped back, putting himself under the doorframe. "If you need anything, I'll be here." He pointed to the room at his back.

"All right. Thanks."

He nodded and disappeared under the doorway.

I stayed in the same spot for a couple of minutes, taking in the place and, more importantly, trying to get used to the nasty smell. Yeah, that would take a couple of days. Or months.

The place was like a long, wide corridor with several doors on each side, but only two or three led to actual rooms, like the office Jimmy was holed up in now and the tack room. The other doors were stalls, where the horses were. It was easy to see that several stalls were empty, the horses probably out with Hannah and her group.

There were metal plates beside each stall, indicating the horses' names. Leo's horse, Minuano, was here, as were both Bia's horses, Preta and Midnight, and Garrett's mare, Felicity. Of course, Hannah's beloved horse, Argus, wasn't here. After helping him through a major trauma, she fell in love with that horse. Sometimes I thought she loved him as much as she loved Leo.

Past Argus's stall, near the back gate, was Belle. I thought she would be out with the group since Hannah always said she was such a docile and calm horse, great for beginners or leisure riding.

Slowly, I put one foot before the other and walked along the corridor, looking at each stall, trying to familiarize myself with the fact that I was surrounded by horses. Even if they were secured in their stalls, I was still surrounded by horses.

My hands sweated.

The last stall caught my attention. The door's top part was closed, unlike the other stalls, and the wood boards around it were reinforced. That was where Hannah had kept Argus while she was helping him. That was where she kept all violent and problematic horses until they were doing better.

I racked my brain, trying to remember if my sister had mentioned having a new one. She was always talking about horses; I couldn't keep track.

The sound of agitated hoofs stomping to one side and the other and something like a loud snort let me know the stall wasn't empty. Of course it wasn't. Hannah had a big heart, and when it came to mistreated animals, it was even bigger. If animal control or a desperate owner came knocking on her door, asking her to treat their problematic horse, she would never say no.

I didn't want to get too close to that stall, although I wanted to go see Belle, and her stall was right beside it.

I paused and stared at Belle's door. I could always come back later, when this other horse was gone. But what if it took months to make him or her better? I would have to wait to face the next fear on my list. I wouldn't make any progress. Then what? I couldn't put my life, myself, on hold and hope everything would be all right. I wanted to be whole again, to be free and happy, to enjoy little things without being afraid.

I had to do this.

*I can do this.*

Eyes closed, I took a deep breath, preparing myself to push past my fear.

"Hey, you."

I shrieked and, on turning toward the voice, tripped on my own foot, stumbling to the side and reaching for the nearest pillar to steady myself.

Gui reached out, but I was able to stabilize myself before I fell on my face.

"Gosh," I muttered, my hand on my throat.

"Sorry," Gui said, hiding a smile.

"First Jimmy, now you." I took a deep inhale, trying to calm my racing heart.

"Sorry," he repeated, his accent thick, thicker than usual.

"It's okay." I straightened, suddenly embarrassed about being here.

I noticed Gui's eyes gliding over me, taking in my outfit. That was when I noticed he was wearing his practice clothes—tight white pants, the Montenegro polo shirt, and black knee-high boots.

A smile spread on his lips. "I don't think I've ever seen you dressed like that. It suits you."

"Um, thanks." I wiped my sweaty hands on my jeans. "What are you doing here?"

He cocked his head to the side. "What are *you* doing here?"

"Looking for my sister." I lowered my eyes so he couldn't see my lie stamped on my face.

But Gui was smart. "You wouldn't have come all the way here looking for your sister, knowing she could be out. No, you would have called first to make sure she was here." He glanced at the whiteboard on the wooden wall between two stalls. "And I see here she's out right now. In fact, she'll be out for a long time." He crossed his arm, his chin jutted out. "What is it? Why are you here?"

I opened my mouth, but nothing came out. Two feelings I knew too well, embarrassment and fear, engulfed me and I couldn't bring myself to say the truth. "It's nothing, really." I hooked my thumbs on my jeans' front pockets and started walking past him, to the stable's main gates.

Gui's hand shot out and, gently, he closed his fingers around my wrist, making me stop and instinctively jerk back. He pulled his hand to himself. "Sorry." He frowned, looking unsure. "About grabbing you like that. I know—"

"I-it's okay," I said quickly, hoping he would take the hint that I wasn't up to talk about it. "I should just go." I started walking again.

"Hil, wait." Gui turned with me. "I know you're not a fan of horses, so if you're here, it must be for a good reason. What is it?"

I narrowed my eyes at him. "Why all this curiosity?"

"It's not just curiosity. It's intriguing. You always intrigue me."

First, I gasped, shocked. Then rage course through my veins. "Oh, like that girl is so crazy, it's intriguing."

"No." He gave a step closer, his eyes on mine. "Like that girl is amazing, but she's hiding behind a wall. If only she would let someone break through."

The rage faded as fast as it had surged up. I watched him as he watched me, confused and intrigued too. Gui had just called me amazing. If I were still my sixteen-year-old self, I would be doing an internal happy dance right now. The truth was, it did mess with my insides; I just wasn't sure how.

"Tell me," he said, his voice soft, gentle.

Something in his eyes or his stance or his voice, or all of it together, cracked me a little. I sighed. "I had a panic attack last week during one of my final exams, so I sought out my therapist to help me. I'm tired of the panic and the fear. She suggested I make a list of my fears, from any stupid little thing to the things that give me panic attacks. Getting close to horses and riding them is on that list." I clamped my mouth shut, a little stunned that I had just blurted the truth out.

"I see." Gui narrowed his eyes at me. "And why didn't you ask Hannah for help?"

"I love my sister, but she wants to help too much. She'll act like a therapist and I can't deal with that. I just need to take this slow."

He stared at me for a moment, those blue eyes too bright, too interesting. "I can help you."

My heart skipped a beat. "W-what? Why?"

"Because I would like to see you break through that wall you hide behind." His eyes ... his expression ... he was serious.

Why was he serious about this?

"I don't know," I whispered, lowering my gaze. "This is pretty stupid."

"I don't think it is, otherwise it wouldn't be on your list."

He was right, of course. I just wasn't ready—it wasn't easy—to admit that out loud. It was one thing to let my therapist in, with whom I was taught to open up and share important things, but to share my fears with Gui? Yes, he was practically part of my family, but it wasn't the same thing. I didn't like to be seen as the girl with the one hundred problems, even if it were true. Those problems, those traumas were private, and exposing them like this, as if I was really considering doing it, made me feel vulnerable, weak, and afraid.

"I don't know," I whispered again.

"Come on, I promise I'm pretty good with horses." He flashed me one bright, reassuring smile. "And I promise I won't tell anyone if you don't want me to." He paused, giving me time to think, but then he nudged me with his elbow. "Come on, say I can help you."

I didn't know why, but the word spilled from my mouth before my brain could process it. "Okay."

# 12

GUI

When I had come to Hannah's ranch, I would never have guessed I would find Hilary there. And, to be honest, I was quite glad I did.

Then, when I entered the stable and saw her standing there in jeans, a plaid shirt, and cowboy boots ... damn, she looked so, so hot. The jeans seemed molded around her ass, and the shirt was fitted enough that I could make out her thin waist and her full boobs. I felt a new heat wave wash over me, going low, low, low.

After her shock at seeing me here had passed, and she agreed to let me help her, I leaned on the doorframe of Belle's stall. Slowly, Hilary walked back and halted on the other side of the doorframe, careful not to lean on it, though.

With her green eyes wide, Hilary stared at the mare across the door from us. Belle, though, was as calm and quiet as ever.

"So." I crossed my arms. "You're afraid of horses." She only nodded. "And I thought you didn't like them because of the smell."

One corner of her lips tugged up and she rolled her eyes at me. "That too."

I chuckled. "Why are you afraid of horses?"

She remained silent while staring at Belle for so long that I thought she wouldn't tell me. "You see, Hannah has loved horses since she was a few months old, and by the time she was four, she was riding ponies by herself. So, right after I was born, my father pushed me toward horses, expecting me to be like Hannah. But I never liked them, not really. They were big and scary and smelly." Hilary scrunched her nose, and I realized she was too cute like that. "But my father kept pushing, so finally at four, I gave in and told him I would ride with him. He brought his most prized stallion out and, even though I was shaking so hard, he put me up on the back of the horse. He was going to come up with me, but I think, I don't know, that the horse felt my fear and he reared up. I fell and hit my head. I don't remember much, but my mother always says I was knocked out and the horse almost trampled me." She closed her eyes for a minute, taking in a long breath. "I was taken to the hospital and had to stay in observation for two days." Her hands were shaking. I fought the urge to reach over and take her hands in mine. "After that, my father kept on pushing me, and of course, he said I couldn't give up this easily, but my mother sided with me and helped me with the arguments. After a couple of years, he just stopped trying."

"I'm sorry," was the only thing I could think to say.

She shrugged, but her hands were still shaking. "It was a long time ago."

I frowned. "It might have been, but if you add riding horses to your list, that means you're not really over it. Haven't you ever thought about trying again?"

She huffed. "My life is surrounded by horses. My house, Hannah's ranch, the club, now you guys. Of course I've thought about it, but ... have you looked at them?" She gestured toward Belle. "Look how tall they are, how thick their thighs are, and those hooves." She inhaled sharply. "They scare the hell out of me," she confessed in a low voice.

This time I did reach out and held her hand in

mine. With wide eyes, she stared at our hands. "It's okay, Hil." I squeezed her hand. "We'll get you through it. I promise that I'll help you get through your fears, and you'll be riding a horse like a champ."

She smiled and tugged her hand free of mine. "Thanks, Gui."

I did a mock bow and tipped an invisible hat. "You're welcome, ma'am." That earned me a wider smile and it took my breath away. Damn, I had to make her smile more often.

Mirroring me, she leaned on the doorframe and crossed her arms, hiding her still shaking hands. She stared at me with those big green eyes, a little amusement shining in them. "And what are you doing at Hannah's ranch on a Friday afternoon? Didn't you have practice or something?"

"*Bom* ..." I ran a hand through my hair. "I pretended my shoulder was hurting so I could get out of practice early, so I could come here and steal one of Leo's shirts."

Her delicate brows shot up. "Why?"

"It's a surprise the guys and I are planning for him for the bachelor party."

"Wow, you guys are already thinking of the bachelor party. And why one of his shirts?"

"We're going to have it bedazzled. He'll have to wear it during the bachelor party."

Her smile widened again, and I swore I could feel my heart beating faster in my chest. "I'll need to see pictures of that."

I chuckled. "I promised we'll take several and I'll show them all to you."

"I'll hold you to that." She tucked her hair behind her ear before looking at Belle again. "So, what do we do about this?"

"We take it slow."

"And that means?"

"That means that you just spent several minutes leaned against the door of a stall, only a few feet from a horse, and you did quite well." Her eyes turned back to me, and they were full of wonder. "I think we're done for today, but we should already schedule our next meeting."

"Meeting," she muttered.

"Unfortunately, I can't meet often because of my practice and game schedule."

"And now I'm working full days too," she said.

"Yeah, so, how about next Thursday?"

She seemed to think about it for a moment. "Yeah, I guess that will do."

I grinned. "It's a date, then." And this time, I meant it.

# 13

HILARY

"I LIKE THESE." MARGOT PICKED UP THE THREE samples of fabric I had chosen and placed them side by side on her table. She took a few steps back and tilted her head, analyzing them. "Oh, I love these. I'm definitely using them."

The tension slipped away from my shoulders, and I beamed, proud of myself. "Thanks."

Since last Thursday, I had been helping Margot with one of her bigger projects. It was exciting and I was learning a lot, and now I was thrilled that she had liked my suggestions.

Dread was also playing its part inside me, though. It was Tuesday afternoon of my second week here, and I hadn't been assigned any project of my own, like Fallon said I would. Maybe she changed her mind and wanted to delay the start of my designs? Maybe after a week working here, she realized I wasn't as bright as she thought I was and was having second thoughts about hiring me.

It was hard to concentrate on other projects, on someone else's projects, or even my project for college—which I tried to think about as often as I could—when those ideas kept bouncing inside my mind. I succeeded for about a few minutes, then doubt charged my mind and I had to fight a small panic attack.

At 4:15 p.m., the landline phone ranged on my table.

"Hilary here," I said upon answering, knowing it was either Sonya in the front or Fallon.

"Hilary, come to my office, please," Fallon said from the other side of the line. Her tone was deadpan, and I froze for a second.

"On my way," I muttered before hanging up.

Taking a deep breath, I stood from my chair. I glanced around, sure three pairs of eyes would be on me, analyzing me, curious about the call, interested in its outcome. But Christine, Margot, and Karl were deep into their own worlds, not even acknowledging my presence. Which was a relief.

My hands were shaking when I knocked on Fallon's door.

"Come in," her voice came through loud and clear.

After another deep breath, I opened the door and stepped inside her office.

"Did you want to—?" I saw who was seated across Fallon's desk and lost my words. "Hannah, what are you doing here?"

My sister stood and opened her arms to embrace me. "Hello, Hil."

I glanced at Fallon, as if I needed permission to hug my sister, and she nodded.

"Hi," I said, wrapping my arms around my sister. I stepped back and looked at her. "What are you doing here?"

She sat back down and gestured to the chair beside me. Again, I looked at Fallon and she nodded. I sat down and stared at my sister.

She smiled. "Well, I need a dress for my wedding. My mother, my maid of honor, and my bridesmaids need dresses too."

"Oh, great," I said with a smile. She had come to the right place. "Fallon is the best. You'll love working with her."

Hannah shook her head, and I heard Fallon chuckling. "No, silly, I want you to design our dresses."

My jaw fell open. "But I thought ..." I wasn't sure what I thought.

"You've been designing clothes since you were four, and you always gave me great fashion tips. Come on. Did you really think I would have anyone else design the most important dress of my life?"

I was in shock. When she put it like that, I understood. If our roles were reversed, I would have her design my dress too. Emotions filled my chest—pride, excitement, anticipation, happiness. Tears sprang to my eyes.

"I told you I would assign you your own project during your second week here," Fallon said.

Oh, this was amazing!

I flung myself at my sister and embraced her again. "Thank you! Thank you!"

She hugged me tight and laughed. "Of course, Hil. I wouldn't have it any other way."

---

I ARRIVED TWENTY MINUTES EARLY TO PREPARE myself for the challenge I was going to face today. I hadn't expected to find Gui's Jeep already parked beside the stable. I parked my car beside his and spied into the stable. He was probably busy with the horses and hadn't seen me arrive yet, so I had a little time to myself.

I closed my eyes and worked on the calming and focusing technique my therapists taught me. Images of Fallon's studios, lots of colorful fabrics, Hannah in a beautiful wedding dress, and models on a runaway wearing my creations filled my mind. Things that made me happy. Things that made me confident.

With a renewed spirit, I got out of my car and headed toward the stable. Gui appeared at the open gates.

"*Boa tarde*," he said. His eyes raked down my body, taking longer at my legs. Warmth spread through my cheeks. Maybe choosing to wear cutoff jeans shorts hadn't been the best idea, but it was so damn hot today. At least I was wearing a modest green T-shirt that hid everything.

"Good afternoon," I answered him, taking him in. He wore worn jeans, a fitted white shirt, a black Montenegro baseball hat turned backward, and brown cowboy boots. Even though I had sworn off men and he was practically family, I couldn't not notice how gorgeous he looked. It was no wonder he was a god with the ladies.

Gui straightened, all business-like. "Ready?"

I bit my lower lip and shook my head. "Not really."

His eyes glanced to my lips before returning to my eyes with a different gleam, one I was sure I was imagining. "It's okay. I've got you. We can go as slow as you want to." My eyes widened this time. A second later, his mouth rounded in a silent oh. He pulled off his hat, ran his hand through his hair, and then settled the hat back in place. "You know what I meant," he said, his tone strained.

I looked down at my boots, to hide my cheeks, which were probably scarlet red. "I know." What, did he think I didn't know what he thought about me? What he said the other day, about me being an amazing girl hiding behind a wall ... well, the hiding behind a wall was right, but I was sure he threw that amazing in there to make me feel better about my messy feelings, about my scarred soul. He thought I was damaged, broken, like everyone who knew about what had happened. And I guess they were right. With my fears and my panic attacks, I certainly wasn't anywhere near being whole.

"All right." He stepped back into the stable. "Come with me."

I followed him, taking note of each step, each

stall we walked by, until we were crossing the back gates into the arena out back.

"Where are we going?"

Gui pointed to another set of gates on the other side of the arena. "To the round pen."

"Oh-kay," I muttered. I barely knew what stable and arena meant. If he started throwing specific horse-related terms my way, I wouldn't follow.

He chuckled. "You know what a round pen is, right?" I stared at him, letting my silence do the talking. "Wait. You've been around horses all your life."

"Nope, I haven't. They have been behind my house all my life, but I stopped going near them when I was four. End of story."

He narrowed his eyes at me, probably remembering the story I told him the other day. "A round pen is a closed place to train horses, and it happens to be round. Some are reinforced—" He pointed to a third set of gates to our left. "—for horses like Argus." He halted beside the wooden fence that made up the round pen he had led me to. "And some are just regular round pens for basic training, like this one."

Movement caught my sight, and I leaned closer to the fence, spying between the wood boards. "Belle is here."

"*Sim.* I brought her here before you arrived."

I jerked my head to him. "What time did you get here?"

He shrugged. "About thirty, forty minutes ago."

Why had he arrived so early, even earlier than I had? Wasn't he busy with training and promoting his team?

I closed my eyes and inhaled.

*Okay, Hilary, stop questioning everyone's intention. Not everyone has a hidden agenda.*

At least I hoped not.

Nevertheless, I believed Gui pitied me, was sympathetic with my cause, and for some inexplicable reason, decided to help the troubled girl. I wouldn't waste my time explaining to him how I hated pity and sympathy, because I knew he would bail once I did, and I kind of needed someone to help me with this. As much as I hated asking for help, I knew I couldn't scratch this item off my list alone.

"Okay, so ... what now?"

"Now." Gui climbed the fence, swung his legs to the other side, and sat atop of it. "We just get used to this." He opened his arms to the round pen.

"Oh-kay," I said, not really sure what he wanted me to do.

He chuckled. "Come on up, Hil. The fence won't bite you." I stared at him. "Well, it might have a few splinters, but those don't count as bites, so ..."

I sucked in a quick breath and climbed up the fence. Swinging my legs to the other side, now that was a challenge. I swung one leg, straddling the fence, and my body swayed to the side. I was sure I would lose my grip on the fence until Gui closed his hands around my forearms and steadied me. I froze, staring at his hands on my skin. A man's hands on me. And it didn't make my stomach roll in disgust or fear. No, but it certainly made me anxious—if that was the first step before fear, or anxiety for something else different, I couldn't tell nor did I want to. I wasn't ready to overanalyze anything.

With Gui's strong hands guiding me, I swung my other leg over the fence and sat a good two feet away from him. When he was sure I wouldn't fall, he retreated to his side.

"So ..." I said, looking at Belle, who trotted in the round pen. At first, I thought she was distressed by being here, but now looking at her, she seemed to be playing.

"So ..." Gui repeated.

"What do I do?"

"I meant it. We sit here and let you get used to being here with Belle close by."

"But we could have done that in her stall like we did the last time."

He shook his head. "It's not the same thing. There you had her door between you, and she didn't have a lot of space to run. Here, she's free, more or less, and you're on the inside of the fence." He looked at my legs for a brief second, and then returned his gaze to the mare in the pen. "Even though I would like to see you standing in the pen with Belle, I think giving some distance from where she is but still being close is a good first step."

It made sense. In her stall, with her stall door between us, she couldn't hurt me. It was a controlled environment. Here, she was out in the open and I was inside the fence. If I were to stand inside with her, there would be nothing between us. Belle was a good mare, but I was nervous around horses. If I spooked her, the situation would be more complicated to control.

Gui fell silent, his gaze on Belle. For the first ten minutes or so, I also focused on Belle. She was a good-looking horse, with strong legs, long neck, and shiny brown coat. Even though she wasn't the youngest out there, she was energetic and playful.

Perched up here, it was easy to enjoy this moment. To feel eager about moments to come. I would never be like Hannah and Bia, but looking at Belle now, I felt quite hopeful that I could also love horses someday, just like them. Well, maybe not all horses, but one horse. One mare, actually.

A breeze blew by, whipping my hair across my face. I turned my face in the direction of the wind and ran a hand around my ear, tucking in the messy strands. As I was about to return my gaze to Belle, my eyes caught Gui's. He was staring at me. Just staring. His jaw was tense, his lips pressed into a thin line, the slightest wrinkle on his forehead. He looked serious, almost painfully so.

Did it hurt him so much to look at me?

My sixteen-year-old self would have asked him what he was staring at without hesitation. My nineteen-year-old self? This version of me wanted to hide, to jump off the fence and run to her car and pretend this never happened.

I tucked in my chin in my chest, letting my hair fall like a curtain between us, so I could compose myself before I broke down right here, right now.

"Don't hide," Gui said, his tone low but sure. "I'm sorry if I keep staring, but you're just too beautiful. Don't ... you don't need to hide."

My head snapped back to him, and I gaped at him in shock. He thought I was beautiful?

I remembered being called beautiful hundreds, thousands of times before. I remembered hearing I would be stunning when older even more times. However, that was all before what happened to Hannah and me. Before the news spread and everyone in our circle, in our town knew what Eric had done to us. Before he left me damaged and broken, and I became the hottest gossip around for months. Before everyone looked at me with pity and sympathy. Since then, nobody had told me I was beautiful, not anymore.

Gui could be teasing me, playing a trick on me, but he wasn't that cruel, was he? I didn't know him that well to know if he was capable of such things.

I didn't know him well enough. Truth be told, I didn't know him period.

The fear of being around horses was replaced by my deepest, scariest fear: of being alone with a man.

Panic filled my chest, rising within my throat. The shock froze me and I barely breathed.

Gui noticed my reaction and retreated. "It's okay, Hilary. You're fine. I promise I won't hurt you. I will never hurt you." He jumped off the fence, inside the round pen, to give me more space.

Regardless, the panic attack had already started, and I could do nothing to stop it now.

I held on to the fence to try to stop the shaking. I closed my eyes and focused on trying to stop my vision from blackening, and on my lungs to try to stop the rapid breathing, the shallow gulps. Nothing worked.

Something snapped in me and the dam broke. I wanted to run from here, to hide in my car, inside Hannah's house, anywhere but here. I didn't want Gui to see me like this.

Still shaking, I swung my legs over the fence. My foot caught on the highest board, pulling me backward, making me unstable, and with the momentum, I tumbled toward the round pen. Somehow my flailing arms worked and caught one of the boards, pausing my fall. My right shoulder and hip hit the fence, and I didn't even yell when the pain exploded in my limbs.

My vision darkened a little more, making me dizzy, nauseated. I wanted to scream, to run, to crawl out of my skin. I think I tried doing all that, but I was lost. Lost in my mind, swimming in panic and debilitating fear.

Gui knelt before me. He was speaking, but I couldn't hear him. I could barely see him. Suddenly, he jumped up and turned his back to me, his arms to the side, trying to signal someone, keep something away? I remembered a part of my brain asking what he was doing, but it was a small part. The rest was taken up by my feelings, my uncontrollable emotions.

Then warm hands closed around my shoulders. Eric's face appeared before my eyes, and I screamed. I screamed because my life, my soul depended on it.

"Hil," I heard him calling me. "Hilary." I didn't remember his voice being this soft, this ... feminine. "Hilary, are you hearing me?" His face transformed. His hair grew out, his nose and chin thinned, his eyes became green, and then Eric wasn't Eric anymore. "Hilary, snap out of it!" Hannah's beautiful face was two inches from mine. With her hands still gripping my shoulders, she shook me hard. "Hilary!"

Eric wasn't here. Eric was never here. Eric was locked away, in a wheelchair, and he could never hurt me again.

The scream faded, leaving my throat raw. "Hannah," I croaked.

She let out a long, relieved sigh and embraced me. "Thank God," she whispered.

Taking a deep breath myself, I let my head fall on her shoulder. The fight left me. The panic dulled to a numbing sensation, leaving me empty, listless.

Slowly, the world came into focus again.

Gui was holding Belle's reins across the round pen, tension and strain visible in his face, in his arms. Belle jerked against him, and he held her down.

Hannah followed my line of sight.

"Belle got spooked when your ..." She glanced back at me. "When your attack started. Gui held her back, even though she fought him the entire time."

I rubbed my eyes, trying to get rid of the dull pain in my head. "How long did it last?" From experience, I knew that my notion of time was lost when the attacks started. Sometimes I thought it lasted for hours, but it was only a few minutes, and sometimes I thought it lasted for only a minute, but it was much longer.

"I'm not sure. I got here about ten minutes ago, but my guess is that Gui has been holding Belle back much longer than that."

I still stared at him and he stared back at me with worried eyes. Or was it pity? Or maybe it was only fatigue from having to hold the spooked mare for so long. Poor Gui. I wouldn't blame him if he never wanted to help me again.

"Help me get out of here," I said low, my throat still hurting.

Hannah hooked her arm around my waist and helped me up. My legs were still numb and wobbly, making me too heavy for Hannah alone. I leaned against the fence, trying to move by myself. I wanted to get out of the round pen so Gui would be able to stop fighting Belle.

"Can you give me a hand?" Hannah asked, looking behind me.

I looked over my shoulder and saw Jimmy walking up to the round pen. Nodding, he opened the gate and passed one of my arms around his shoulders. Hannah still clutched my waist. Together, they carried me out of the round pen. Jimmy pulled the gate closed.

"I didn't lock it," he yelled.

"I got it," Gui answered.

Despite everything, I glanced over my shoulder and saw Gui walking across the round pen toward the gate, his expression closed and his eyes on me.

## 14

HILARY

Jimmy and Hannah laid me on the sofa, and Hannah pulled a blanket over me. I was still shaking, but I didn't tell her it wasn't from the cold. It was the remnants of the panic attack.

Jimmy retreated to the door and Hannah followed him. They exchanged a few words, all whispers, then he left and she knelt beside me.

"What can I do for you?" she asked, concern written all over her face.

"I just need to rest and calm down."

"All right." She looked me up and down a few times. "You've got a bruise on your shoulder." She pointed to a bright red spot on my shoulder. "Does it hurt?"

I was still numb. Nothing hurt. The only things

I felt were mortification and exhaustion. "Not yet." Remembering I had hit more than just my shoulder, I lifted my T-shirt and saw the reddish mark on the side of my waist too.

"What do you remember?" my sister asked, her voice gentle, cautious.

I didn't really want to think about it anymore, but I also had a few questions. "Hm, I'm not sure. The panic started and I tried to run. I didn't want Gui to see me like this," I muttered, embarrassed. "But I ended up falling inside the round pen. By then panic had already consumed me." I didn't want to tell her I had seen Eric ... I wouldn't. "How did you get there?"

"I was coming back early from a private lesson with two young sisters. I hadn't seen anything until Gui called me. He was holding Belle back. I handed off the girls to Jimmy and rushed to the round pen. Then Gui told me you had fallen. He wanted to help you, but because you were already having the attack, he wasn't sure if touching you was the best way to go or not. Before he could decide what to do, Belle got spooked and he held her back until I arrived."

I sucked in a long breath. "How long was that?"

"Accordingly to Gui, it was about thirty minutes." Her tone was low, careful as if she didn't want to admit that to me.

Oh my gosh, Gui held Belle back from me for thirty minutes? No wonder he looked so strained and tired when I came to.

I buried my face in my hands.

"Shhh." Hannah rubbed my back gently. "It's okay, Hil. You're okay now."

Taking a deep breath, I looked into her. "Thank you."

"For?"

"I don't know." I shrugged. "For being there, for snapping me out of it somehow, for carrying me in here."

She waved her hand, dismissing my thank you. "So, are you hungry? Do you need anything to drink?"

Hannah would be over me like a mother hen until I gave her something to do, so I lied. "Yes, I'm hungry."

"What do you want?" she asked. I hesitated, not sure what to ask. What would buy me some time to be alone? She filled in the silence for me. "How about a loaded grilled cheese? And some iced tea?"

"Sounds good," I lied again. Not that I didn't like her loaded grilled cheese and iced tea. I liked them, but right now, my stomach didn't want anything.

"I'll also bring ice for those red marks. They look like they will hurt soon." She jumped up. "Be right back." She marched to the kitchen.

Sighing, I laid my head back and closed my eyes.

The brief memory of the terrors of my panic attack rushed to the front of my mind, and I stifled a sob. A single tear escaped my eye. Then another. And another.

The front door opened, and I sat up, wiping away the tears.

Gui stepped inside, his baseball hat in his hands. His brown hair was damp from sweat, I realized. He stayed by the door, eyeing me with worry.

"Hi," I said, feeling mortified by what he witnessed.

"Hey." He still stood by the door. "Are you okay?"

I nodded. "I guess so." A new batch of tears made their way to my eyes, but I wiped them. "I'm sorry about my reaction. Somewhere, deep in my mind, I knew it was you beside me. I knew you would never hurt me. I knew there was no reason for me to panic, but I couldn't help it. It was stronger than me." The tears won, and a couple ran down my cheeks. "I kept seeing his face and there was nothing ... nothing I could do. I'm—"

"Hey, hey." Gui took two steps toward, but stopped, his frame rigid. "It's okay. I know that. Don't worry about me."

Again, I wiped my tears away as if I could erase all from my mind. "I'm sorry."

"Hil, it's okay. I swear." His knuckles were white around his hat. "Just tell me if you're okay now."

For some reason, I couldn't lie to him. "I'll be okay."

Gui stared at me for a minute, his eyes shining with worry or ...caution? He was probably afraid of getting close to me again, of triggering another attack.

Interrupting the awkward moment, Hannah came back from the kitchen with a tray. Looking from me to Gui and back to me, she deposited the tray with my sandwich and drink on the coffee table.

"Here you go, Hil." With a forced smile, Hannah handed me the ice pack. Then, she stood, her hands on her back. "Gui, hmm, may I speak with you for a minute? In the kitchen, please?"

My curiosity piqued as Gui followed my sister

into the kitchen, but I lay back on the sofa, holding the ice pack to my shoulder with my eyes closed, just too tired to care about whatever she wanted to talk to him about.

I wasn't counting, however, in being able to hear part of their whispers from here.

Hannah started. "... you doing here? And her? ..."

"Hil said she would help me with something for the wedding ..." My sister replied something I couldn't hear, and Gui continued, "It's supposed to be a surprise."

"...her clothes. That's not like her."

"I guess she wanted to get in the spirit of things."

"What things?"

"Told you. It's a surprise ... won't tell."

Hannah muttered something else, and then came back to the living room. "You didn't even touch your food."

Gui stayed by the hallway door, his eyes cast down.

"I don't feel like I can eat right now," I admitted.

"All right." Sighing, Hannah sat down on the coffee table beside the tray and leaned forward, getting closer to me. "I want to help you, Hil, but

I don't really know what to do. Tell me what to do."

"I just want to relax for a minute. I'll be okay soon."

She frowned, as if she was suspicious of something.

Tires crunched the stones on the entrance road, signaling an incoming car. Hannah looked out the window and stood. "I'll be right back."

I glanced out and saw Leo parking his SUV beside Hannah's car. She rushed out and down the porch steps to greet him, and I turned away.

Gui walked into the living room, but still maintained his distance.

"I want to thank you for trying to help me, and especially for holding Belle so she wouldn't stomp all over me," I said, trying to make a joke with the stomping part. Then I remembered that was what made me afraid of horses in the first place, and worse, how Eric ended up in a wheelchair. Hannah's horse, Argus trampled him. My stomach revolved.

"It was nothing."

Of course it wasn't nothing. It must have been hard to hold back a spooked horse. He was probably tired, aching, and pissed at me.

"I'm sorry," I whispered again.

"Stop apologizing, Hil. There's nothing to apologize for. You're all right now; that's all that matters."

I opened my mouth to argue, but the determined and almost irritated look on his face made me clamp my lips again.

I looked out the window and saw Hannah and Leo talking, and Leo's expression changing—a knot appeared in his forehead and his jaw tensed. Then, he looked up, through the window, past me. I glanced back and found Gui staring back at his cousin. Gui gave a sharp nod, then shifted his gaze to me.

"Be right back." He marched from the house.

As Gui approached Leo, Hannah walked to the stables.

I couldn't hear them, and from their position, I couldn't even try to read their lips, but I could see their body language. Leo and Gui were arguing. They both pointed to the stables and to the window from where I spied on them a couple of times. They were arguing about me. I could imagine the whole discussion. Leo was telling Gui to stop being stupid and stop helping me. I was damaged and would drag him down with me. Coming to his senses, Gui finally realized he had a moment of delusion. Why was he even bothering with me anyway? But Gui surprised me. Instead of agreeing with Leo, Gui retorted fiercer and fiercer, until finally he clenched his fists, as if he was holding back from punching Leo, yelled one last time, and then stomped down the porch stairs and didn't stop until he was inside his Jeep and leaving the property.

Leo stared at him, shaking his head. After a long moment, Leo turned to the front door and I lay down, pretending to be asleep on the couch.

---

I PLACED THE HOT TEA MUG ON THE NIGHTSTAND and climbed in my bed. I leaned against the headboard and pulled the covers up to my waist. I grabbed my Kindle from the nightstand and opened to the romance book I had started reading two days ago. I reread the same sentence about ten times before I gave up and laid the kindle beside me.

It was good to be home—Hannah had insisted I spent the night at the ranch, or at least she wanted to drive me to town, because according to her, I was too distraught to drive. Maybe she was right, but I didn't give in. I wanted my place—even if it was temporarily rented—my bed, my stuff. I wanted to escape her scrutinizing gaze and her motherly overprotection.

So, after a long argument, Leo intervened and convinced Hannah to let me go, with the condition that I had to call as soon as I parked my car in the building's garage.

A long bath and some reheated leftovers for dinner later, I was ready to turn in for the night. My mind didn't agree with me, though. It kept re-living the day, moment by moment, making me nauseous, mortified, and afraid again.

I closed my eyes and tried my therapist's trick to calm down. I conjured images of my family: Hannah's excitement about her wedding, her telling me I was going to design her wedding dress, the girls laughing around a table during girls' night out, my design project classes, my professor telling me I had a chance of having my work presented at next year's exhibition, and then a new image I hadn't really associated with happiness until now. Gui, in the ranch stable, telling me I was amazing, and then Gui seated on the fence, telling me I was beautiful.

A ding came from my phone, and I snapped my eyes open, suddenly afraid of my happy thoughts.

I checked the message and held my breath.

Gui: *How are you doing?*

Me: *Hi. I'll be okay.*

Gui: *Sorry I left the ranch without saying good-bye. Leo got on my nerves.*

Me: *It's okay.*

He didn't reply right away, so I entered a text before I lost the nerve.

Me: *So, I don't think I'll need your help anymore.*

What I wanted to say was something more like "I understand if you don't want to help me anymore," or "I'll save you the awkward moment where you tell me you don't want to help me anymore, and tell you I don't want your help anymore," because really? After today's fiasco, why would he still help me?

But at the same time I hit enter, a new text came.

Gui: *I realized we didn't schedule the next day we'll meet.*

I stared at my phone. Wait, what?

Instead of a new message, my phone rang with a new call.

I sighed and answered, "Hey."

"You're not giving up, right?" Gui asked, his tone severe.

"Well …"

"What?"

"It's just ... after what you saw today, I didn't think you would want to help me anymore," I confessed. There was a long pause on the other side. "Gui?"

"Are you afraid I'll trigger another panic attack?"

"Gui ... it wasn't you. I mean, the fact that we were alone out there didn't help, but it wasn't just that. It was several small gestures and situations that clicked in my mind and put me in that state."

"But it was me too."

"No. Yes. I don't know." I sighed. "Look, I'm just too vulnerable right now, and I probably won't have the courage to step in the stable, let alone face a horse, for the next couple of weeks. I need to get myself in check first." I hated admitting these things to him, but I didn't want to lie to him. He was a good guy and he deserved to know the truth. "So, since I won't be going back to the ranch, I won't need your help."

"For now?" he asked, a little bit of hope in his tone.

"For now," I lied, knowing that I needed to erase that item from my fear-defeating list.

"Okay." He cleared his throat. "*Bom*, if you change your mind, you know where to find me."

"Okay. Thanks. Good night."

"*Boa noite*," he said in Portuguese before hanging up.

I plugged my phone in the charger and left it on the nightstand. Then I lay in my bed and stared at the ceiling.

My chest constricted and new tears found my eyes. I couldn't even scratch the first item on my list off. How did I hope to go through all of it? It was hopeless.

# 15

---

HILARY

"I don't think you should erase that fear from your list," Dr. Walker said. She was seated on her chair, notepad in hand.

I crossed my legs on the chaise long. "I don't want to just erase that item from my list. I want to throw my list away."

After wallowing in my apartment almost all day Friday, I finally gave in and called my therapist Friday night. She rebuked me for not having called sooner and scheduled an appointment first thing on Saturday morning. And that was why I was at her office, confessing my embarrassing panic attack in front of Gui and Hannah at 7:30 in the morning.

"Why would you give up this easily?"

I snapped my head at her and gaped. "Easily? I tried. I really tried and even had a freaking panic attack!"

"You had panic attacks before and you didn't give up." She set down her notepad. "How many panic attacks have you had this year?"

I counted in my head. The one from two days ago, then the one in May during a final exam, another one in February when Evie's husband showed up for the first time at the women's center and threatened her and me. And before that, one in December, but that didn't count as this year. "Hmm, three."

"By this time last year, how many panic attacks did you have?"

I rummaged my mind, but couldn't remember the exact numbers. "I don't know, four?"

"Seven," she said. "I think three is an improvement from seven, don't you think?"

When she put it that way ... "It doesn't matter. Obviously, this is the wrong way to go about my fears."

She leaned back in her chair, tapping her pen on her notepad. "Explain."

"I already did. I tried and I had a panic attack."

"So you're giving up."

"No. We just have to find another way."

"There aren't many ways to go about this, Hilary. And the list is a great way to progress. You just have to stick with it a little longer. Take some time off from it. Don't go to the ranch for a couple of weeks. Avoid talks about horses and whatnot, but once you're feeling better, once you're sure you can't feel a panic attack around the corner, try again. You owe it to yourself to try again."

I sighed. "The old don't give up meme."

"Yes. It's old, but it's true. You know you won't succeed if you give up now, but there is a good chance you might succeed if you try again."

"I'll think about it," I said, not really feeling it. But I had to say it, otherwise she would bother me about this for a long time.

"Good. Meanwhile, I want you to visit the women's center. Try to make more friends there. Some of them need more help than you do."

"Like Evangeline."

She nodded. "Like Evangeline. Help her and that way you'll be helping yourself too."

LEAVING DR. WALKER'S OFFICE, I MADE A MENTAL note to go visit Evangeline sometime during the week, but as soon as I got back home and looked around—and still had no clue what to do for my design project for school—I decided there was no better time than now.

So, I called her, intent on asking her to go to the movies with me or meet me for coffee, but my heart hurt a little when I found out she was at the women's center. Again.

Without thinking, I just turned around and drove there. I stopped by reception to ask about Evie, when a nurse came over from behind the desk and gave the receptionist some fliers.

"Please, hang these up somewhere," the nurse said, before turning on her heels and marching away.

I stared at the fliers as the receptionist set them aside. It was about self-defense classes that would be taught here at the center. That was new. I wondered if Evie would like to take those. It would come in handy if things got too ugly with Mike. I groaned; things were already too ugly with Mike.

Finally, the receptionist turned to me.

"Evangeline is in the garden," she said.

Of course.

I found her seated on one of the benches

hidden among the flowerbeds in the garden. Her eyes were swollen and red as if she had been crying.

I sat down beside her. "Want to talk about it?"

She shook her head and then sighed. "I don't know."

"It's all right," I told her. "We can talk about something else. How's work?"

She groaned. "Not good. I've been arriving late and sometimes missing an entire shift, because ..."

Okay, not a good topic. I remembered she commented the other day about exercising, to take her mind off the bad parts of her life, to feel a little better. I asked her about that.

"I don't seem to find time to exercise," she answered.

I knew what she meant by that. It was Mike. It was always Mike. Jealous and possessive the way he was, he didn't let her go to the gym.

Everything I could talk about involved Mike. So, instead of asking about her, I told her about me. Actually, I told her about Hannah. She already knew a lot about Hannah, of course. Everyone in town knew since what had happened to my sister and me, and to Eric, ended up in newspapers and on news channels everywhere. But Evie didn't know much about my sister's wedding. Not yet.

I set out to tell her about the engagement party, about the preparations, about the dress, trying to paint it as a fairy tale.

"If Hannah can find her happy ending, you can too. I'm sure of it."

Evie looked me with tears in her eyes. "Not just me. You too."

I sucked in a sharp breath. "I ..."

She went on. "I know I wallow in my problems and pity myself too much, but deep down, I have to believe there is something better out there. For me." She offered me a small, forced smile. "And for you too."

THE HOT WATER IN MY BATHTUB WAS ALMOST TOO much for my sensitive skin, but I didn't care. I needed this alone time, this soaking time, to recharge.

Although, my sister and our friends didn't think so.

Two minutes after settling in the bathtub, lying back, closing my eyes, and hoping I would take a late nap, my phone started dinging like crazy.

Hannah: *Are you meeting us at the event? Or should we pick you up?*

Bia: *It's almost parteeeeee time! This event is going to rock. What are going to wear?*

Iris: *I can't decide. Can I send you pics and you help me choose?*

Gabi: Droga, *I wish I were there! I want to go to the party too!*

Hannah: *Hil, you're going to the event, aren't you?*

Bia: *I'm thinking a little black dress with cowboy boots. To make a statement, you know.*

Iris: *I love polo, I love our boys, but some of these events are just exhausting. I would prefer staying home, snuggled with my man, watching some boring movie.*

Some of the messages had been sent in private to me, some had been sent to our girls' group. Even though I didn't answer any of them, I couldn't help but grab my phone and read the texts with each new ding.

Hannah: *Hilary, why aren't you answering?*

Because I didn't want her to try to convince me to go. She would make me feel guilty, and I would relent, even though all I wanted to do was relax in my bathtub, then settle in my bed and read. Or design a new dress. Or work on my school project, the one I hadn't started yet.

I understood how important this event was to the guys. Their sponsor, Jeep, was opening a new store in Santa Barbara and, of course, the team would be the special guests. The event organizers had even set up a small field with fake grass so the guys could play polo for fifteen minutes. It was supposed to be huge and reporters from the newspapers, magazines, and news channels would be there. I was happy for them. Attention like this was great. It brought money to their sponsor, to them, to their team, and they could keep playing and winning longer.

I just didn't feel like I needed to be there. I didn't feel like being among a crowd, cameras, and attention right now.

The next text was the one that shocked me.

Gui: *Hey, Hil. You're coming to the party with us, right?*

For some reason, I wanted to reply to him. What would I tell him? That I had given up on my list of fears and had declared myself a coward who was hiding from her life? No, thank you. I preferred staying silent and letting them imagine whatever they wanted. Surely, it couldn't be worse than the truth.

A new message from Hannah followed, again asking why I wasn't answering. This time though, she threatened to call and, if I didn't answer that too, she would stop by on the way to the event.

Groaning, I typed a text to her.

Me: *I think I have a cold. Took some meds and I'm in bed. Going to sleep now. Have fun!*

Then I turned off my phone before she could call me and accuse me of lying.

## 16

GUI

I KNEW HILARY WASN'T COMING, BUT I STILL couldn't stop myself from looking for her in the crowd every ten seconds.

The guys and I were wearing sleek black suits and dark blue shirts, with a bluish-silver embroidery Jeep over the pocket on the left of our jackets. We looked good and everyone wanted to take pictures with us. We could barely walk three steps before being stopped by someone who quickly introduced him or herself and launched into conversation as if we had known them our entire lives. Most of the time, we didn't.

This part of polo—the attention, the flashlights, the cameras, the interviews, the pictures—it didn't happen often, but I always loved it.

I still did, but for some reason, my usual excitement was missing tonight.

For some reason. As if I didn't know the fucking reason. What? Now I was going to lie to myself?

The reason was Hilary. There. I confessed. Big difference it would make. She still wouldn't come. And it made me very, very fucking miserable. And acknowledging that made even more miserable.

I had known I was attracted to her since the first time I laid eyes on her, but when had I become the guy who held his breath every time a blond walked past, hoping she would turn around and I would find Hilary smiling at me?

I sighed.

What did I expect? That after two days she would have recovered from a panic attack. Damn it, I didn't even know she still had them. I thought ... I thought she had recovered from them. I knew she wasn't totally healed yet, but I had no idea it was still that bad.

"Hey," Hannah said, slipping her arm around my waist and posing for a picture. "Smile, *guri*."

The mask slipped into place and I smiled, wide and happy. Nobody would ever know I was considering leaving this party to go check on a girl. A beautiful, sweet, quiet girl who was growing on me.

Gathering courage, I asked in a low voice, "How is Hilary?"

Hannah's smile faltered for a brief second. "To be honest, I'm not sure. My mother said she went to her therapist this morning, so I'm hoping she's better. She doesn't talk much about that, no matter how much we beg her to."

I nodded. Yeah, I could see her closing in more after the other day.

Which was why she had to let someone in. Me, maybe, if I helped with that list of hers. And, I wanted to help her. I felt like … like I should. Like I needed to.

Fucking stupid.

Leo halted beside Hannah, then Bia came to my other side, and more pictures were taken.

Then, I excused myself and went to the bar. Waiters were waltzing around the crowd, making sure everyone's glasses were full, but I wanted a moment to myself.

I ordered a whiskey on the rocks, and then leaned my back on the counter, watching the crowd, but not really seeing anyone. Still, it seemed my mind wouldn't cooperate, and all it did was look for a pretty blond with the most beautiful smile I had ever seen.

A girl leaned on the counter beside me, ordering a flute of champagne from the bartender. From the quick flash I got when she walked into my peripheral vision, I knew she was tall, had wavy black hair, and was wearing a red dress.

Drink in hand, she turned around and stayed there, by my side.

"Hm," she finally said after a long while. "Maybe the rumors are wrong."

I turned to her. "What rumors?"

A lazy smile spread over her bright red lips. "That the renowned Guilherme Fernandes likes to have company during parties."

She was pretty. I would give her that. Under different circumstances, I could see myself flirting with her, trying to gain her favor, so maybe she would take me to her house. But the spark, the desire, the excitement of something new and crazy, the longing for that high—it wasn't there.

I turned my attention back to the crowd. "Not *all* parties," I said before taking a long sip of my drink.

She humphed and stormed away, probably not used to being turned down. Truth was, I also wasn't used to turning girls down. My infamous reputation was worse than reality. Yes, I slept with several girls and never dated, not seriously. The closest I ever got to that was sleeping with the same girl for more than two or three months. However, it wasn't as if I screwed a girl every weekend after every party. That ... that didn't even sit well with me. The rumor was there, though, and some girls seemed to like it, so I never did anything to stop it.

Until now.

Now, when I thought of a certain blond hearing more and more about said rumors, I cringed.

I pushed against the bar and walked to our little group. Leo, Hannah, Bia, and Garrett talked about the game we had played on the improvised field the event organizers had set up, laughing that we had to strut around on our horses in such a tiny space, and also wearing suits and dress shoes. Ri, Pedro, and Iris were right beside us, talking.

I smiled. The guys looked great. I knew that. I had looked in the mirror before leaving my apartment. But the girls looked stunning. I narrowed my eyes for a moment and pictured Hilary beside us, wearing a beautiful party dress, probably green to emphasize her pretty eyes, smiling at the cameras, and laughing at the jokes we told when posing so we all would smile and laugh more naturally. She would complete the picture and make our group richer. Whole.

If only.

---

## 17

HILARY

THE TELEPHONE BESIDE MY COMPUTER RANG.

"Hilary speaking."

"Your three o'clock appointment is here," Sonya said. "Design room three is free."

"Great. Take them there, please. I'll be right over."

With a smile, I hung up and stood from my chair. I straightened my pencil skirt and shirt, picked up my A3-sized folder from my side desk, and headed to design room three.

I opened the door and stepped in. "Hi, ladies."

"Hilary!" My sister rushed to me and embraced me. "How are you?" she asked in a low whisper. "I was worried about you."

"I'm good," I told her. It wasn't entirely a lie.

Next in line was Bia, then Iris. Gabi was face timing through Bia's phone.

I grabbed the phone from Bia. "Hi, *guria*. Nice of you to show up."

Gabi laughed. "Yeah, right. I wish I was there."

"But you're coming soon, right?" I asked, taking a seat on one of the white leather sofas. "You need to try your dress on prior to the wedding, you know."

"I know," Gabi said. "I'm in Greece right now, and I plan to go back to Brazil in three weeks, but now I'm thinking of detouring through Santa Barbara so I can try it on, or at least, so you can get my measurements right."

"That sounds great." I handed the phone back to Bia and opened a large drawing pad. "So, Hannah, wanna tell me what you have in mind for you and your bridesmaids?"

Seated all around me, the girls turned their gazes to my sister.

"Well," Hannah said. "You know me. I want something romantic, something with a sweet country style, but not hillbilly or heavy country, please. No plaid or flannel, I mean." She moved her hands all over the place and she was rambling. Yup, my sister was anxious about the wedding. "I've decided on yellow for you guys." I groaned and she froze, staring at me with wide eyes. "What?"

"I'm blond and pale. Yellow will look awesome on me," I said, my words dripping with sarcasm.

Hannah's eyes bugged. "No, no, don't say that to me now. I've been thinking about this for weeks. It took me a long time to decide on yellow, and—"

"It's okay," I interrupted her. "It's your wedding, and I'm sure yellow will look pretty." Just not on me. But that wasn't the point.

Hannah kept on talking about the several designs she had in mind, the ones she had seen in magazines and on TV, and how she wanted everyone to look like. Then she rambled about her dress. Bottom line, she wasn't sure of anything other than the colors. White for her, yellow for the girls and me. I took some notes about some tiny details she mentioned, and I planned on incorporating those in my drawings before presenting to them.

While Hannah went on, I took their measurements, and we already scheduled another meeting in a few days so we could go over the designs and fabrics.

At some point, Sonya brought coffee and pastries, and the appointment became a friendly get-together. Now we just needed some drinks and we would call it happy hour!

Of course, the girls stayed until my quitting time, and they tried to convince me to go to a pub, one that allowed eighteen and older, and continue our happy hour. I lied that I was still feeling a little under the weather from the fake cold I had gotten during the weekend. Hannah's gaze told me she knew I was lying, but I didn't care.

I wasn't ready to go to a bar for happy hour again.

I wasn't ready for anything.

---

I WAS PAYING ATTENTION TO MY PHONE WHEN THE elevator doors opened and I stepped in. Noticing someone was inside, I looked up. An uneasy feeling spread through my arms.

"*Bom dia,*" Gui said, pulling the earbuds from his ears. He had on dark gray sweatpants, a black Montenegro shirt, and black sneakers.

"Morning," I said, standing beside him.

He pressed the underground button on the elevator's panel for me, retreated to the other side of the elevator, far from me, and we both stared at the closed doors while the elevator moved down.

Gui shifted his weight. "Going to work?"

"Yes." I glanced at him. "And I guess you're going running?"

He nodded. "*Sim.*"

The elevator doors opened in the lobby, and Gui stepped out.

"Have a nice day," I said as the doors started closing.

When I thought I was able to breathe, Gui shot out his arms between the closing doors and they opened again.

"All right, I can't just leave like that," he said, standing right in the path of the elevator's opened doors.

"What do you mean?"

"I mean, I want to know how you're doing. I would love to hear you're doing better and I certainly would like to know why the hell you didn't go to our event on Saturday."

My jaw dropped. "Hm."

"So?"

I glanced around him. "You can't just hold the elevator like that."

"Fine." He stepped inside and the doors closed. I stepped back, bumping my back against the mirrored wall as the elevator started going down again. "Wait. Does this bother you?"

"W-what bothers me?"

"Being in a closed space, alone with me." He stayed as far away as he could. "I'm sor—"

"No!" I felt offended that he would suggest that. But then again, I never gave him a reason not to think that. "The problem isn't you, Gui." I sighed, not believing I was about to confess one more thing to him. "The problem is males. Men in general."

He relaxed a tiny bit. "Okay, now tell me, how are you?"

The elevator doors opened and he stepped back, exiting the closed box. I followed him, noticing he was walking me to my car.

"I'm fine," I said. An automatic response. What did he want me to say? I wasn't unwell, but I wasn't one hundred percent either. "I'll be fine."

"You always say that."

"What?"

"That you *will* be fine, as in you aren't fine now, but one day you will be."

Hurt flashed through me. "Well, I do hope I'll be better one day, otherwise what reason do I have to live?" My voice was much louder than I had intended.

Gui flinched. "I'm sorry. I didn't mean to make you upset."

"And I didn't mean to yell."

I unlocked my car, but Gui leaned on the door, not allowing me to enter and flee from his sudden questioning.

"What are you doing to make yourself feel better?"

I shrugged. "Working, drawing, worrying about Hannah's wedding."

"I understand you love your work. I love mine too, but that's not everything. You have to have more."

I put my hands on my waist and stared at him. "Oh, yeah, do you have more?"

"Friends, family, parties. I'm always out and about."

I knew what he meant by out and about. Gui was known for partying more than necessary and for having several girlfriends—or actually, a new girl every other week.

I scrunched my nose. "I'm more like a homebody."

"That isn't what I heard. I heard you used to be a firecracker. You were always out and about too."

"That was before ..." I trailed off, averting my eyes.

"I know. I just wish you had that fire in you

again. I really would like to see that. It's probably a beautiful sight."

I crossed my arms. "What do you want me to say, Gui? I suffered a major trauma, and my therapist says I've made a lot of progress in the last three years. If all goes well, it'll continue like that and one day *I'll be fine.*"

"I want you to say you'll let me help you again."

I shook my head. "I'm not sure that is a good idea."

"Why? Are you afraid of me?" He gave a step back, finally freeing my car's door. "I told you I would nev—"

"Never hurt me. I know." To prove my point, I reached over and rested my hand on his upper arm. My mind registered that my palm rested on his hard biceps. I gulped, but didn't move my hand away. "I trust you, Gui. I swear I do. The problem isn't you. It's me. I'm a wimp, I'm weak, and I'm really, really scared."

Surprising me, Gui rested his hand over mine. Heat passed from his warm skin to mine, and I swear I could feel that in my core. "I don't want you to be scared anymore. Please, let me help you."

How could I say no when he looked at me with

those big, pleading, pretty eyes? When he had his hand on mine? When he leaned close and I felt the tiny sliver of safety emanating from his tall, strong frame?

I sighed, knowing I was going to regret my next word. "Okay."

I TOOK IN A DEEP BREATH AND STEPPED INSIDE THE stable.

"*Oi*," Gui said with a lopsided smile. He stood in front of a stall that I remembered being empty before.

"Hi," I said, coming to stand beside him. The stall wasn't empty anymore. Belle was in there. "Why is she here?"

"Because she's away from the other horses here."

I looked up at him. "You put her there?"

His grin flashed bright. "*Sim.*"

I frowned. "How long have you been here?"

He pulled out his phone from his pocket and checked the time. "Twenty, maybe thirty minutes?"

I gaped at him. Why did he come so early again? To talk to Leo maybe. But Leo's SUV hadn't been in the parking lot when I parked my car.

Shouldn't he be, I don't know, training? Doing something more useful with his time?

"I ..." I what? What would I say to him? I couldn't ask him why he came so early because I was afraid of the answer. I cleared my throat and watched Belle again. "So, what are we doing today?"

"We're taking a step back," he said. "Instead of letting Belle loose and having you get used to her like that, I isolated her, so no other horse can interfere, and you'll approach her here with the lower half of the door between you two."

In my mind, I saw Belle snorting at me and retreating to the back wall of the stall, far from my reach. But so far, she stood there, right in the center, curious about what was going on.

"Oh-kay, so I just stand here?"

Gui took a step toward me and reached out with his hands. Before he could touch me, he stopped and looked in my eyes. "May I?"

I gulped and nodded.

His right hand rested on my lower back while his left hand clamped my left upper arm. He put pressure on my back, and I took a step forward, bumping the tip of my boots on the door. Sliding his hands down my arms, Gui grasped my wrists and placed my hands on the door.

"Stand here." He withdrew his hands from me, but he didn't retreat. I was painfully aware of how his body was a couple of inches away from mine.

My arms shook—if it was from horse-related nerves or from Gui-related nerves, I didn't know.

"Now what?" I asked, my voice low.

"Horses can sense your emotions. Belle will know if you're stressed, nervous, or afraid. So just stand there, look at her, and will your fear and nervousness away."

I scoffed. "If only it was that easy."

A warm hand clasped my shoulder, squeezing gently. "I know it won't be, and it won't be fast either, so just try to relax as much as you can. Small steps. This is all about small steps."

Gui squeezed my shoulder once more, then withdrew his hand. Instantly, I felt a cold rush seep through my skin where his hand had been.

I shook those thoughts and feelings from my mind and body, and focused on why we were here. Exhaling a long breath, I rolled my shoulders and looked at Belle. She stared back at me. I swear, her gaze was intense, as if she were reading my soul and taking notes of all my sins and flaws. It was unnerving.

I wondered if this was something similar to what Hannah did with the problematic horses, to get close to them, to gain their trust. How long did she have to wait? Five minutes? Thirty? An hour? I wasn't sure I was that patient.

After several minutes, Belle huffed and advanced a couple of steps. I gasped and tensed.

"It's okay," Gui whispered, his voice close to my ear. "Relax. You're doing great."

I was dying here. I didn't know how many more minutes passed in this tense game, but finally, Belle was within reach.

"Go on," Gui whispered. "Touch her."

I stopped breathing. Touch her? Was he sure? He had mentioned small steps. After having her get close to me on her own, touching her seemed like a giant leap.

"She's okay, Hil. She's used to people. Maybe she remembers what happened the other day, but she's fine about that now. You're the one holding back."

Once more, Gui guided me. He closed his hand around my wrist, steading my shaking arm, and reached forward. He leaned over me, his chest almost touching my back—I could feel his body heat and his breath on my ear.

Surprising me, my fear didn't spike. I had been tense just standing here; now, with him so close, I was even tenser. However, the usual fear that came from being so close to a man was nowhere to be found.

Carefully, Gui guided my hand until it was resting on top of Belle's head, right between her eyes. She didn't flinch or snort or run away—like I expected her to. A long exhale escaped my throat, and I smiled.

Belle pushed her head against my hand, and still holding my wrist, Gui slid my hand to under her chin.

"Scratch her. Gently," he said. I did it and Belle let out a sound like a loud sneeze. "It means she likes it."

Gui slipped his hand from mine, sliding it up my arm until it rested on my shoulder. I turned to face him and froze. His face was only about three inches from mine. My eyes flicked to his mouth. He pressed his lips in a thin line, lowered his gaze to the ground, and stepped back.

"You're doing great," he said, his voice tight.

My emotions surprised me once more; disappointment made its way through my chest. As best as I could, I ignored the unwelcomed feeling and turned my attention back to Belle. I was still petting her and she still let me.

I ran my hand up and down her face and neck, feeling her smooth, shiny coat, her strong muscles, her blood rushing inside her. Meanwhile, my thoughts drifted someplace else. To someone else. Why hadn't I flinched when Gui touched me? Why hadn't I felt sick with fear when he got that close? Why hadn't I run away crying and screaming when he stared into my eyes?

A mix of feelings overwhelmed me, confused me, and still I felt the absence of fear.

A single tear broke free and ran down my cheek. "Thank you," I whispered, turning my eyes to Gui again. "Thanks for insisting on helping me through this."

His pose still stoic and guarded, he nodded. "You're welcome. But just to be clear, this—" He gestured to my hand on Belle. "—is just the beginning."

# 18

BECAUSE OF HAVING TO DESIGN A BRIDE'S DRESS, A maid of honor's dress, three bridesmaids' dresses, and a mother of the bride's dress to be ready in a little over two months, I ended up working late on Thursday.

It was almost six in the evening when I left Fallon's studio. Of course, she was still there, laboring away.

My car was parked on the thin strip of concrete Fallon called a parking lot. At least it fit our cars, parked tightly at the back of the lot, and about four or five other compact cars. Maneuvering in or out wasn't always easy, but today, there was only Fallon's and my car there.

As I turned the corner from the sidewalk into the parking lot, something charged me and rammed my body into the building's wall. My back hit the concrete wall with a loud thud, and the pain radiated through my body. My lungs compressed and I gasped for air, which didn't come, as a clammy, strong hand closed around my throat.

I scrambled to focus, to regain composure, to understand what was happening. A face appeared before my eyes, only a couple of inches from mine. A man's face. A man's face I had seen only once before.

Mike, Evie's abusive husband.

Panic rose from deep inside my chest.

"What do you think you're doing, bitch?" he asked, his voice rough. His breath reeked of alcohol.

I gasped. Even if I knew what to say to him, I couldn't. Fear paralyzed me, and his hand on my throat was tight enough to make speech difficult.

"Mike," I tried, but it came out as a croak. "Let ... let me go." I pushed on his shoulders, but the man didn't budge. "Please."

He punched the wall, half an inch from my face. Desperate tears filled my eyes, making my already blurred sight worse. "It doesn't matter what kind of ideas you put in Evie's head, she'll always come back to me. Always." He jerked me off the wall, only to push me back hard into it. My head slammed against the facade, and my vision went dark. "You'll regret it, bitch."

His hand tightened around my throat. I was swimming in a dark sea made of oil. Even though I moved my arms and legs, fighting with each stroke, the oil carried me further and further from the shore, until it swallowed me, and I couldn't do anything other than let it take me.

A gush of air rushed down my throat, burning its way to my lungs as I slid down the wall and fell on the concrete ground in a numb heap. Through the pain and burning, I gasped, willing my lungs to work. Slowly, my hearing focused and my vision cleared.

With a bloody nose, Mike spat at my feet, then turned and ran.

Gui knelt in front of me.

I stared, in shock. He had a cut on his lower lip and a red bruise on his left temple. His eyes, though, his eyes looked at me with pure concern and fear.

"Are you hurt?" he asked. I still stared, not sure what had happened. "Hil, answer me, please. Are you hurt?"

I started shaking my head, but pain radiated through my skull. "Ow," I muttered, closing my eyes and pressing my hands on the top of my head.

Gui cursed under his breath. "All right, let's go." He took my hands in his and pulled me up. Still shaking, I could barely stand. A wave of dizziness overcame me and I leaned against the wall for support.

"Just ... give me a moment," I rasped, my throat still burning.

"Where are your car keys?"

"Purse. Outside pocket."

He glanced around and found my purse on the ground, my portfolio case next to it. He picked up my things, grabbed the car keys, clicked the button to open the car, slid the strap of my purse up his arm, put my portfolio case between his knees, then he slid one arm around my back and the other under my knees and lifted me as if I were a rag doll.

"What ...?" I started protesting, but with the shaking and the dizziness, I could barely take two steps on my own.

Somehow, Gui picked up the portfolio case with one of his hands and carried me and all my stuff to my car. He stopped by the door, raised one knee, and rested my bottom against his leg, while he opened the door and threw my stuff in the backseat, and then he picked me up again and deposited me on the passenger seat. He ducked inside the car with me, and pulled the seat belt around me. I could feel his arms and hands touching me, and I knew that another time, another day, I would actually like this, but today I was too numb to think about him like that. One good thing I realized as he raced around the car and slipped into the driver's seat was that, even though I had all the reasons to have a panic attack now, it didn't come. And I should have been cowering from him too, and I wasn't.

Gui started the car. "What's the closest hospital?"

"W-what?"

"Hospital. You're hurt and I'm taking you to the hospital."

I pressed a hand where my head had hit the wall, then stared at it. It still hurt like crazy, and every time I moved my head too fast, the pain radiated everywhere, but there was no blood.

"I'm fine," I said.

"No, no, you're not. I'm taking you to the hospital. Tell me where the nearest one is before I search for one on my phone."

Looking into his eyes, I laid my hand on his extended arm. "Gui, I'm fine now. Yes, it hurts, but I think I'll only have a bump. Please, don't take me to the hospital. I *hate* hospitals." In my gaze, I tried to show him I was serious, I was honest.

I saw the battle in his eyes. His knuckles were white around the steering wheel and his jaw popped every few seconds. He wanted to argue, he wanted to disagree, but with an exasperated sigh, he nodded and backed out of the parking lot. I watched him as he turned the car toward our building, and for the first time, I noticed his clothes. He was wearing black sweatpants and a blue Montenegro T-shirt and sneakers. His hair was disheveled and his phone was strapped to his arm.

"You were out running," I said.

"Yes. I change my course every few days, so I don't get bored. I started running down this street three days ago. *Graças a Deus*."

"Thank you."

Eyes on the road, he shook his head. "You have nothing to thank me for. I just wish ..." He pressed his lips tight.

"What?"

"I wish I had been able to knock the guy unconscious and call the cops. Or at least landed a few more punches on him before he got away." He stole a quick glance at me. "*Que merda*! What happened? The guy was robbing you? Or ..." He shut his mouth, probably too afraid to say the R word. I was too.

"Neither." I looked down at my hands. They still shook. "His name is Mike. His wife, Evangeline, is one of the women at the women's center I visit every couple of weeks. We became friends and she told me all about him." A tear slid down my cheek and I wiped it away. I hadn't even noticed I was about to cry. "He's ... There are no words to describe him. He's the worst kind of man there is. But Evie is too afraid to confront him and leave him. So, every now and then, she goes back to him. Then she comes back to the women's center. I'm trying to help her, to convince her to leave him for good." I snorted. "Me and all the staff at the center. But, for some reason, she's not strong enough. A few days ago, I visited her and we talked a long while about that. She said she would finally do it, and I believed her this time. I checked with her a few days ago, and she still hadn't done it, but my guess is that she left, or tried to, otherwise ..."

"He wouldn't have come after you," Gui finished for me.

"I never thought he would do something like that. I didn't even know she had mentioned me to him, but apparently she told him enough."

"He knows where you work." Gui punched the wheel, startling me. "Sorry, sorry."

I just nodded and focused on him. Because if I didn't, if I let my mind wander, if I let myself think about what had happened, if I let my emotions creep into me, I would succumb to the worst panic attack I had since the night that started this mess.

Taking deep breaths, I ignored my hands shaking and watched Gui as he drove the few blocks to our apartments. His hands clenched and unclenched the wheel, his arms taut, the muscles flexing with each of his movements. The blue shirt had a big wet spot on his back and his chest. His shirt clung to his skin, revealing the strong muscles beneath. His face was serious, almost feral, his lips pressed together, his brows furrowed, his jaw hard. His damp, messy hair framed his beautiful face. I gulped down the realization that Gui was more than handsome. He was stunning. Like underwear-model slash rock star slash movie star stunning.

At a red light, Gui glanced at me.

"What?" he asked.

"Hm?"

"You're staring at me."

Warmth flooded my cheeks. "I'm trying not to think about what happened, and you're the only thing to stare at here."

One corner of his lips tugged up. "Are you trying to make me relax or something?"

The truth was, I was trying to make *me* relax. "Is it working?"

The frown between his brows deepened and his lips lost their almost smile. "I might be furious, and ready to throw a punch at someone, but I swear, I would never hurt you. You know that, right?"

A lot of men who had said that had lied. I also knew women felt incredibly safe with their boyfriends or husbands before they turned violent—or before they were raped. But for some reason, deep in my heart, I knew Gui was different and that he would never, ever hurt me. "I know."

We remained silent the rest of the way, and I kept my mind busy, so as not to give in to the panic and fear.

Using the remote control, he drove past the gate and into the parking lot under the building. He parked my car in my reserved spot, killed the car's engine, and turned to me.

"I still wish you would let me take you to the hospital. Or to your doctor. Or your therapist."

I took in a deep breath and let it out, calming my nerves before I spoke. "Gui, something big just happened. I was assaulted by a known violent man." Gui flinched as if I had hit him. Each word was paused as it hurt saying them out loud. "I have the right to slip into one of my panic attacks. I thought I would have slipped into one by now—probably the biggest one since that day—but for the first time in three years, I'm staying in control. For the first time, I can feel the panic coming, and I'm not surrendering to it. I'm pushing it back. I'm not sure why I'm able to do this now, or how, but I am." That wasn't entirely true. I kind of suspected my newfound strength had something to do with Gui's presence, but I didn't want to give much thought to it. Not yet. "Please, please, don't spoil that by taking me to my doctor or my therapist. If you take me to them, I'll break down, and I really, really don't want to break down right now." A stubborn tear escaped from my eye.

Gui reached over, cupped my face, and wiped my tear with his thumb. His hand lingered, the warmth of his skin seeping into mine. "You're strong, Hilary. Stronger than you think, and I'm proud of you right now."

"Thanks," I said, offering him a tiny smile.

As I averted my eyes, Gui pulled his hand away and opened the car's door. "All right. Let's get you home, then."

# 19

GUI

I HAD A SLIGHT IDEA OF THE TIME HILARY GOT OFF work, so I showed up half an hour before and waited on the sidewalk. I walked up and down the street, kicked loose stones on the pavement, watched the cars go by, browsed Facebook, answered some emails, and waited.

Over an hour later, I thought about going inside and asking for Hilary. Maybe she had gone home early, and here I was, a freaking puppy waiting with a sad face. Or maybe she had listened to me and taken the day off. God knew she needed to rest after what happened yesterday.

I closed my eyes as rage coursed through my veins. I couldn't even remember it without my blood boiling. And when my mind went further and I thought about what could have happened if I hadn't decided to go running yesterday. That bastard could have raped her, killed her. I clenched my fists and allowed my rage one more minute before I got it under control.

I counted to twenty and took three long breaths. Then, I reached for the front door, but it opened before I could touch it and Hilary stepped out.

She halted when she saw me. "Gui? What are you doing here?"

"Hey, Hil." I took off my baseball hat, ran my hand through my hair, and tucked the hat on my head again. "I ... I just wanted to make sure you were safe today." I glanced to the sides. No signs of any evil characters.

"Oh, hm." Her cheeks reddened. "Thanks."

"I've brought you something," I said, grabbing her little gift from the back pocket of my jeans. I handed it to her.

With a frown, she picked up the small red plastic bag and spied inside. "Pepper spray."

I shrugged. "I hope you never have to use it, but I thought that, after what happened yesterday, it might make you feel safer."

"That's ... that's a good idea. Thanks." She turned the pepper spray in her hands, and then put it inside her purse. She opened her mouth, and then closed it again.

I took a step toward her. "What?"

She wrapped one hand around the strap of her purse, squeezing it tight. "Last night, after you brought me home, I was thinking that I should know how to defend myself." She shook her head once, making her blond hair spill over her shoulders. "I don't know why I didn't think of this before, right after what Eric—" She pressed her mouth tight. "Anyway, I heard of a self-defense class, and even though my size—" She gestured to her delicate frame. "—might be a disadvantage, I could learn how to break free long enough to run or call for help."

"That is a great idea," I said. Pride filled my chest. "Do you have a place in mind?"

"No. I'm going to research more online this weekend. I remember seeing a flyer at the women's center my mom and I go to, but it won't start for another eight weeks. I don't want to wait that long. I'm sure I can find a class somewhere."

"No need to research." I took a step toward her and grabbed her hand. "I know just the place."

I pulled her with me, to my Jeep, which was parked across the street.

"Wait, hm, my car is in the parking lot."

"I can drive you back here afterward, if that's okay," I suggested, opening the passenger door for her.

Hilary stared at me, those green eyes wreaking havoc in me. "Okay," she whispered.

She hopped in the Jeep. I closed her door and rushed to the other side. When I slid into the driver's seat, Hilary had already buckled and she sat completely still.

"Are you okay?" I asked. She nodded, glancing at me for a second, before returning her attention to her purse on her lap. "Have you changed your mind? You don't have to do this now, you know."

She looked at me, her eyes conveying much more than she let on. "I know. It's okay. Let's do this now." She sighed. "If I don't, I might spend too much time researching and thinking about doing this and never actually doing it."

Instinct hit me and I reached over, grabbing her hand. "I'm proud of you for taking action." I squeezed tight.

She stared at our hands. "Thanks," she whispered, squeezing my hand back.

It felt too fucking good to have her hand in mine. I had to control myself not to entwine our fingers. To not tug her to me. To not pull her into my lap. To not grasp her hips and leaned her down to me, and not to claim—

Clearing my throat, I pulled my hand away. "All right. Let's go."

The drive took only a couple of minutes. Hilary eyed the building as I parked my Jeep in the parking lot. I remembered the first time I saw it years ago. The building looked like a gray box with a few windows, and in desperate need of a new paint job. The metal sign In Shape over the door looked precarious, like it was going to fall at any second.

"I know it doesn't look like much," I said, killing the engine. "But it's a good place. The guys and I come here at least three times a week to work out."

"They offer self-defense classes here?" she asked.

"*Sim*. Once every two or three months, I think. Let's go in and check it out."

I opened the front door for her. As we walked to the reception desk, I noticed she scanned the place, taking it all in. At least it looked better on the inside. New flooring, well taken care of machines, updated couches in the waiting area, a nice snack bar, and in the back, the lockers and the large classroom with a wooden floor, a mirrored wall, and a glass wall that overlooked the main gym floor.

"Hello, Gui," the receptionist said with a smile.

"Hi, Janice," I said. Hilary snapped her attention to the receptionist. "This is Hilary. She's interested in self-defense classes."

"Oh." Janice looked at Hilary from head to toe and back, her expression disgusted.

I suppressed a sigh. Janice had been flirting with me since she started working here a few months ago, and even though I knew she was serious about hooking up, I wasn't. I wouldn't sleep with her once, twice, three times at most, then send her away, just to have to see her all the time here. It would be too awkward. And who knew how she might react? She could try to sabotage one of the machines so the weights fell on me and killed me. I had vengeful girls attack me like that before. I knew it was bound to happen again.

If I ever slept with a random girl again.

I glanced at Hilary.

She knew about my reputation and she probably had heard the worst version, the one that was ten times worse than the truth. I never treated a girl badly, not before, during, or after being with her. All the girls knew that I didn't like getting too involved before hooking up with me—I wasn't trying to be a jerk. It just wasn't in me. I had my career and my family to keep my mind and heart filled. I always thought that was enough.

Until now.

Hilary was also watching Janice, her eyes narrowed. Fuck. Knowing my reputation, Hilary probably thought I had already slept with the receptionist.

"So," I said, breaking the sudden weirdness in the air. "Any classes opening soon?"

Janice turned her attention to the computer screen behind the desk. "Nope. The next one is scheduled to start in October. If we have enough sign-ups."

"Shit," I muttered.

Janice looked from me to Hil and back again. "But a new class started last week. I think John could be convinced to let you join."

John was the gym's owner. He was always around when the guys and I were working out, and he always talked to us. He was a nice guy in his late fifties. I was sure I could convince him to let Hilary join in the class.

"Nice," I said. "I'll talk to John. When is the next class?"

"Wednesday next week," Janice said. She pulled out a clipboard and form from under the desk and looked at Hilary. "If you could fill out this form, please, I'll enter your name on the class roster."

"Thanks," Hilary said, taking the form.

She took a few steps back and sat down on one of the couches.

I sat beside her, careful not to be too close though. I knew how she could snap and feel crowded. Especially after yesterday.

As she filled out the form, I took my time and looked at her, really looked at her. And, *Meu Deus*, once more it hit me, taking away my breath, how beautiful she was. I had never seen a more beautiful woman in my entire life, and I had seen a lot of women.

But Hilary was special. She was above all others.

Her hair was pulled to one side, over her shoulder, and I just now noticed she was wearing a thin scarf around her neck. On a hot summer day.

Without thinking, I reached over and pulled the scarf down. I sucked in a sharp breath and rage flooded my body as I took in the red marks around her neck.

With wide eyes, Hilary pulled the scarf back up, and let her hair fall like a curtain between us as she continued filling out the form. Now her hands were shaking and she could barely write.

Feeling like a jerk, I grabbed her hand in mine, squeezing the pen between our palms, and with my other hand, brushed her hair back, so I could see her pretty face.

"I'm sorry," I said. "About not being there sooner yesterday and—"

"That wasn't your fault."

"—for pulling your scarf just now. I didn't mean to spook you again."

She looked at me, her green eyes shining with unshed tears. "It's ... it'll be okay."

Again with the "will be" okay. I hated that. I wanted her to be okay now.

I lifted her hand and placed a kiss on her knuckles. "If you ever need help or ... anything, you know where to find me."

One corner of her lips curled up and she nodded. Then she pulled her hand from mine, wiped her unshed tears, and went back to the form.

While I started imagining all the ways I could break Mike if I ever found him again.

# 20



HILARY

I DID ALL I COULD TO AVOID GOING TO LUNCH ON Sunday at the club, but my mother threatened to disinherit me. At least Hannah was going too.

I met them at the usual balcony where we ate appetizers, had drinks, and talked. Before we moved on to the main dining room, my mother held on to my arm to keep me in place.

"What is it?" I asked.

Hannah sat back down, watching us.

"We're having lunch out here today," my mother said.

"Why is that?"

She didn't need to answer me. Eloisa and Reese approached our table and took the seats across from us.

"So nice of you to join us for lunch," my mother said.

"Our pleasure," Eloisa said.

In a matter of seconds, my mother had involved Eloisa and Hannah in a conversation, purposely leaving Reese and me out. However, we didn't stay quiet for long. Reese started a conversation with me too. How are you doing? How's college? I heard you started an internship in town. How's that going? And other mundane questions. Politely, I answered all his questions and asked a few too, so as not to look like I was snubbing him.

After lunch, I lied that I had errands to run. My mother protested it was Sunday, but I said I was busy during the week with work, so I had to use the weekends for errands.

As I stood and excused myself, Reese stood too.

"I'll walk you to your car," he said.

I wanted to tell him there was no need, but he had already walked around the table, offering me a bright smile. I didn't want to be mean. Besides, the glare my mother shot my way told me I better not argue about this. Not right now.

Okay, she had won this round. Letting him walk me to my car didn't have to mean anything. I hoped Reese got a hint of that soon.

Hannah shot me an I'm-sorry look when I waved goodbye.

"So." Reese walked by my side, his hands on the pockets of his dress pants. "Busy week ahead of you?"

"A little busy, yes," I lied. I only worked about thirty hours per week, and my plans this week were to meet my mother and Hannah to go over the wedding plans.

"Mine too." He mentioned training and preparing for a tournament, plus some dinner with their sponsors. To be honest, I didn't even know who the Knight House sponsor was.

We walked down the path to the parking lot while he still told me about his day and affairs. Apparently, he wanted to buy a new horse. "I need to ask your sister if she has any recently born foals, or if any of her mares are pregnant."

"She would be glad to answer you," I said, not really interested in the subject. A few more steps and I stopped in front of my car, which was thankfully parked right off the main path. "Here I am."

Two car rows down, I saw Gui, Ri, and Pedro coming our way, walking from the back of the parking lot to the main building. They had their polo attire on for an afternoon match. Gui saw me first, then he stared at Reese, his eyes widening.

Getting closer, Ri and Pedro saw me and waved. I waved back.

Reese glanced over his shoulder and greeted the guys before turning his attention to me.

"So," he continued. "I was wondering if you would go out with me some time."

My eyes glanced at Gui, long enough to see his step falter. But it could have been my imagination as he continued on, his jaw set, his hands clenched, and his steps sure.

"Hilary?"

I snapped my eyes back to Reese, my mind blank. What were we talking about? "Hm, oh, well. I am busy right now with work, and the new apartment and helping plan my sister's wedding."

He narrowed his eyes and nodded. "I understand."

"I should go," I said, reaching for my car door.

"Hilary?"

I stopped, my hand on the handle. "Yeah?"

A small smile appeared on Reese's lips. "I won't give up that easily."

---

I HAD JUST LEFT MY BATHTUB, DRIED MYSELF, PUT ON pajamas shorts and a tee, and was walking into the kitchen to raid my freezer for ice cream when the doorbell rang.

I stared at the closed door, wondering who it could be. I spied through the magic eye and gasped. Gui? What was Gui doing here? At this hour of the night! And I was only in my flimsy shorts and tee.

The doorbell rang again and, confused, I opened the door.

"Hey, I—" Gui's words died on his lips. His eyes traveled down and up my body. They grew wide, his mouth pressed into a thin line, and his jaw popped. When his gaze returned to mine, his pupils were dilated and the intensity of his stare robbed the air from my lungs.

"Hi," I said, a little breathless, fighting the urge to cross my arms in front of myself. "Is there something wrong?"

He closed his eyes for a second and shook his head. "No, no." He swallowed. "I just wanted to talk to you about the wedding stuff. You know, I'm the best man, you're the maid of honor."

"So?"

"I don't know. Brazilian weddings are different. I don't know what kind of crap I'm supposed to do. The guys and I were talking about the bachelor party last night. I have no idea how Americans do bachelor parties." He ran his hand through his hair. "I might need help."

I stepped back and gestured for him to come in.

"Thanks," he said as he walked by me.

I closed the door and went back to the kitchen. "I was going to dig into a tub of caramel ice cream. Want some?"

He sat down on an armchair. "I'm not much of an ice cream fan."

I turned and stared at him, shocked. "What? I didn't know people like you existed!"

He chuckled. "Yeah, well. If you have hot chocolate fudge, then I'll have that, with half a scoop of ice cream. Otherwise, no ice cream for me."

"Well, I have a bar of dark chocolate."

He offered me a sly grin. "Now we're talking."

I grabbed the tub of ice cream from the fridge, the chocolate bar, and a bottle of coke, and brought it to the living room. Gui helped me set it all down on the coffee table.

I settled down on the couch across the coffee table, pulling my legs under me and holding the tub of ice cream for dear life.

I noticed Gui's eyes wandering to my legs again. "So, about the bachelor party," I started. His eyes snapped back to mine. "I guess you can do whatever you want. If you want to do a Brazilian bachelor party, go ahead."

"That's the thing. Even though people talk about bachelor parties in Brazil, most guys don't have one. Nobody in my family ever had one."

Slowly, I pulled an accent pillow to cover most of my legs, hoping Gui hadn't linked my current action to his previous one. "Well, then again, I say do whatever you want. Take Leo and the guys bowling or clubbing or invite a respectful, bachelor party-experienced stripper to your apartment, drink until you guys pass out. Oh, wait, Leo doesn't drink."

"Nope, he doesn't." He sighed. "I guess I'll just ask him what he wants to do, and I'll try to go from there."

"Sounds like a good idea."

"I'm also helping him plan the honeymoon."

"Oh, will you tell me where he's taking Hannah?" So far, Leo had been mysterious about the destination.

A slow grin spread on Gui's lips. "Only if you promise not to tell your sister."

"I promise!"

He chuckled. "The first week he's taking her to Brazil, to visit Rio and São Paulo. He'll take her to the ranch he grew up on and where we used to practice. Then, he'll take her to the Maldives."

"Oh my gosh, she's gonna love it!"

"I hope so." He took one big bite of his chocolate bar and chewed it. After he swallowed, he asked, "Okay, what else am I supposed to do?"

"Ha, not much. My mother is going crazy over the wedding. She'll take care of every detail. Don't worry." I paused, and then added, "Have you guys already been to a tailor to do your tuxedos?"

"Hm, no."

"No? Oh no. Most tailors need to be booked in advance by like months. You need to see that ASAP."

"*Bom*, guess I'll be opening Google Maps and typing in tailors in the search box."

"What? Oh no, that won't do." I picked up my phone from the side table. "Here, I'll send you a text with some names. I just hope you're not too late."

He shrugged. "We can always rent."

I gasped. "You did not just say that."

He chuckled. "Relax. I was kidding."

"God, I hope so."

"Sort of." The twinkling in his eyes told me he enjoyed teasing me.

I groaned and threw the pillow at him. With a

wide smile, he caught it. Then his eyes fell on my legs again and his smile was gone. Damn it. I had thrown the pillow at him without thinking.

This feeling blooming inside my chest ... it was new. Well, not exactly new. I had felt something like this plenty of times before the incident that changed my life, that changed me. But I hadn't felt like this in three years. There were times when I thought I would never feel like this again.

Like a little satisfaction taking root in my gut for noticing that a guy was noticing me. For liking it. And the complete absence of fear.

However, this guy shouldn't be noticing me, and I shouldn't like it.

With a loud huff, Gui reached for the coke on the table and took a long swallow. Then, he shifted his gaze to me. "So, when are you going out with Reese?"

I snorted. "Never."

"But I heard ..." He tilted his head, examining me. "I heard him asking you out."

"He did, and I said no."

"Oh," was all he said.

He kept staring at me, holding the bottle of coke tight.

Then, all of a sudden, he set the bottle on the coffee table and stood from the armchair. "*Bom*, it's getting late and I have a workout early tomorrow morning."

I stood too and walked behind him to the front door. Surprising me, he turned around and looked down at me. Taken aback by his height and intensity, I almost stepped back. Almost.

"Thank you," he said, his tone gentle. "And I'm sorry for having disturbed you so late."

I scrunched my nose. "You didn't disturb me."

"That means I can come raid your pantry for chocolate bars more often?" Mischief glinted in his eyes, followed by a cute smile.

The corners of my lips tugged up. "Only if you start bringing me some ice cream in turn."

"All right. I'll keep that in mind." He reached behind him and turned the knob. Without breaking our stare, he exited my apartment. "*Boa noite.*"

"*Boa noite,*" I repeated. With the image of his surprised expression forever etched in my mind, I closed my door.

---

I ARRIVED AT MY HOUSE—WELL, MY PARENTS' HOUSE —at the agreed time on Monday, but Hannah was already there. I found my sister and my mother in the sunroom with lots of open books and magazines and portfolios taking over every single table and seat.

"Good afternoon," I said, entering the room.

When she saw me, Hannah shot me a help-me look. "Hi!" she squealed as if I were a breath of fresh air.

My mother didn't even look up from the sheet of paper she had on her hands. "Hello, Hilary."

I picked up a portfolio from an armchair, took its place, and set it on my lap. "I thought we agreed to meet here at five, so I had time to drive from Santa Barbara."

"I called Hannah this morning and asked her to come earlier," my mother explained. "We have too much to do."

"Okay. And how is it going?" I asked them, looking around.

"We have to decide on the cake," Hannah said, pointing to a pile on the coffee table. "The flower arrangements." She gestured to some magazines on the loveseat. "The band." She pointed to a pile of CDs on a side table—who the hell still had CDs around? Then she opened her arms wide, encompassing the entire room. "And many other little details."

"I see." I switched the portfolio on my lap for the pile of cake choices. "What do we have decided so far?" We had met once before, almost a month ago, to decide the big things, like venue, guests, date, and the invitation design, and to send out the save the date card. After that, I knew Hannah and our mother had met a few more times, and I hoped they had done a lot of the things on the to-do list.

"Well, we decided on the date, of course, the venue—here, we sent out invitations last week, and we also decided on the color yellow, the types of flowers in the arrangements, and my bouquet, and who is going to make my dress." She shot me a sweet smile.

"You two haven't done almost anything since we met a month ago. What the hell have you been doing?'

"Hilary!" my mother snapped. "Language!"

"Sorry," I muttered, making a face at Hannah since my mother wasn't looking at me.

Hannah rolled her eyes at me and grunted. "Mostly, we just argue."

I shook my head. "Ugh, you two." I reached for the embossed to-do list my mother had done before our first meeting. "All right. We won't leave this room until we cross the big things off this list.

And if that means we won't sleep all night, so be it."

Hannah's shoulders relaxed. "Thank you," she mouthed.

I HAD BEEN SO ABSORBED IN MY WORK THAT, WHEN the phone on my desk rang, I jumped from my seat, startled.

"Hilary speaking."

"Your eleven o'clock appointment is here," Sonya said.

I frowned and turned to the computer. "I have an appointment this morning?"

"Yes. He called about an hour ago and scheduled it."

I had only checked my schedule when I arrived, right after nine this morning. Seeing nothing important for a Tuesday morning, I delved into my drawings, forgetting about the rest of the world.

"Oh-kay," I said. "Where are you taking the client?"

"Conference room two."

"Be right there. Thanks."

I hung up and straightened my flowy skirt and

fitted blouse. After making sure everything was in its place, I picked up my drawing pad and favorite pencil and went to conference room two.

As my hand touched the knob to open the door, I heard voices. Loud, male voices with a lilting accent.

Oh my ...

I pushed the door open and stared at them, my jaw slack. Ri was sprawled on the white leather sofa, his feet on the coffee table. Pedro sat in an armchair, his nose in a magazine. Leo sat on the arm of the sofa, his foot fidgeting. Garrett stood in front of the window, but instead of looking out, he was messing with his phone. And Gui was seated in the other armchair, one of his feet draped over his knee.

"Hilary!" Gui said, standing up.

I stepped into the room and closed the door behind me. "What are you guys doing here?"

"Surprise," Leo said, sounding like he was ready to prank me. Or this was the prank.

Pedro lowered the magazine. "Gui said we needed tuxes, so here we are."

I tilted my head at Gui. "But the names I gave you?"

"I was going to call them," he started. "But then I realized you designed clothes. So I called this morning and asked if the studio also made male clothing, more specifically tuxes."

Fallon was picky about the projects she worked on, and bridal clothing was even rarer. She had shown me a couple of wedding dresses and tuxedos she had made over the years, but as she said it, I had the impression she was done with that kind of work. She was now focused on a larger fashion industry, even if her clientele was selected.

However, this wouldn't be a project for Fallon. It would be for me.

"You want me to design your tuxedos?" I asked, my voice tentative.

"Is that so hard to believe?" Gui asked.

"Sort of," I admitted.

"It's true." Leo stood. "So, Hil, are you going to design our tuxes or not?"

A smile crept across my face and pride that these men would trust me with this task filled my chest. "I will."

## 21

GUI

BEFORE THE GUYS AND I LEFT THE STUDIO yesterday, Hilary approached me and asked me to go to her first self-defense class with her. I didn't tell her, but I was planning on going anyway. Like a fucking stalker, I had already planned everything. I would go out for a run, and today's path would include the front of the gym. I would remember about her class, and stop my run to go check it out. Hopefully, it wouldn't look too bad.

As bad as a fucking stalker.

So, on Wednesday, I went down to the building's lobby almost thirty minutes prior to the start of her class and waited for her.

When, ten minutes later, the elevator's doors

opened and Hilary stepped out, I stopped breathing.

She was a vision. A freaking goddess from a dream. And she was totally clueless. Her long hair was tied in a ponytail, but a few strands got loose and framed her beautiful face, and she wore workout clothes—a sports bra, a tight top, and an even tighter cropped pants—that hugged her perfect body the way nothing, no one should.

*Only me.*

Closing my jaw—which I hadn't noticed had fallen open—I did my best not to stare at her perky breasts or round ass, but it was too hard. Too damn, fucking hard.

She turned her face to me, her bright green eyes shining with worry and fear. "Hey," she said.

I inhaled, forcing my lungs to breathe again. "*Oi.*" I glanced away from her, not sure I could trust myself. "Ready to go?"

She nodded.

We exited the building and, side by side, we walked the three blocks to the gym. On the way, Hilary looked nervous, like she could bail at any second. I had to distract her.

"So, is my tuxedo ready?"

That made her smile. "Ha, sure! You can pick it up tomorrow."

"Wow, your studio is really great. Super fast. I'm gonna recommend it to everyone I know."

She chuckled. "I just started drafting some ideas today," she said. "I want to do something new, but not too new, you know. I don't want the guests to look at you guys and wonder what the hell you're wearing."

"That would be ideal."

She rolled her eyes. "But I want to give your tuxedos a special touch. Something unique."

"I'm sure you'll think of something," I said, glad she had relaxed a little. "Are you working on anything else besides the dresses and tuxedos for the wedding?"

She hesitated. "Well, actually, I have a design project for school due at the end of summer. After a couple of weeks just thinking about it, I think I finally came up with an idea." She glanced at me, a little mischievousness shining in her eyes. It made my heart pump faster. "But it's a secret for now."

"Oh, come on. You can't tease someone like that. Tell me at least one detail."

Her smile widened. "Nope."

My chest squeezed. Shit. She was too beautiful for her own good, and when she looked at me like that, when she smiled like that, I was a goner. I knew I was a goner, and I knew I should have turned the other way and run as fast as I could … but that was the thing. I couldn't.

My interest in her had grown, and it was out of control. Out of my control. The more I spent time with her, the more I saw a side of her I didn't know before. Before, she had been hiding from the world, even from her friends, from us. Now I knew her better than the others did, probably even better than her sister did, which made me a little proud.

I let out a long breath.

She tilted her head toward me. "Are you okay?"

The question caught me by surprise. "W-what?"

"You're always asking me that, but I never get to ask you if you're okay. And you just let out a huge sigh. What is it?"

"Nothing, just polo stuff," I lied.

"Oh. Okay." She lowered her gaze.

What? I had to think like a chick here, or I was going to lose her. What would Gabi or Bia say? That Hil was upset I wasn't telling her what my problem was. But how could I tell her that my problem wasn't polo, it was her?

Not wanting the moment to end, I searched for something to say. "A club from Florida has been asking me to go play with them for a few months now, and it's getting harder and harder to say no." Which, in the end, wasn't a lie. It was true that a Florida team had been asking for me, but that wasn't a problem.

"I thought you liked doing the visiting player thing."

"I do. It's just that with Leo and Hannah's wedding coming up at the end of summer, I would like to be around." I pulled on my shirt as if I were straightening my tuxedo jacket. "Best man, you know."

She smiled again.

*Meu Deus.* I let out a long breath. It was all I could do not to pull her to me and kiss her right then.

At the gym, I introduced her to John, who I had already talked to. He didn't need much convincing to let Hilary join the class. She followed him inside the classroom, her hands shaking.

A sudden urge to go to her, to hold her tight, to tell her everything would be all right swept through me. I even took a step toward her before I stopped myself. I was a fucking idiot.

To pass the time, I worked out on the weight lifting floor. *Graças a Deus*, the classroom had a glass wall and I could watch Hilary every few seconds. Otherwise, I would be going nuts now, trying to imagine what she was doing in there. To be honest, if the glass wall didn't exist, I would probably peek through the door after each rep set.

There were only eleven women in the class, and John and another instructor who helped him demonstrate the moves. As I expected, Hilary looked nervous and reserved. It took her at least twenty minutes to relax a little and put some effort into the movements.

As the minutes passed, Hilary's stance shifted. She stopped shaking and acted. Her movements became surer and determine, and during an exercise with John, she was the one who escaped from him the fastest.

He said something to her, making her smile. I smiled too.

"What's that sappy grin for?"

Surprised, I turned and found Malcolm behind me.

"Hey," I said, not surprised to see him here. He lived nearby, and the guys and I bumped into him here a lot. "Working out late today?"

"Yeah. Practice ran late today. And you?"

I shrugged. "Was bored."

He chuckled.

I started a new rep set, and he settled on the machine beside the one I was using. When he finished his rep set, his eyes scanned the place. He did a double-take at the classroom.

"Is that Hilary?"

Did I pretend I didn't know she was here? I sighed. "Yup."

"Man." He let out a low wolf whistle. "She looks absurdly hot in those clothes."

Rage flowed through my veins and I clenched my fists. After another long breath to calm me down, I shrugged. "She's okay, I guess," I lied.

"You know, I think Reese has a thing for her."

"What?" I knew Reese had a thing for her, otherwise he wouldn't have asked her out, but I wasn't prepared to hear that from his teammate.

"He's always trying to get close to her when she's at the club, and whenever the topic is girls, he keeps going on and on about her." Malcolm tilted his head, thinking. "Yeah, I'm sure. He certainly has a thing for her."

What did I say to that? Ask him where Reese was so I could threaten him? Tell him if he ever tried anything with Hilary, I would punch him?

Like a fucking stalker.

"I didn't know about that," I lied again.

"It's fucking annoying actually. He's smitten."

I frowned. "I didn't know they were friends, or that they were close."

"They aren't. As far as I know, Reese and Hilary have only spoken a few times, but he has been watching her since he joined the team and he's definitely smitten." Malcolm shook his head. "Which I don't get. Reese knows about what happened, with Eric, you know. Even though I admit Hilary is one of the hottest girls I have ever seen —" He gestured to her as she again escaped from John. "—she is damaged. I'm not sure I would date a girl like that."

The rage I had been fighting exploded, and I let it out on the machine, almost breaking it with the force I was exerting.

When I was a little less prone to strangle Malcolm, I spoke up. "It was not her fault. She was a victim and I don't think she deserves our pity. I think she deserves our admiration. She has gone through so much, but look at her now." I jerked my chin to the direction of the classroom. "She's fighting it. Maybe it'll take her a long time to feel whole again, but she'll get there."

Malcolm paled. "Hey, I didn't mean it in a bad way. I was just commenting. Sorry if it's a touchy topic." He stood from the machine he had been working on. "I forgot you and her are practically family now. You must know her better than the rest of us."

I cleared my throat. "Exactly."

"Sorry again. Didn't mean to assume anything."

"It's okay," I lied. It was so not fucking okay.

Malcolm walked toward another machine, one far away from me. Good for him, otherwise I would have beat him to a pulp.

However, his words clung to me. *I forgot you and her are practically family now.*

It was true. One more reason why I could never, ever act on this infatuation.

# 22

HILARY

I WOKE UP THE NEXT DAY ENERGIZED. I DIDN'T KNOW why, except that last night I had had my first self-defense class, and even though I still wasn't prepared to take on an attacker, I somehow felt lighter. More confident. And happy. Which was odd since it wasn't even the weekend yet, just a normal Thursday with a day full of work.

That energy turned into nervousness as I parked my car at Hannah's ranch in the evening and didn't see Gui's car there.

Hm, had I gotten the day or hour wrong? I pulled my phone from my purse and checked the messages. Nope. I was here at the right time. Thursday at 5:30 p.m.

So ... where was Gui?

I walked by the stable—not even Jimmy was there—then checked at the arena, and finally came back to my car. I still held my phone and considered calling Gui, to ask him if he was on his way or if he had forgotten.

I chewed my lower lip. I didn't want to impose, though. If he had forgotten, it was because he had something better to do than play the Good Samaritan. Who was I to blame him? I certainly didn't understand the appeal of helping me.

Sighing, I opened the door of my car. Better to go home and work on my school project—the one I still had no idea for. At first, I thought about the wedding clothes and during the presentation, I could tell the story of how Hannah and Leo met, but that was too personal. I could avoid mentioning Eric, and what he had done to Hannah and me, but it was still too close. And I didn't want to associate the wedding with something so horrible.

I slid inside my car.

"Hilary!"

I froze upon hearing my name, just a whisper on the wind. Slowly, I climbed out of my car and looked around, searching for the voice that had called me.

"Here," it said again, a little clearer, a little closer.

I turned toward the entrance road and gaped.

A beautiful dark brown horse trotted on the road, approaching the parking lot, and Gui was on top of him.

I took several steps back as the horse approached, but Gui pulled on the reins and the horse came to a complete stop twenty yards from me. The fashion designer in me couldn't help but notice he was wearing dark jeans, black polo shirt, black cowboy boots, and a black and orange baseball cap.

"*Oi*," Gui said, smiling.

"H-hi," I managed to say.

"Sorry I'm late. I wanted to surprise you with Pampa, but it seems I miscalculated how long we would take to gallop from our ranch to your sister's."

I frowned. "Pampa?"

Gui patted the horse's neck. "Yeah. This is my horse, Pampa." He dismounted the animal and, grabbing the reins, took a few steps closer. "Pampa, this is Hilary. Say hi."

I smiled, amused by the way he talked to the horse, but then Pampa moved his head up and down, as if he was nodding at me, and I gaped.

"Oh my …"

Gui's smile widened. "See? He's a good boy."

"That's incredible," I whispered. I took in the rest of the horse. He was tall and strong, with thick thighs and neck, and his dark coat was shiny and lush. The color of his coat darkened near the extremities, giving the impression that his legs were black. "He's beautiful."

"Thanks. He was born on our ranch in Brazil five years ago and, when it was time to move, he was the first thing I chose to come with me."

That was so sweet.

"It still boggles my mind how you guys brought horses from another country."

"Me too." Gui turned his baseball cap to the back. "Come with me. Let's put him in a stall." He gestured for me to walk with him.

I stood my ground for five seconds, while trying to rein in my fear, but then I took a deep breath and went with him. I kept a safe distance from Gui, and Pampa was on his other side. Besides, I knew Gui could take control of his horse in case he decided to lunge at me. As if horses just lunged at people for no reason.

I shook my head, getting rid of that ridiculous thought. "So, you play polo with him?"

Gui let out a chuckle. "I see you don't know much about polo, do you?"

I scrunched my nose. "Sorry?"

Gui chuckled some more, then explained as we walked in the stable together. "No, I don't play with him. In fact, Pampa never played polo. There are certain breeds that are better for polo, and certain requirements, like a certain height range, and Pampa doesn't fit those. Which is fine by me, because polo ponies don't last long. On the field, I mean. We have at least two polo ponies for each player when playing because the horses get too tired and they need rest. And polo is a sport that wears them out too fast." He opened an empty stall and guided Pampa inside. "Polo ponies retire too fast, even if they don't get injured while playing."

"I see." I observed as Gui locked the stall and turned on the water system. "So, all of you have horses like Pampa and Minuano, and also the polo ponies?"

"*Sim*. Although, we don't get too attached to our polo ponies. Don't get me wrong. We still take good care of them, but they don't become our friends like this one." Standing in front of me, he jerked his chin toward his horse.

"Understandable." At least, it sounded like it. I

looked at Gui and found him staring at me with a lopsided grin. "Hm, so, what are we doing today?"

Still sporting that mischievous smile, Gui turned to Belle's stall. "How about we give the round pen exercise another try?"

I sucked in a sharp breath. "What if I panic again?"

"Do you think there is any reason to panic again?"

I stared at him and realized there was no reason to panic again. Not right now at least. We were alone, and he sometimes looked at me in ways that made my stomach fill with butterflies, though I didn't think he did it on purpose, but we had been alone several times before. Gui had proved to be a good friend, and I knew he wouldn't hurt me.

"No," I said, my voice sure.

He nodded. "Good. Then let's go."

THE PERFECT FRIDAY NIGHT: MY PJS, ME SEATED ON the floor, my drawing pad on the coffee table in front of me, my pencils and charcoals and accessories spread around me. And the tub of ice cream in the freezer that I would soon devour.

I stared at the drawing pad and nothing came to me. Nothing.

How would I pass this class, present this project, if I couldn't even come up with an idea? What did they want me to do with a design that has a history or a story? The wedding dresses and tuxedos popped in my head again.

And from there, I imagined Gui in a tuxedo. Next, was an image of Gui with his tuxedo riding Pampa. A smile tugged at my lips.

Last evening had been good. Gui had taken Belle to the round pen, and she ran and ran as we settled on the fence and observed her. After a while, she approached us and I touched her with my feet. When she didn't pull away, I leaned down and brushed my hand over her forehead.

"Now, jump in," Gui said.

I stared at him, frozen. Until he jumped down and extended his arms to me. I let him help me down, and for a moment, I didn't know what I was more stunned about. That Gui kept a hand at my waist, or that Belle hadn't run away and was sniffing me.

I didn't ride her, I didn't try to make her feel crowded, but that hour I spent in the round pen just walking around Belle, having her walk around me, and touching her smooth coat every few minutes ... that hour had been amazing. Practically magical.

Mindlessly, I had started drawing a horse on my pad. Sure, why not design a clothing line for horses?

I chuckled.

The doorbell rang and I froze.

Slowly, I stood and walked to the door, knowing who it was. I looked down at myself, at my short shorts and my tight tee. Crap, if he kept on showing up like that, I would have to buy new pajamas.

Swallowing my sudden nervousness, I opened the door. My mouth went dry.

Gui stood there—in jeans, a casual T-shirt, and sans baseball hat. In fact, his hair looked a little damp, as if he had just showered. His blue eyes shone and he had a half-grin on his lips.

He held up the ice cream tub he had cradled on his hands. "*Oi.*"

I smiled. "Buying free passage?"

"Sorta."

I stepped aside and let him in, wondering what the hell he was doing here on a Friday night.

He was already opening the ice cream over the kitchen's counter by the time I snapped out of it and closed the door.

He looked around the kitchen. "Where are the bowls again?"

"I'll get them." I strode into the kitchen and grabbed two ice cream bowls from a cabinet.

He shook his head at me. "No ice cream for me. But I do accept chocolate, if you have any."

I smiled and reached for the chocolate in the pantry. "What if I didn't have it?"

"Then I would have to run home and grab some," he said as he served me what looked like three big scoops of ice cream.

Holy crap, did he think I could eat all that and not worry about gaining weight. I was a girl. Girls tended to gain weight easily. Ugh.

I took the bowl from him before he added a fourth scoop. "Thanks." I settled back on the floor of the living room, hiding my bare legs under the table.

Gui sat on the couch behind me, just to my side. "That's ... wow, I didn't know you could draw like that."

I narrowed my eyes at my drawing. "It's not that great." And it wasn't. I sort of knew a little about art since I had to draw a lot for my class, and this wasn't close to what art students could do, what real artists could do.

"I can't even draw stick figures." He unwrapped

the chocolate bar. "To me, this looks perfect." He tilted his head, taking in my drawing. "I can see the lines and the strand of the coat and the shadows. I would say this horse's face is perfect."

"Shut up," I muttered.

"But ... hm, why were you drawing a horse?"

"It wasn't my intention. I was trying to work on my project for school, but nothing came to me, so I guess my mind went to yesterday evening, to playing with Belle in the round pen, and I just ... drew a horse."

"Not any horse. Belle."

What ...? But he was right. I could see her now, the way the hair on top of her forehead always swept to the left, and the little mark under her right eye. It was Belle. And I hadn't even noticed it.

"I guess you're right."

Gui placed the empty chocolate wrapper on the side table, then leaned forward, resting his elbows on his knees, putting his face a mere foot from mine. I gulped.

"So, how is the secret project going?"

I chuckled. "Well, it's so secret, it wants to remain a mystery even to me."

One corner of his lips tilted up. "Wow, Hilary Taylor can crack a joke. I'm impressed."

I swatted his shin and he made a face, pretending it had really hurt. "Shut up, Guilherme Fernandes." I narrowed my eyes. "I don't know your middle name. In fact, I don't think I know many things about you."

He rested his chin on his hand, and that made his face even closer than mine. Gosh, he was ... he was handsome. With those blue eyes and that chiseled jaw and that full mouth—

"What do you want to know?"

"We can start with a middle name," I said quickly.

"It's not common to have middle names in Brazil. We have two last names, though. One from our mother's family and one from our father's family. So, I'm Guilherme Duarte Fernandes."

"Duarte is your mother's and Fernandes is your father's."

"Yes, that's why Leo, Bia, Ri, and Pedro have the same last name, because our fathers are brothers. Their other last name, though, or what you here call middle name, is their mother's so it's not the same as mine."

I nodded. "I get it. It's odd, but I get it."

"What else do you want to know?"

"I know you're twenty-four. You love polo, in fact, you live for polo. I also know you like to party. You seem to like exercising since I've seen you going to the gym or going running a few times."

"I can't say I love exercising, but I'm always glad after, when I know I've done it."

I tapped my chin, thinking. "You seem to be a good friend and your cousins love you, and ... I don't know anything else, I think."

"Then ask something else."

I leaned back, my side resting on the couch, and Gui straightened, sitting up so he didn't have to twist to look at me.

What could I ask him? I wanted it to be a good question.

Staring at the half-grin, I thought and thought until it struck me. "Tell me something you did as a teenager, something that was sort of embarrassing but you don't regret it."

He gaped. "What kind of question is that?"

I waved my hand at him. "Just answer it."

He looked around the living room for a moment, probably thinking of something outrageous to tell me. I bet he had many entertaining tales of a rebellious youth. I almost laughed.

"*Bom*." He ran a hand through his hair and returned his eyes to mine. "I used to be on an *invernada*."

"A what?"

"*Invernada.* That's what we call a group of people who dance traditional dances from my state in Brazil."

My turn to gape. "You danced?"

Gui chuckled softly. "I know you're either imagining me in tights dancing ballet, or in loose pants that are barely hanging on my hips. That's not it." He pulled out his phone from his pocket and opened the YouTube app. "I'm gonna show you an example."

He typed *dança folclórica gaúcha* in the search box and thousands of videos popped up. He browsed through a few, and then clicked on one.

A melodic but heavy beat came from the phone's speakers, and the dancers, always couples, swayed from side to side, sometimes stomping their feet on the floor, along with the music, or clapped their hands or twirled. Gui switched to another video, then another, showing me different rhythms and clothing—though it was always the same style. The men wore pants that were loose in the legs, but tight on the hips and shins. Some were plain, but others had designs and details on the side. The look was completed by shirts, also with some kind of frill or detail, a scarf of sorts around their necks, boots, spurs, and hat. Odd shaped cowboy hats. The women wore dresses with many, many details and laces and frills and fringes. Some dresses went to their necks, and some showed slight cleavage. Some had long sleeves; some were short. However, all of them were round, full skirts that brushed the floor. Their hair was also brushed in beautiful waves, and they had something in their hair that matched their dresses—a flower, a tiara, a bow.

It looked pretty, powerful, and all the dancers, all of them, seemed proud and happy to be dancing the dances of their state.

"It's so ... meaningful."

Gui nodded, a small smile on his lips. "It is. I'm glad you see that. We *gaúchos* are proud of our state and its unique culture."

I narrowed my eyes at him. "And you danced that?"

"I did. Pedro pushed me into it. There were these girls from school ..." Gui ran a hand through his hair again. "We had a crush on them and we knew they danced with an *invernada* group, so we joined. The thing is, he and I actually liked it. We danced with them for over a year, long after our crushes were gone."

"Why did you quit?"

"Polo. We were getting too good at polo and we were at a point in our career where we had to choose. Play polo for fun and keep going to the *invernada*'s rehearsals, or dive into polo with all we had, which meant practice and practice and practice some more." He shrugged. "So we quit."

"That's a shame. I would have liked to see you and Pedro dressed like that and dancing those dances."

Gui shot to his feet. "*Bom*, I don't have the clothes here with me, but I still know how to dance. Or at least, I still know the basic steps." He extended his hand to me.

I just stared at it. "What?"

"Come dance with me," he said, as if that was the most normal thing ever. I kept staring at his outstretched hand. "Just come." He leaned forward, grabbed my hands in his, and pulled me up. He pushed the coffee table to the side and played one of those videos on YouTube. Then he turned to me, hands open. "May I?"

I swallowed the sudden self-consciousness and nodded.

Gui stepped into my personal space, took my right hand in his left, and placed his right hand on my waist, while I rested my left hand on his shoulder.

Those big, blue eyes were on mine. "Just ... let

me guide you." His voice sounded a little hoarse to my ears.

He swayed us, two steps to my right, one step to my left. "Two, two, one," he whispered. So far, so good. Next, he moved us around while we kept up with those two-two-one steps. Soon, I got the hang of it. Then he fancied it up again by pulling one of the legs to the back during those steps, causing me to move to him, and my body bumped into his. Our chests and stomach touched, and I suddenly became very aware of the big, powerful male holding me.

A trickle of fear snaked up my spine and I went rigid, which made me miss the next step, and Gui, not noticing my sudden panic, halted, thinking I had tripped.

He chuckled. "That was pretty good for your first time."

My cheeks heated and I forced myself to move, to stamp the panic down, to focus on the now, on the present. Nothing happened. It was just a silly dance between friends.

Breathe in, breathe out.

I took a step back. "Thanks."

He lost the smile. "Are you okay?"

"Yeah." I nodded, forcing my face muscles to relax. I didn't need to smile; I just had to look normal. Okay. "That was fun." It really had been, until I crashed into him. Time to focus on the former. It had been fun, which was all I needed to think about now.

"That was nothing, I mean, compared to what we used to do." He sighed, taking his seat back on the couch. "I miss it sometimes."

Following his lead, I sat down too, just this time I took an armchair across the coffee table. "Would you go back to it?"

A knot appeared on his forehead. "I don't think so. It was fun, I miss it, but now polo is more important to me. I won't take time from polo."

I looked at my hands. "You're taking time from polo to help me out."

He shook his head. "No, I'm using my free time to help you out."

"Even worse!"

He chuckled. "Not really. It's a nice way of spending my free time."

I sucked in a long breath. Why, gosh, why did his words always hit me so hard?

Then, looking into his eyes, I had a clear vision. All of a sudden, an idea for my project popped in my head.

A smile spread across my face.

"What's that smile for?" Gui asked.

"I think I figure out my school project."

He leaned forward, his elbows on his knees again. "Oh. Care to share?"

"Nope." I shook my head like a defiant child. "Not yet."

"Bah, you and this secret project. I hope you show it to me after you present it to your professors, or there'll be unfinished business hanging over my head when I die."

I rolled my eyes at him. "Shut up."

He laughed and I laughed too.

# 23

HILARY

RI TURNED TWENTY-EIGHT DURING THE WEEK AND he had simply announced he had plans for the day—I could only guess he had a line of girls waiting for their turn outside his apartment.

But on Saturday, João Pedro wanted to throw him a party, so we all went to the Fernandeses' ranch for a Brazilian-style barbecue.

I still wasn't up for a party, but I thought it would be only the Fernandeses and my family, so I would be among know, familiar faces and would feel at home.

Wrong.

The Fernandeses had invited a lot of people. Many people from the club were there, and others I didn't know or how they knew them.

"Wow, this place is packed," I said, embracing Bia after I had parked my car along the entrance road, because there didn't seem to have another free spot in their parking area.

"Tell me about it." She grabbed my hand and pulled me inside the house. I waved and said hi to the people I knew as we walked past them. "The party has barely started and I've been all over, helping with serving drinks and appetizers. I wish we had hired some waiters."

"It can't be that bad."

She brought me into the kitchen. "You'll see." Then she shoved a tray in my arms with what looked like a big plate of sausage and ...

"What's that flour thing?"

I heard his chuckle from behind me. Clutching the tray to my chest, I turned around and found Gui entering from one of the many archways. I sucked in a sharp breath. He looked great, as usual, in jeans, a plaid shirt with the sleeves rolled to his elbows, and cowboy boots. No hat this time. "What's so funny?"

He halted before me, smiling. "That's *farofa*. It's a toasted cassava mixture we usually eat with our barbecue."

"Oh,"

"Here." Bia grabbed a toothpick, stabbed one

through a piece of sausage, smeared it on the *farofa*, then raised to my mouth. "Try it."

I stared at it for two more seconds before opening my mouth and letting her feed me. I chewed and ... well, it was good. A little dry, but good. And a little spicy.

Gui raised an eyebrow at me. "*Então*?"

"It's good." I nodded. "Probably not something my mouth would water over, but good."

Gui shook his head. "That's not the right answer. You gotta say it's one of the greatest things you ever ate."

I rolled my eyes. "Now you're pushing it."

Bia clasped my shoulders and steered me toward one of the doors leading to the porch on the back. "Just go around, say hi to people, and offer them the sausage and *farofa*."

"How much are you paying?" I teased.

"I'll give you a glass of coke afterward." She winked.

I shook my head as I headed for the open door. There was music coming from outside and I knew the music. The rhythm sounded like the songs Gui had played for me last night. *Dança folclórica gaúcha*. I smiled, proud of myself for remembering.

Before I could cross the doorway, Gui took the tray from me. "I'll do that."

With a slight bow, he left the kitchen and walked along the big, wooden porch, stopping at every circle or group and offering them the appetizer, always with a smile and lots of words. He was like a social bee and everyone seemed to think he was a nice guy. A great guy.

I walked out the door and regretted it instantly. Reese was to the right with his teammates. Upon seeing me, he approached with a big smile.

"Hey, there," he said. "I was wondering if you would show up. Nice to see you here."

"Hi, Reese." I smiled at him, though I wasn't particularly pleased he had found me. "How have you been?"

"Good, good. Lots of practice. We have a big tournament in L.A. starting next week."

"Oh yeah, so I heard." Gui had mentioned the tournament last night when he was at my apartment.

"So, I was won—"

"Hil!" Hannah ran up the porch stairs and embraced me. "There you are." She smiled at Reese. "Hi, Reese. Do you mind if I steal my sister for a minute?"

He looked unsure but smiled. "Go ahead."

Hannah grabbed my hand and pulled me down the steps, into the crowded backyard. Again, I waved to the people I knew as we walked past them, until she pushed me into a group of people. Our group. Leo, Ri, Pedro, Iris, and Garrett. My parents were to our left, talking to two couples from the club. And João Pedro and Agnes were a few yards to our right, around what looked like a tall rectangle made of brick.

Hannah caught me staring. "That's a Brazilian-style grill. They call it *churrasqueira* and it's made of special bricks that don't get damaged with the heat."

"That looks like such an odd thing," I whispered.

"I know. Some things are still odd to me."

I glanced at her. "Thanks, by the way. For the rescue."

"You're welcome." She nestled against Leo.

"What rescue?" Gui asked, stepping between Hannah and me, sans tray.

"Reese was all over Hil," Hannah said. "Again."

Gui raised one eyebrow at me. "Really?"

"Really, what?" Bia asked, joining our group. She was carrying another tray with what looked like ... omg, those were chicken hearts. I had heard

Brazilians liked eating chicken hearts, but I had never seen it before.

"Nothing," I said, trying to steady my breathing so I wouldn't gag.

"What's with that face?" Bia asked.

"Hm ..." I pointed to the tray on her hands. "That."

Hannah gasped. "You've never had a chicken heart?"

I shook my head.

"Oh, you're gonna love this one," Gui said. He picked up a toothpick and got a big chicken heart with it.

"No way." I pressed my hand over my mouth. "If I eat that, I'll throw up."

"No, you won't," Hannah said. "It's good. I promise. You'll like it."

I shook my head again.

"Just try it, *guria*," Leo said, joining the team. "It's really good."

They bugged me for another couple of minutes until I finally nodded my head, took the toothpick from Gui, and shoved the chicken heart in my mouth. I almost gagged right then, but the flavor exploded on my taste buds and my eyes widened as I chew. This was good. Really good. Much better than the *farofa*.

"So?" Gui asked. Everyone was watching me.

Instead of using words, I used my toothpick to get another chicken heart and put it in my mouth. Okay, even better the second time. I could get used to this.

"I think she likes it," Bia said, smiling.

After chewing and swallowing, I said, "Yup. This one is really good."

Gui chuckled. "Glad you like it."

After that, Bia strode off to continue offering chicken hearts to the guests, Garrett went with her, Ri walked off to receive more guests, Pedro took Ivy to dance, and Leo did the same to Hannah.

A smile on my lips, I watched as they danced like Gui and I had danced last night, but much better.

Gui brushed his fingertips on my elbow. "Hey."

I looked up at him. "Hm?"

"Want to say hi to Pampa?"

"I would love to."

## 24

GUI

HILARY EXTENDED HER HAND OVER THE STALL DOOR and brushed Pampa's muzzle. The horse took a step closer, pressing against her touch.

"He likes you," I said, smiling.

*I* liked her.

Fuck, she looked so beautiful today. She wore a floral green and white dress with high heels that wrapped around her ankles, and her golden hair fell into waves down her back. I knew she had makeup on, but it was only a small touch that accentuated her beauty, the fullness of her lips, the bright shine of her green eyes.

Right now, she looked feminine and hot.

She turned that wide smile to me and I inhaled sharply. Damn, she would kill me.

"I like him too," she said, pulling her hand from my horse. Slowly, she turned around and looked at the other stalls in our main stable. "So, if Minuano, Preta, Midnight, and Felicity are all at Hannah's ranch, whose are all these other horses?"

I beckoned her to walk along the stable's main corridor with me and presented her to all the horses. There was Poncho Negro, Astro, Limão, Charrua, Generoso, Trovão, Ricardo's horse, Crioulo, and Pedro's horse, Coronel. All the others were João Pedro's horses.

"All of these are from Brazil?" she asked, peering into Astro's stall. He was a horse with a dapple coat—a pretty mixture of white and gray that looked like splotches of paint all over his body.

"No, not all, but most."

Suddenly, the song coming from the big speakers Ri and Pedro installed this morning died, grabbing my attention. What was happening? Would Ri stand up on a chair and thank everyone for their presence?

Hilary and I walked to the stable main gates and looked out. In the distance, everything looked normal. *Tio* João Pedro handling the *churrasqueira*, *tia* Agnes helping him out while also in charge of the kitchen, and the guests min-gling, talking.

"That's odd," Hilary said. "It's like, the speakers lost power."

"I'm gonna check it out." I took a step toward the house when a new song played from the speakers.

All the *gaúchos* cheered. This song was like a little anthem to our people.

Hil gasped. "Wasn't this the one you played yesterday while trying to teach me how to dance?"

I noticed the emphases she put on the word trying.

"*Sim*. The one and only."

Ri, who probably was changing songs looking for this one, rushed down the porch steps and grabbed *tia* Agnes, taking her to the spot that now doubled as a dance floor. Leo and Hannah, and Pedro and Iris were already there. Then, Bia showed up with Garrett. Soon, *tio* João Pedro paused his work at the *churrasqueira* and took Ri's place to dance with *tia* Agnes.

A sudden pride and urge filled me in.

I extended my hand to the girl beside me. "Want to dance with me?"

She gaped at my hand, and then her eyes shifted to the crowd behind the big house. "Hm."

I lowered my hand and disappointment made its way into my chest. "Sorry, I shouldn't have asked."

"No, it's okay." She made to reach for me, but stopped and clasped her hands behind her back. "It's just ... big crowd. I don't really know the dance, and ..." She reached to her feet and pulled her shoes off. "Ah, much better." She let the shoes fall beside her and spread her toes in the grass. "Damn these new shoes. They were assassinating my feet."

I looked down and saw angry red marks on her ankles and her toes.

"Oh yeah, you wouldn't want to dance with those." I frowned. "Those look bad, though. Want to go in and grab some ice? Or something else to help out?"

She waved her hand, dismissing it. "It's okay. It doesn't hurt too much."

Silence fell over us as we watched the dancers.

Ri, dancing alone in the middle of the dance floor, tripped on his own feet and fell.

Beside me, Hilary laughed, unbound and free, and I glanced at her, admiring how beautiful she was when she let her walls down. That smile, that laughter ... I wanted to see them stamped more often on her pretty face.

When the song was done, Ri yelled from the floor, "*De novo! De novo!*" and someone restarted the song.

Chewing her bottom lip, Hilary turned those big, green eyes to me. "I changed my mind."

I lifted an eyebrow. "About?"

"Dancing with you." My eyes widened. She raised a finger and said, "One condition, though. We have to dance here."

I laughed, and then took her hand in mine. "I can do that."

I pulled her to me—trying to focus on the fact that we were two friends having a good time, and not on the fact that she was too hot and looked so beautiful and fragile and small without her shoes, and that she was too close to me, looking up at me with a big smile—and we danced.

## 25

HILARY

AFTER A QUIET SUNDAY, MONDAY WAS BUSY AT work. Margot and Karl showed me their projects and asked my opinion, which led to long conversations about the best color, the best cut, and the best details. Then there were the wedding clothes, which took a lot of my time.

Thirty minutes late, I left work and found Gui pacing on the sidewalk in front of the parking lot.

"Gui?" I called, approaching him. He stopped pacing and turned to me.

"Hey."

"What are you doing here?"

He pulled off his baseball hat and ran a hand through his hair, then tucked the hat back. "I heard there's a great new ice cream shop around the corner, and I know how much you like ice cream."

A knot marred my forehead. So, he had come here to take me to eat ice cream? That didn't make much sense.

A trickle of fear ran up my spine as a burst of yearning filled my chest, but yearning for what?

Both emotions made me feel self-conscious. I drew in a sharp breath, well aware that my cheeks were probably red right now.

Gui shifted his weight. "I thought ... I thought you would like to go check the place out."

I snapped out of my trance and cleared my throat. "Yeah, why not?"

Stuffing his hands in his jeans pockets, Gui turned to the street and I fell in step with him. We walked the first half block in complete silence.

Then I suddenly halted. "Wait. You don't even like ice cream?"

He stopped beside me and shrugged. "But you do."

As if not wanting to talk more about it, Gui jerked his chin toward the street and started walking again. Still dumbfounded by the sudden revelation, I resumed walking too. After scurrying for four steps, I caught up with him and decided it was best if I didn't say anything else for now.

But ... what the hell was going on?

"I'm going to Los Angeles tomorrow morning."

"Oh yeah, the tournament, right?

"*Sim*." We turned the corner and Gui pointed to a yellow and blue sign almost a block away. "There."

The Blue Bowl was the name of the place, and yeah, it was new because I didn't remember seeing it before.

"How did you hear about this place?"

"*Bom*, I—"

"Gui!" someone shouted.

Both of us stopped and turned to the voice. Shock hit me in the face as I saw a pretty girl with long, black curls jogging toward us, a big grin on her face.

"Gui!" she exclaimed, throwing herself at him. Her arms were around his neck before I could blink.

But Gui looked as shocked as me. His arms were slack beside him, and he didn't seem to breathe until the girl pulled away and smiled at him.

"Haven't seen you in a while? How are you?"

"Hey, Ashley."

She clasped his biceps. "Hm, someone has

been working out. How is polo? Still the love of your life?"

I couldn't help the crazy feelings that swelled in my chest. Jealousy, disappointment, and embarrassment. Always embarrassment.

Without meaning to, I took a few steps back as the girl chatted with Gui, and he seemed ... lost? Surprised? Ashamed for being caught with one of his many girls?

Another pang of jealousy exploded in me. Damn it. I couldn't feel this way. It was not right. Gui was nothing more than a friend. He could do whatever the hell he wanted, and if he wanted to change our ice cream plans to go out with this girl instead, so be it.

The girl wore a short dress that hugged her perfect body. With that hair, that face, and that body? Why wouldn't a guy want to spend time with her?

I looked down at myself. Pencil skirt and a loose blouse and pumps hiding what wasn't there —my small breasts, my narrow hips, and my thin legs.

I snorted. Dr. Walker would be proud of me at this moment. I was finally showing more emotions than I had in years. I hadn't felt jealous or cared if a guy found me attractive in three years.

Before, when I was desperate for being rid of my past and the weight it held over me, I would say that this kind of self-consciousness and the jealousy would be welcomed at any time.

Now, I wasn't so sure.

I turned to leave.

"Hil, wait," Gui called out. He took two steps toward me, then stopped and looked back at the girl. "Sorry, Ashley, but I'm here with Hilary. See you around." The girl, finally seeing me, shot me daggers with her eyes as Gui turned his back to her and halted in front of me. "Sorry about that. I hope you're still up for ice cream."

I opened my mouth to ask him why. Why was he doing this? Why was he ignoring this girl, and not doing whatever the hell she wanted, to take me to eat ice cream, which he didn't even like? Why was he wasting his time with me? Why?

But the words didn't form. They got stuck in my throat. The truth was, I was afraid of what would happen if I did utter them, if I asked him all that.

I wasn't that brave. Actually, I wasn't brave at all.

So I swallowed those words and came up with new ones. "Yeah. Let's go."

THIS TIME, I ARRIVED EARLIER. HALF AN HOUR earlier. I wanted to beat Gui and be the first one at the ranch. To do what, I had no idea. I just wanted to beat him.

To no avail. His Jeep was already in the parking lot—at eight in the morning on a Saturday. We had scheduled for Thursday evening, but Gui had sent me a text asking if we could change the date and time because of the tournament in L.A.—to a Saturday morning. Seeing as I had nothing more interesting to do, I agreed.

"Did you sleep here?" I asked as soon as I entered the stable and found him at Belle's stall, brushing Belle's coat.

"Nope." He continued brushing Belle. "And *bom dia* to you too."

I tilted my head and examined him. As usual, he wore jeans, a Montenegro polo shirt, and a baseball hat. As usual, he looked good. "You always come so early. Much earlier than me."

"It's because I need to set up for whatever we're doing. I don't want to waste your time just watching."

Okay, but he was wasting his time preparing something for me. I didn't get him.

"You know, you could let me help you set up. I might not be able to saddle a horse, but I could learn. I mean, it'll probably take me a few tries to calm down and do it, but I would like to try."

He stopped brushing Belle and looked at me. "Okay." He exited the stall and beckoned me to follow him into the tack room. "How was the rest of your week?"

Despite this past week in which I knew Gui had been at the tournament, I didn't see Gui around too much. Sometimes I wondered if we really lived in the same building. Or maybe he spent so many nights out, partying or with girls or both, that it was hard to bump into him there.

"It was okay," I said, watching as he placed the brush in a box of similar brushes, and stopped in front of a wall where all kinds of equipment hung on hooks. "I called Evie the other day, to check on her. She was hiding at the women's center. She apologized for Mike's behavior, but it wasn't her fault." Even if she had given him details about me, it wasn't her fault. I knew she didn't mean to. I bet that if a man was hitting or threatening me, I would also blurt out any information he wanted.

His jaw tensed as he watched the stuff on the wall. "Did the guy show up again?"

"No. I don't know. I've been careful to leave

only when someone else does, so I'm never alone. If he was there and hiding, I didn't see him."

Gui picked a saddle, stirrups, and reins. "I wanted to be there every time you went or came back from work, just to make sure you were okay, but I have this damn tournament and—"

"You're still in the tournament?" I asked.

He nodded, chuckling. "Yeah. Why? Thought we were that bad and we were done already?"

"No, but ... your text. You said you couldn't come Thursday, so I thought you had a game. Then you texted again saying you could come today, so I thought you guys had lost and were out."

"*Não*. We're still in the tournament."

I gaped at him. "That same tournament? In Los Angeles? What are you doing here, then?"

He smiled, taking my breath away. "It's okay, relax. When it's close, it's easy to come and go as we want. I canceled on Thursday because I had a game that afternoon and wouldn't make it back in time, but I didn't have a game this morning, so here I am."

"You could have canceled today too. I don't mind."

His smile slipped away. "I didn't want to cancel."

I gulped and lowered my gaze, feeling too hot

under his stare. "Okay." I turned to the equipment. "What do I do with this?" I gestured to the things he had laid on a bench in the middle of the tack room.

"You will only watch this time." He picked everything up and jerked his chin to have me follow him again. We stopped by Belle's stall. "I'll tack her up, explaining everything I'm doing. Take notes, I might quiz you later."

Like a good girl, I paid attention to every detail as Gui saddled Belle, but I doubted I could do that alone if he had asked me to. I was still afraid of touching and being too close to horses, and I would probably get too nervous and forget all the steps. Besides, I wasn't only paying attention to what Gui was doing. I was also paying attention to him.

As much as I tried to fight it, there was no way to resist. He was too handsome for his own good. Being a designer, I sometimes wondered if his clothes were made for him, because they fitted him like a glove, revealing enough of his hard body to leave me wondering what else lay under there.

In shock, I realized I was lusting after a guy. Not only admiring how cute he was, but I wanted the guy. A man. A male. Lusting. Wanting. That was huge! I hadn't felt this way since before that terrible night three years ago. Giddiness bubbled inside me.

There was still hope for me!

Then it all came crashing down. I couldn't feel this way about Gui! He was my brother-in-law's cousin. He was practically family. No, damn, it wasn't right.

"What?" he asked, exiting the stall, pulling Belle out with him with the reins.

"Nothing," I said too quickly. Gui narrowed his eyes at me, but didn't prod me for more. He finished tacking her and turned to me. "What now?"

"Now we ride." Gui effortlessly jumped onto Belle and extended his hand to me.

I gaped. "You're kidding."

"Nope."

I gulped. "I ..."

He leaned forward and reached for my arm. "Come on, Hil. I promise you'll be fine. I'll be here with you the entire time."

*Okay, okay. Deep breath in and out. I can do this.*

With my stomach twisting in knots, I rested my hand on his and let him help me onto the horse, right behind him. Immediately, I scooted closer to him, gluing my chest to his back, and my thighs to his, and wound my arms around his waist.

Gui chuckled. "I was going to tell you to hold on tight, but I guess I don't need to anymore." He jerked the reins and Belle started moving. "Here we go."

My arms started shaking and my breaths came in small snippets. If I weren't so nervous and scared, I would have enjoyed the warmth of Gui's body pressed against mine, and the spicy scent of his deodorant.

Belle walked slowly, but each step she gave, her entire body moved, which meant the saddle moved, and I swore I could see me falling headfirst and then her hooves falling over me. I buried my head in Gui's back.

"You're okay, Hil." He rested one of his hands over my interlaced hands on his hard stomach.

Slowly, Gui guided her away from the stable. I dared a peek or two, and saw that we hadn't left the arena. It was large enough for us to walk around in circles for a while.

After a few minutes, I stopped shaking, but my muscles were still wound up. Every time Belle moved in a different way or stomped a hoof or did anything I didn't expect, I tensed even more and dug my nails into Gui's stomach.

"Sorry," I whispered, trying to loosen my hold on him a little bit and failing.

He chuckled. "It's okay." Absentmindedly—or not, Gui ran his hand over my forearms, from one elbow to the other and back. "Tell me, what's the next fear on your list?"

That question surprised me. "Why?"

He shrugged. "Just curious. Maybe I can help you with that too."

I didn't have to pick up the list to look at the next fears. I knew the list by heart even before I wrote it down. I didn't answer his question right away, though. Admitting having fear of horses wasn't too bad—I bet lots of people were at least skeptical about these massive four-legged animals, but admitting to the rest? That would expose more of me to him, and I wasn't sure I was ready to make holes in the walls I had put around myself.

*You're stupid, Hilary. Can't you see there are already holes in that damn wall?*

I groaned. Yeah, I knew there were holes there. Brand new holes that Gui had helped open.

"Sorry," Gui whispered.

"For what?'

"I swear I'm not being nosy or anything like that. I just thought you were becoming good friends and good friends talk to each other."

He was right. Damn it. "It's okay. I was just gathering the courage to tell you."

"That bad, huh?"

"Not really. It's more like embarrassing."

He sighed. "Don't worry, Hil. I promise I won't judge you." Belle jerked as a squirrel ran across the arena and I tensed, burying my nails into Gui. "*Ai.*"

I relaxed my grip on him. "Sorry." He chuckled again, and I decided to blurt it out before I lost my nerve. "The next two items on my list are fear of heights and fear of going to a club."

"Going clubbing?"

"Yeah, I used to dream about going clubbing with my friends before, but now ... it's because of the crowd and the bodies bumping against each other and there are always drunk guys ..." I stopped right there. He knew what I meant.

"I see."

Gui didn't offer any other comment and that bothered me. "That's it? I just confessed to you two of my fears, and you're not even encouraging me to beat them."

"I'm thinking."

"About?"

"How to help you with those fears." He pulled Belle's reins and the horse turned to the left. Tensing, I tightened my grip on Gui again. "I'm not sure about the height fear yet, but going clubbing is easy. We just need to get all the gang together and go. Like we have done so many times before. But this time when we invite you and you say yes, there will be no tricking us."

"But—"

"You'll be with us. I promise I'll be by your side all night and make sure the girls are around you all night, and we'll take care of you. What do you think?"

I shook my head, my forehead brushing against his back. "I'm not sure."

"That's okay. You don't have to decide now."

Why was he trying to help me? Why was he being so nice about it? I really didn't get him, and I was too scared to ask him why—that was another fear I could include on my list right now. To confront Gui and ask him why the hell he was bothering with troubled me when he could be doing anything else. No, I couldn't do that. Not yet. I was too scared of his answer.

With no other sudden movements from Belle, other than her rhythmic walk, I relaxed against Gui's back. We remained in silence as Belle walked around the arena for a couple more laps. Finally, at ten in the morning, Gui guided her to the stable.

He jumped off the horse first, then put his hands on my waist and helped me down—his eyes one mine.

Warmth crept up my cheeks. "Thank you."

He smiled at me. "My pleasure. You did well."

I rolled my eyes. "Yeah, right."

"I'm serious. Soon enough, you'll be a pro." He took a step back, releasing me. "I need to get going." He sidestepped me and started taking Belle's tack. I wanted to ask him where he was going, but now I didn't want to look like the nosy one. Thankfully, he answered it anyway. "I have a game this afternoon in L.A."

"What? You said you didn't have a game today."

"No, I said I didn't have a game this morning." He glanced at his phone. "If I leave now, I should be in L.A. just past noon. Plenty of time to have lunch and warm up before the game."

"You're crazy. You should have canceled with me."

"I didn't want to," he said, staring at me as he closed the door to Belle's stall.

The intensity of his gaze was too much. Too hot. I would get burned. Lowering my eyes, I took a step back, telling myself it was to give him more space so he could walk past me to the tack room, but deep down, I knew that was just a part of it. I stepped back because I wasn't sure what I would have done if I didn't.

I helped him carry the equipment to the tack room and put them in the right places. Then we walked out the stable and to the parking lot together.

"*Por favor*, take care of yourself," Gui said, turning to my car. "Don't give that guy a chance to get to you again." He clenched his hands.

"I will." I opened my car door. "Good luck at the game this afternoon."

"Thanks." I slid inside my car and he leaned down a little, so he could look into my eyes. "Text or call if you need anything, okay? L.A. is just two hours away. I can come and go anytime."

I smiled. "Okay. Thanks."

He stepped back. "All right."

"Bye," I said, reaching for the door.

"*Tchau*," he said, closing the door before I could.

I fumbled with my purse, pretending to look for something while I watched him walk to his Jeep and climb into it from the corner of my eyes.

*Wake up, Hilary. Stop being so stupid.*

I snapped back to reality and started my car before Gui noticed I had been watching him like a starstruck girl. Because I wasn't a starstruck girl. I couldn't be. Not with Gui.

With a frustrated sigh, I drove away from the ranch as if I could leave the starstruck girl behind.

---

SUNDAY WAS A LAZY BUT RATHER BUSY DAY. THE only things I did were have lunch with my mother and her friends at the club, then spend the afternoon at Hannah's ranch. Leo was at the tournament in L.A. and the other girls were busy. It had been a long time since my sister and I had spent some time alone. We made our grandmother's special cookie recipe while talking about the wedding and horses and me—though I didn't tell her about Gui's help. Hannah was happy I was facing my fears, and she could see me becoming quite the Amazon warrior like her. I snorted.

She wanted to go riding, but I wasn't ready to ride by myself. What if Belle got spooked again? I wouldn't know how to control her. Hannah thought I could do it, but hey, I wasn't ready.

Or maybe I didn't want to because this was something I shared with Gui. For now.

Maybe.

Anyway, all the coming and going made me tired, and by seven in the evening, I was back in my apartment, in my pajamas, and ready for my ice cream.

That was when the doorbell rang.

I frowned, wondering if it could be Gui. But he had a game today. In the afternoon. He couldn't be back here so fast, could he?

"*Oi*," Gui said after I opened the door. His hair was damp and he had on fresh jeans, a polo shirt, and a big grin.

"First, why the hell do you always arrive right when I'm opening the freezer to grab my ice cream? And two, what are you doing here?"

"Get dressed," he said, stepping into my apartment.

"What?"

He closed the door, clasped his hands on my shoulders, spun me around, and pushed me toward my bedroom. "Get dressed."

I dug my heels and glanced at him over my shoulder. "Why?"

"It's a surprise. You'll like it, I promise."

"I need more than that."

Gui shook his head. "Sorry, can't say more or it'll ruin the surprise."

"A surprise?"

"Hil, go get dressed, please?"

With those big blue eyes begging me, how

could I say no? "Okay, okay." I disentangled myself from him. "What kind of clothes?"

"Casual. Jeans and some shirt. Blouse. Whatever girls wear."

"Be right back," I muttered before slipping inside my bedroom and closing the door behind me.

My mind spun as I went through my closet, considering what to pick. I didn't wear jeans often, but I had a pair I loved, so no questions there. But what about a blouse? There were so many options. A graphic tee that screamed casual and friend-like outing? An off-the-shoulder top that had a hint of sexy but still covered everything? Or a lacy strapless and fitted top that had sensual written all over it?

I opted for the dark green off-shoulder blouse, cute brown ballet flats, and a bracelet made of brown leather to match. I quickly brushed my hair and pulled it in a tight ponytail, applied some mascara and a pale lip gloss, and headed to the door.

As my hand touched the knob, I froze. What was I doing? I was ready to go out alone with a guy.

Me. Alone. Guy.

I pivoted to the mirror and stared into my eyes. A few weeks ago, heck a few days ago, I wouldn't consider this. It wouldn't even cross my mind, and if someone, a guy, had suggested it, I would ignore it. Now? Now I was ready. I had even dressed up a little. Wow. Was this me? Could I possibly be healing?

Before I allowed my fear and panic to slither back into me, I exited my room and met Gui in the living room.

## 26

GUI

I sat down to wait for Hilary, thinking it would take her forty minutes or an hour to get ready. Well, that was how long Gabi used to take to get ready—more actually. But that had been when we lived together, years ago. Who knew? She might have gotten worse with time.

Surprising me, Hilary stepped out of her bedroom much sooner than I expected.

My breath caught and, before I knew what I was doing, I stood. My eyes widened and my mouth hung open for two seconds before I recovered and relaxed my expression. Only my expression, because the rest of my body was reacting to everything else right now.

My eyes lingered on her long neck and exposed shoulder, and I couldn't help but imagine how it would feel, how it would taste to graze my lips on her smooth skin. Would she shiver? Would she moan?

"Gui?"

I shook my head and focused on her beautiful face. "Ready?"

She shrugged. "It depends on where we're going."

I smiled. "Just ... trust me."

After she locked her apartment, we rode the elevator to the underground level, where we got in my Jeep. I drove us to another building, a few blocks from ours, and parked the car on the street.

"What is this place?" she asked, exiting my Jeep.

"Just a building. What I want to show you is on top of it."

She raised one eyebrow. "On top?"

Hoping she didn't have time to consider and be afraid, I grabbed her hand and pulled her inside the building. The doorman nodded at us as we took the elevator all the way to the top floor. The elevator doors opened to a small room with long glass windows and a glass door that lead to the open roof.

Hilary stepped out of the elevator and froze, her eyes wide.

"Oh my gosh," she whispered.

I tugged on her hand. "Come on."

She shook her head. "I'm dreaming, right?"

"Nope." I chuckled.

"There's no way a helicopter is sitting on the roof of this building."

"Yes, way. It's right here." I tugged on her hand again. "And we're going to ride it."

"I-I can't."

I stepped in front of her and grabbed both her hands with mine. "There's an item on your fear list that says you're afraid of heights. If you come with me in this helicopter, and we fly around for a bit, you'll be able to scratch that item off your list. One step closer to be rid of all your fears." She shifted her wide gaze from the helicopter to me. I could see her internal battle. I squeezed her hands. "You'll be okay, Hil. I promise."

She gulped. "How do you know?"

"That you'll be okay?" I asked, and she nodded. "I know the pilot and I know he has lots of experience. I wouldn't take you on a helicopter ride if it weren't safe. I promise. Besides, when have I let you down?" She stared at me long and hard. I could see I was winning. "Just hold my hand and don't let go. I'll keep you safe. Okay?"

Finally, she nodded.

I smiled and, still holding her hand, took her to the helicopter. I could feel her shaking and when we sat side-by-side in the helicopter, I could see her chest rising and falling fast. I let go of her hand long enough to adjust our headphones and seat belt, then took her hand in mine again.

Hilary probably thought I was doing it—keeping her hand in mine—for her benefit, but it was for mine too. I wouldn't admit it out loud, but it was fucking great to hold her like this.

The helicopter went airborne. Hilary let out a yelp and squeezed my hand. Two seconds later, she turned to me with her eyes closed and rested her forehead on my shoulder.

I leaned my head closer to her, lifted her headphones, and told her, "I'm right here. I won't let anything happen to you. You're safe."

Slowly, as the helicopter stabilized and started its smooth ride, she lifted her head and stared into my eyes. For one quick moment, my eyes flickered to her mouth—to her fucking perfect and kissable lips. I couldn't help it. Kissing her was constantly on my mind, and when she was this close, looking at me this way, it was too damn hard to resist the pull.

I cleared my throat and pointed outside. "Look." Still close to me, she turned her head to look. We were exiting Santa Barbara, going along the coast. From here, everything looked like tiny dots of light—the sky, the town, and even the sea.

As the minutes went by, Hilary relaxed and she even leaned closer to the windows. "It's beautiful," she said.

"Yes, it is," I said, looking at her.

She turned to me with a small smile. "Thanks."

I lifted her hand to my mouth and planted a little kiss there, my eyes on hers. "You're welcome."

## 27

HILARY

"Here you go." My sister handed me a glass with whiskey and coke from across the kitchen's island. She immediately turned around to grab another glass to serve someone else, and I handed my drink to Bia. I wasn't a drinker. In fact, I hadn't had a drink since before that fateful day. I wasn't sure why drinking related to that, but my therapist thought it was because men tended to abuse women, physically or even verbally, when drunk. She said it might also be because I was afraid of losing control.

"*Obrigada*," Bia whispered, winking.

While Hannah busied herself with the drinks and finger food, the guys played video games in their living room. They had just come back from the tournament in Los Angeles, which they had won, and they wanted to celebrate.

"Here," Agnes said, handing me a glass with coke. She and João Pedro had joined us for the celebratory dinner, though João Pedro was with the guys in the living room, complaining that playing video games wasn't the right away to celebrate and that finger food was an appetizer, not a proper dinner.

"Where's the steak? The pasta? The lasagna?" he had asked once we started passing around the cheese bites and lobsters rolls.

I mouthed a thank you to Agnes and turned around on my high stool to glance at the TV. Well, to be honest, I was watching Gui.

He had one of the joysticks in his hands, taking a turn at the violent game flashing on the TV. Leo sat on his left, and Garrett sat on his right. Ri was seated on the loveseat, Pedro had one armchair, while João Pedro was in the other.

Ri told them some joke in Portuguese and the guys laughed. Even João Pedro couldn't hide his smile. After the laughter quieted down, the guys focused on the game, but a big grin stamped Gui's handsome face. He looked boyish, with the hard lines of his jaw and chin smoothed, and his bright blue eyes shining.

As if sensing my gaze, Gui turned his head to me. His grin widened, making me smile in return.

"Hey, *presta atenção*, Gui!" Leo said.

Gui snapped back to the game. "Okay, okay."

He was a puzzle to me. I didn't understand him at all. Why was he hanging out with me? Why was he helping me? Why was he spending so much of his time with me? Of course, my brain came up with several explanations. I was troubled and he felt sorry for me, or I was a challenge. Or, he had a traumatic experience during his teen years and now wanted to redeem himself through me. Or, the most absurd of all—but the one my brain and heart seemed to think of the most—he liked me. More than as a family member. Like the way I liked him.

There, I said it. Or thought it. I had finally admitted it to myself. I liked Gui more than I should. Which probably meant I should stop hanging out with him before things got complicated. And there were several reasons why this could get complicated. One, I could reveal my feelings, find out he didn't feel the same way, and make things awkward between us. Two, I could reveal my feelings, find out he did feel the same way, and make things awkward for us and everyone around us. Dating the cousin of my sister's husband? That was a mess in the making. And three, what about my fear of commitment? Or kissing a guy? Of actually surrendering my heart, soul, and body to him? As much as I wanted to believe I was healing, I didn't think I would be ready to sleep with a guy for many, many years.

Besides, I was sure Gui didn't feel the same about me. He hooked up with pretty girls all the time. For what, a month? A week? I knew he went through them like going through shirts during the week. I didn't want to be one more. Which brought me to number four—what if I was some conquest? He enjoyed the challenge of breaking down my walls, of stripping my soul bare, of taking me to his bed, and then of throwing me away. Then things would not only get awkward between our families; they would get ugly too.

A different array of emotions swirled within me. Elation, wonder, frustration, hope, worry, nervousness, but mostly confusion. I was so, so confused. And if I stopped to analyze it, I became even more confused and nervous, and then my panic and fear flared. Like now.

My breathing grew shallow and my heart beat faster.

Bia sat on the stool beside me, a new glass of whiskey and coke in her hand. "What are you staring at?"

I lowered my gaze and whirled back to the kitchen. "Nothing." I scanned the area, trying to find something to comment on, so she wouldn't ask me more about it. Trying to calm myself down, I settled for her glass. "How many of those did you have?"

"Your sister keeps making them and passing them around," Bia said. "I think everyone has had about ten. Each," she joked. Yeah, right. She would have puked her guts out and then passed out on the bathroom floor.

It didn't take long for Leo's parents to leave—I guess they preferred to celebrate at their ranch, which was what they originally wanted, but the guys insisted on doing it here.

Not thirty minutes after, Bia walked in front of the TV, drawing some shouts from Ri and Gui, who were playing the game.

Cursing, Ri paused the game. "What?"

"This party is dying down," she said with her hands on her hips. "What are we? A bunch of old people? Nu-uh!"

My sister chuckled from across the counter. "I guess she drank more than I thought she had," she whispered. I rolled my eyes. Did Hannah not notice she kept pouring drinks to everyone all night long? I guess those wedding jitters were getting to her, and she had to keep busy somehow. Getting people drunk seemed to be the night's choice.

"Bia, what are you doing?" Garrett asked.

She smiled. "I'm telling you guys that we're going clubbing!"

Pedro and Leo groaned, Iris and Hannah smiled as if they approved the idea, and Gui shifted his attention to me. His eyes were serious, focused. He was trying to send me a message and I was trying to ignore it.

"Turn this game off," Bia said, reaching for the joysticks. "We're leaving."

Ri hid his joystick behind his back. "Let us finish this fight, then we'll exit the game and go. Sound good?"

"*Sim.*" She stepped out of the way and strutted to the kitchen. "And you?" She pointed at me. "You're coming too. No excuses this time, and no getting away from us."

Hannah looked at me with worried eyes. "I would love for you to come, but I understand if you don't want to."

I opened my mouth to tell them I wasn't feeling well, to tell them a lie, but closed it again. Why not tell them the truth? I wasn't comfortable going to a club. I was afraid to go to a club. My eyes found Gui's again. He had handed the joystick to Leo and stared at me with such intensity. Until he turned his gaze to his phone and typed. Once more, I opened my mouth to tell the girls something, anything, as to why I wouldn't go to the club, when my phone dinged.

Gui: *It's one more item you can scratch off your list. Come to the club, por favor.*

I snapped my head back to him, my eyes pleading. *Please, understand.*

My phone dinged again.

Gui: *We'll all be there. I promise I'll stay by your side all night and won't let anything happen to you.*

I shook my head.

Gui: *Pretty please.*

I smiled and looked again at him. This time, his eyes were pleading.

"Hil?" Hannah called me, snapping my attention back to Bia and her. "What is it?"

"Are you coming or not?"

I took a deep breath and, even though I was shaking from head to toe, I said, "Yes. I'll go to the club with you."

I RODE TO THE CLUB WITH LEO AND HANNAH, BUT right after Leo parked and we exited his Grand Cherokee, Gui was by my side, walking with me toward the entrance.

"Are you okay?" he asked, his voice low.

"No," I confessed. I still shook so much I thought I would miss a step and fall flat on my face.

He inched closer to me, as much as he could without holding my hand like the other couples in our party were doing.

"I'm right here."

I nodded, focusing on each step I had to take. However, each step became harder, heavier, and made me shake even more.

In front of the club, I paused and took a deep breath. Oh my gosh, I was doing this. I couldn't do this. I would freak out. I was already freaking out. What if—?

Gui's hand closed around my upper arm. "Hey." I looked at him. There was concern in his furrowed brow and hard jaw. "Whatever is going on inside that head of yours, shut it out. Focus on us, your family and friends. You're here with us and only us."

I nodded, keeping his words front and center in my mind.

*I am here with family and friends. They won't let anything happen to me. I am fine.*

I exhaled and let Gui, who was still holding my arm, guide me toward the VIP line. Five minutes later, we were inside the club, walking in a line to wherever Ri was taking us. The music blared from speakers, bouncing inside my head, and the lights flashed, all colors swirling in the dark, making me a little dizzy. At least, Hannah was in front of me, and Gui was behind me, his hand resting on my back, giving me strength while I stared at my sister's head.

We went up a flight of wide concrete stairs lined with red carpet to a balcony that overlooked the dance floor. Several rooms were separated by waist-high walls made of reddish brick and glass, and leather sofas, chairs, and low tables filled the spaces. Ri took us to one of the largest of the VIP areas, and I let out a long breath once we all had made it safely inside.

Anyone who looked at me would think I had just walked through a war zone, because it was a war zone to me. As everyone got settled on the sofa or ordered drinks, I approached the silver railing and looked over the balcony to the dance floor, the

DJ standing in the center, the tables and chairs around the room, and to the bar. Everywhere, guys flirted with girls; men hit on women. Couples—new or old—kissed. This, clubbing, was all a game to see who would end up with whom, even if for a night. I didn't understand why my sister and our friends liked clubbing so much. I remembered dreaming about clubbing because I was young and single, and I wanted to flirt and be watched and desired. I wanted to find a guy to love, to love me, and what better way than a nightclub? That was my sixteen-year-old train of thought. At that age, I couldn't get into clubs so I did all that at the parties my friends threw. But what about Hannah and the others? They were all couples. They didn't need to find someone to love—well, except for Gui. And Ri, but Ri didn't count. From what we all knew, he would be single forever.

"Here," Gui said, standing by my side and handing me a glass with ice. I stared at it. "It's only coke."

"Thanks." I took it and the liquid sloshed to the rim. My hands still shook.

Gui glanced at my hands then looked into my eyes. "You're fine here, okay? We're inside this area and nobody will come in here uninvited."

Didn't he know that meant nothing to me? Eric had been Hannah's boyfriend for two years before he started getting impossibly possessive and violent. He had been a part of the family. My father had loved him and welcomed him like a son. One thing I learned was that we never really knew anyone. A person could be one thing in front of us, and then completely different behind our backs.

Before I dropped it or spilled it, I set my glass on an end table to my right and returned my attention to the dance floor. Maybe, if I stared at the place and the people long enough, I would get used to it.

I doubted it.

With a deep breath, I sat down on the sofa beside Leo. Maybe if I stayed right here, immobile, time would pass. I wouldn't see anything, feel anything, and then it would be time to leave and I would go back to the safe haven of my bed.

Leo saluted me with his coke. "Kinda boring, isn't it?"

Boring? No. Scary? Intense? Out of control? Yes.

"Don't you like coming here?"

He wrinkled his nose. "I do, most of the time. But clubbing reminds me of a part of my past I want to forget." When he was younger, Leo had a mishap on his path to being polo's absolute leader. As a prodigy, he started playing at a young age and ended up missing classes and failing most of them. Because of that, his father forbade him to play tournaments until he finished high school. Jealous of seeing his brothers and cousin playing, Leo rebelled. He went down a dark path he wasn't proud of. Thank goodness he came back around, and he always said part of it was because of his twin sister, his brothers, and his cousin, and the other part was because of Hannah. "Besides, everyone around me is drinking and I'm not, so that makes it even less fun."

I picked up my glass of coke and raised it to him. "You're not alone there."

He smiled and clinked his glass on mine.

Shaking a tiny bit less, I took a sip from my drink and looked around. Hannah danced with Bia and Iris, while Ri and Pedro argued about polo—visible from their gestures. Garrett was focused on the plate of appetizers that had arrived, as if we didn't have enough food before coming here, and Gui leaned against the rail, his back to the dance floor, his eyes on me.

"Ohmygosh!" a girl shrieked.

I knew that voice. My head snapped and I saw

Megan standing outside our VIP area. Of course, Blaire and Andrea were with her.

With a wide smile, Hannah welcomed them in and offered them drinks.

Leo groaned when Hannah smiled at him and gestured for him to go stand with her and say hi to her friends. I held back a laugh as he stood and shot me a glare.

Bia took Leo's place. "I don't like them very much," she said, her voice normal. How much could this girl drink before she was drunk?

"Why is that?"

"When we first arrived here, they were intent on getting with the guys."

"What? I didn't know about that."

"Oh yeah. Megan and Leo kissed, and—"

I gasped. "No!"

"I'm serious!" Bia shook her head. "Blaire tried hooking up with Pedro, but he turned her down. And Andrea went after Gui."

My heart skipped a beat and my throat felt dry. "And?"

"He didn't give in right away, but I saw them together a couple of times last year. I think he slept with her once or twice."

I sucked in a sharp breath, trying to fight back the bile rising in my throat. Despite myself, I glanced at Andrea, and she was staring at Gui. "What happened then?"

"I think he got tired of her. I'm not sure." She paused. I shifted my gaze to Gui just in time to witness when his eyes left mine and went to Andrea. His lips pressed into a thin line and his jaw tensed. He nodded at her and she smiled at him, batting her eyelashes. Oh, crap. "You know how he is. He's not the worst out there, but he certainly doesn't seem to have any intention of settling down."

Yes, I knew that. I just needed to be reminded of it. Repeatedly.

A couple of minutes passed and Bia stood to go dance in the middle of our room with Garrett. The rest of our group mingled. Then, on the prowl, Andrea walked up to Gui and leaned against the rail beside him.

I couldn't hear them over the music, and I didn't want to.

Gui glanced my way and heat overtook my cheeks. What the hell was I doing? I shouldn't care.

*I don't care.*

Averting my eyes, I twisted in my seat until I couldn't see them anymore—unless I snapped my head back and I wouldn't do that.

If I were more courageous, I would stand up

and leave. But I wasn't brave. I was a wimp. Standing up and leaving would mean I had to walk by all those people downstairs by myself and the thought of that made me almost as sick as watching Andrea flirting with Gui.

I didn't allow myself to look back and find out if he was flirting back.

An eternity passed as our group continued being social, and all I wanted to do was crawl into a hole and never, ever leave again.

Why the hell had I come here?

It was all Gui's fault. He had promised he wouldn't leave me, that he would be by my side the entire time. And what was he doing now? Probably planning to leave with Andrea.

Surprising me, Gui sat down by my side. I gaped at him, then on instinct, looked for Andrea. She was back with Megan, Blaire, and Hannah, and her eyes were shooting daggers at Gui.

"I guess you know about Andrea," he said.

I took a long breath and looked back at him. "I heard some things, yes."

"I ... there's nothing going on with her. Not for almost a year now."

Why was he telling me this? He had no obligations toward me. He could do whatever he wanted. The feelings inside my chest—jealousy and disappointment—were mine and mine alone. He didn't need to know about them.

I forced a fake bravado. "It's okay. You do whatever you want to." He tilted his head and narrowed his eyes at me, as if trying to spot my lie. I wouldn't give him the satisfaction. Before he could say anything else, I attempted to smile. "So, I guess I can scratch another item off my list."

"Not yet." He had a glass of water in his hand. I had noticed that he drank, but he kept pausing, drinking water or coke between each glass of whiskey.

"Why not?"

"You're at a club, but you aren't clubbing," he said. I frowned at him, confused. Was he trying to trick me with a riddle or something? "You haven't danced."

I turned my gaze to the girls in our room. All of them dancing right there, including Megan, Blaire, and Andrea. This time, even Garrett and Ri had joined in, while Leo and Pedro hovered close by, pretending to dance.

"It seems a little weird to dance in here," I said, gesturing to them.

He shook his head. "Not in here. That doesn't count."

I stared at him, his eyes serious. Understanding hit me and I gasped. "You want me to dance down there?" I pointed to the sea of people grinding their bodies together. His silence was a loud answer. I shook my head. "No way."

"Why not?"

"Because ..." My cheeks burned with embarrassment. Anger? Frustration? I wasn't sure. "I just can't."

Gui reached over and held my hand between his. "I'll go with you and I promise that I won't let anything happen to you." He kept saying that, and I wanted to believe it was true, that he could shield me from anything. "Have I ever done something for you to doubt me?" he asked. My thoughts flew to moments ago when he was talking to Andrea and jealousy flared in me. I had no right to be jealous. Besides, he had left her standing alone to sit by me.

"People will bump into me and I'll freak out. I just know it."

He squeezed my hand. "People bumping into you is part of clubbing. You have to let that happen sometime. What better time than now, when your family and friends are right here with you? While I'll be right by your side the entire time?"

"I don't know," I whispered.

"I'll give you a minute to let this sink in, but I'm

not taking no for an answer. You're here. You're so close to getting this done, to overcoming this fear. I won't let you go home with it half done."

Gui was right. Damn, he was always right when it came to my fears. And he had helped me through so many of them. He had walked me through, held my hand, and never once came close to disappointing me. I was ninety-nine percent sure he wouldn't disappoint me now—the other one percent was my insecurity talking—so why not trust him and let him guide me once more?

Before I gave in to my fear, I nodded. "Okay."

He beamed at me for a second. Then he forced his expression to a blank state and stood, tugging my hand. "Let's go, then."

Taking a deep breath, I stood and my legs felt wobbly.

Nobody noticed as we slipped from the VIP room—except for Andrea—and descended the staircase to the first floor. The entire time, Gui kept me in front of him, his body a wall behind mine, even though we weren't touching. Only his hand was firm on mine. Attentive, he extended his arms around me each time someone stepped back and almost bumped into me. So far, he kept me protected as he said he would.

Regardless of that, my hands sweated, my breathing came in hard gasps, and my heart beat so fast, I thought it would take flight and jump out my chest.

At the edge of the dance floor, I froze. Inches from my back, Gui leaned forward and slid his hands on my arms. "It's all right, Hil. You can do this."

*I can do this.*

People danced, smiled, screamed, twerked, kissed, grounded against each other as if they were ready to have sex, right there, right then. Some guys circled around groups of girls, waiting for the right moment to attack. Some girls looked eager to have the guys' attention; some looked disgusted. All that mixed with the loud *thud-thud* of the electronic song and the colored lights coming from all sides was enough to make me feel sick again.

I wasn't so sure I could do this anymore.

Gui leaned closer, his mouth right in my ear. "Close your eyes."

I snapped my head toward his, surprised by his suggestion, but even more surprised to find his lips only an inch away from mine. His eyes fleeted to my mouth for half a second. Gulping, I turned my face away. "I don't—"

"Trust me. Close your eyes."

Taking a deep breath, I closed my eyes.

Gui snaked his hand around my waist and took a step forward, gluing his chest to my back. I sucked in a sharp breath. He walked forward, pushing my legs with his, making me walk too. After only ten steps or so, he stopped. Without taking his arm from my waist, Gui whirled me around, my body brushing against his.

Though he didn't tell me to, I opened my eyes and lifted my chin so I could look at him. As I suspected, he was looking down at me, an intense shine in his eyes. Now I was nervous for an entirely new reason.

A corner of his lips tilted up. "Forget about everyone else in here. Focus on me now. On us."

He had no idea what he had just said to me—not the way I took it, at least.

Slowly, Gui started swaying side by side. His hands, still on my hips, applied some pressure, trying to make me move too.

All right, I could do this.

*Focus on him.*

That shouldn't be too hard.

I sighed. It was and it wasn't. Yes, it was easy to concentrate on Gui's handsome face, on his hard body against mine, and the way he looked at me as if we were the only ones in this world. However, at the back of mind, I felt the pressure of everything else. The people, the dancing, the flirting, the music, the lights ... it made me dizzy. But no more dizzy than looking into Gui's eyes, than moving my body side to side with his, than having his strong arms around my waist, holding me close.

It was all too confusing. Too consuming.

Gui broke the spell when he stepped back, pulling me with him. "Watch out," he said. Someone had stumbled back and would have bumped into me if it weren't for Gui and his attention. It was impressive how committed he was in making sure nobody other than him touched me.

I tensed all over again.

Gui ran his hand up and down my back, making me shiver. "Relax," he whispered, close to my ear.

Relax with him so close in a place like this? I had no idea how I still hadn't broken down in the most terrible panic attack in the history of panic attacks.

He pulled back and looked into my eyes. With his palm flat on the small of my back, he pushed me closer, making me straddle one of his legs and my breasts to squish against his chest. I stopped breathing as he moved his hips side to side, more vigorously this time, taking my hips with his.

I laid my head on his chest, with my forehead nestled in the crook of his neck, and my ear over his heart. It beat hard and fast, almost as hard and fast as mine. For some reason, that brought me a little satisfaction and I was able to relax a little bit.

I moved to the rhythm of the music, brushing my body against Gui's. Nothing fancy—I wasn't ready for that—but bold enough for me to feel almost like my old self. Almost.

After a few minutes, I felt confident, secure. I twirled once, twice. On the third time, Gui's hand shot out and grabbed my waist and pulled me back to him, my back to his chest. His hand slid to my stomach, his fingers opened wide, and he pushed a little more. Something long and hard pressed against the small of my back. Realizing what that was, I sucked in a sharp breath and jumped away from him.

Oh my gosh, oh my gosh. A guy. Touching me. Desire. Strange people around me. Kissing. Laughter. Loud music. Bright lights. Hard to breathe. Hard to stand. Hard to see.

"Hey, hey," a voice said through the haze. "Hil, come back to me. It's all right." Gui reached out and clasped his hands around my upper arm. He pulled me a little closer and leaned down to look into my eyes. "You're okay, Hil. Nothing is happening." He shook his head once. "Breathe, Hil, breathe." He inhaled and exhaled, showing me what to do. Dizzy, I followed his lead and did as he instructed. "I'm so, so sorry. I lost my mind for a minute. It's just ... you're so amazing, so beautiful, so irresistible. But that's no excuse. I know. I should have better control over myself. I'm sorry."

I didn't trust myself to speak, because I was sure I would scream if I did. Instead, I just nodded, accepting his apologies.

"Want to go back to the VIP area?"

I shook my head. "I want to go home."

His shoulders drooped and I swear he flinched as if I had slapped him. "Okay. I can take you home."

Gently, I disentangled myself from him. "No. I'll take a cab. I'm sorry."

I turned and dashed through the crowd, yelping each time someone bumped into me. Outside, I inhaled deeply, as if I had emerged from underwater after hours fighting for fresh air. Shaking, I hailed a cab.

At my apartment, I started getting undressed as soon as I closed the front door, throwing each piece of clothing on my path, as if I were throwing them into a bonfire. I went directly to the bathroom and sank into the bathtub. Then, I opened the faucet. I suppressed a yelp when the cold water hit me, but thought I deserved it for being so stupid. Then, the hot water replaced it and I sank into it, hoping I could drown my worries, all my fears, all my sins.

# 28

Sᴌᴇᴇᴘ ᴇᴠᴀᴅᴇᴅ ᴍᴇ. I sᴛᴀʏᴇᴅ ᴄᴜʀʟᴇᴅ ɪɴ ʙᴇᴅ, replaying each moment, each gesture, and each action that happened at the club. Everything, from the moment we arrived, to dancing with Gui, and then leaving alone.

I thought I was going to have a panic attack; I was sure of it. I cried on the cab ride home, but the soaking in the bathtub helped. Then there was the ice cream. And after an hour of tossing and turning in bed, I got up and made tea, to see if that would calm me down enough to sleep. No go. It was almost five in the morning and I still hadn't closed my eyes.

I couldn't. With my eyes open, I replayed what had happened. With my eyes closed, I felt it all again. Gui's hand on me, his body pressed against mine, his breath on my neck, his erection ...

I sat up, frustrated. What did I have to do to get some sleep? I wasn't in the right mind to read or even watch a movie ... but maybe I could put on the TV. Maybe the background sound would help me sort through my thoughts. Or at least numb them.

I grabbed my phone from the nightstand, and while walking to the living room, I glanced at the screen. There were several messages and calls from Gui, Hannah, and Bia.

*Where are you?*

*Why did you leave?*

*What happened?*

*Are you okay?*

I stopped reading them.

As I lay on the couch and turned on the TV, my phone vibrated with a new message—a voice message from Gui.

I stared at it, wondering what to do. I could delete it and forget about it, but that would be acting like a kid and I wasn't a kid.

Taking a deep breath, I put the phone to my ear and listened to the message.

"Hil, I know you're mad at me, and with good reason, but please don't shut down. Don't shut me out. You've made amazing progress these past few weeks, and I would hate myself if because of one moment, one mistake of mine, you threw all that away." He paused. "I'm standing outside your door, wondering if I should knock. I need to make sure you're okay. I need to make sure you made it home okay, but I'm too afraid of knocking and you ignoring me." He paused again. "You're amazing. I know I've said this more than once, but you are. I know you don't believe me and that was something I planned on working on. Your confidence. Your belief in yourself. Because, Hil, you've got it all, and once you lower your guard, you'll see I'm right. You're perfect, Hil." He cleared his throat. "Anyway ... please, call your sister, or send her a text letting her know you're okay. She was worried sick when I told her you left. I ran after you, and even though I saw you entering the cab safely, I am worried sick too." He paused again. "Okay. So, talk to you soon. I hope."

The message ended and I stared at the front door. He said he was at my door. Was he still here?

Without thinking, I stood from the couch, walked to the front door, and opened it. And there he was, seated on the floor, his back to the wall across the hallway from my door. He looked tired, disheveled, and incredibly sexy.

Gui jumped to his feet, his eyes on me. And what I saw made my heart ache. Concern, guilt, kindness, relief, sympathy. And something else I wasn't sure I was seeing right.

"Hil, I—"

Something snapped in me. I acted on that new, awoken feeling, and in two steps, I reached him, cupped his face with one hand, clutched his shoulder with the other, and on my tiptoes, I grazed my lips to his. I felt him stiffen under my palms, and his lips didn't move with mine.

Shock and embarrassment began its trip around me—had I misread everything?—but then he woke up from whatever daze he had fallen into. He leaned down, giving me better access to his mouth, wound his arms around me, pulled me closer, and finally moved his lips with mine, taking control.

His kiss was gentle, tentative. It was as if he was afraid that if he pushed too far, I would jump off. And I still could, but right now ... right now I wanted more. I teased his tongue with mine, and he groaned, deepening the kiss. He backed me up until we were inside my apartment, then he kicked the door closed. He spun me around, pushing me against the door. I yelped in surprise, until his body molded over mine, his hard parts pressing against my soft ones, one hand on my hips, the other on my nape, urging me to give more. And more. I moaned.

It had been so long since I last felt like that. Correction. I had never felt like this. I had had a few dates with a couple of guys from my high school, and kissed a few, even thought about going further, but never acting on it. It never felt right. It never felt this way.

My head spun, my body buzzed, my blood pumped.

His mouth left mine and I took a deep inhale, as if I had been underwater for too long. But my relief was short lived as his lips traveled from my mouth to my jaw, leaving a searing trail I was sure would never wash off. His breathing was hard in my ear and, sliding both hands down, he gripped my hips and pulled me to him. His hard-on was more than evident, and for a brief millisecond, I panicked. I really did. But then, I closed my eyes and pressed my hand over his heart and paid attention to the beat under my palm and the breath on my neck, and I reminded myself of the way he looked at me, the way he cared about me, the things he said. He grazed his teeth on the soft part of my neck and I moaned again.

Without warning, Gui slammed his mouth on

mine again, and this time, his kiss was more urgent, as if he had to taste me before I melted away.

And I did melt away.

I placed my hands on his shoulders and gently pushed him away. "Slow," I whispered. "Slow down, please."

Without hesitation, he stepped back, but his hands were still on my hips. "*Claro*. Of course." He looked into my eyes, a shine of concern in them. "Are you okay?"

It seemed the question he asked me most.

"I think so," I said. "But I need to slow down." I walked around him, putting some distance between us. "Give me a minute, please."

He gave me a minute and more. He stood there, in front of the door, while I paced in my living room.

Inside me, I battled so many emotions, so many thoughts and actions. I was elated by Gui. More than that, I was dazed and dazzled. I was surprised I had kissed him first, and even more surprised that he had reciprocated it. More than that, he had kissed me as if he had been planning it for a long time. The idea made me giddy, nervous, happy, and scared, all at the same time.

My heart beat fast and my hands shook.

Until a few seconds ago, my mind had been

blocked against even kissing a guy. Thinking beyond that? I couldn't. I still couldn't. If I tried, the memories rushed forward, taking over my thoughts, and panic set in.

I hadn't given in to panic at the club, and I hadn't given in to panic after kissing Gui.

I wouldn't give in to panic now.

After a long while, he finally spoke. "Please, talk to me, Hil."

Taking a deep breath, I forced those thoughts away.

"I'm sorry, Gui, but I need more time to process this," I whispered, afraid of his answer.

Surprising me, he nodded. "I understand." Then he took a couple of steps toward me and took my hand in his. "I just want you to know that —what just happened here." He gestured to the door behind him. "I don't regret it. In fact, I hope it happens again."

Blood rushed to my cheek, and I felt hot.

Staring at my eyes, he kissed my hand with soft lips, and then left the apartment, closing the door behind him.

I just stood there, gaping at the door and wondering if I had heard him right.

"I HAVE SOMETHING TO SHOW YOU," I SAID, LEANING forward in my chair and handing the piece of paper to my therapist.

With a wary frown, she took it. Her eyes scanned the paper and her eyebrows shot to her hairline. "Oh, wow. I didn't expect this. And so fast."

"Me neither," I whispered.

I had called Dr. Walker's office in the early morning and, thankfully, her assistant was able to add me to her schedule for late afternoon. So, I came over right after work.

"You braved horse riding." She raised one finger. "Fear of horses? Check."

"I didn't ride alone."

"Not yet, but still, riding horses even with someone else is progress." She raised a second finger. "You went on a helicopter ride. Fear of heights? Check." She raised a third finger. "You went out to a club. Fear of crowds and clubbing? Check." Another finger went up. "And you kissed a guy! That is great!"

It had felt great then. I didn't feel too great now.

Sunday morning, I had sent texts to my sister and Bia, because, as their several texts said, they wanted to make sure I was all right. I wasn't all right, but they didn't need to know that. Gui also sent a couple of messages during the day, checking in. I didn't answer him, though. I didn't know what to say to him. I was afraid of bumping into him in the elevator or parking garage at our building, because I didn't know what to think about what happened.

"Tell me about it," Dr. Walker said.

I gaped. "About what?"

"About the boy and the kiss. Do you like him?"

I cringed. "It isn't that simple."

"Ah, of course not. Nothing is simple."

"It's just ... I'm not sure about it."

"It? The kiss?"

"No. Yes. I mean, everything." I sighed. "I ... I like him, more than I should, but I don't know about his real feelings. And I don't want to know. I'm not ready for that. What if I'm just one of his conquests? What if he kissed me back because I'm a female and I was available? Worse, what if he really likes me too? He's the cousin of my sister's fiancé. We're practically family. We can't date. I can't have feelings for him, and he can't have feelings for me."

"We don't choose whom we fall in love with."

My mouth fell open. "I'm not in love with him."

"I didn't mean to imply that. Let me rephrase. You can't choose whom you'll be attracted to."

"But I can choose to ignore it."

"Yes, you can. But do you really want to?"

"I just said he's like family!"

"He is the first male you've felt attracted to since the day Eric made you distrust all other men on this Earth. And apparently, he has been good to you; he has been there for you, which tells me he cares for you, maybe as much as you care for him. I don't think the fact that he's the cousin of your sister's fiancé will be too much trouble."

"It would be if we started dating." I gulped, still not sure how I was able to say these words out loud. "Then broke up and had to face each other at family reunions and parties. Besides, he's in my friends' group right now. If we broke up, I would probably stop hanging out with my friends, making me sink deeper into my fears. I'll be miserable."

"And do you think it'll be easier to hang out with him knowing there could be more between you two, but you didn't even want to try?"

"That's the thing. We're here talking about a relationship I'm not even sure exists. That kiss might have meant nothing for him."

Dr. Walker raised one eyebrow at me. "Are you sure?"

"What?"

"Are you sure the kiss meant nothing to him?"

The memory of his mouth on mine, his body pressed against mine, his hands on me invaded my mind and heated my body. My cheeks flamed at the same time my hands shook.

"I don't know," I muttered. "I'm so confused."

Dr. Walker left her chair to sit beside me. She took my hand into hers. "I know trusting your heart with a man, even one you know and trust, might be too hard for you right now. But you're going in the right direction. You're stronger than you think you are. Just don't overthink each one of your actions and feelings too much. Let them happen. They might surprise you, in a good way."

# 29

HILARY

THE GIRLS AND I WERE IN ONE OF THE HUGE, FANCY fitting rooms at the studio. Even Gabi had arrived last night. She had come to try on her dress, and she would stay a few days before returning to Brazil.

The room was a large rectangle with white leather sofas in the middle, four dressing stalls on each side, each with a booth and tall mirror, a floor-to-ceiling mirror taking over the entire back wall, and a short, round podium lined with white carpet in front of it.

Hannah stood on the podium, tears in her eyes as she looked at her reflection in the mirror.

"I hope those are happy tears," I said from behind her.

She nodded, unable to speak.

Around us, Iris, Bia, and Gabi stared at Hannah, also with tears in their eyes.

A knock echoed from the door. A second later, the door opened and Sonya walked in, bringing a tray with a champagne bottle and crystal flutes.

Her eyes widened as she saw my sister. "Wow, Miss Taylor, that is beautiful!"

"Thank you," Hannah and I said together.

After Sonya left, the girls put on their dresses. Taking turns on the podium, the girls chatted happily, admiring themselves and talking about their expectations for the party. Catching me off guard, Gabi sneaked beside me.

"*E aí, guria*, how are you?"

I offered her a small smile. "I'm good. And you?"

"I'm better now that I'm here."

"I'm glad you were able to come. I was really worried you would arrive only a few days before the wedding, and we would have gotten some measurement wrong and your dress would be all messed up."

"That would have been terrible." She looked down at her delicate, yellow dress. "It's so beautiful."

"Thank you. But it's not finished yet. It'll look even better."

"I've always heard about your talent, and now I can say nobody lied to me. You're truly amazing."

My heart squeezed. She called me amazing, which reminded me of her brother calling me amazing. I had managed to avoid him so far, but I wouldn't be able to keep avoiding him forever.

I swallowed the lump in my throat. "That's an exaggeration." She stared at me, her bright blue eyes so like her brother's, shining with mischief. "How's Brazil?"

She rolled her eyes. "The same."

"Is it so bad? To live there, I mean?"

"Of course not, but ..." She sighed. "There's just my parents and me now, and it isn't the same, you know. I grew up with Gui and Leo and Bia and Ri and Pedro, like they all are my brothers and sister, and now they are all gone. It sucks to be there, left alone."

When she put it that way, I understood why she wanted to come live here so badly. "Sorry."

"It's okay." She shrugged. "I believe things will work out the way they are supposed to."

Those words ... she was talking about herself, but they rang true deep within me.

Smiling, Gabi stepped away from me and

joined the other girls in front of the mirror—drinking champagne and talking about the dresses and the wedding.

Watching the girls, seeing how happy they were, how they all seemed to have found what made their life special, brought a little pang of jealousy to my chest. What made my life special? Designing dresses? That was my calling, my talent, but it didn't enrich my life, it didn't make me a better person, did it? I felt so confused.

Noticing the girls were caught up in themselves, I slipped away from the fitting room and went back to my desk, hoping that if I immersed myself in a new project, I would be able to keep my mind busy, blocking all thoughts of Gui and our kiss. Our fantastic kiss.

I shivered.

At least I had my self-defense class tonight and could burn off some of my frustration while punching a target dummy.

# 30

GUI

PPRACTICE HAD RUN LATE TODAY SINCE WE HAD BEEN trying out a new play, and I arrived at the apartment after seven in the evening. Gabi was alone in the living room, watching what looked like an old season of The Bachelor.

"Don't you ever get tired of that show?" I asked, dropping my bag on the couch beside her.

"*Não*," she said with a smile. "The drama is so good. I mean, terrible but good, you know?"

I chuckled. That was the purpose of reality TV —to enjoy the suffering of others. I walked to the kitchen, grabbed a water bottle from the fridge, and then sat on a stool, turned toward the living room. Still sweating and probably smelling, I didn't want to sit on the couch with my sister. I paid attention to the show for two minutes and couldn't take it anymore. I stood and reached for the remote control on the side table. "This is ridiculous."

Gabi almost jumped on me. "Don't you dare turn it off."

"If you're gonna watch that shit, then I'm out of here."

She wrinkled her nose. "You should get out of here. I don't want to be near you with that smell."

With a grin, I opened my arms and pretended I was going to hug her. She yelped and darted away. Laughing, I threw the remote back at her.

"Come here!"

She laughed and retreated several steps, putting two sofas between us. "You wouldn't!" However, she knew I would. I had done it before, and she had loved and hated every second of it. "You better start showering at the club when I come live here. I don't want this smell all over the apartment."

I froze, my arms dropping. "What?"

She lost the smile. "If ... I meant if I come live here."

"Where is this coming from?"

"What do you mean where? Since you guys

moved here, I've been nothing but verbal about wanting to come too."

"I know, but I also know mom and dad would never allow that."

She shrugged. "Well, *tio* João Pedro didn't allow Bia to go to Colorado, and she went anyway."

"That is not the same thing."

She sighed, sitting on the couch again. "I know. But I want to, Gui." Her eyes were pleading. "You're all here and I'm there alone."

"You have Mom and Dad, and your friends. Aren't you applying for *vestibular* in several colleges soon?"

"I don't want to go to college there."

I knew that. In fact, I was well aware that my sister didn't want to go to college at all. She wanted to play polo, like our cousins and me.

"Gabi." I let out a deep breath. "I won't say yes or no or maybe, because I'm not Mom and Dad, and because you're nineteen—old enough to make most of your own decisions. If you really want this, you have to talk to Mom and Dad. Make them agree with you. If they say yes, then my apartment is yours."

"If I talk to them and they say maybe, would you talk to them for me?" she asked. *Merda*, I didn't want to get in a fight with my parents, especially not over Gabi. Then she pressed her hands together and stared at me with huge, begging eyes. "Please?"

I cursed under my breath. "Okay. But only if they say maybe."

"Yes!" she said, jumping up on the sofa. So happy, she raced to me and almost embraced me. Then she wrinkled her nose again. "Yeah, um, I'll want a hug, but only after you shower."

I laughed. "You win." I turned my back to her and headed to the hallway. I itched all over, wanting to ask her how her afternoon with Hilary was, but I held on. I was surprised that I was strong enough and didn't ask. "I'm out of here. I'm gonna take a shower, and then we'll order some dinner for us."

"Sounds good." Her smile changed from sweet to mischievous. "As long as we get to watch more of The Bachelor."

I shook my head and marched to my bedroom, thinking of ways to disconnect the cable.

# 31

HILARY

WE HAD SCHEDULED OUR NEXT MEETING AT THE ranch before we had gone to the nightclub on Saturday. Before we had kissed. I wasn't sure if Gui was coming, since I had ignored all his texts and calls, but I thought he deserved a face-to-face explanation.

So, Thursday after work, I went to the ranch, like we had agreed.

For some reason, I thought he wouldn't come, but I should have known better. Gui was honorable and didn't back down from anything. Even when I was giving him the cold shoulder, he honored our agreement and arrived before me, as usual.

I parked my car between his Jeep and Hannah's car—I thought she would be out with my mother right now—and walked the few steps until I was standing in front of him. I lifted my eyes to him and sucked in a sharp breath. He was seated on the hood of his Jeep, wearing dark jeans, a red T-shirt, black baseball cap, and black cowboy boots. His eyes were hard, and his jaw and shoulders seemed tense. I could feel the tension in his entire body, and I hated that I had put it there.

I especially hated that I couldn't not noticed how good he looked, even when mad at me. He was still the most handsome man I had ever seen.

"I wasn't sure you would show up," he said.

"I said I would come, so I did."

"All right. Let's continue with what we were doing." He jumped off the hood and stood in front of me.

I took two steps back. "Gui ..."

Ignoring me, Gui turned to march to the stable. His movements were hard, rigid, much like the vibe coming from him. He was mad at me, but would still help me with my fear of horses?

I shook my head. "Gui," I said louder. He halted but kept his back to me. "I don't ... I don't think we should do this anymore."

He turned to me, his expression blank. "Because of what happened Saturday?"

"Yes," I whispered.

"Don't worry, Hil. It won't happen again."

All right. I would admit that having him say that hurt more than I thought it would. A part of me wanted it to happen again. A part of me wanted him to try that again, even when I was here, standing in front of him, looking into his eyes and lying to him that it was a mistake.

"I believe you. If you say it won't happen again, I know that nothing will happen."

"Then, what is it?"

I groaned, deciding to lie a little more. "You were probably intoxicated and ended up k-kissing me without meaning it. So, I decided to give you an easy way out."

His jaw popped. "One." He lifted a finger. "I wasn't that intoxicated, and right after the kiss, I told you I hoped it happened again. Two." He lifted a second finger. "That has nothing to do with the riding lessons. I think we're mature enough to keep our lessons without getting involved, if that's what you want. You can trust me on that."

I swallowed, hoping my nervousness went along with my saliva. "But I don't trust myself. I ... I like you more than I should, and I think these lessons, or whatever this is, will only make me like you more."

Gui's jaw dropped and his shoulders sagged. After a couple of seconds, he straightened and took three long steps toward me. There were only two feet between us. "If you like me, why have you been avoiding me?" he asked, losing the hard edge to his voice.

I retreated a step. "Because!" I threw my arms out, as if an easy explanation would simply fall in my lap. "There are so many reasons."

He crossed his arms. "Explain them to me."

"I'm ... we ... that's ..." I groaned again. "I don't know, Gui. It's just too much. We're practically family. It would be too weird." He started shaking his head, but I continued before he could say anything, "And I'm not ready yet. Kissing a guy I like is on my list of fears, but I didn't really think I would get to it so fast. To be honest, I thought I would never get to the last few items on my list, and—"

"Wait. What are the last items on your list?"

I shook my head. "That's none of your business!" He winced as if I had hit him. I immediately regretted my words. "I'm sorry. I didn't mean it that way. It's just ... it's too personal. I had a really terrible time sharing them with my therapist."

"I thought we were connecting."

"We were ... but there are bridges I'm not ready to cross yet." I sighed, feeling exhausted by our conversation. "I don't regret the kiss, Gui. It was amazing. But I'm not ready for more than that. Not yet. And I won't tell you to wait for me, because I don't know how long it'll take for me to heal. If I ever heal. It's not fair."

"You can't make that call for me."

I ignored what he said and went on. "Like I said, we're practically family. Even if I was able to go on, to kiss you again—" My heart raced. "—to try something with you, can you imagine how awkward it would be when we broke up? Having to sit together during family events would be too much."

"And you think that from now on it won't be? Now I know you like me and you know I like you too."

He liked me? I forced that thought away and focused on what I came to do here. "Yes, but just the two of us know about that right now. If we pursued a relationship, I'm guessing the rest of the family would know. That's too much pressure. Even if we tried, this—" I pointed from me to him and back. "—is doomed from the start."

Gui tilted his head, his eyes studying me. "I won't change your mind, will I?" I shook my head. He sighed. "And about the lessons?"

"No. I know myself. In our time together, I'll

fall even more for you and it'll only make things worse for me."

He nodded. "I understand, but I don't agree." He reached forward, and this time I didn't have the strength to pull away. He cupped my face and looked into my eyes. "I wish you would trust me and let me kiss you again," he whispered, leaning down. I should have run away, I should have stepped back, said no, screamed, but I was powerless. Gently, Gui brushed his lips on mine, drawing a sigh from my throat. "I wish you would give us a chance." He rested his forehead against mine. "I understand. I don't agree. But I'll respect your decision." He stepped back and, dizzy, I almost fell forward.

I caught myself and took a deep breath. "Thank you," I choked. Deep down, I wanted him to fight for me. But why? Wasn't this what I wanted? What did I need? In the end, I would just turn him down. I would disappoint him. Letting me go was the best, for him and me. "I ... I guess I'll see you around."

I spun on my heels and rushed to my car. Inside, I turned my head down, so he wouldn't see the tears in my eyes. Pretending to be strong, I turned on the engine and drove away without looking back.

# 32

GUI

I SHOULD HAVE FOUGHT HARDER. I SHOULD HAVE held her and not let her go. I should have told her how I felt about her—it was more than saying I liked her. It ran deeper in a way I never felt for any other girl. It scared me a little, but mostly, it excited me.

Until Hilary slammed the door in my face and locked it.

I paced in front of my bed, trying to calm down, trying to think through the frustration, the rage.

I should have grabbed her shoulders and pinned her to her car, and only let go when she understood the turmoil in me. Then she would run—scared of my actions, of the angry shine in my eyes, of the strength in my hands. No, no. Unfortunately, only time and patience would work on Hilary. Nothing else.

I groaned and punched the wall. I gritted my teeth as I watched the pieces of paint fall to the floor.

*Merda.* Patience wasn't my best trait.

I was already battling with myself over going to her apartment right now and imploring her to talk to me, to listen to me, to understand me. Like a fucking stalker again.

I groaned again and almost punched the wall again. The pain radiating from my red knuckles stopped me.

This was stupid. So fucking stupid. I shouldn't be this worked up because of a girl. I was stronger than this. No girl had ever made me feel this powerless, and it wouldn't start now. I would take control of this situation, and it would start right now.

I pulled out my phone from my back pocket and pressed João Pedro's number.

"*Oi*, Gui. Everything okay?" he answered, his Brazilian accent thicker than mine.

"Is that team from Florida still asking for me?"

A pause. "The Blue Orchard, yes. Why?"

"Do we have any important tournaments coming up, or can I go?"

Another pause. "You can go if you want."

"I want to."

"Okay." I heard the shuffling of pages as if he was turning pages of his calendar. "I'll call them and set everything up. I'll call you later with details."

"Thanks."

I turned off the call and strutted into my closet, pulling a duffel bag out.

That was me taking control of the situation. That was me finding some way to have patience, to wait.

As soon as João Pedro called me and confirmed the transfer, I was leaving.

## 33

---

HILARY

THE NEXT MORNING, I WAS DEEP INTO DRAWING MY school project when Hannah called. She said she would be in town and wanted to go out to lunch with me. I started protesting, saying I had lots to do, but she said she knew I could make my own hours at work, so she wouldn't take no for an answer.

At 12:15 p.m., I met her at a deli place two blocks from work.

We sat in a booth in the middle of the deli, ordered our lunches, and talked about mundane things for the first fifteen minutes. I had eaten half of my panini when she opened up about the real reason for meeting me.

"So," she started.

I rolled my eyes. "I knew this wasn't a social lunch. Okay, what is it?"

"It is! Can't I have lunch with my sister?"

"Of course you can, but I know you. You're far too busy, especially around lunch, and you've never invited me to lunch before."

"Well, that was a mistake." She brushed her long, dark hair over her shoulder and stared at me with her big, green eyes. "You're more than my sister, you're my friend, and we should have more lunches together."

I tilted my head, watching her. "I would like that. However, I know there's more to this lunch than simply spending quality time with me. Lay it on me."

"Well," she started again. "I ended up coming back early from the riding class last evening, and I was at the stable when you arrived at the ranch and met up with Gui."

My eyes grew wide. "Oh my ..."

"I saw you two kissing," she said.

My cheeks flamed. "Oh my ..."

"Are you going to tell me what's going on, or do I have to ask Gui about it?"

"No! Don't ask him." I sighed. "Oh, man. Well ..." I didn't know what to tell her, so I decided to start from the beginning. I told her about my therapist's idea of creating a list of my fears from the mildest to the scariest and about working on going through the list, scratching off items as much as I could, but also taking my time. I told her about being at the ranch to face my fear of horses and bumping into Gui there. I told her about his interest in helping me, not only with horses, but everything. I told her about the helicopter ride, the late night ice cream and chocolate, and that night at the club when we noticed we had more going on between us. And I told her about the kiss in my apartment. "After that, I avoided him. I didn't answer his texts or calls, and I was careful when coming and going so we didn't run into each other. But we had agreed to meet yesterday for another riding lesson several days ago, before the kiss, and I honor my agreements, so I went, but I stuck to my plan. I told him we shouldn't meet anymore, that I was done with his help."

She lifted one eyebrow at me. "Was kissing him yesterday in your plan?"

"Of course not. And I didn't kiss him. He just ..." I shook my head. "It doesn't matter. It won't happen again."

She stared at me, and I could see the wheels in her brain turning. "Now that I think about it, I guess it was always obvious that Gui had a thing for you, for quite a while actually."

"W-what?"

"Yeah, I mean, before I thought it was like Leo watching Bia, you know, like family interest, but now I see it. He was always watching you, asking about you, or making small comments like, 'Wow, she's so pretty,' but then he would change the subject and nobody ever put two and two together. Until now."

Gui had always watched me? He had always thought I was pretty? That was ... wow. I had no idea.

"It doesn't matter," I said, trying to convince myself.

"Why not? I can see you like him too."

"Do I really need to explain myself?" I asked, lowering my voice. "For starters, he might not be a huge playboy, but we both know he's a heartbreaker. He changes girlfriends every month." I made air quotes to emphasize the word girlfriends. Gui didn't do girlfriends. "I would be just one more, and then I would have to see him at our family events all the time. It would be too awkward, too painful. And the most important reason is me. I can barely understand how I kissed him, because just thinking about doing it again sends a jolt of fear through me. A new panic attack isn't far behind. How can I even consider dating someone if I can barely kiss him? And he'll expect more, much more. It's not fair to him."

Hannah reached across the table and rested her hand on mine. "I understand your reasons, but I don't agree with them."

Groaning, I pulled my hand away. "That's exactly what he said yesterday. Though he said he would respect my decision."

She offered a sweet smile. "What kind of sister would I be if I didn't try to convince you otherwise?"

I groaned again. "The kind I need right now?"

"Hil ..."

"Don't Hil me, please. I'm not ready, Hannah. I want to be, I swear I want to be, but I can't force it. I sense I'll break down again, and it'll be even worse this time. I'm not sure I can recover this time."

She nodded. "All right. I'll give you some time, but be warned that I'll bug you about this again. Soon."

I sighed. "Just don't do it too soon, deal?"

"Deal." She finished her juice, and then looked at me with serious eyes again. "Just one more thing."

"What?" I asked, my voice harsher than I intended.

"I think Gui isn't taking your decision too well," she said. I raised an eyebrow at her to continue. "João Pedro called Leo this morning, saying Gui had agreed to play with another team for the next three weeks. A team in Florida." She paused, letting the information sink in.

So, Gui was going to Florida. For the next three weeks. That was okay, right? Better this way. I wouldn't have to be so careful to avoid him in the building or anywhere else now. Why had a sudden pain wrapped around my heart and squeezed it tight, then?

"Oh." I squared my shoulders, as if I could shield myself from any blow with a perfect posture. "When is he leaving?"

"As far as I know, he's not required to be there until the middle of next week, since the tournament doesn't start until the following weekend, but Leo mentioned he might be going this afternoon."

"Oh." My heart sank. It seemed Gui also didn't want to run into me anymore. "That's ... okay. Good for him. I hope he does well there." I pushed my plate away with half of my panini untouched. "I ... I should get back to work."

"Oh, yeah, of course," Hannah said, her brows knitted.

I stood to leave and Hannah grabbed her purse and followed me out.

"Bye," I said, turning in the studio's direction.

Hannah reached out, closing her hand around my wrist. "Hey, Hil, I'm here for you, okay? Whatever you need, whenever you need. I meant what I said about being more than sisters. Okay?"

I nodded. "Thanks."

# 34

HILARY

Driving into the parking garage at my parents' house, I saw two cars I didn't know parked in the visitors' area.

I frowned, wondering what the hell my mother was up to. She had called this morning to make sure I would be going to the club for our Sunday lunch, but I lied about not feeling well. Later, she called saying that, since I wasn't going to lunch, I owed her and had to come to the house for dinner. I argued I was still not feeling great, but she said she would come over, give me some Advil or Tylenol, make me tea, and would make sure I was okay enough to come to dinner. Knowing my mother, I believed her, so to save her the trip—and hours of agony for me—I agreed.

Until now, I thought it was only going to be my parents and me, but now I saw those two cars, and Hannah's car in her spot beside mine.

I looked down at my outfit. Pink flowy skirt with a white and silver swirl pattern, white blouse, and tan sandals, matching my thick tan leather bracelet. I always dressed up for dinner at my parents, but I had almost come in my fav jeans and a simple blouse this time. I was glad I didn't.

I entered the house through the kitchen access, and Rosa greeted me with a tray of hors d'oeuvre.

"What's going on?" I asked her.

"Your mother invited some friends over, and you know how she is. There are only four times more people than usual and it's already like a banquet."

I laughed, trying not to snort out the little shrimp puff I had swallowed. After looking down at my outfit again to make sure nothing was out of place, I entered living room number one, as Hannah and I used to say when we were little. That was the biggest living room in the house, where my mother liked to receive visitors.

At first, I only saw the back of the visitors' heads, seated on a long sofa in front of the massive, unlit fireplace.

"Hilary, you're here," my mother said, standing

from the armchair she always liked to sit in. It stood in a privileged position in the room, with a matching chair right by its side—their thrones, Hannah and I always teased.

My mother was dressed in an elegant dark green dress, and her second best diamond jewelry set. Uh oh, whatever this dinner was, it was big.

"Hi," I said.

The visitors stood and turned, and my jaw dropped open.

"Hilary, how are you?" Eloisa said, reaching to me. Oblivious to my shock, she kissed my cheeks twice, and then introduced me to her husband, James.

"Nice to see you again, Hilary," Reese said, taking my hand and planting a kiss on top of it.

"Hey, there," Lucas said. I knew he was Reese's cousin, but when he reached for me, I stepped back, the images of Hannah's engagement night still fresh in my mind. Fear and dread choked me.

Hannah appeared by my side and nudged me in the waist.

Forcing myself to move past my shock, I waved at Lucas. "Hello." I plastered a fake smile on my face and looked at my mother. "I didn't know we were having a party."

"It's not a party," my mother assured me. "It's just a get-together with dear friends."

It was definitely a party, and these people were not my parents' dear friends. As far as I knew, this was the first time they'd ever set foot in our house.

"I see," I muttered.

Breaking the ice, Rosa entered the room with a tray full of hors d'oeuvre. She walked around the room with the tray, and I seized the opportunity to sit beside Hannah and Leo, and a big, round side table, making sure nobody else sat near me.

"Did you know about this?" I asked Hannah in a low voice.

"No. I'm as surprised as you are," she said in an equally low tone. "Though I can guess why mom invited them over."

"Me too."

"I don't know," Leo said.

"Mom is trying to set Reese and Hil up," Hannah explained.

Leo's eyes went wide. *"O que? Não!"*

She frowned at him. "I thought he was sort of a friend of yours."

"He is," Leo said. "I think he's a great guy, but Hilary deserves better."

A tiny smile took over my lips. "You're so sweet." He turned his face to the other side, waving me off, but not before I saw his lips widening into a smile. "It's a shame there aren't more guys like you."

He snapped his head and stared at me again. "There are. My cousins are all like me, or much better actually. And I know of one who is currently available."

My smile slid away and I gaped at Hannah.

She elbowed him in the ribs and offered me a weak smile. "Sorry. I tried to keep it to myself, but you didn't want to talk about it. Gui didn't want to talk about it. I wanted to tell Bia, but I knew you would be mad at me, so I told Leo."

"You're unbelievable."

"Don't worry," Leo said. "I won't bother you about it. Much." He winked and I groaned. "Though I will bother Gui. Going away to play with another team was a shitty move. He should have stayed and fought for you."

I shook my head. "I didn't give him that option."

"I don't—" Leo started.

I shook my head again. "Please, Leo, like I told Hannah on Friday, I need some time before I can talk about this." And hopefully, by the time I was ready, everyone would have already forgotten about it.

"*Tá bem*," he said, his voice dejected.

To lighten the mood, Hannah told us about one of her riding groups this afternoon. Apparently, a girl and a boy, both around sixteen, had gotten lost from the group.

Leo laughed at that. "*Claro*, lost."

"I know, right?" Hannah said, explaining everyone had noticed they had run off to make out. Or more.

As my sister continued her tale, I heard my name from across the room.

"It's Hilary," my mother said to Eloisa. "Hilary is making all our dresses."

"That's fantastic," Eloisa said, smiling at me. "You must be talented. Congratulations."

I frowned. "Thanks."

Reese and Lucas were talking among themselves, but Reese's eyes kept shifting to me every few seconds.

My mother boasted about me some more while Eloisa did the same with Reese. It was as if they were comparing our attributes, making sure we matched. At least, my father and James were talking about horses, not us.

"Soon, Mom will open the dowry negotiation," I half-joked.

"If they do, we'll kidnap you," Leo said with a wink.

I smiled to him. Seriously, Hannah was one very, very lucky girl.

My mind went from Leo to Gui. The one who haunted eight out of ten of my thoughts. It was impossible to stop thinking about him. I told myself it was only a matter of time. I was enamored with him because, besides his looks, he had been gentle and caring when I needed him to be. He had been a friend and supporter. If I kept my distance, I would go back to normal, to doing my stuff without his help. I wouldn't care about his opinion, and then we could be friends-slash-family again.

For the sake of this family, I hoped I was right.

When Rosa called out dinner was served, my mother announced she had exact places for everyone at the table. She positioned me between Hannah and Reese. Leo sat on Hannah's right, while Lucas sat across from me, snuggled between Eloisa and my mother. Both older men, my father and James took the heads of the long table.

During the first two courses, Hannah tried to keep me busy by talking to her. I knew it wouldn't last though.

"How have you been?" Reese asked me.

I cut into my steak, considering ignoring him. Or being rude. No, that wasn't fair. He might have shown interest in me, but mother had gone to great lengths to set us up.

With a forced smile, I glanced at him. "I'm doing all right. How about you?"

"Pretty good." He flashed me a wide smile. "I hear you've been pretty busy with so many design projects and helping plan your sister's wedding."

"True."

I didn't know what else to say. Thank goodness, Leo was paying attention and saved me.

"Reese, I heard you guys have been training hard lately," Leo spoke up, so the entire table would listen. "I also heard that you guys are training so hard because you want to challenge Montenegro."

Reese paled. "What? No. Who told you that?" His reaction seemed genuine, and I couldn't decide if the rumors were true or not.

Artfully, Leo also involved Lucas, James, and my father in the conversation, mixing the topics between polo and horses and ranches.

Under the table, I squeezed my sister's hand. "I love your fiancé. I mean it," I whispered to her.

She smiled at me. "Sorry, he's taken."

I sighed. "A shame."

"But you know, Leo meant what he said. Gui and Leo are similar in several aspects."

I glowered at her. "Stop. Stop it right now. I don't want to get mad at you too."

"All right, all right."

My mother tried to cut into the men's conversation several times. Thankfully, Hannah had a way of catching all the female attention to her. Once she opened her mouth and uttered the word "wedding," Eloisa and my mother were at her mercy.

The dessert was served back in the living room, quickly followed by coffee. I excused myself and went to the kitchen to find me some ice cream, since I didn't have a taste for these fancy cakes my mother liked to offer.

I was seated on one of the stools around the kitchen island, devouring a bowl of ice cream, when my mother barged in the kitchen.

"Hilary! What do you think you're doing?"

I pointed to the bowl of ice cream. "Eating?"

She frowned. "You're being rude. You should be out there with our guests. They came especially to see you."

I set the bowl on the island, not in the mood for my dear sweets anymore. "Why? So you can arrange a marriage? Did he propose yet? Did his parents like my dowry?" She gaped at me, but didn't say anything. "I'm not one of Dad's horse. I won't be sold like that."

"This is the twenty-first century, Hilary. We're not arranging your marriage."

"It sure looks like it."

She straightened her already perfect posture and lifted her chin. "Well, Eloisa and I seemed to agree that Reese and you would make a great couple."

"Have you asked us if we think that?"

"I don't think it's necessary to ask Reese. He seems enamored with you."

I groaned. "But I'm not enamored with him. I ..." I sighed, trying to calm my boiling blood. "After all I went through, I thought you understood I'm not ready for this kind of thing." I gestured to the kitchen's door leading back to the living room. "I feel like I'm a song on repeat, because I say this all the time, but it seems I need to say it again. I. Am. Not. Ready."

"But, Hilary, it has been three years. That's plenty of time to move on."

I flinched. "For most people, I agree that three years sounds like enough time, but unfortunately, I'm not most people. I've made major progress in the last three years, but I'm nowhere near healed."

She watched me, her features softening. "I

thought ... you look so well. You're in school, you're working, you're helping with your sister's wedding, and you've even gone out. And you've been around men, especially Leo's brothers and cousin. I thought you were better."

What did she mean by that?

"I wish I was."

My mother walked around the kitchen island and embraced me. "I'm sorry."

Surprised, I embraced her back. "It's okay. Just ... don't try to play matchmaker anymore, okay?"

She pulled back and smiled at me. "I'll try." She looked around the kitchen, trying to recompose herself. "Now, we have guests over and I have to entertain them until they leave. But if you want, I can tell them that you weren't feeling great and went to lie down for a little bit. How does that sound?"

I smiled. "Great. Thanks, Mom."

She kissed my cheek. "You're welcome."

Then she strutted out of the kitchen as if we didn't just share a rare sweet moment. I could be mad at her most of the time, but thankfully, after what happened with Eric, my mother started listening to Hannah and me. Sometimes it took us a few tries to make her understand what we were saying, but in the end, she listened to us. She understood us.

Feeling lighter, I walked onto the back porch and looked over my parents' beautiful estate. The lush green expanse of the back garden, dotted with lamps, illuminating my mother's prized flowers.

Hannah's wedding would be right here and it would be beautiful.

I was happy for her and Leo. They were great together. I wished them more of the same: love and happiness. I wished someday I would heal and find a love like that too.

Past the garden, atop a green hill, sat the main stable, where my father's stallions were housed. Before I noticed what I was doing, I walked across the garden, on one of the side stone paths, until I was standing in front of the stable's wrought iron gates.

Maybe it was rubbing on me, or maybe I was just starting to pay attention to these beasts for the first time, but I realized horses were growing on me. As I walked past the stable main corridor and looked inside the stalls, I was amazed by how beautiful these animals were. Long necks, massive torsos, strong legs, shiny coats, and some had manes and tails like they visited the hairdresser every week. Well, maybe they did. I was sure my father had the best horse groomer in town. Maybe even in the state.

Okay, I had to admit, I was falling for horses. A sudden pain rushed through my heart, and I wished I were at Hannah's ranch, walking her stable and stopping by Belle's stall. Because she was the horse I was falling for.

My first instinct was to reach for my phone and text Gui about my sudden realization, but with a frown, I remembered we hadn't parted on good terms on Thursday, and right now, I wasn't sure we were even friends. I pocketed my phone and stared at an empty stall.

Footsteps snapped me out of my stupor.

Reese entered the stable, followed by Lucas. A rush of fear went through me and I retreated several steps.

"Oh, hey," Reese said, sounding surprised. "Your mother said that you went to lie down in your bedroom because you weren't feeling well."

I shrugged, not sure what to say.

Reese turned to Lucas and said something to him. Lucas nodded and left. Though my fear had surged because of Lucas, now it spiked because Reese had sent Lucas away, leaving us alone in the stable.

"You didn't know we would be here tonight, did you?"

"No," I confessed.

"Yeah, I figured that when you arrived. You looked shocked."

"Well, I was."

"I swear this dinner wasn't my idea." He stopped just past the front gates, his hands in the pockets of his dress pants. "When my mother told me your mother had invited us over, I thought you knew about it, and I thought it was a great way to talk to you, to get to know you better in a familiar place, with familiar faces. It cuts the edge from a real first date. However, if I had known you were in the dark, I wouldn't have agreed to it. I wouldn't have cornered you like that. I'm sorry."

I offered him a small smile. "Thanks, I appreciate your honesty."

"I'm honest and most of the time I'm direct too," he said, the corner of his lips tipping up. I raised an eyebrow. "During dinner, you mentioned being busy with work and the wedding plans. Are those the real reasons you never got back to me about going on a date with me, or are there other reasons?"

I gulped. When he said he was direct, he meant it. "I ... I have truly been busy." If not with actual stuff to do, my mind and heart had been busy these past few weeks.

"All right, I'm not stupid. I understand a no when I see one."

"I ... I didn't mean it like that," I said quickly, feeling bad for cutting down his hopes.

He stepped closer, but not too close, and looked into my eyes. "I know what you went through, and I can only guess what it has been like these past three years. It must not have been easy. In fact, I guess it was exactly the opposite." He paused. "I kind of hoped your rejection isn't because of me per se, but because you're still dealing with the damage it caused you."

"Y-yeah, it kind of is," I confessed, feeling like fate had punched me in the gut. I never had a guy be this honest with me before. And he wasn't stepping on eggshells around it as if I would break. It was refreshing.

"In that case, I'll be honest again and say I can wait." He reached to me and grabbed my hand. I almost pulled back. Almost. "I'll be here, I'll be your friend for now, but when the time comes, I'll remind you of how I feel."

He kissed my cheek and walked out of the stable.

## 35

HILARY

"You'll be fine," I told Evie as I parked my car beside Hannah's at the ranch.

She gripped the seat belt and stared at the stable. "How can you be so sure?"

I smiled. A few weeks ago, I had been in her place. Honestly, I still got a little nervous every time I approached a horse, but now I knew how to push through my fear.

After the realization I had at my parents' last night—that I actually liked horses more than I ever thought I would—I decided I would bring Evie for a ride with me. From Hannah, I knew horses could be used for therapy, and I thought Evie was in need of all the help she could get. Unfortunately, she still hadn't left Mike, and today she was sporting a new purple bruise on her right shoulder. She hid it under her T-shirt and pulled her hair over it, but it didn't matter. I still knew it was there.

Since I didn't have a lot of experience with horses, I contacted Hannah and Bia and asked them to help me out. With two of them and two of us, I felt confident nothing would happen. And, if it did, if something went wrong, Hannah or Bia was capable of handling it, whatever it may be.

Convincing Evie of my idea, though, that had been hard. She had given me several excuses from being sick, to not wanting to aggravate Mike. In the end, I found out she was also afraid of horses, and she had never been near one before.

"Because I've been where you are right now," I told her. "I was afraid of horses, still am a little I guess, but now I can face it, and a few weeks ago, I started riding. And, truth be told, I kinda love it." She still stared at the stable with fear in her eyes. "Don't worry. I promise. I've brought two specialists to help us out."

"Specialists?"

"Come and see," I said, sliding out of my car.

Inside the stable, I found Hannah and Bia tacking Preta. Belle, Argus, and Midnight were already tacked and ready. As we walked through the stalls, I introduced Evie to each one, then showed her the tack room, and even narrated each piece as the girls tacked Preta.

"Wow, are you really my sister?" Hannah teased. "Until a few weeks ago, she wouldn't even step inside a stable."

"Very funny," I said. "Evie, this is my sister, Hannah, the ranch's owner. She is a master with horses. She is even like a horse whisperer. You know, she can turn abused horses around."

Evie's eyes grew wide. "Oh."

"Nice to meet you, Evie," Hannah said with a smile.

"And this is Bia. She's the twin sister of Hannah's fiancé." Even I frowned at that long description. "She is also a master with horses. She has been around horses all her life, and her brothers and cousin are famous polo players. And she goes to vet school because she wants to take care of horses."

"Wow," Evie whispered.

"*Prazer*," Bia said.

"Oh, yeah, she's Brazilian so sometimes she slips a few Portuguese words out."

Bia shrugged. "Sorry about that."

"It's okay," Evie said with a tentative smile.

"We're glad you're here," Hannah said. Then

she switched to her tour guide/instructor voice and explained to Evie all we were doing.

Soon after, we were on our horses, riding through the gates of the arena onto the path of the easiest riding trail.

***

IT WAS ONLY TUESDAY, BUT I FELT LIKE MY DAYS were getting busier as the week went on. Maybe it was because I had scheduled several dates after work. Yesterday was riding with Evie; she was actually starting to relax and enjoy it. Today was a girls' night out at a restaurant before Gabi left for Brazil the next morning. Finally, tomorrow, my mother, Hannah, and I were meeting at a quaint restaurant to see more wedding-related stuff.

"Iris just texted," Bia said as we sat around a round table in the center of the restaurant. "She will be a little late, but told us to order her drink."

The waitress came and we ordered drinks and appetizers while we waited for Iris to arrive.

"Ready to leave?" I asked Gabi.

"Not really," she admitted. We all knew she wanted to stay.

"Because of Mateus?" Bia asked.

"Who is Mateus?" I asked.

Gabi rolled her eyes. "My ex-boyfriend."

"Uh-oh," Hannah said.

"We dated all through high school, and then he went to São Paulo for college," Gabi explained. "He wanted to keep dating, but I don't do the distance thing, so we broke up. Now he's back in Porto Alegre. He transferred there a month ago, and he's been calling me, asking to see me. I have avoided him so far, but I know he'll corner me at some point."

"You two were so cute together," Bia said with a smile.

"I thought so too, but we broke up several months ago. At first it was hard, but I like being single now." She sighed. "I'm not ready to face him. He was part of a good phase in my life. I don't want to end up being rude to him."

"Hopefully, he'll realize you moved on as soon as you two meet, and you won't need to be rude," Hannah said.

"Yeah, that would be better," Gabi said. "I can't wait to be back for the bachelorette party and the wedding, though. Do you guys want to kidnap me so I can stay in the U.S. forever?"

We laughed, but I knew her joke had a bit of truth.

The waitress came back with our drinks and

appetizers, and we then talked about the bachelorette party. As maid of honor, I was planning it. The girls tried to guess what I was coming up with, but I wanted most of the details to be a surprise.

"There will be strippers, right?" Bia asked.

"I'm not telling," I said.

Then, Hannah's cell phone dinged. Then Bia's. Then Gabi's. I frowned as they grabbed their phones, stared at the screen, and frowned.

Hannah turned to me, her eyes wide. "You kissed Reese?"

I sputtered the soda I was drinking. "W-what? No! Why would you say that?"

They all looked at me as if I had committed the crime of the century. I fished my cell phone from my purse and looked at it, expecting to see whatever they had seen, but there was nothing.

"Leo just texted me saying you kissed Reese Saturday night in our parents' stable," Hannah said.

"No! That's not true. I didn't kiss him. And he didn't kiss ..." The kiss on the cheek. Reese had kissed me on the cheek. Oh my gosh, what was he telling people?

My cell phone rang and, startled, I almost

dropped it. I looked at the screen and swallowed hard.

"Hi," I said once I answered.

"You kissed Reese?" Gui asked, his tone harsh.

"Why are you all asking me that?" I asked, looking at the girls.

"You all? Who is asking you that?" he asked. "No, wait, first answer me. Did you kiss Reese?"

I stood and rushed out of the restaurant, barely aware that I bumped into Iris as she came in to meet us. I halted on the sidewalk, where I was far away from known faces and ears.

"No! I didn't."

"Why is he saying that, then?"

"I don't know. Where did you hear about that?"

"Apparently, Reese told Lucas, who told Malcolm, who told Justin, and then Carlos heard them talking about it—"

Malcolm and Justin were on the Knight House team with Reese, but ... "Who's Carlos?"

"A guy who works at the club. He heard Malcolm telling Justin, and then he gossiped to Leo, Ri, and Pedro when they were leaving practice this evening. Leo, who I guess knows about us somehow, called and told me." He paused before continuing, his voice tight again. "Reese was gloating about having dinner with you and then, before he left, you two had a moment and kissed."

I groaned. "Reese twisted what happened—"

"So something happened?"

"Yes, no." Rage slipped over me. "It's none of your business!"

Gui inhaled sharply. "You did kiss him." I was about to explain—again—that I had not kissed Reese, but he spoke up before I could. "You know what, you're right. This is none of my business. You made that clear when you told me you didn't want anything with me and even after I told you I wanted to give us a try. So, yeah, it's none of my business. I'm sorry I called."

He hung up. Just like that.

Frozen on the sidewalk, I gaped at my cell phone.

I didn't know how many minutes or hours went by until Hannah came outside. My sister hooked her arm around my shoulders and brought me inside the restaurant. I sat in my previous chair and found four faces staring at me, worried and curious.

"Do you want to talk about it?" Gabi asked, reaching across the table and squeezing my hand.

Even though I shook my head, I said out loud, "I didn't kiss Reese."

"If you say you didn't, we believe you," Hannah said.

"We do," Bia agreed. "But why is Reese saying you guys kissed, then?"

"I didn't kiss him, I swear." I glanced first at Hannah, then to the other girls. "Last Saturday, our mother invited us for dinner at our parents' house, which is sorta normal. We always have brunch or dinner on Saturdays together. Anyway, when I arrived, I found out we had guests. Reese and his family."

"Our mother is trying to set up Hilary with Reese," Hannah explained.

"What? No!" Bia spoke up. "Reese is nice and good looking, but you deserve better."

I smiled, thinking it must be a twin thing because Leo had said the same thing to me the other night.

I lost my smile. "I sneaked out after dinner and went to the stable."

Bia gasped. "You? At the stable? You went there by yourself? Without even taking Evie with you as an excuse?"

"Yes. Can we focus on the main topic here?"

"Sure, but I want to know all about this urge to go to the stable later," Bia said.

I rolled my eyes. "Anyway, I went to the stable

and Reese found me there. He told me that even though my mother is pushing it, he really likes me and would like to go out with me. I told him … I'm not ready to date yet." I shifted my eyes to Hannah, the only one who knew about Gui and me. Gosh, the way things were going, soon everyone would know and the level of awkwardness would be unbearable. "He told me he knows what I've been through and he respects the time it's taking for me to heal. He also said he'd wait for me, then he kissed me on the cheek and left."

"Oh, he sounds like he's in love," Iris said dreamily.

"If that's what happened, why did he say you two kissed?" Bia asked.

"Maybe he didn't," Hannah said. "Maybe he told the right story, but from what Leo told me, the story traveled through several people. Someone must have added to the story or heard wrong."

"Or both," Gabi said.

It made sense. I hoped Gui heard that theory. Ugh, why did I care so much? Maybe if he thought Reese and I had kissed, he would move on quicker. To be honest, it was hard to imagine Gui hung up on me, but when we talked, he made me believe he was. Maybe now he would be mad at me for a few days, then move on and things wouldn't be awkward between us anymore.

One could only hope.

"What are you going to do about it?" Bia asked.

I frowned. "What do you mean?"

"I don't know, are you going to talk to Reese, see where the story derailed from the truth?"

I hadn't thought of that. Did I care about it? Ignoring that deep down I did care if Gui knew the truth or not, I didn't care if the rest of the town believed Reese and I had kissed. Perhaps people would stop thinking of me as damaged now.

"I don't think I'll do anything." I grabbed the menu from the table. "Are we ready to order, or are we only staying for drinks and appetizers?"

Getting the hint that I was done with that topic, the girls picked up their menus and started browsing. Over their menus, I felt the weight of Hannah's knowing stare. I did my best to ignore her too and focused on trying to relax with my girls.

# 36

HILARY

I COULD HAVE WAITED UNTIL SUNDAY, WHEN I WAS going to the club to have lunch with my mother and her friends. I knew Reese would be there then, but I just didn't want to wait.

Last night, when meeting with my mother and Hannah to taste the food that would be served at the wedding, my mother told me she had heard Reese and I had kissed last Saturday. Oh my gosh, this was going too far. I wanted to clarify this situation now.

I took the afternoon off on Thursday, promising Fallon I would work later on Friday and next week to compensate. She just shrugged, not caring about my work hours. Since I didn't have Reese's number, even though my mother had wanted to give it to me on several occasions, I called the club in the morning and found out what time his next practice was with the Knight House. At 1:30 p.m. Figuring he would arrive early, I had a quick lunch at my apartment and then drove to the club. I arrived there a little after one in the afternoon.

I parked my car in the almost empty parking lot and waited. Soon, Malcolm, Justin, and David arrived. They watched me as they walked to the practice field. I just crossed my arms and waited, leaning against my car's trunk.

Ten minutes later, Reese arrived. He parked his car beside mine and hopped out with a big smile. Until he saw my face.

"Oh, shit," he muttered. He walked toward me, his hands at his sides, palms out, like in defeat. "You heard the rumors."

"Yes, I did, and I want to know why you lied?"

"I didn't lie," he said, looking straight into my eyes. "I told the guys I had kissed you on the cheek. That was all. Then they told other people and exaggerated, and things got out of hand." He ran his hand through his hair. "I'm sorry. I didn't think they would tell people."

Worse than girls. "I didn't think you would tell others about any of it."

"I thought we had a moment. Can you blame me if I was too excited about it and wanted to share it with my friends?" he asked, his tone soft, almost pleading. I guess I couldn't, so I shook my head. "Besides, is it so bad if people think we kissed? Is the thought of kissing me so disgusting to you?"

"No." I shook my head. "Of course it's not disgusting. But ... I don't like having lies going around, especially about me. If any guy I greet or shake hands with goes around telling everyone and exaggerating it, I'll soon have slept with the entire club."

"I understand." He nodded. "I'm sorry about that. I'll set it straight, okay?"

"That's all I want. Thanks."

He started taking a step toward me but stopped. "I was going to kiss you on the cheek again, to prove to you I still meant all I said that night, but I guess it's better I don't, right?"

I opened my car door. "Right."

"Wait, Hilary." Reese held on to the top of my car's door. "We're still good, right? I mean, I hope this hiccup hasn't ruined my chances with you."

I sighed, not sure what to say to him. Before this mess, I hadn't considered going out with him, not really. Not when someone else occupied my thoughts. Now, though? Now I was sure I wouldn't give him a chance. I knew this wasn't his fault, but he hadn't done anything to undo it so far. It was hard for me to trust anyone, and he already started with a mishap.

In the end, I decided on half the truth. "I don't know, Reese."

---

MY HANDS BEGAN SWEATING EVEN BEFORE SONYA called my desk telling me my 10 a.m. appointment was in fitting room four. Until I arrived early this morning and looked at my schedule for the day, I had forgotten the guys were supposed to come today. Thank goodness their attire had been ready for the first fitting since the beginning of last week.

After Sonya announced their arrival, I wiped my hands on my pencil skirt and trudged to the fitting room. I stopped before the closed doors and took a deep breath.

*I can do this.*

I could, couldn't I? Gui and I were still friends, right? Maybe things would still feel a little awkward, but soon it would be like old times. I would just look at him, think in the back of my mind that he was too handsome for his own good, and go on with my life as if I had never felt anything else—anything stronger—for him.

I wiped my hands on my skirt one more time, raised my head high, and opened the door.

"Hey, Hil," Leo said, his voice cheerful.

"Hi, guys," I said, scanning the crowd as they all greeted me. Leo, Ri, Pedro, and Garrett. But no Gui.

Pain sliced through my heart.

Gui hadn't come to the fitting. I mean, I kind of expected it since he was in Florida, but I thought he would take a flight, be here for the fitting, and then go back to Florida.

After lots of how are you doing and how was practice and all that, I showed them their tuxedos and waited while they disappeared inside the fitting stalls. Leo was the first out. He hopped on the podium in front of the mirror, and I marked the few adjustments needed. Then the others came out, but before I had a chance to mark their tuxes, Sonya came into the room.

Like last time with the girls, she had brought in champagne and I almost laughed at the face she made when she walked in and saw all these gorgeous men dressed up.

Another point for my future. I was able to admit they were all gorgeous.

Ri, Pedro, and Garrett got lost in the champagne.

Like a sneaky cat, Leo approached me in the back of the room. "*Tudo bem*?"

I forced a smile. "Sure."

He frowned at me. "You're not good at lying."

I grunted. "Well, to be honest, I've been better. And that's saying something."

He nodded. "Is it because of Gui?" I lowered my gaze, not sure I should engage in this topic. "It's okay. You know I know about you two."

That didn't make talking about Gui with him any easier. I cleared my throat. "He should have come for the fitting. I can't have a perfect tux for him without any fittings."

"He was ready to come last night," Leo said. "He was taking a flight last night, just to be here this morning."

A knot weighed down my forehead. "What happened?"

"*Bom*, he heard that you went to see Reese yesterday afternoon at the club."

"What?" I yelled. The others looked at us, so I turned my back to them and lowered my voice. "How does he already know about that?"

Leo's eyes widened. "So you admit it? You went to see Reese yesterday?"

"I did, but it isn't what you're thinking. Even my mother had heard about the non-kiss. I didn't have his phone number and I didn't know how else to reach him. So I went to the club and asked him why the hell he was spreading those rumors." I knew Hannah had already explained to Leo what had happened that night. I was glad I didn't have to repeat myself now. "I guess that after hearing the rumors people must have seen us talking and thought we were having some kind of date. I didn't even leave the parking lot!"

"I get it," Leo said. "Do you mind if I tell Gui?"

"Does it make a difference?"

Leo nodded. "It does. He's been kind of a jerk lately. Even far away, he can get on our nerves. Even my father said he got a few calls from the other team's coach, complaining about his attitude."

I frowned. "I don't want to give him hope though."

"Why not? What are you afraid of?"

"Hasn't Hannah told you?"

"Actually, no. She said it was your problem, and she had already said too much to me." I could kiss my sister for that. "So, will you tell me?"

I opened my mouth to lie, but then closed it again. This was Leo. My sister's fiancé. The guy who was there for her, who helped her heal much faster than I did. I trusted him with my life.

"A lot of things. I'm afraid of the level of awkwardness it'll be if we give this, whatever it is, a try and it doesn't work. Of falling in love and having my heart broken. Of finding out Gui isn't the guy I think he is."

Leo nodded. "I understand."

I narrowed my eyes at him. "You do?"

"Unfortunately, it's all about your past. You trusted someone before, you thought highly of him, you thought he was something, and in the end, he disappointed you." Disappoint was such a weak word. "I get why you're so guarded and afraid to trust again ..."

Leo seemed to want to say more, but Ri called out, "Hey, you two. Will you stop gossiping?"

Pedro turned to me, his hands in his jacket. "Hil, is this right?"

I took a deep breath and pushed thoughts of Gui away from my mind. Instead, I focused on my progress, on how well I was doing. A couple of months ago, I would cringe before entering a room alone with these guys, even though I knew them all and trusted their girls. I would be on the defensive the entire time, fighting a panic attack every time one of them got too close. Now, here I was.

Deep down, my gut was still tense, and I kept re-visiting some of the self-defense moves I had learned in class, but I was feeling confident and strong enough to be here without feeling scared or fighting a panic attack. In fact, I enjoyed their company.

I forced a smile on my lips and went to help these four men with their tuxedos.

# 37

GUI

I KEPT THINKING I SHOULD HAVE GONE TO SANTA Barbara last night, regardless if Hilary was with Reese or not. However, because I had decided to act like a fucking child, I felt bitter and decided to stay in Orlando, even though there had been no game today and there wouldn't be one until Sunday afternoon.

For the most part, this trip had helped. Because the team was new to me, we practiced a lot, which took a lot of my time and kept my mind busy. But, whenever I had down time and had nothing to do besides go back to my hotel and binge on some series on Netflix or stalk everyone on Facebook—mostly Hilary, though she rarely posted anything there—it was fucking lonely and boring.

I wished I hadn't come. I wished I were there with my family. I wished I were there to face Hilary and ask her about Reese.

Disgust and rage swept over me, and I dragged my feet to the kitchen for another shot of whiskey. Late this afternoon, Dan, the team's best player—after me, of course—had called, inviting me for a dinner at his house. I didn't know why, but my brain conjured an image of a nice townhouse with the team plus a couple of other people having a nice quiet dinner. I should have known better. I had been here only a few days, but the guys liked parties as much as I did.

Dan's house was a freaking mansion almost as big as the Taylors' mansion in Santa Barbara, and it was packed. Besides the team members—Dan, Austin, and Zack, the coach and his wife, and a couple of the wealthy club members, I had no idea who all these people were.

In the kitchen, I didn't even need to ask for a whiskey, or find the bottle. A waitress saw my empty glass and exchanged it for a full one.

"Thanks," I said, taking it from her. She smiled then turned to some other guest.

I exited the kitchen and weaved through the

crowd, finding a living room with big glass doors opened to an outside patio.

I had been to Florida only a handful of times, and I always forgot how hot it could be during the summer—too fucking hot for my taste. I took a sip of my whiskey and leaned on the patio's rail, looking at the starry sky.

And the first thing on my mind?

Hilary.

*Que merda!* I thought that putting some real distance between us for two or three weeks would work like a charm. It is just an infatuation, I told myself. As soon as I stop spending time with her, my feelings would be gone, I assured myself.

Right. As if I didn't know my feelings had changed from simple interest to …

No, I wouldn't go there. She had made it clear she wasn't ready for anything. I could wait, I wanted to wait, but I also didn't want to wait. I wanted her. Now.

But it was like she had said before: What guarantee did I have that she would be able to push through her fears and allow herself to be with someone? To like someone? To like me?

This was so fucked up.

If only I found a way to get her out of my head.

"Hm, what is a hot guy like you doing out here all alone?" a sultry voice said.

I glanced over my shoulder and saw a girl standing a few feet behind me. She was pretty, with long, fake blond hair, bright red lips, and too much makeup. Her dress was too tight and too short, accentuating her generous curves and screaming, "Take me now," which was what she was going for.

"Enjoying the view," I said with a grin, entering game mode. I hadn't acted like a player in weeks, but it came back to me as if it were second nature.

With a flute of champagne in her hand, she sauntered closer and leaned her ass on the rail beside me. "So, you're the one that came to save my cousin's team?" I raised an eyebrow. "I'm Brenda. Austin is my cousin," she said, as if it didn't matter. "So, are you said hero or not?"

"I don't know about the hero, but I can help most of the time." I extended my hand to her. "I'm Gui Fernandes."

She shook my hand and narrowed her eyes at me. "Oh, I detect an accent. Where are you from?"

I pulled my hand back. "Brazil."

Her grin widened and she leaned closer. "I had heard Brazilian guys were hot. Now I can confirm that." She licked her lips. "I also heard that

Brazilian guys are good in bed. I would love to confirm that too."

She extended her hand and slid her finger up my arm. I expected to feel a shiver, a course of desire, something.

Nothing.

What was the fucking problem with me? If it had been two months ago, I wouldn't have thought about it twice. Actually, I wouldn't have thought about it at all. She was hot, free, and offering. There were no warts or fungus on her that I could see. Nothing that could disgust me later. Besides, if I drank two or three more shots of whiskey, even that wouldn't matter. It would be too damn easy to lose myself in this girl, to erase the thoughts in my mind, the images of the other girl haunting me each second of the day, even if only for a few minutes. Perhaps that was how I would recover from her rejection.

Having made up my mind, I leaned toward the girl to say something dirty that would tell her I could confirm her suspicions when my phone rang. I froze, taking three seconds to decide if I should ignore it or not.

It was Leo. I sighed, as if his phone call could save me from making a huge mistake. "*Que foi?*" I answered with a bite.

"Get your head out of your ass, *tche*," Leo said. "I have something important to tell you."

I turned my back to Brenda. "What?"

"I talked to Hilary today."

"I guess that is a given since you went to the studio."

"*Não, veado*, I mean I talked to her about yesterday. About her meeting with Reese at the club."

I groaned. "I'm not sure I want to hear this."

"*Sim*, you do. Apparently, even her mother had heard about the non-kiss—her words, not mine—and she went to the club to confront Reese about it. She wanted to know why the hell he was spreading rumors. She was pissed. And sad."

"So ..." I took a deep breath, trying to clear the haze in my mind. "So, she wasn't there to see him? To spend time with him?"

"*Não.*"

"And what he said to her? About the rumors?"

"He said it got out of hand. People distorted the truth, and he felt proud that everyone thought they were together. Apparently, he apologized and said he would fix it. At this moment, she can't stand him."

I cursed under my breath. "So I didn't go back there last night for nothing."

"*Sim*. Told you it wasn't as bad as you thought

it was. You can't assume anything until you know the facts."

I pressed a thumb and forefinger to my temples. "Easier said than done."

"Yeah, I know," Leo said. "But, Gui, seriously. You're a brother to me, and Hilary is like a sister—"

"When you say it like that ..." I groaned.

"—don't mess this up. I have no idea what you intend to do, if you intend to do anything, and I won't interfere, but I want you to remember that, whatever happens, it's bigger than just you. It's bigger than just the two of you. We're all going to be a big family now, and I would love if it didn't start with problems and weirdness."

I sighed. "I ... I don't know what I'm gonna do."

It was the truth. As much as I wanted to leave this party right now and grab the first flight to Santa Barbara, go to Hilary's apartment, bang on the door until she opened, sweep her in my arms, and kiss her until she confessed her feelings for me, until she was so wrapped around me she would never let go, that wasn't what she wanted. Not right now. She had made that clear. It hurt, but I would respect her wishes.

"Are you all right?"

"Yeah. *Sim*, I am." It was an automatic answer;

one that both Leo and I knew wasn't entirely honest.

"I need to go. Hannah needs me to help her with closing the stable for the night."

"All right."

"If you need anything, call, okay?"

"Yeah." I sighed. "Thanks. For letting me know."

"No problem. *Tchau.*"

"*Tchau.*"

I turned off the call, and when I spun on my heels to tell Brenda something had come up and I would have to go, I found her spot empty. Relieved, I let out a long breath. I glanced at the stars one last time before I left the party and went to my hotel. Alone.

# 38

AFTER THE LAST COUPLE OF DAYS I HAD, IT WAS NICE to relax.

On Saturday afternoon, the urge to go to Hannah's ranch and see Belle, and go for a ride with her, hit me fast and hard, something I had never expected to feel.

However, it was here now and it was welcomed.

So, without an announcement, I drove to Hannah's ranch and, when she saw me there, I invited her to go for a ride with me. The smile she shot me ... I didn't think I had seen my sister smile at me like that before.

Leo was there and I invited him to come with us, but he waved us off, saying he had to go do something with Ri and Pedro. Okay, then. If he said so.

"This is so nice," Hannah said as we rode along one of the many riding trails on her ranch. She was with Argus, of course, and I had Belle. "I have to confess. Never in a million years would I have imagined you and me riding together." She turned that thousand-kilowatt smile on me again. "I love it and I hope this is the first of many."

I nodded. "I know what you mean. I would have laughed at anyone who said this—" I pointed to her and me and the horses. "—would happen." I returned her smile. "I'm glad that I was wrong, though. I ... I love this." I opened my right arm, en-globing everything around us. The path, the trees, the green, the smell of the leaves and flowers, the sound of the birds and the clop-clop of the horses' hooves. "It's peaceful."

Hannah took in a long breath. "It really is."

I looked down at the mare under me and ran a hand over her neck. "Hannah, I want to ask you something."

My sister lost the smile and her eyes gained a worried shine. "What is it?"

I bit my lower lip. "Hm, I hope you're not of-fended, but, well ... will you sell Belle to me?" Hannah stared at me with huge eyes for three seconds before breaking into a loud laugh. I couldn't fight the small smile tugging on my lips. "Hannah! It's not funny."

"Sorry." She inhaled deeply, calming down a little. "It's not funny, I know. It's just so awesome and it makes me so happy, the need to laugh for joy was too big to ignore."

I rolled my eyes at her. "Will you sell me Belle or not?"

"Of course not, silly."

Shock locked my limbs. Wow, I hadn't expected that. I mean, I thought she would say no at first, but then I would talk her through it and she would give in.

"W-why not?"

She offered me a half-smile. "If you want her, she's yours. No need to buy her from me. I'll have the papers drawn up this week. In a few days, she'll be officially yours."

My heart stuttered for a moment and tears welled in my eyes. I wanted to jump off Belle and hug my sister. I settled for reaching to her and squeezing her hand. "Thank you," I said, my voice breaking.

"You're more than welcome."

I leaned over Belle. "Hear that girl?" I hugged her neck. "Soon, you'll be mine. For real."

THE PHONE ON MY DESK RANG.

"Hilary speaking," I said, knowing it was Sonya.

"A client of yours is here," she said. "He says he doesn't have an appointment, but he wanted to see if he can have his fitting sometime today." My throat closed and I plopped down on my chair. "Hilary? Did you hear me?"

"Y-yes."

"His name is—"

"Guilherme Fernandes, I know," I said, trying to recover from the surprise. Which was impossible, so I just barreled through it. I glanced at my computer screen and opened my schedule for the day. "He can have his fitting right now, actually, if we have a fitting room available."

"We do," she said. "I'll bring him to fitting room one, then."

"Okay. I'll be right there. Thanks."

I put the phone down and stared at it for a long time, not sure what to do next—other than get up, stop by the closet area where all the clothes were hung when not being worked on, pick up his tuxedo, and meet him in the fitting room.

My palms became sweaty and my breathing grew shallow.

Oh my gosh. Gui was here.

Slowly, I got up and moved through the motions until I had his tuxedo folded over my arm, and I stood in front of the door of the fitting room one.

After a deep breath in and out, I knocked on the door and opened it.

Gui was standing in the middle of the room, his eyes on me. My breath caught. He looked gorgeous, as always. He had his Montenegro baseball hat backward, and wore a pair of fitted jeans and a blue and white polo shirt, and brown cowboy boots. How he made it all work together, I had no idea. That would never be an outfit I chose for anyone, but on him, it worked.

But what really got to me was his eyes. They shone with so many unsaid words. Most of them I couldn't decipher, but I could see the frustration in him, the worry, the caring, and the relief too.

"*Oi*," he said.

"Hey." I closed the door and walked closer.

"Sorry I didn't come last Friday."

"It's okay. You're playing away." I frowned. "You still are, right?"

"I am. I came last night after my game, and I'll

be going back tonight because I have a game tomorrow."

"Oh." I held out his tuxedo for him. "Let's get to it, then."

He picked the tux up. "Just change into this?"

"Yup," I said, nodding.

Gui turned to one of the stalls on the side of the room and disappeared behind the thin opaque glass door. I scanned the room, looking for something to focus on, so I wouldn't think that Gui was undressing just a few feet from me. This room was a smaller version of the room I met the girls and the guys in the other day. However, it still had the same elegance, the same mirror wall, and the same podium in front of the mirrors.

I heard the ruffle of clothes as Gui stripped it all. Searching deep in my thoughts, I remembered seeing him shirtless once or twice over a year ago, and the only thing that came to mind was that his chest was ripped back then. I could only imagine if he was still that ripped now. I swallowed.

Then he surged from the stall and I had to swallow again.

Oh my ...

Gui in his usual clothes was hot. Gui in his polo uniform was hotter. But Gui in a tux? It was hotter than the sun. He had forgone the baseball hat, and the cowboy boots, opting to put on the dress shoes that were kept inside the fitting rooms. Even though the tux still needed a few adjustments, he looked edible.

"Is it all right?" he asked, opening his arms and looking at himself. "I mean, I know you made it, but I'm wondering if the measurements are good."

"Hm." I stared, having completely forgotten how to speak. "Hm," I tried again, pulling the professional out of me. Damn it was hard. "I think we can adjust the shoulders, and maybe the length of the pants."

"Oh."

"Come here," I said, beckoning him to stand on the podium in front of the mirrors.

One corner of his lips tugged up as he stepped onto the small podium. "I feel a little silly standing here."

I reached for a box of pins in the drawer of a shelf to the side and then knelt beside him, focusing on the hem of his pants. "The guys said the same thing the other day, but the girls loved it."

He let out a soft chuckled. "I bet."

I folded the hem on the place I thought looked best, placed one pin, stood, and stepped back to look. Even though I tried not to, I lifted my eyes to his and found him looking at me.

"How's the tournament?" I asked, trying to lighten the mood a little. "Winning?"

"Yes," he said. "That's what I was hired for. To make the team win."

I knelt in front of him again and adjusted the hem a little more. "I thought you were hired to help the team win."

"Well, that's a polite way to say it, but face it. They wouldn't hire someone in the top ten in the world and pay a ridiculous price to have us help. They expect to win."

I placed more pins in the right places and stood. "I'm glad you're winning, then." I looked up at him, briefly wondering how I would get to his shoulders if he was already much taller than me without the podium. Standing on it? I needed a ladder. "Hm." I considered standing on the podium with him, but it was too small. I would have to be too close to him, and that would be ... awkward. "Can you come down, please? I need to reach the shoulders of your jacket, and with you up there ..." I didn't finish.

"Oh, right." He stepped down and right in my face. I sucked in a long breath, taking in the spicy tang of his aftershave before I gave a step back.

"Thanks," I said. I avoided looking at his face, at his eyes, because I was too afraid of what I would see. Instead, I examined his shirt. "How's the neck of your shirt?" The problem here was, to touch his clothes, I had to be close to him. I gave a half a step toward him. With the word professional in my mind, I reached up and hooked a finger inside the shirt's neck, to feel how tight it was. *Not* feeling the warmth of his skin, I tugged. "We can tighten this one-sixth of an inch more, too. It'll look better."

"If you say so," he said, his voice a whisper.

His breath teased my cheek, and I did my best not to turn my head toward him.

"Now, the shoulders," I said, reaching to his left arm. Damn it, he was too tall. I could touch it, but I couldn't get a good look to pin it right. Why had I worn flats today? I stood on my tiptoes. Still not good. "Hm, could you—?"

I gasped as Gui's hands closed around my waist and raised me up and deposited me on the podium. His hands stayed on my waist, his body too close to mine, my head—my mouth—just an inch higher than his. He stared into my eyes.

"Better?" he asked, his voice low, but coarse.

I didn't trust myself to speak. I just nodded.

Disappointment invaded my chest, surprising me as he withdrew his hands and turned to the side, giving me better access to his left shoulder.

I cleared my throat. "Try not to move or I might pin you."

"Duly noted."

I pressed the fabric, moving it tighter, and pined it in the right position. I leaned back, examining how it looked, then applying light pressure on his shoulder, had him turn his right shoulder to me. He kept his head high, his gaze straight, right over my shoulder, and I wondered what he was thinking, what he was feeling. Was I the only one worked up here? Was I overreacting? He didn't seem too affected by what had transgressed between us.

"This is how it's going to be from now on?" he asked, making me lose the pin I was about to plunge in the fabric.

I snatched another pin. "What do you mean?"

He turned his face toward me and I froze. There were only a few inches between our lips.

"This." He pointed a finger at me, then him. "This coldness, this awkwardness. Every time we meet. Is this how it's going to be from now on?"

I sighed. "I hope not."

A knot appeared on his forehead. "You expect me to just go on being friends with you as if we haven't kissed? As if you didn't confess to me that you like me? Or did that change already and that's why you're acting so okay with all this?"

"I'm not—" I pressed my lips tight and took a deep breath. "I'm not acting okay. I'm a nervous wreck on the inside." The words were out before I could stop them. Damn it.

"Then you're a better actress than I thought."

I gasped. "You're such a—" I snapped my mouth shut. A what? A jerk? A selfish bastard? But I knew he wasn't. Not really. He might be—used to be?—a playboy, but he was never a jerk about it. All the girls who got involved with him knew what to expect from him. Including me. "We already talked about this, Gui. What else do you want me to say?"

He stared at me for a long time, as if he wanted me to read it in his expression. I tried not to.

His forehead creased. "I don't know."

A couple of months ago, being this close to him would have made me nervous. I would be shaking like a leaf and ready to bolt. Now? He still made me nervous, but it was for other reasons. I wanted to be close to him. Even closer. The problem was ... how close was too close? I could handle this distance. A simple kiss. His hands around me. Would I be able to handle more? My brain seized each time I thought about that, which indicated my body would seize too if I tried. I didn't want to freak out while making out with him, while ... doing more with him. He had already bothered too much with me, more than he should have. I didn't want to become a problem in his life. He was so much better off without me.

If only he understood that and stopped being mad at me.

No, Gui wasn't a jerk or a selfish bastard, but right now, he was infuriating. Groaning, I finished straightening the shoulder of his jacket and stepped off the podium.

"We're done here," I said, my voice firm, resolute. "You can change back into your clothes. Leave the tux on the hangers inside the stall. I'll come pick it up later." I turned and head to the door.

"Hil, wait," Gui called.

I didn't look back. "Good-bye, Gui."

I exited the room and, once the door was closed behind me, I rushed to the nearest bathroom, where I locked myself in and fought not to cry.

# 39

HILARY

GUI WAS BACK. HE HAD WON THE TOURNAMENT IN Florida, and he was now number three in the world ranking. It wasn't official yet since the federation wouldn't announce it until next week, but Gui had invited everyone to his apartment to celebrate.

My first thought was hell no. I shouldn't go. Last time we saw each other, we had parted on such a bad note. I didn't feel like facing him. But during the afternoon, I thought about it. Wasn't I the one insisting on going back to the way things were before we started spending so much time together? Before we kissed? If I didn't stand behind what I said, how did I expect him to do it? Besides, I would have to face him sooner or later. It was only three weeks until the wedding now and we lived in the same building. We were bound to run into each other sometime soon. So, I decided to have some control over when and how I saw him again.

After lots of fake meditation and weak relaxation techniques, I got ready for the party and went upstairs a little after the appointed time. I wanted to make sure I wasn't the first one to arrive.

I kept messing with the skirt of my dress the entire elevator ride. I had chosen a casual black and pink summer dress with a flirty skirt and pink sandals. I had pulled my hair into a tight ponytail and applied a little makeup. Not too fancy, not too casual.

My stomach revolved as I knocked on the door. To my relief, Iris opened the door.

"Wow, you look pretty!" she said, moving aside so I could enter.

"Thanks," I said, scanning the place as I stepped into the apartment.

As usual, Leo and Garrett were playing video games, while Ri and Pedro were with them in the living room, waiting for their turn. Hannah and Bia were in the kitchen, preparing drinks and the finger food that would be passed around.

I didn't see Gui and my feelings divided into

relief and disappointment. Wasn't this his party? Where was he?

I followed Iris to the kitchen where Hannah handed me a whiskey with coke, which I passed to Bia. To occupy my mind, I went around the kitchen island and helped Hannah with everything. If I just sat on a stool beside Bia, my thoughts would make me more nervous and scared than I already was.

Hannah handed me another glass with whiskey and coke. "Take it. You'll need it," she whispered.

"Why?" I asked, setting the glass aside. I wouldn't drink this, no matter what.

She just shook her head and spoke up, talking about the wedding. And that was how the girls distracted me. They asked me about their dresses and the bachelorette party, and we talked about other light topics.

I could handle this.

But as the minutes passed, I wondered where Gui was.

Finally, almost thirty minutes after I arrived, the balcony glass doors opened and Gui stepped inside the living room. With a girl trailing behind him.

She said something as she halted beside him, and he chuckled.

My heart stopped.

Beside me, Hannah tsked. "Are you sure you don't want some alcohol?"

"W-who is she?" I asked, my voice low.

"Her name is Amanda," my sister said. "But I don't know her. Gui introduced her to us when she arrived, just a couple of minutes before you did, and then Gui took her to the balcony."

The balcony made an L around the living room, going to the bedrooms. Gui could have been anywhere in the apartment with this girl. Nausea rolled in my stomach.

Gui's eyes found mine across the room and his smile dropped. He nodded to me and I raised my hand, waving my fingers at him. The girl turned to me too and smiled wide.

"Hi," she mouthed. I waved at her too.

She turned back to him and she clasped her hand around his upper arm. Gui returned his eyes to her and his lopsided grin appeared again.

How I was able to stand here, wave at them, and watch them, I had no idea.

I had known coming here would be awkward, but I was willing to push through that. We had to; otherwise, we would never be friends again. But I hadn't expected to find him with another girl already.

I turned my back to them, leaning my butt against the kitchen island.

"What can I do for you?" Hannah asked.

I shook my head. "I don't know."

Just the other day, I had told myself he wasn't a jerk. Now I wasn't so sure anymore. Maybe Gui didn't feel the same for me, as he led me to believe, but he knew how I felt about him and he knew my reasons for not being with him. They might not make sense to him, but they did to me. I expected a sliver of respect from him. Of consideration.

"Everything okay?" Bia asked. I looked at her over my shoulder. "Hannah has a murderous look on her face, and you have your shoulders slumped. What is it?"

"Nothing," I said before Hannah invented some other lie. "Just had a bad week at work."

"But I thought the internship was amazing," Iris said.

I nodded. "It is."

"What's the problem, then?" Iris asked.

I almost cringed as I fabricated a lie. "One of my co-workers is a jerk, that's all."

"Tell us all about it," Bia said. "Let us talk bad about the bastard."

A tiny smile took over my lips. "Thanks, but I would rather not talk about this anymore."

Across the room, my eyes met Gui's again. Hannah started a new topic, grabbing the girls' attention while mine remained with Gui. He turned to Amanda, grabbed her hand, and pulled her to sit down at the dining table. They took side-by-side chairs, and Gui put his arms over the back of her chair, leaning closer, with his lopsided grin brightening his gorgeous face. Amanda certainly looked smitten, but she also played the same game. Her arm, which had been lying on the table, slid under, probably to touch his thigh ... or someplace else.

My stomach turned over.

I placed both hands on my belly, as if that would help. I wanted to be strong, I wanted to face this, but it was too much too fast. I wasn't ready for this.

"I'm not sure I can stay here," I whispered to Hannah.

She entwined her fingers with mine and squeezed. "It's okay. I'll help you with a white lie if you want to."

I groaned, not happy with it. "Okay."

I turned around, facing Bia and Iris across the kitchen island, and behind them everyone else in the living and dining room. I opened my mouth to say something, anything that would maybe get me out of here, but Hannah's actions were faster than my addled brain.

She reached behind us, grabbed a two-liter bottle of coke, uncapped it, and, when turning back to us, she tripped on her own foot and bumped into me, spilling coke all over the side of my dress.

I gasped, not believing she had done that. I glared at her, ready to kill her. My night had been terrible so far, and now she had just put the cherry on top of the sundae by ruining my dress.

"Oh my ..." I hissed.

"I'm so sorry," Hannah said, her tone loud and clear.

"*Meu Deus!*" Bia shrieked, jumping from her stool. Iris wasn't far behind. With Hannah, they all found rags under the sink and dabbed them at me and on the floor.

The game was paused and the guys stood, looking in our direction with worried expressions, probably thinking we had cut ourselves with the knives or something. Gui was among them. Amanda had stayed at the table a few feet behind him.

"What happened?" Leo asked, looking from me to Hannah and to me again.

"I'm a klutz," Hannah said, forcing her voice to sound too sweet and innocent. "I tripped and the bottle fell on Hilary."

The liquid pooled around my feet, and my skin felt sticky wherever the liquid had dripped down—my right arm and the outside of my right leg.

I took a rag from Hannah and wiped my arm. The excess was gone, but I still could feel it as if the gooey thing had seeped into my bones. Gosh, I could kill my sister.

"That's one big mess," Iris said. "And that's one ruined dress."

Angry, frustrated, disappointed, and humiliated, my eyes filled with tears.

*I'm a big girl. I won't cry. Not here, at least.*

I sucked in a deep breath. "Excuse me," I said to Bia, who was cleaning the floor around me. I leaned against the island while I took off my sandals and cleaned my feet with the rag, before stepping away from the mess. I just hoped I wasn't dripping coke anymore.

"I'm so sorry," Hannah said. This time she stared into my eyes, and I knew what she meant.

"It's okay," I said. I put the rag in the sink and

turned to the crowd watching me, forcing a smile. "Well, I guess I'm gonna go home."

"Yeah," Bia said. "It shouldn't take you more than what? Fifteen minutes to clean up and change?"

"We promise we won't talk about anything interesting while you're gone," Iris said with a sweet smile. "But I might eat all of Bia's *pão de queijo* by then."

I forced a chuckle. "Be right back," I lied.

As I walked from the kitchen, through the hallway between the living room and dining room to the front door, I felt everyone's eyes on me. I wanted to shrink and disappear.

I walked by Gui and I couldn't help it. I spied him from the corner of my eyes. He was watching me too. A knot adorned his forehead, and his mouth was pressed together as if he was holding back from saying something, from yelling something. A tear escaped and I was sure he saw it.

I hurried my steps and left the apartment as if it could bite my ass. At the elevator, I looked into the mirror and another tear escaped as I promised myself I would skip the next get-together. No matter the circumstances.

# 40

GUI

The tear broke me.

I had tried so hard to keep up this I-don't-fucking-care facade, but in the end, as she left my apartment and glanced one last time at me, a tear rolling down her face, I felt broken. Stupid. Empty. A fucking jerk.

Because that was what I was. A fucking jerk.

The girls cleaned the kitchen while the guys settled down to continue playing, everyone a little quieter than before.

Amanda leaned into me, her hands closing around my arm. "How about you show me your room now?" she said, her voice holding a sensual note.

I stepped back, pulling my arm from her hold.

I didn't want anything to do with her. Even before I had seen the dull glint in Hilary's face. And that was why I was an even bigger jerk. I had met Amanda a few months ago when I went clubbing with Malcolm, Justin, Reese, and Lucas. We almost hooked up that night, but I didn't even remember what happened. She went dancing and I found some other girl? It was the most probable outcome. I hadn't seen her since that night, until I arrived at the airport this afternoon. She was there dropping off her sister, and we started talking, and then before I realized I had invited her over for dinner. For a quick heartbeat, I was mad at myself, but it didn't last. I was mad and hurt and wanted to make Hilary feel the same. I wanted to make her jealous. I wanted her to feel what it was like when I heard the stories about Reese and her.

I was proud of myself for moving on.

Then Hilary saw Amanda with me. I watched as she broke right before me. That much pain, that much sadness ... I didn't wish it on anyone. Until then, I didn't really believe she liked me. She couldn't have meant it. Otherwise, how could she let me go so easily? It hurt like hell to respect her wishes and stay away. How did she do it?

So I pushed it. I went to the dining room with Amanda and let the girl touch me and lean on me as if we were ready to hook up. Inside though, I was disgusted with myself. All the while, Amanda only had ten percent of my attention. The other ninety was on Hilary.

Because of that, I knew Hannah and Hilary had engineered a way for Hilary to get out of the party without questions. I wasn't sure Hilary had agreed to Hannah's plan, but it worked. She was out.

And I felt like a fucking jerk.

I sighed. And I was about to be a fucking jerk again.

I crossed my arms. "I think it's time for you to go."

Amanda gaped at me. "What?"

"I need you to go. Now."

She clenched her hands. "You're fucking kidding me?"

"Nope. Please, leave." It killed me to say please to her, but I really wanted her to go.

"Jerk!" She tried to punch me, but I deflected.

That got the attention of everyone. The video game was paused again, and the girls had frozen.

Amanda tried hitting me one more time, but I stepped out of the way and pointed to the door. Hissing, she marched away and slammed the door on her way out.

"What was that?" Leo asked.

"Whoa, what did you do this time?" Ri asked.

I shook my head. "I don't want to talk about it." I ran a hand through my hair, but unfortunately, that didn't help with my confusion, with my frustration. It was never that easy.

I wanted to go to my room and punch a wall, but I had asked my family to come celebrate with me. I couldn't just leave them here. Pushing down the knot in my chest, I sighed and joined the guys in the living room.

"I want to play," I said, extending my hand to Garrett and Pedro—they were the ones with the joysticks. I wanted to play this game, to spend my built-up energy by killing some villains.

"So moody," Pedro teased, handing me the joystick.

"Just shut up and watch as I blow your score out of the water," I said, my voice harsher than I intended. Still a fucking jerk.

The guys exchanged a look but said nothing. Great, because I wasn't in the mood to talk. If they tried, they might get my fists in their noses. And right now, I would enjoy it.

# 41

HILARY

I parked my car in the studio's parking lot, checked the mirrors, and looked out for any sign of Mike, or anyone else who could rob me—a habit I had developed since Mike almost killed me in this same spot. When everything looked okay, I exited my car and walked to the studio's door, my chin high, my eyes half-closed, enjoying the warmth of the sun on my skin. It was not even nine in the morning on a Monday, and the sun wasn't already hot. It made me wish for a day on the beach. Or poolside.

I had just stepped inside and greeted Sonya when my phone rang.

I glanced at the screen and frowned. "Hi, Evie. How are you?" I asked, concerned. She rarely called me. I heard a gasp and a sob and stopped dead in my tracks. "Evie? Talk to me." The hallway leading to the main studio floor and the offices and meeting rooms was empty, so I leaned against the wall and spoke up, "Evie!"

"I-I'm here," she croaked.

My heart sped up. "What happened?" She let out a whimper. "Where are you?"

She inhaled. "At the c-center." She took another deep breath. "The nurse here is taking care of me."

Fear jolted through my chest. "I'll be there in a few minutes, okay?"

"O-okay," she whispered.

I turned off my phone and went straight to Fallon's office. I would be sorry if I interrupted an important meeting, but this was important to me too. Fallon could fire me if she wanted. There were only two weeks left on this internship anyway. I soon would be back to L.A. and wouldn't worry about another internship until next summer.

Thankfully, Fallon was alone.

"Hilary, so great to see you." She smiled at me. "Only two more weeks, huh? I'll be sad to see you go."

As much as I wanted to bask in her compliment, I had more urgent matters. "I'll be sad to go too," I said. "But I just received a phone call … something urgent came up and I need to leave for the day."

Her brows furrowed. "What happened? Is it your mother? Your sister?"

I shook my head. "No, they are fine. It's a friend. She's in trouble and I need to go see her."

"All right, I understand." She spread her hands over the planner on her desk. "Take the day off; it's no problem. But, if you can, I would like you to come in tomorrow. The wedding clothes are all done, and I would like to take a look at them with you."

I nodded. "Thank you. I'll be here tomorrow, I promise."

I left the studio in a hurry. To be honest, I didn't even know how I drove to the women's center without getting into an accident, because my mind was elsewhere. My hands shook and my heart beat faster.

At the center, I went to the nurse's office. The door was closed, so I knocked and waited. Ten seconds later, a woman with a blue uniform opened the door.

"What can I do for you?" she asked, her voice sweet, calming.

"I believe Evangeline is here with you."

"Hilary?" Evie's voice came from inside the room.

"Yes," I answered, loud enough so she would hear me.

"She can come in," Evie said.

The nurse stepped to the side and let me in, then closed the door again.

My gaze landed on Evie and my heart skipped a beat.

It was as if she had been hit by a truck. Her right eye was swollen shut, a big purpling bruise around it that extended down to her cheek. Her lip was also swollen and split. Her neck had ugly scratch lines and ... were those bites?

"What ... How ...?" I didn't know what to say, what to ask.

The nurse spoke up. "I wanted to take her to the hospital, but she refuses."

Evie shook her head. She stopped and closed her eyes, hissing, as if it hurt too much. "I-I won't go to the hospital."

She should not only go to the hospital, but also to the police and file a restraining order. This was ridiculous. Mike couldn't do this to her and get away with it.

Rage boiled in me. I wanted to shake her shoulders and demand for her to see reason.

The nurse finished closing a bandage over Evie's neck. "I'll give you two a moment to talk." Then she exited the office, closing the door behind her.

Silence filled the room as I thought over what to say. A tear rolled down Evie's face, breaking a little more of my beat-up heart.

I reached over, taking her hands in mine. Oh my gosh, even her wrists had bruises. I took a deep breath, trying to calm down. "Do you want to talk about it?"

She shook her head. One more tear fell. "The only thing I want to tell you is that I'm done. I'm done."

Something like hope pushed against the rage. "You're done?"

"With him. I'm done." She stifled a sob. "I'm moving out. I don't know how, I don't know exactly when or where I'll go, but I'm way past done. I'm moving out."

I wanted to jump and take her into my arms and squeezed her tight, but I was afraid of scaring her and adding to her pain. So I settled for squeezing her hands. "You have no idea how much I love hearing you say that." I offered her a supportive smile. "I'll help you with the how, when, and where. Don't you worry about a thing."

She tried smiling, but it was forced and only lasted two seconds. "Thanks, Hilary. You're the best person I know."

---

I DECIDED TO GO IN AN HOUR EARLY TO THE STUDIO on Tuesday to compensate for having taken the day off yesterday. My plan was to go in an hour early and leave an hour late every day this week.

The elevator doors opened and I was about to enter, but I saw Gui inside and froze. He stared at me while I stared at him. The doors began closing before I could react. Gui shoved his hand in the way, making the doors open again.

"Are you coming?" he asked, his tone flat.

As if he had slapped me awake, I stepped into the elevator and stood beside him, facing the closed doors.

The elevator started moving down, and the awkwardness reached a new high.

It didn't help that he wore sweatpants, a T-shirt, and sneakers, with his earphones around his neck. He was either going running or working out.

Inhaling my pride, I decided to be the bigger person here. "How have you been?"

"*Bem. E você?*"

"Me too," I answered. Automatic questions and answers.

The doors opened to the first level and Gui walked out. Before the doors closed, he reached out and put his arm in the way, causing them to open again. I had a terrible case of triple deja vu.

"About Amanda," he started.

I lifted my chin. "I don't want to know."

"Nothing happened," he continued, even after my comment.

"I don't care," I insisted.

"But I do," he groaned. What the hell was that supposed to mean? "Nothing happened. I sent her away right after you left."

"Okay," I said, trying not to read between the lines.

He stepped back, taking his arm from the doors. "I just wanted you to know that."

The doors closed, and I stared at them with my jaw hanging open.

I wanted to yell, what was that supposed to mean?

Instead, I swallowed my comment and, at the underground level, walked to my car as if nothing had happened. Because it didn't matter if Gui had done something with Amanda; it shouldn't matter.

On the drive to the studio, I shoved Gui out of

my thoughts by focusing on Evie and her situation. I had spent yesterday afternoon looking for a new place for her to live and other necessary things.

The small apartment I had found—far away from Mike's place—would be available on Thursday. I planned on taking the afternoon off again to help her with the move.

As long as she stuck to our plan, Evie would be okay.

At the studio, I sat down at my desk and my phone rang.

"Hilary speaking," I answered.

"Good, you're here," Fallon said. "Meet me in fitting room three, please."

She hung up and I trudged to the assigned room. Fallon stood in the middle of the place, admiring the many dresses and tuxedos hanging from poles placed around the room.

She smiled at me. "I wanted to check on these with you, but mainly, I just want to congratulate you on a job well done. These are incredible."

I blushed. "Thanks."

"I confess I was a little skeptical when your mother called and asked me to consider you for an internship," she said. I gaped at her, but, still looking at the dresses, she didn't acknowledge my shock and went on. "But you surprised me the moment you walked into my office. I loved your portfolio then, and I love it even more now. Keep that up and I'll hire you to work for me every summer."

She patted my shoulder and left the room.

My knees weakened and I almost fell on my butt.

My mother did *what*?

After a long time—I wasn't aware of the time passing—I sat down on one of the white leather couches in the fitting room and called my mother.

"Good morning, Hilary," she said, her voice poised and firm as always. "How are you?"

"Not very well since I just found out you asked Fallon White to give me my internship!"

"Well, I asked her to consider you for an internship," she said matter-of-factly. "She wasn't obligated to hire you. She started with an interview, didn't she? She could have said no."

"An interview on a day you knew I had a test with a lenient professor, who would allow me to take the test another time."

"I told her when you could be available for an interview, so what?"

I gasped. "You can't interfere in my life like that."

"I'm your mother. As long as I live and

breathe, I'll help you, or as you say, interfere in your life, as much as I want. Besides, Fallon called yesterday. She said she's impressed with you, that she was glad she hired you, and that you will go far. Even if I nudged her to give you this internship, how well you did was all up to you."

Damn, she was right.

Fallon could have said no after the interview, or she could have hired me, hated me, and fired me in a week. Or she could have said nothing this morning about how well I was doing. Still, it hurt a little knowing my mother had gotten me this internship. How would I be able to look at Fallon again knowing that?

I swallowed my pride. "I won't say thank you … yet. But you're right. Fallon could have hated my work and apparently she doesn't."

"She loves your work, Hilary." I didn't say anything, because I wasn't ready to thank her yet. I had to get my pride in check first. So, my mother broke the ice. "I'll see you Sunday for our lunch at the club, right?"

"Yes, ma'am."

"Great. And Hilary?"

"Hm?"

"I'm proud of you."

A small smile spread across my lips. I could thank her for that. "Thanks."

***

"So, what do you think?"

Evie stepped into the living room of the small apartment, looking around. "It looks ... great." She offered a small smile. "Better than great."

Well, I wouldn't say it was better than great, but I was good for an apartment I whipped up in three days. I scoured the internet on Monday morning, after seeing Evie at the women's center. I found a few possible options and went to check them out. I chose the nicest, cleanest one—it was small, a living room and an open kitchen with a high counter that served as an eating area, and two small bedrooms and one bathroom. I already signed the documents. The agent said it had never been done so fast, but I was offering to pay six months' rent in advance, plus a special fee for how fast he could do it all. Then, in the afternoon, I went furniture shopping. I bought simple things and had them delivered on Wednesday, a couple of hours before some handymen came to assemble everything. Then last night, I went grocery shopping and stocked the kitchen, and, knowing she would leave in a hurry with only one or two suitcases, I bought her some new clothes and shoes.

However, in my opinion, the best feature was the distance from Mike's place: far away.

"It's a starting point. I know that, with time, you'll do better."

She turned to me with tears in her eyes. "You have no idea what this means to me. I can't even begin to describe it." She wiped her hands on her cheeks. "It's amazing, Hilary. You're amazing."

I smiled. "You're welcome." I sat down on the couch and opened my laptop. "Now let's go looking for a new job for you."

She sat down beside me. "My job is fine." She made a face and I laughed. "Okay, okay. I agree. My job stinks. Let's look for a new job."

---

THE LIMO WAITED IN FRONT OF THE BUILDING.

Hannah screamed as we stepped through the front door. She smiled at me and then ran to the limo. Bia, Gabi, and Iris—all dressed in pretty party dresses—were beside the limo, waiting for us. They let Hannah and I enter first, then followed suit.

The seats in the limo were arranged in a rectangle, leaving the middle open, except for a small table where the champagne, the chocolate, and the strawberries lay in pretty crystal vases.

"This is so cool," Gabi said, reaching for a strawberry.

"*Por favor*, tell us where we're going," Bia asked.

I just shook my head.

Hannah couldn't sit still. She bounced her legs and looked from side to side, taking in everything.

Iris grabbed the champagne bottle and popped it open. "How about we bet?"

"Bet what?" Gabi asking, holding the crystal flutes for Iris.

"Where Hilary is taking us," Iris said.

"You'll never guess," I said, smoothing the flowy skirt of my black dress. I rarely wore only black, and black to a bachelorette party seemed a little depressing, but I thought it was fitting for what I had planned for today.

Bia shot me a fake glare. "Let us try."

I smiled. "Be my guest."

They bet on everything possible: stripper club, normal club, hotel room with strippers. There were always strippers in their guesses, but they all got it wrong.

The limo took us to the outskirts of Los Angeles, to a big stadium and track.

"Oh ..." Hannah said. Her eyes were wide as she took in the place, and her mouth was turned into a little O.

"So, was it a surprise?" I asked as we enter our little VIP box. The girls faced the track, all with their mouths hanging open. "I'm guessing you're all surprised, right?" It was funny, really, how they all stared at the track, then at me, then at the track again. I knew going to horse racing wasn't a usual spot for bachelorette parties, but we all loved horses and I wanted to do something different. I fished a check from my purse and showed it to them. "Here's my father's gift for us. We can bet on all the horses all day if we want." The check was absurdly high, and Hannah gasped in surprise when she saw it.

The fun began. And I really mean it. I hadn't had that much fun in so, so long. We bet on horses that won and horses that lost, we ordered fancy food and drinks, we yelled and whistled and laughed, and some of us drank too much. And, for the three hours we were there, I was surprised to realize I hadn't thought of Gui once.

Okay, that was a lie. I thought of him often, but I didn't acknowledge it.

After the horse racing, the limo took us to a Brazilian Steakhouse, where I had reserved a private space with handsome guys dressed as *gaúchos* served us—the closest we would get to strippers all night. The girls drank more and flirted with the guys, and I laughed and laughed.

It was two in the morning when the limo took us home. Most of the girls had passed out in their seats.

Half asleep, Hannah reached for me and entwined her fingers through mine. "Thank you. My bachelorette party was perfect. I mean it."

I leaned into her and rested my head on her shoulder. "I'm glad you liked it."

"I really did." She kissed my head.

Ten seconds later, I could hear her soft snoring.

# 42

HILARY

EVEN THOUGH I PROMISED MY MOTHER I WOULD GO to Sunday lunch at the club, I tried getting out of it. Without luck. She wouldn't have it, and then Hannah said she would go too, along with Bia, Gabi, and Iris.

I was certain we all looked like shit after such a long, fun night, but nobody commented on it.

Of course, Reese was there and he joined us after lunch. I wanted him to leave before I did, so he wouldn't try to walk me to my car, but I had no luck there either. I had agreed to meet Evie at her new apartment at four, and it was now three and I still had to stop by my apartment to grab some things I had bought for her.

Groaning on the inside, I excused myself from the post-lunch coffee, and Reese stood with me.

Once we had left the balcony and were out of earshot, he turned to me, without his usual smile.

"I take it you still don't forgive me," he said, his tone flat.

"Actually, I think I have." It had been so long, I didn't really think about him or the rumors anymore. However, people were looking at us now. We might be initiating new rumors at this exact moment.

"Oh." A small smile took over his lips. "So, that means you might want to go grab a coffee with me some time?"

I sighed. "I really don't want to hurt your feelings, Reese, because you seem like a nice guy, but no. I forgave you, but I don't want to go out with you. And not just because I'm not ready to start dating. I don't like you that way."

"Ouch," he muttered.

"Sorry."

He tsked. "It's okay. I admire your honesty. I just didn't think it would hurt this much."

"Sorry," I repeated, feeling bad. I shouldn't have said anything, but then he would always think there was hope that something would happen between us, and that wasn't true. No, I was doing the right thing. He might be hurt now, but he would be okay soon. At least one of us should be okay soon.

"No need to apologize, really." He narrowed his eyes at me. "Your answer was so sure and ready, I have to ask, is there someone else?"

I glanced at the spot where usually Gui parked his Jeep—it was empty now. The guys had had their bachelor party last night too. I bet they were all still sleeping or nursing a hangover.

"That's not relevant," I said, lowering my gaze.

"I see," Reese said. He saw where I looked, and he knew who always parked there.

We stopped in front of my car and I turned to him. "Thanks for walking with me."

"My pleasure." He grabbed my hand and kissed the top. "See you at your sister's wedding."

I nodded, entered my car, and left before more club-goers saw Reese and me talking. The next thing I knew, they would spread rumors I was the next one getting married.

Late, I stopped by the apartment, grabbed Evie's gifts, and then drove to her apartment on the other side of town.

When I arrived, she was in the kitchen, mixing the ingredients to bake a cake.

"I haven't baked a cake in ages!" she exclaimed with a wide smile on her face.

She looked much better now. It was as if she could finally be happy, feel happy, or at least hopeful for a better future. And her bruises were healing nicely too. Seeing her like this made me happy. She had endured so much—more than any woman should—and I was glad to be helping her pave a new path for herself. My only wish was that she had been this strong before, and left Mike months ago.

Better late than never. She was still young and had her entire life ahead of her.

I leaned against the counter and watched as she finished mixing the last ingredients, poured the mix in a baking pan, and put it inside the oven.

She turned to me with a wide smile. "It should be ready in about thirty minutes."

"That's good." I raised my arm and showed her I was holding a big bag. "You can look through these in the meantime."

Her eyes widened and she reached for the bag. "More gifts? Hilary, I'm serious, please stop. You're gonna spoil me rotten." Her eyes filled with tears. "Besides, I don't deserve it."

"Yes, you do." I gestured to the bag. "Now, open it!"

She rushed to the couch and sat down, the bag on her lap.

As she opened it, the doorbell rang.

"I'll get it," I said, already walking to the door.

Still smiling, I opened the door and barely registered who was standing there before I was shoved to the side and hit my head on the wall behind the open door.

Mike strode in and the door slammed closed.

Evie stood. "W-what are you doing here?"

"What are *you* doing here?" Mike asked, advancing toward her.

Shaking, Evie retreated until she had put the kitchen's high counter between Mike and her.

Fighting the dizziness that spun my mind and made my vision blur for a few seconds, I pushed from the wall and placed my hand on the back of my head. It wasn't bleeding.

I took a deep breath, gathering my strength and my courage. "Mike, you should leave."

He didn't even look at me as he said, "Stay out of it, blondie, or I'll finish what I started in that parking lot."

With wide, scared eyes, Evie looked from Mike to me and back to Mike. "H-how did you find me?"

"Easy. I just followed blondie here. I knew she was bound to come visit you at some point."

My chest deflated.

No. How could I have been so stupid? I should have known he would be watching me. I should have been careful. I should have watched out for him. If I had seen him following me, I would have lost him somehow. Now it was too late.

Mike grabbed my arm with force and pulled me with him as he took a few steps toward Evie.

Tears spilled from her eyes. "Please …"

"Please, what, baby? Please take me home? Please forgive me?" He pushed me down and let me go, making me fall on my knees right beside the kitchen counter. He rounded the counter, getting close to Evie. She took a few steps back, but I knew what was going through her mind. She was thinking about surrendering, because if she resisted and he caught up with her, it would be so much worse.

"Evie, don't," I said.

She spared me a quick, terrified glance. "I don't know what to do," she cried.

"You know what will happen to you, right, baby?" Mike asked. He closed the distance between them and wrapped his hand around her arm. Tight. He pulled her to him and she whimpered. "That's my girl." His eyes on me, he licked her cheek. "What shall we do about her, baby?

Hm, should we punish her for what she did to us?"

Panic and fear made its way through my veins.

The door wasn't too far behind me. I could run and scream for help. I would be safe, and Evie might be, if someone came to help in time. But if no one came, Mike would beat her up, would abuse her more, and she would let him. Worse, he would take her away and I was sure I wouldn't be able to help her again.

Fighting my instinct wasn't easy. I pushed the panic and fear down and tried to think this through. Mike was a big man. He could hurt Evie and me without breaking a sweat.

"Please, Mike, don't," she whispered.

He pulled his arm back and slapped her hard enough that her head whipped to the side and she lost her footing, toppling into the counter. I gasped, my fear spiking.

His teeth bared like an animal, Mike turned to me. "It's all your fault."

I started to push up, to stand, but he grasped my shoulder and pushed me hard, making me lose my balance and fall back down. I hit my head on the kitchen's hard floor and darkness surrounded me.

Before I could recover, Mike pulled me up by

my hair. I heard Evie's cry and fought against the dizziness and the darkness.

Mike shouted something. Then pain exploded on my cheek and I went barreling to the floor again. The darkness took over again. There were more shouts; they seemed to be coming from underwater. A new, terrible pain exploded in my stomach, taking my breath away. I wheezed, certain I was drowning.

Minutes passed—or seconds?—and finally my breath steadied enough that I could take a long inhale and the dark spots in my vision retreated. Mike had Evie backed into a corner. She barely moved as he landed punch after punch on her.

"Mike," I called him, but my throat hurt and nothing came out. I pushed to my knees and tried again. "Mike!" I yelled. He didn't stop.

Holding on to the top of the counter, I pulled myself up. My hand lay beside my purse and a thick rolling pin. I quickly grabbed my cell phone and the pepper spray.

I dialed 911 and yelled, "Help!"

Then, Mike roared as he let go of Evie—she slid to the ground—and advanced on me. He took the pepper spray and the phone from me before I could finish rattling the address to the operator, and threw them both on the other side of the room.

I didn't pay much attention to the blood on his fists as he raised them to hit me, or I would give in to the fear trying to break me.

I grabbed the rolling pin from the counter and swung it at him. A sickening crack followed as the rolling pin connected with the side of his head.

"Bitch!" he yelled, taking the rolling pin from me. That did it. He roared and lunged at me.

But this time, I wasn't going to let him take me down that easily.

From somewhere inside me, I pulled strength I didn't know I had. I sidestepped him and picked up a pan that was on the range. I brought it down, as hard as I could, and hit him in the back. Groaning, he turned around again, and easily hit my arm hard enough that the pan went flying. Then he slapped me with the same hand, making me stumble to the side. I didn't even register the pain anymore as he closed his hand around my neck and backed me against the wall.

"Bitch! Now I'm gonna finish what I started that day," he said, spitting his rage on me.

He pressed his hand tight, and on purpose, lifted me up so I couldn't even stand on my tiptoes. I closed my hands on his wrists, trying to push them apart, to break free. But he was a monster, an animal. He was too big and too strong for me.

Thank goodness, I had learned how to deal with guys like him.

Still holding on to his wrists, I used them as leverage so I could pull my knees up and then kick him in his stomach with both feet, as hard as I could. Surprised, his rigid stance wavered and his grip on my neck loosened enough so I could pull them apart and break free. I ducked as he made it to grab me again. He corrected himself too quickly and was able to grab my arm as I tried to run away. He closed both hands around my right wrist. I twisted, so the narrow side of my arm was against his thumbs, and then pulled it hard toward me. Even a big guy like him couldn't hold on like that, and then as his hands were pried open, I kept pulling my arm up, bending it so my elbow hit his chin hard. His head snapped back and, aiming for the center of his chest, I used both hands to push him back. He stumbled, coughing.

I didn't waste time. I ran to the door.

Before I could open it and call for help, Mike caught up with me. He closed his big hand around my arm and pulled me back into the living room as if I didn't weigh more than a rag doll.

Mike threw me on the couch and leaned over

me. "I'm gonna kill you, bitch. But first, I'm gonna enjoy you a little." He punched my cheek. Pain exploded on my face as my head snapped to the side. My vision blurred and I could swear I had lost a tooth.

I fought against the darkness taking over just to see Mike reaching for his belt and opening his pants. Pure panic rose in me. No, no, no. Not again. Not like this. Not the same way.

The panic rose, rose, rose. I felt like I was drowning, but now I knew how to swim.

I swam through my panic, fighting it every inch of the way, and acted.

Like before, I used both my legs to push Mike back. He stumbled over the coffee table, and I bolted up and to the side, to where he had thrown the pepper spray. I looked for it for five seconds, five precious seconds before Mike recovered and darted after me.

Then I found it. A rush of hope cut through me, and I picked it up and used it on him, half a second before his hands would have closed around my neck.

Mike yelled and clawed at his eyes and mouth. I kept pressing on the spray, not letting him recover. He backed up from me, and doubled over, as if he could get rid of the sting by bowing down.

But I was done here. I took a step closer and brought my knee up with all my might, first into his face—his head flew back and he stumbled again—and then to the middle of his legs.

His screams died and he fell on his knees, defeated, even if only a moment.

But a moment was all I needed. I ran to the kitchen where I had seen some duct tape on the counter and came back to where Mike was still a little disoriented. Without wasting a second, I started wrapping the tape around him.

"What the ...?" he croaked. Realizing what was happening, he started fighting me. I grabbed a picture frame from the end table and broke it into his head. That wouldn't make him unconscious, but it would make him pause long enough for me. I grabbed both his hands, pulled them behind his back, and wrapped tape around them. Then continued wrapping it all around him.

"Bitch!" he yelled once more.

Feeling dizzy, I crawled around him and next wrapped his ankles—again I had to distract him by throwing something at him, otherwise he wouldn't have stopped kicking at me. He kept on yelling obscenities, so I taped his mouth too.

I stood back on my knees and admired my work.

There was tape everywhere around him. I just hoped it would hold him while I found my cell phone and called 911 again, just in case they couldn't trace my phone call before.

The dizziness was overwhelming now, but I kept on swimming. I had to. I finally found my phone. It was broken beside the wall. I picked it up but nothing work.

"Damn it," I muttered.

Where was Evie's phone? Oh gosh, Evie. She hadn't uttered a word in the last few minutes.

"Evie?" I called, but I was distantly aware that my voice wasn't above a whisper. I wiped my nose and was surprised to find blood on my hand. Shit.

I started crawling to the kitchen, but dark spots danced in my vision and my limbs felt heavy. I knew how to swim now. I didn't want to drown. I couldn't drown. But the current was stronger and took me under.

## 43

"Can you bring that one over?" I asked.

"Sure," Magnum said.

Squinting against the sun, I pulled my baseball cap lower and leaned over the fence.

After the bachelor party last night, I couldn't sleep. I tried for hours and I just couldn't. Every second of the night, I fought the urge to go to Hilary's apartment and ask her how their bachelorette party had been. What if she had hired strippers? What if she had hooked up with one?

Paranoid, I went to Gabi's bedroom, woke her up, and asked her how it went. She threw one of her pillows and yelled at me to get out of her room. Well, I deserved that.

Still, I couldn't sleep. We had the day off—no games or practice, but I knew João Pedro wanted to go to Fresno soon to check on some polo ponies. In Brazil, our ranch bred and trained polo ponies so we never had to worry about buying them until we moved here. Unfortunately, it was easier to buy them around here than to fly them from Brazil. Leo and I were trying to convince João Pedro of expanding the ranch here and start breeding polo ponies here too.

Anyway, I called him first thing in the morning and told him I could go right away.

"Are you sure?" he asked. "You guys didn't have a big party last night?"

"It's okay. I'm fine," I assured him.

"Okay, let me call them and see if I can schedule something for today."

Ten minutes later, João Pedro called me back, saying he had been able to schedule it for that afternoon. That was too far away, but I figured I could go early and kill the time there, even if that meant I had to stop by a coffee shop and wait it out.

As it turned out, I was stuck on the interstate for well over one hour because of an accident and arrived at the ranch in Fresno only a few minutes before the appointment.

"This is Speedy," Magnum said, showing me the pony.

I went over the fence and approached them.

The pony was young. If I bought him, we would have to keep him at the ranch until he was old enough to be trained. But he looked strong and spirited. After years watching polo ponies from the time they were born to when they were shining on the field, I knew this guy would make a fine one.

We were discussing prices when my cell phone rang. A peek at the screen told me it was Leo, so I ignored the call. I could call him when I was on my way back.

But he called again. And again.

"Excuse me," I said, stepping back. "I gotta take this."

"Sure," Magnum said.

I walked a few steps farther into the field and answered the damn call. "I'm in the middle of a negotiation; it better be good."

"It's Hilary."

My heart skipped a beat. Leo's tone was grave and it chilled my veins. "What happened?"

"She's at the hospital now and—"

"At the hospital?" I shouted. I noticed Magnum and the others raising their eyebrows at me, so I walked farther away, already in the direction of where my Jeep was parked.

"Yeah, hm ..."

"Just say it, man!"

"We don't know details yet, as the police only allowed Joyce in her room so far, but apparently, she was at a friend's house when a guy broke in and assaulted them."

My step faltered. "A-assaulted?"

"Like I said, I don't know details. I'm here with Hannah and we're waiting until they let us in her room."

"But ... how is she?"

"Honestly, I don't know."

"*Merda.*" I jumped over the fence. "I'm on my way right now."

"All right. I know you're in Fresno and I know you're upset, so *por favor* be careful. The last thing we need is someone else in the hospital."

"Yeah, yeah." Behind me, Mangum and the others called for me, but I just kept running to my car. "I'll see you in a couple of hours."

## 44

"Take it easy," Hannah said, holding my arm.

"I can do it." I pushed her away and stood from the bed on my own.

"Sorry, just trying to help."

I sighed. "I know. Sorry."

I was just too stressed, too frustrated, too disappointed.

The 911 operator was able to trace the call from my cell phone, and she sent cops to Evie's place. Apparently, they arrived there moments after I fainted. The cops arrested Mike and called an ambulance, and Evie and I were sent the hospital where we were ushered to a double room and examined by doctors and interviewed by a lot of cops. I remembered having answered the same questions at least five times. Plus more times for my mother and Hannah and Bia and Gabi ... the list went on. I was so done with this day.

After many examinations and x-rays and lots of probing, the doctors said I needed to stay a little longer to get a CT scan because of the concussion, and for observation. If I didn't show any more problems, I could go home later that evening.

My mom stood from the armchair she had been lounging in and followed me to the bathroom.

"Are you sure you don't need any help?" she asked, leaning into the doorway.

"I'm sure."

I closed the door, careful not to slam it into her face, and turned to the sink. I splashed some water on my face and made the mistake of looking into the mirror.

I winced at my reflection. More pale than normal, heavy sunken eyes, and dark, red bruises all over. By the looks of it, I had just survived a war zone. Which, in a sense was true.

Besides the bruises and the concussion, I didn't have anything bad. On the other hand, Evie had a broken nose and two broken ribs. She would stay the night and, pending a family member to come pick her up, go home under supervision. As far as I knew, she didn't have anyone else.

I might have begged a little and my mother moved some mountains. She had secured a room for Evie at the women's center, where she could stay for the next month while recovering.

After using the bathroom, I washed my hands and came back to the room, with Hannah and my mom hovering over me like two shadows. They kept their hands outstretched, as if they were expecting me to fall and they wanted to catch me before I hit the floor.

Dragging my feet back to my bed, I looked at the second bed in the room. Evie was in the second bed, sleeping—probably from a mix of exhaustion and morphine. After what happened, I didn't know how she wasn't in a worse state. Thank goodness, she was resting now. She had a lot of recovering to do and sleeping was the first step.

I winced as images of the incident flashed in my mind.

"Are you okay?" Hannah asked, reaching for me.

I nodded and let her help me back into the bed. Let her mother me a little, it was better than arguing over so little.

I lay down on the bed and closed my eyes, feeling a little safer.

No, actually I felt a lot safer. Because of me.

I still couldn't believe I had taken him down by myself. That I had beaten a man that size. That I had called for help and hung on tight until the cops arrived. This evening during the cops' visits, I heard time and time again about how brave I was, and how great the self-defense classes and the pepper spray had worked out. I even heard an atta-girl once or twice.

And, as if my mind conspired against me, that brought thoughts of Gui. Maybe because he had been the one to give me the pepper spray or to take me to my first self-defense class? I didn't know. Still, I wondered where he was. I mean ... well, I knew I had told him to stay away from me, and who knew what was going on with him right now, but I thought ... I felt silly thinking that now, but I thought he cared about me. Had cared about me. At least enough to come see me.

Maybe ... maybe he had called. My phone had been smashed into the wall. Even if he had called, I would never know.

I opened my eyes and looked up at Hannah. "Can you go out and buy me a new phone?"

She stared at me, stunned. "Now?"

My mother settled back into the armchair and started reading her book again.

I shrugged. "It doesn't seem I'll be out of here any time soon, so, why not?"

Hannah glanced at our mother, and then returned her knowing eyes to me. "Leo called him as soon as we heard about it," she whispered, so our mother wouldn't hear it. "Gui was in Fresno. From what Leo told me, he is worried about you and he's driving here right now."

I nodded, not sure what to say. If my cell phone had been with me, I think I might have called him to let him know I had been strong enough, that I had been able to defend myself and Evie, and that I even used his pepper spray. Even though I should let this go, I wanted him to feel proud of me.

Which was silly and selfish. I was feeling proud of myself for being able to take care of myself, and that was enough.

Soon after, a nurse came back and gave me pills for pain. "They will make you a little sleepy. Try to rest before your next exam," she said.

As if by magic, the pill's effect was almost instant. That, or the adrenaline was finally wearing off and deep exhaustion was catching up to me. I turned to my side, hugged the pillow, and soon I was in dreamland.

# 45

GUI

WHEN I GOT TO THE HOSPITAL, EVERYONE HAD already left, except for Leo, Hannah, and Mr. and Mrs. Taylor. Since they all couldn't stay in the room with Hil, everyone else got a chance to sneak into the room at some point, say hi to her, then leave.

I found Leo and Mr. Taylor in the waiting area.

"How is she? Where is she?" I asked, approaching them.

Mr. Taylor frowned at me while Leo stood up, draped an arm around my shoulder, and steered me to the hallway.

"She's fine now," he said, his voice low, probably not to disturb the other people in the waiting area and the many other people at the hospital.

I crossed my arms and braced myself before asking. "What happened?"

So he told me.

Rage, fury, disgust, nausea, dread, and another million emotions filled me and fought for attention, asking me to react. Punch a wall, break something, vomit, scream.

However, another emotion I wasn't expecting cut through all those others.

Pride.

I was proud of Hilary for standing up for herself, for helping her friend, for saving them both.

That didn't lessen my want, my wish to be able to turn back time and be there to help her, and break every fucking bone in that guy's body.

At least now I knew why the calls I made to her while driving back to Santa Barbara went directly to voicemail—because that piece of shit broke her phone. Damn it, I could kill the guy.

I closed my eyes, inhaled deeply, and then let the air out slowly. I snapped my eyes open and looked to my cousin. "I want to see her."

"I know," Leo said, nodding. "I'll check with Hilary and her mom if you can enter. Just wait here."

As Leo turned, we saw Mrs. Taylor coming our way. She barely nodded at us, then approached her husband, and invited him to go to the cafeteria and eat something.

I lifted an eyebrow at Leo.

He shook his head. "It's your lucky day."

He took me to Hilary's room and opened the door slowly.

A pang squeezed my heart upon seeing Hilary sleeping on the hospital bed. With her hair undone and the white gown, she looked so fragile, so small, so helpless. A burning sensation itched behind my eyes.

Hannah approached us at the door. "She fell asleep not even fifteen minutes ago," she said.

"Can I come in and sit by her? At least for a little while?" I asked, hoping my eyes looked like abandoned puppy eyes.

She glanced at Leo before returning her eyes to me. Finally, she nodded. "Be careful not to wake Evangeline." She pointed to the second bed that had been concealed by the half-opened door. "She's in worse shape and needs to rest."

"Will do," I whispered.

Then, Hannah took Leo's hand and they both walked away.

Slowly, I stepped into the room and closed the door behind me.

I gasped and the burning behind my eyes increased as I approached the bed and saw the bruises on Hilary's face and neck.

Fuck.

I pulled up a chair and sat right beside her bed, from where I needed to reach over and stroke her hand, her arm, her face.

I didn't know how long had passed. I just stared at her, still wishing I could have done something to prevent this from happening, to have interfered, to have saved her, even though she had done a good job of saving herself. Still, the bruises. Fuck. I didn't think I could ever get over that.

I was swearing under my breath when Hilary stirred. Her eyes fluttered and then she was staring at me, confusion written all over her face.

"*Oi.*"

"Hey." Hilary turned her face down, letting her hair fall over her face. Over her bruises.

I lifted my hand and slowly, gently brushed the hair away from her beautiful face. Because she was beautiful, she was gorgeous, even with the red-purple marks on her skin.

"No need to hide from me." My voice broke and the tears finally won, making their way to the front of my eyes. I blinked hard, trying to stop them before she could see them.

"It's just ..." She motioned to her face, then

shook her head. With a sigh, she snaked her hand to the side of the bed and, pressing the button, lifted the head of the bed until she was in a semi-sitting position. "How long have you been here?" She sounded a little groggy, as if the pain meds were still strong in her system.

"Not long." I had wanted to do so many things, to say so many things. Now that I was here, no fucking words came to me.

I had come to make sure she was okay, to see with my own eyes, because ... because what I felt for her didn't go away, wouldn't go away, even after she told me to leave her alone, to forget her, to go on and live my life without her.

Suddenly, I felt fucking stupid for being here. Hilary had been the one to tell me to go, to leave her alone, and here I was, feeling like my heart was bursting out of my chest. And for what? To have her shut me down again?

"I ... I was worried," I confessed. "I need you to know that I never wanted something like this to happen to you, I ne—"

"It was not your fault."

"I know." I let out a long breath. "I know, but I can't help but feel like I should have been there. I should have—"

She rested her hand over mine. "It's okay, Gui.

I'm fine now." She offered a tiny smile. "Before I fell asleep, I was thinking about you."

"Really?"

"Yeah. I was thinking about telling you that the pepper spray and the self-defense came in handy after all."

I shook my head and squeezed her hand. "How I wish you would never need to use both of those things."

Sighing, she let go of my hand. "Me too. But … I'm glad I had those tools, you know?"

I nodded.

Damn, this woman. She made my heart hurt and swell with pride and with—

I gasped, realizing something that had been obvious for a while now, but I had been too blind to see.

"Hil, I—"

The door opened and a nurse came in. "Hi, Miss Taylor." She smiled warmly at the girl in the bed. "I came to take you to your CT scan."

"Oh, okay." Hilary looked at me. "Hm, thanks for stopping by." With the nurse's help, Hilary stood from the bed.

"Y-you're welcome," I whispered.

Fifteen seconds later, Hilary was out of the room and I was left alone with too many feelings and thoughts. Once more, the urge to punch the wall hit me hard and fast. The girl on the second bed moaned and stirred, and that was the only reason why I didn't.

I scurried out of the room.

# 46

SOMETIMES I THOUGHT MY MOTHER COULD MOVE more than mountains. Entire islands maybe. Well, it was a better way of thinking than acknowledging that she had money to buy everything and everyone.

After leaving the hospital on Sunday evening, my parents escorted me to their house—no way they were leaving me alone at my apartment in such a state. Even Hannah spent the night at my parents' house with us.

Hannah's and Leo's wedding was next Saturday, so we had scheduled a three-day visit to a local, famous spa for all the girls right before the wedding. But with my bruises—the ones on my body and the ones in my soul—my mother called the spa and was able to squeeze Hannah and me earlier.

They both had planned everything while I rested in my old bedroom on Monday morning. Hannah even went to my apartment and packed a bag for me. Then, right before noon, she pushed me in her car and we were off to the spa.

Just like that.

Note: They didn't even ask me if I wanted to go.

On the drive there, Hannah made her best to convince me it was for the best. Even though my mind was quieter and more at peace than it had been in three years, my body had been abused and I needed time to relax and heal before the wedding.

It seemed crazy that I was feeling better about myself after such a tragic event, but it was true. I had talked to Dr. Walker this morning on the phone, and she told me that was natural.

"I'm very proud of you," she said. "I'm sure you'll believe me now when I tell you that you'll feel whole again soon."

I did believe her now. I did feel it now.

We checked into the spa and, with a big smile, Hannah hooked her arm with mine. "Now, let's see what we'll do first!"

THE BIG DAY WAS HERE.

Five days at the spa had been a little too much, but it was exactly what I needed. I had great bonding time with my sister, I relaxed, I was taken care of, I ate and slept well, and I knew I was safe. Nobody could get to me here. Then Bia, Gabi, and Iris arrived, and we all bonded a little more. At first, they were all walking on eggshells around me, but then, I don't know, I felt different. It was as if an old part of me had broken loose from the walls I had erected around me long ago—a fun part, a more relaxed and so-cial part. I still wasn't the old sixteen-year-old Hi-lary—I guess I never would be again, after all, I had grown up—but I wasn't so scared and re-served anymore.

On the last day, Bia hugged me and said she was so glad to see this new side of me. Gabi seemed excited about this new development in my personality too.

As for me, I was still processing all that had happened these past few days. Dr. Walker stopped by twice during the week—I bet my mother was paying for these overpriced exclusive clinics—and we talked for a while. She also mentioned I looked lighter, and by our second meeting, I was smiling more on my own.

I guess knowing I wasn't defenseless against a 250-pound man helped defeat most of my fears.

Now I just had one more fear on my list to scratch off, and I was coming up with a plan for it that included the wedding.

My mother had designated two of the guest bedrooms on the east side of the house for the guys to get ready, while Hannah, the girls, and I were camped in Hannah's and my bedroom on the west side of the house.

Gabi zipped up my dress and looked at me in the mirror over my shoulder.

"You look beautiful," she said.

I smiled. Yeah, I guess I could say I did look nice. I still didn't like the yellow Hannah had chosen for our dresses—it didn't go well with my fair skin and blond hair—but I like the dress and accessories enough to compensate for it. Besides, I liked my sister, and if this was what she wanted for her big day, that was how she was going to have it.

The yellow of my dress was a different tone than the other girls. It was brighter, more open, while the girls had a soft yellow. My dress was strapless with a tight bodice encrusted with little fake diamonds and a flowy skirt that opened up from the hips. A rip on the right side came up to almost thigh-high, showing off a little skin. Fake diamonds adorned the hem of the skirt—and the rip. A heavy, real diamond bracelet sat on my left wrist, and I had thin but long diamond earrings. My hair was pulled up in a tight ponytail decorated with several thin braids, but a few strands were pulled on the front, forming side-swept bangs. Fake diamonds spread through the length of my hair completed the look. I had designed it all, so it was a given I liked it, but oh, I really liked it.

"Thanks," I said, taking a step to the side so she could be in the mirror too. "And you too."

It was incredible how all the Fernandeses looked amazing; they all had come from a top-model-making tree or something. That was the only explanation. And Gabi was no exception. With her long, wavy dark hair, bright blue eyes, and fair skin, she had the face of a fierce angel. Like me, soon she would be twenty, and I found it hard that no guy had snatched her up yet.

She twirled and the skirt of her dress flared up. "Thanks. This dress is perfect."

This was Hannah's and Leo's day, and as maid of honor, I had to make sure *everything* was perfect.

Just like Hannah.

Still smiling, I turned around and looked at my sister. She was in front of the other mirror, applying lip gloss on her lips for the hundredth time —her hands shook slightly.

"You're gonna use up all that lip gloss today," I joked.

She sighed and offered me a small, nervous smile. "I know!"

Gosh, if someday I got married, I hoped I looked half as great as she did. Her dress was also strapless, but a custom lace fabric covered the bodice, coming up to her neck. It was sleeveless, but she wore gloves from the middle of her hands to her elbows with the same lace fabric. And the skirt was made of ruffled lace and silk juxtaposed, all with tiny, fake diamonds, forming a rain pattern that got heavier at the bottom. Her hair was pulled up in an intricate bun with several specifically placed loose strands here and there, and a real diamond tiara—a gift from our parents.

She looked every bit like a princess. A real princess living her fairy tale. Her happily ever after.

Hannah smiled at me. "What?"

"You ... you look amazing."

Her smile widened. "Half of this—" She gestured to herself. "—is all your doing. Thanks, by the way, for the most gorgeous wedding dress I have ever seen."

I shrugged, a little embarrassed and a lot proud of the compliment.

A few seconds later, my mother entered the bedroom. "Charles just told me the boys are all ready and waiting for us. They want to know if you're ready too."

We all looked around. Everyone seemed ready.

"We're ready," Hannah said.

"All right," my mother said. "I'll tell Leo that he can go, then."

Hannah smiled faded. "Oh my God," she whispered.

My mother grabbed her hand, worried. "What?"

"It's happening," Hannah muttered. "Oh my God, it's really happening."

We all laughed.

"Yes, it is." My mother squeezed her hand. "And it's going to be perfect. See you out there." She kissed my sister on the cheek and, after smiling at the rest of us, she walked out the bedroom.

I stepped into my mother's place and took Hannah's hand. "Come on."

As a group, the girls and I went down the stairs —everyone was forbidden to enter the house for now. The only ones allowed were my parents, Leo's parents, the guys, and us. Even so, my parents and Leo's parents were being watchful so Leo and Hannah wouldn't cross paths before the actual wedding.

Hannah stayed behind with my father in the living room, while the rest of us went to meet the guys in the solarium, from where we all would exit to the backyard, where the guests were waiting.

The guys wolf-whistled when we entered and the couples reunited. No way to avoid him now. Not that I wanted to.

I sighed. I had seen him before in a tuxedo—it had been an unfinished one, but still it looked pretty good. Now he looked way better. It was easy to see he had gotten a haircut—though not too short—and he had applied a little gel or mousse, though I guess only I could tell the difference from his usual super messy style to this on-purpose messy style, since I was probably the only one who had paid that much attention to his hair.

And the tux ... it was sin on him.

"You look beautiful," Gui said, approaching me. He was serious, his eyes intent, shining with too many unsaid words. "You are beautiful."

My cheeks warmed. "Thanks. You don't look too bad either."

"I guess I can blame the designer." One corner of his lips tugged up. "She's a pretty great fashion designer, you know."

I shook my head, but I couldn't help the small grin that popped onto my lips.

His eyes ... his impossibly blue eyes were killing me. I could read so much in them—his worry, his concern, his caring. But was it enough? Was it as much as I wanted it to be? If it weren't, then I would make a fool of myself.

My mother and father entered the solarium, followed by João Pedro. Because of their Brazilian background, we tried to mix the ceremony, make it as Brazilian and American as we could. For that, Leo was already outside with his mother, Agnes, waiting for my mother's signal.

"Everyone ready?" my mother asked. We all nodded. "Okay, then. See you all outside."

She and João Pedro exited to the backyard. My mother signaled the musicians, and they started playing a song Leo and Hannah had selected. Leo and his mother walked through the arch on the white wall erected between the house and the backyard. Then my mother went with his father.

Then it was time for us.

Gui offered me his arm. "Ready?"

I smiled and took his arm.

Together, we walked down the aisle followed by Ri and Gabi, Pedro and Iris, and Bia and Garrett. After we all took our places at the altar, we waited. Five nerve-racking minutes until the musicians started playing the nuptial march.

Like a princess, Hannah emerged from the arch with our father.

There were exclamations all around, but I was paying attention to Leo. His entire face brightened; his smile was the widest and purest I had ever seen. Happiness filled my core. Happiness for my sister.

The wedding proceeded as planned.

After Hannah and Leo were married, the guests were guided deeper into our backyard where the tables, chairs, and buffet tables had been set around a large wooden dance floor and stage, all under fancy gazebos.

We made toasts, a few of us said a few words—me, Gui, Bia, João Pedro, Megan—we ate the food, and the real party began. My mother had bought enough food and drinks and paid waitresses and the band well enough to last all night long. We wouldn't leave this shindig before it was morning again.

Hannah and Leo had opened the dance floor with a waltz. Our parents followed them, and then the other couples of the family joined them. Gabi, Gui, and I were the only ones left. Finally, Gui's mother—whom I finally got to meet—insisted Gui took Gabi dancing. And I stayed behind alone.

I sat at our table, happy for Hannah and Leo and my family, but suddenly feeling alone at this amazing party. Which was ridiculous. I shouldn't feel lonely just because I didn't have a partner to dance with.

In fact, I wouldn't allow myself to feel embarrassed, ashamed, or lonely. No. I was done with all that. It didn't matter if I had anyone to dance with. I could mingle and talk to my mother's friends, to Hannah's friends. I bet they all would be happy to say hi to me, to learn more about the details of the party and the dresses. I had been getting questions about the dresses and tuxes all evening.

As for my plan, it wasn't going as I had imagined, but there was still time. The night was young.

I stood and walked three steps before halting again.

"You look stunning," Reese said, standing in my way.

"Thanks," I said.

He looked around. "This all looks great. The food was delicious too. I heard you did all this?"

"Not alone."

"Congratulations."

"Thanks."

He looked to his feet, then turned worried eyes at me. "I heard what happened last weekend. I'm sorry about that. How are you feeling?"

This was the worst part of it all. Of course, most people here had heard about what happened last weekend. How could I have forgotten that? So all these people weren't staring at me because I looked pretty, or because they were impressed with my designs or the party organization. They were staring at me because, in their minds, I was even more damaged than before.

I wouldn't let that stop me from having a good time. Yes, I had gone through some bad patches, through some terribly damaging events, and I had survived. I had made it. And even though these events hurt me, I had grown from them, and I was proud of that.

I smiled. "I'm fine, actually."

Reese leaned closer. "Is it true you beat up a three-hundred-pound man?"

The rumors ... people already had made Mike bigger than he was. "Yes, I did."

"That's ..." He cleared his throat. "I'm sorry you had to go through that, but I'm glad you were able to defend yourself and your friend. Good for you!"

I knew he meant every word and that made me hopeful that other people would see it that way too. "Thanks."

"So, hm ..." Reese ran his hand through his hair. "I was wondering if—"

"Excuse me," Gui said, appearing out of nowhere and stepping between Reese and me. He stared at me with such intensity, my knees wobbled.

"Hey!" Reese protested, coming to stand beside Gui.

Ignoring him, Gui extended one hand to me. "Dance with me."

I didn't think twice. I simply slid my hand into his and let him guide me to the dance floor. As I walked by Reese, I mouthed, "I'm sorry." I was sorry for leaving him hanging like that when I knew he was about to ask me to dance too. But I wasn't sorry Gui had asked first.

In the middle of the dance floor, Gui stopped and turned to me. He placed his hands on my waist and pulled me close, all the while looking straight through me. I didn't break the stare as I slid my hands up his arms and rested them on his shoulders.

The song was a slow, romantic ballad. And suddenly my plan was back on track—though with a few modifications.

"I know I said it before, but you are especially beautiful today." His voice was low and careful, a gentle caress to my ego.

"Thank you." I tilted my head to the side and suppressed a smile. "So ... why didn't you let Reese ask me to dance?"

"Oh. I'm busted. Damn," he joked, a small grin illuminating his handsome face. "I wasn't sure if he had already asked or not. Once I saw him talking to you, I don't know. Something hit me hard. Right here." He briefly let go of my waist to tap his chest, right above his heart. My breath caught. "I just knew I couldn't let you dance with him, and I knew it was just a matter of time until he asked, and you wouldn't say no, because you're polite like that."

"I hope Gabi wasn't mad about being dumped on the dance floor."

He chuckled. "Nah, she was glad to be rid of me. I know she wants to go around the party and see if she can find a guy to flirt with."

"She's not like that!"

"I know. I'm just kidding." He frowned. "But you know, sometimes I wonder if she would look for a guy, an American guy, and get hitched just so she would have an excuse to stay here."

"She wouldn't do that."

"Wouldn't she? She wants to come live here so badly."

"I know, but she wouldn't go so low as to get married to any guy just to stay here. I know that if it's really meant to be, she'll find another way to make that happen."

Gui raised an eyebrow. "Are you talking about Gabi right now?"

"Maybe, maybe not."

His expression grew serious again, and his stare turned concerned. He lifted one hand and caressed the cheek where I had a fading bruise hidden under pounds of makeup. "I'm sorry you had to go through something like that again." His fingertips lingered on my face for three more seconds, and then he set his hand back on my waist. "But I'm very proud of you."

"I'm proud of me too," I whispered.

The song changed from one corny romantic ballad to another, and the tension grew thick between us. I was barely aware of other couples dancing around us, because in my world, there was only Gui and me. Now, if only I could make sure he still felt that way too.

All of a sudden, he exhaled and let out, "Okay, I wasn't able to tell you all I wanted to last Sunday. I need to tell you. I was out of my mind when Leo called me. I was so pissed that, of all days, I decided to go to Fresno that particular day. I wanted to get to you as fast as I could. I never wished for a teleportation device as much as I did while I was driving back here. I wanted to be by your side. I wanted to make sure you were okay, see you with my own eyes, because only hearing Leo tell me on the phone what was going on was killing me. Actually, I wanted to have a time travel machine, so I would be with you when you went to your friend's house and I would have kicked that bastard's ass to the moon and back." He raised his hand to my face again and placed two fingers on the hidden bruise. "I would kill him for laying a hand on you. I'm so sorry for not being there for you."

I placed my hand over his. "Don't apologize. There was nothing you could do. And, unfortunately, I'm convinced that was something I had to go through. By myself. Alone. I had to face him because if I didn't, I would never know what I was capable of, how strong I am, and how I can take care of myself if the need ever arises."

"I hope the need never arises again." He sighed. "If only you gave me a chance, I would take good care of you."

That was all I needed to hear.

With a smile, I knotted my arms around his neck, tried to stand on tiptoes—hard with four-inch heels—and raised my face, angling it just right.

"Are you sure about that?" I asked, holding my breath.

"I was never this sure about anything else in my entire life."

I raised an eyebrow. "Even polo?"

He chuckled. "Even polo."

I was okay with that. Screw a grand gesture; besides, this was Hannah's big day. I would already steal her spotlight enough with a little gesture. Still smiling, I tugged on his neck, so he would know exactly what I wanted.

His eyes widened for a millisecond, and then he leaned down and met me halfway. His lips claimed mine, first slow and soft, as if he was afraid of scaring me away. But I wasn't scared any-more. I parted my lips and increased the intensity of the kiss, showing him exactly what I wanted. Who I wanted. His arms wound around my waist, and he pulled my body flush with his. A sigh escaped my throat as my delicate figure molded to his hard frame.

Someone cleared his throat beside us.

We broke the kiss, but we didn't spring apart, as we looked to the source of the noise. It was Leo, watching us with a big smile. Hannah was with him, of course, and she winked at us.

"Not fair," she said, her tone teasing. "It's my big day, but everyone will be talking about you two from now on."

I let myself look around. Sure enough, everyone was watching us. Everyone. My parents had wide eyes, Gabi jumped up and down as if her day had been made, Bia shook her head with a wicked smiled, Pedro and Ri gave us the thumbs up, and Reese stared at us with disappointment. And Gui's parents ... well, I wasn't sure what the expression on their faces meant, but I hoped it meant they were willing to meet me.

My cheeks extremely hot, I hid my face in Gui's chest. He chuckled and kissed the top of my head. His arms tightened around me.

"I've got you," he whispered in my ear. "You're okay, Hil. You're fine now."

His words rang true. I used to answer with I'll be fine. For the first time in so long, I felt strong enough to answer, "I am fine," and that brought me an amount of pleasure and pride that I couldn't even begin to describe.

I stopped hiding in Gui's chest—even though he had a nice chest and I wanted to hide there every day—and raised my head high. I was proud of me, I was proud of Gui, and I was most certainly proud of us.

I stared him in the eye and smiled. "I really am fine." Once more, I wound my arms around his neck, and with a grin, he leaned down and kissed me again.

And this time when our family and friends cheered, we didn't stop.

# 47

## HILARY

After spending the Sunday tucked in with Gui at my apartment—but he went back to his own apartment for the night—Gui took me to Los Angeles the next morning. I was a bundle of nerves on the passenger side of his Jeep, alternating between chewing my nails, chewing my bottom lip, or wringing the skirt of my dress.

Gui reached over and rested his right hand over mine, stilling my compulsive movements. "It'll be all right, Hil. You got this."

Did I?

I hadn't touched this project in so long and had to scurry to finish it this past couple of days—and yesterday, when Gui insisted on seeing the project, I didn't let him. All the time, my laptop had been turned away from him while I put my presentation together.

Now we were here, with three of my design professors, plus the professor that got me this chance and two T.A.s, all in the first row of the auditorium-like classroom. Gui had stayed in the back, so he wouldn't disrupt the presentation, and my focus, in any way.

I stood in front of them all, with the big, white screen at my back.

I started the PowerPoint and the first thing that popped on the screen was a video from YouTube —a video showing a group dancing one of the dances from Gui's state in Brazil.

I tried not to, but I couldn't help myself. I glanced at him and saw the surprise stamped on his face.

Then I launched into my rehearsed text, telling the professors about Rio Grande do Sul and the many dances only performed there. I told them about my brother-in-law's family, that they had been living here for over three years now and that I learned a lot of things about their culture. I showed them pictures of the different food and the different drinks, I played a few seconds of different songs, and I showed them a second video of the dancing.

"And that was my true inspiration for this project," I said, changing the slide. The main two of my designs for this project popped on the screen. It was a dress like the *prendas* wore for the dances, and also the *bombacha* and shirt the men wore. I picked up five A3-sized papers, reinforced by thick cardboard, and handed them to my professors. They looked at the drawings on the papers, probably giving attention to every little detail, every little element that composed the clothes.

Then, to their surprise, I opened my tote and pulled out the *prenda's* dress. I stepped into it and pulled it over my clothes. I had made the dress myself at Fallon White's studio—though I had used my own fabric.

In the back, Gui watched me with a hand over his mouth.

I took a long breath. "Now, for the best part of this presentation." I beckoned for Gui to come down the stairs. He froze for two seconds, and then rushed down.

"What are you doing?" he whispered, as he joined me in the spotlight.

From my tote, I pulled out a *gaúcho* hat I had gotten from Leo and a red silk scarf, and put them on Gui. "Just ... dance with me," I whispered back.

I changed the slide and a new song filled the speakers in the room. And Gui and I danced one of the many *dança folclórica* from his home state, the only one he had tried to teach me. I just hoped I still remember it.

I had cut the song so it only went on for a minute—not too long, but not too short either.

When the song was over, I turned to my professors and bowed. Gui lowered his head in an attempt of a bow, then looked at me with a now-what kind of face.

I smiled and shrugged.

The sound of applause filled the room, and I was surprised to see my professors standing up, applauding some more, and nodding.

"Well done, Miss Taylor," one of them said with a big smile. "Very well done!"

They all congratulated me, wished me well, and by the end, I left the classroom almost certain I had passed this class. Finally.

Gui reached for my hand as soon as we walked out of the classroom and squeezed it hard. "I had no idea that that ..." He shook his head in disbelief. "When did you start this project?"

"The night you first told me about the *invernada* thing."

His eyes widened. "That was a couple of months ago."

"Yup." I pulled him around a corner, guiding him through the long hallways of the building.

"Why? Why choose that as your theme for this project?"

"Because ... it has a story *and* history, which was the requirement for this project, but most importantly, because it has a meaning. These dances, the clothing, these songs, the food, the drink ... they all mean so much to *gaúchos*. To your family. To you." I looked at him pointedly. "Because it means a lot to you."

I gasped as Gui let go of my hand and pushed me back, pressing me against a wall. Without warning, his mouth fell on mine, and his hands slid around my waist. He kissed me with fervor and I felt myself heating, burning. Thank goodness classes hadn't started back and the hallways were still empty.

Gui brushed his lips down my jaw and whispered in my ear, "You're something else, did you know that?"

I wound my arms around his neck. "If you're going to kiss me like that every time you tell me that, then no, I didn't know. You can try saying that again."

He chuckled and returned his mouth to mine. He brushed his lips on mine delicately before pulling back and staring into my eyes. "You're something else, Hilary." Then his mouth crashed on mine again.

# SIX MONTHS LATER

## GUI

IF THIS WASN'T AN EMERGENCY, I WOULD KILL LEO.

I was leaving the building, getting into my car to go surprise Hilary in L.A., when Leo called, saying there was an emergency at Hannah's ranch and I had to go right now. Damn, didn't he know it was Valentine's Day? My first one with an actual girlfriend? And that she had classes until late this evening and couldn't come to Santa Barbara so I was going down there to see her?

I cursed some more as I sped down the road, hoping that the extra acceleration would help get me to the ranch fast, so I could help with whatever emergency it was, and then go to L.A. equally fast.

I turned my Jeep onto the ranch's entry road and almost hit the brakes.

"What the ...?"

Leo's SUV wasn't here, nor was Hannah's car. But Hilary's car was here, parked right in front of the stables. What was she doing here?

I slowed down and parked my car beside hers. As I exited the Jeep, I called for her, but nobody answered. I grabbed my phone from my pocket and called her number, but she didn't answer.

Wary, I walked into the stables.

"Hilary?" I called once more and got no response.

A red piece of paper taped to a closed stall door caught my attention. Approaching it, I saw the red paper was cut in the shape of a heart. A smile tugged in my lips when I saw Hilary's delicate handwriting.

*Gui,*

*Take your horse and follow the red path.*

*Love, Hil*

My horse? The red path? What the hell?

Shaking my head, I opened the top part of the stall and saw my horse was right there—tacked and ready to go.

"What are you doing here, Pampa?"

He neighed as I opened the lower part of the door. I grabbed his reins and guided him from the stables. Instantly, I saw a red ribbon tied to one of the gates on the arena. Chuckling, I hopped on my horse and followed the trail.

There were ribbons tied to trees and sometimes roses on the grass—and I followed it all for about twenty minutes, until I saw her down in a small vale, a few yards from the lake.

Man ...

A heavy picnic blanket was spread on the grass, a large picnic basket in one corner, and a round outdoor fireplace in another—the fire high and bright. Belle was tied to a tree a few yards back, and Hilary had her back to me. She was wearing the dark green cowboy boots I had given her for Christmas and jeans. A heavy blanket wrapped around her shoulders, and her beautiful, blond hair moved with the soft breeze.

Pampa neighed and Hilary turned. Her eyes found mine and she smiled. And I smiled too, my heart squeezing in my chest. She was so fucking beautiful it hurt.

Never in my life had I thought I could feel about a woman the way I felt about her. Never ever. I was happy for Leo and Pedro when they found their matches, and even Bia had found Garrett, but I wasn't sure how they could tie themselves to someone like that. Until now. Until feeling as I did at this moment.

There were so many plans in my mind for her and me, plans I had never thought of before I had met her, before she had bewitched me.

My first plan had been to surprise her in L.A. tonight, and give her something that meant a lot to me, but she had beaten me to it and surprised me instead.

I guided Pampa to the tree, hopped off, and tied him with Belle. My chest hurting, I ran to Hilary and only stopped running when she was in my arms. I bumped into her, wound my arms around me, pressed my mouth to hers, and took her to the ground, being careful so we wouldn't fall too hard. Never breaking the kiss, I deposited her on the blanket on the ground and lay over her, fitting my body to hers. She moaned when I pressed my hips on hers, which only made my chest hurt more. I had missed her. I had seen her a few days ago, but I had missed her. I always missed her, even after only an hour being away.

She wrapped her legs around my waist and shifted under me, pressing her pelvis on my hard on. Damn, this girl drove me crazy. I slid my lips down her jaw and down her neck.

She inhaled sharply. "Hi."

"Hi," I whispered, never taking my mouth from her delicious skin.

She snaked one hand under my shirt, tracing the plains in my abdomen. I groaned, pressing my face into her neck.

"Surprise," she half-whispered, half-giggled.

I lifted my upper body and supported my weight on my elbows, so I could look into her beautiful eyes. "I was going to L.A. to surprise you."

She shrugged. "Sorry?"

"No need to be sorry. This looks pretty good." It looked perfect. Much better than me showing up at her dorm room and inviting her to dinner at a crowded restaurant. I had to work on my romanticizing skills.

She looked at the fireplace. "I think I overdid it a little."

"No, you didn't. This is perfect," I confessed. I ran a finger down her neck, into the cleavage of her thin, white sweater. "You're perfect." I contoured the curve of her breast and her breath hitched. I loved hearing these little sounds she made.

Since we admitted our feelings and outed our relationship to everyone at Leo's and Hannah's wedding, we hadn't done much more than kissing. Okay, that was a fucking lie. Even though it killed me not to go all the way with her, we took it slow.

Hilary had never gone to third base before and I didn't want to rush her, not after everything she had gone through. We advanced, very little, very patiently. In the past six months, we started with heavy make out, then some heavy touching. Three months ago, I explored a good part of her body, having her naked, except for thin panties, and I happily put my mouth everywhere she'd let me. Two months ago, I had made her come just by touching her through her panties. And a month ago, she had slipped her hand under my pants and jacked me off. Her moves were a little clumsy and unsure but the feeling of her hand on me was enough to have me bursting with desire, with need. It had been torture—pure, fucking torture—not to take her right then. But I knew, I just knew she hadn't been ready. And I liked her too much, way too much, to push her.

Besides all the physical stuff, I got to know the real Hilary, the one that had been hidden behind a wall for over three years. She smiled more, she laughed more, and she even told jokes. She loved horses and we went riding together often. She came to all of my matches—except one or two when it was right during a final exam or something serious—and she learned all the game rules and supported me like no one else ever had. We went out with our family and friends, and I learned the girl could freaking dance and drive me crazy with a shift of her hips. She was a free, wild spirit with a kind heart and a beautiful soul. And she was all mine.

Hilary arched her back to my touch, giving me more access to her cleavage.

I withdrew my hand. "Hil?"

Pushing me back until I was sitting on my heels, Hilary sat up. Looking into my eyes, she pulled her sweater over her head and threw it somewhere behind us. Next, she reached around her back and unclasped her bra.

My throat went dry. "Hil?"

She didn't pull her bra off. "I'm ready," she whispered. I could see her shoulders shaking slightly, but the resolve in her eyes was unmistakable. "I'm ready," she repeated.

"I ..." I ran a hand through my hair. "Don't shit with me."

She reached for my T-shirt. "I'm not shitting with you."

"Hil ..."

"What?"

"I ... I can't ... I don't want you to think you're ready and regret it five seconds later."

She cupped my face and looked into my eyes.

"Gui, I won't regret it. You know why?" Holding my breath, I shook my head. "Because I love you."

I didn't waste one second. I jumped on her, took her mouth into mine, pressed my body into her, slipped my hands under her bra, and clasped her breasts. She moaned as I pinched her nipples before sliding down and closing my mouth over her right breast. She gasped as I lapped my tongue on her hard nipple and slid my hand down her stomach. Very, very slowly, I unbuttoned her jeans. I took minutes, giving every chance for her to back off, to say no, but she didn't.

I stopped, breaking the kiss, and pulled away enough to look into her eyes. "You gotta tell me ... if you give up, if you change your mind, it's okay. I'm okay with that. Just say the word and I'll stop."

She lifted her head and brushed her lips on mine. "Don't stop," she whispered.

I swallowed hard. I was probably more fucking nervous than she was. But this was a big deal. It was her first time—after all she had been through—and she was sharing it with me. Damn, a mix of happiness and pride and concern filled my chest. I wanted her all for myself forever. I just hoped she wanted that too.

It was now or never.

I reached into the back pocket of my jeans and

pulled out a slim, black velvet box and offered it to her.

Her face paled and her eyes went wide. "What …"

"Just opened it," I said.

With trembling hands, she took the box from me and opened it. She let out a sigh of relief and I almost laughed. "Your apartment keys," she said with a smile. "For a second there, I thought you were proposing."

Well, she didn't know that, but I thought about proposing a lot. I just knew she needed more time for that and we had all the time in the world.

"You're coming back to Santa Barbara this summer for the internship with Fallon White again, so I thought, instead of renting an apartment, you could move in with me." Pedro was more at Iris's place than anywhere else. That apartment was practically all mine, and I wanted to share it with her.

"M-move in?"

"Yeah." I rubbed the back of my neck. "You come up here every weekend and officially stay at your parents, though you sleep at least one night at my apartment. I thought we could make that a permanent thing." She stared at the key and I started getting anxious. Her parents were still a little wary of me. I wasn't sure why. Maybe because another one of their daughters was dating a Fernandes and that was just weird. Well, at least they weren't giving me too hard of a time about that. But they could be talking to her about it, trying to make up her mind about ditching me. "So?"

Hilary threw her arms around my neck and kissed me hard, long, and deep. She pulled me down until I was lying over her again.

"Yes," she whispered between kisses. "I'll move in with you."

My turn to kiss her hard and long and deep. I continued where we left off minutes ago—my hand sliding under her unbuttoned jeans pants, and she squirming under my touch. I pushed past her panties and touched her right there. She gasped and went still when I slipped one finger inside her. Damn, she was so fucking wet! I groaned and kissed her even harder. Her lips molded to mine, and her tongue took as much as it gave. I moved my finger, sliding in and out, and soon Hilary was panting, moving her hips to match my hand.

"Do you like this?" I asked against her mouth. She nodded and I slid a second finger inside her. She gasped again, but this time instead of freezing, she grabbed my shoulders and held on while she rode my hand. Her half-closed eyes, her parted mouth, and her erratic breathing were the sexiest thing I had ever seen in my life. I increased the speed and pressed my thumb on her clit. She moaned and dug her nails on my arms. She could draw blood if she wanted; right now, I didn't care.

"Please," she gasped.

"Please what?" I asked, loving this game.

"Please ..."

Her sultry voice, it was torture. Without stopping moving my fingers, I leaned on my free arm, and then pulled her bra from her arms and threw it aside. Adjusting myself on top of her, I took one of her breasts in my mouth and sucked. Hard. She knotted her hands in my hair and cried. I lapped my tongue on her hard nipple and increased the pressure of my thumb on her clit. She cried again and then went still for two seconds before breaking out in little tremors. Slowly, I removed my hand from under her panties and slid my lips up her chest and neck until I was looking into her eyes.

Then I just had to take a minute to appreciate the view. She looked so gorgeous and wild and carefree lying under me, with her breasts bare, and her blond hair fanned around her beautiful face. Her expression was pure bliss, but her green eyes sparkled, attentive. My heart squeezed. This ... this perfection was mine. Just mine. It was too much.

"Are you going to stare at me, or are you going to make love to me?"

Man, I almost lost it. Instead, I pulled her pants and panties off, then my pants and boxers, and threw one of the blankets over us.

I positioned myself over her, just right, and she grasped my hips, pulling me to her. I held on, letting her feel my hard on before entering her. She gasped as my erection rubbed on her clit.

"If I hurt you, if you want me to stop, please just say the word and I'll stop."

She cocked her head at me, a mischievous glint in her eyes. "I thought we went over this already. Don't stop." She tugged hard at me and I groaned.

Slowly, I pressed my erection into her entrance. "By the way," I said, a little out of breath. "I love you too."

I slid inside her. Eyes closed, she half-gasped and half-moaned, and went still when I had buried myself in her. Damn, she was so fucking wet, so fucking tight. I wanted to move, to thrust against her, but I fought against myself and held still, giving her time to get used to me.

"Are you okay?" I asked.

She nodded. "Just give me a minute."

"Hil, look at me." Slowly, she opened her eyes and stared into mine. "Are you okay?"

"I am," she whispered, her voice breaking.

"Why are you almost crying?"

"Because ..." She inhaled deeply. "Because there were moments in the past when I didn't think I would ever scratch the last item off my fear list."

"What is the last item?"

"To fall in love, and to give myself, body and soul, to the guy who loved me too."

I smiled, feeling proud I was that guy. "I do love you, you know. So very much. Sorry it took me so long to tell you that."

A tear fell from her eyes and I licked it, and then slid my lips over her cheek until I closed my mouth on hers. She laughed before molding her lips to mine and kissing me slow and deep.

She wiggled her hips, taking me deeper, and then I lost it. Groaning, I started moving. With every ounce of my being, I tried to be gentle and slow, but it was too damn hard. She felt so perfect against me, her skin smelling so sweet and feeling so hot, her sounds so inciting, so addicting. After a few moments, I had to push harder, drive deeper. And she seemed to be okay with it. Well, judging by her moans and the way she dug her nails on my hips, pulling me to her, I would say she was more than okay with it.

It had been so long since I had had sex, and even though I had jerked off a few times in the last few months—always thinking of Hilary and this moment with her—it wasn't the same. Besides, this wasn't having sex. This was making love. It was so much better, and because of that, I wouldn't last long.

"Hil, I ..." I tried to warn her, so she wouldn't be disappointed with me.

"What?" she asked breathlessly. She captured the tip of my ear in her teeth and flicked her tongue on my skin, singeing me down my neck. Cursing, I drove deep and hard one, two, three more times, and she let out a sexy little moan each time. That was my undoing.

My feelings, my sensations, everything exploded inside me and around me as I came—the hardest and most divine climax I had ever had. Gripping her hips, I buried my face on her neck, and she wound her arms and legs around me as my body quivered over hers.

Slowly, the trembles faded, and I propped myself up on one elbow to look into her eyes.

"Are you okay?" I asked.

She was smiling. "I'm perfect."

That was true. I smiled back at her and ran my fingers along the side of her face, brushing aside a few strands of her hair. "I meant it. You know, before." I swallowed. "*Eu te amo.*"

"*Eu também te amo,*" she answered in Portuguese.

I raised an eyebrow. "Did you practice that?"

"Maybe."

Damn, Hilary had planned this entire evening to the millisecond. Leo's urgent call, bringing my horse here, the red path, the picnic blanket, and fireplace, and the food we still hadn't touched, being ready for me, and even saying she loved me in Portuguese. She was too good for me, too perfect, too everything. I didn't deserve her, but I sure as hell would try to because I was too damn crazy about her.

I brushed a slow, sensual kiss on her lips, and incredible or not, my body started answering hers already. Oh, if she let me, we would have a second round, but while I recovered, we could do something else.

"So, what do you got over there?" I jerked my chin to the picnic basket.

"Besides the lingerie I was planning on wearing for the second round?"

I laughed out loud. "*Meu Deus*, you're perfect." I buried my face on her neck again, enjoying snuggling with her.

She ran her hand through my hair. "No, but I'm hoping I'll be perfect enough for you."

"You already are, Hil. Too damn perfect for me."

---

Want to read more books in the Breaking world? Get *Breaking Down*, Gabi's book, now!

# THANK YOU

Thank you for reading *Breaking Through*!
  Reviews are very important for authors. If you liked my book, please consider leaving a review on your favorite retailer and/or on goodreads, please!

Get the next book on the series, *Breaking Down*!

To find out about more books, visit www. julianahaygert.com/books

.   .   .

Don't forget to sign up for my Newsletter to find out about new releases, cover reveals, give-aways, and more!

If you want to see exclusive teasers, help me decide on covers, read excerpts, talk about books, etc, join my reader group on Facebook: Juliana's Club!

# ABOUT THE AUTHOR

While USA Today Bestselling Author Juliana Haygert dreams of being Wonder Woman, Buffy, or a blood elf shadow priest, she settles for the less exciting—but equally gratifying—life as a wife, a mother, and an author. She resides in North Carolina and spends her days writing about kick-ass heroines and the heroes who drive them crazy.

Subscribe to her mailing list to receive emails of announcement, events, and other fun stuff related to her writing and her books: www.bit.ly/JuHNL

*For more information:*
www.julianahaygert.com

facebook.com/julianahaygert

twitter.com/juliana_haygert

instagram.com/juliana.haygert

goodreads.com/juliana_haygert

pinterest.com/julianahaygert

bookbub.com/authors/juliana-haygert

# ALSO BY JULIANA HAYGERT

To find links and more info, go to:

www.julianahaygert.com/books/

*Shorts*

Into the Darkest Fire

Tested

*Standalones*

Daughter of Darkness

*Rite World: Blackthorn Hunters Academy*

The Demon Kiss (Book 1)

The Hunter Secret (Book 2)

The Soul Bond (Book 3)

The Shadow Trials (Book 4)

The Infernal Curse (Book 5)

*Rite World*

The Vampire Heir (Book 1)

The Witch Queen (Book 2)

The Immortal Vow (Book 3)

The Warlock Lord (Book 4)

The Wolf Consort (Book 5)

The Crystal Rose (Book 6)

The Wolf Forsaken (Book 7)

The Fae Bound (Book 8)

The Blood Pact (Book 9)

*The Wyth Courts*

Winter King (Book 1)

Spring Warrior (Book 2)

Summer Prince (Book 3)

Autumn Rebel (Book 4)

*The Fire Heart Chronicles*

Heart Seeker (Book 1)

Flame Caster (Book 2)

Sorrow Bringer (Book 3)

Earth Shaker (Novella)

Soul Wanderer (Book 4)

Fate Summoner (Book 5)

War Maiden (Book 6)

*The Everlast Series*

Destiny Gift (Book 1)

Soul Oath (Book 2)

Cup of Life (Book 3)

Everlasting Circle (Book 4)

*Willow Harbor Series*

Hunter's Revenge (Book 3)

Siren's Song (Book 5)

*Breaking Series*

Breaking Free (Book 1)

Breaking Away (Book 2)

Breaking Through (Book 3)

Breaking Down (Book 4)

9 781954 291034